Praise for th

"A female Walter Mosley."
Eileen Dreyer

"West's talent is bursting at the seams."
Drood Review of Mystery

"West has a knack for creating colorful yet
realistic characters and witty dialogue . . .
[and] will keep readers guessing to the end."
Publishers Weekly

"If you're looking for a great mystery series
with quirky characters, tight plots, a touch of
romance, and a funny, gutsy heroine,
look no further than Chassie West."
Romantic Times

"[A] unique talent . . . [West] delivers
mystery, suspense, and intrigue."
National Black Review

"A new Chassie West mystery is always cause
for great rejoicing and dancing in the streets.
No one does it quite like our girlfriend,
the divine Ms. West."
Helen Chappell

By Chassie West

Killer Chameleon
Killer Riches
Killing Kin
Loss of Innocence
Sunrise

CHASSIE WEST

KILLER CHAMELEON

HarperTorch
An Imprint of HarperCollins*Publishers*

This is a work of fiction. Names, characters, places, and incidents are products of the author's imagination or are used fictitiously and are not to be construed as real. Any resemblance to actual events, locales, organizations, or persons, living or dead, is entirely coincidental.

HARPERTORCH
An Imprint of HarperCollins*Publishers*
10 East 53rd Street
New York, New York 10022-5299

Copyright © 2004 by Chassie West
ISBN: 0-06-054842-8

First HarperTorch paperback printing: October 2004

HarperCollins®, HarperTorch™, and ❦™ are trademarks of Harper-Collins Publishers Inc.

Printed in the United States of America

Visit HarperTorch on the World Wide Web at www.harpercollins.com

10 9 8 7 6 5 4 3 2 1

Acknowledgments

No matter how often it seems that writing a book is a solitary endeavor, especially when faced with that blank monitor screen and a brain completely absent of intelligent thought, quite the opposite is true. So . . .

Many thanks to the members of my critique group for the spark of inspiration they've ignited in me every other Thursday for the last thirty years—Ruth Glick, Randi Dufresne, Patricia Paris, Binnie Braunstein, Nancy Baggett, Joanne Settel, Linda Williams, Kathryn Johnson, Joyce Braga, Cronshi Englander, and Marcia Mazur (in absentia).

To Joyce Varney Thompson, mentor and guide, whose belief in me started it all, my eternal gratitude.

To constant friends, old and new—Maggie Sands, Farris Forsythe, Elaine Flinn, Jean Favors, Dr. Ann Yvette Eastman Ellison Tyler Bynum (whew!), Tex Gathings, and the indomitable Ches Applewhite, proofreader extraordinaire, you've kept me going through good times and bad.

And to the TeaBuds, in a category all to themselves and as dear as family, purple rules!

And to Carolyn Marino, my editor, friend, fellow N.C. barbecue lover, and Ellen Geiger, my agent, who goads with such a gentle hand, life would be far less fulfilling without you.

And to Bob, peeking over my shoulder from the Other Side, all my love.

And to you, dear readers, who make every single lonely, frustrating, agonizing moment in front of the computer worth the effort, thank you, thank you, thank you!

Chassie

1

IT'S ALWAYS THE SAME, A SENSITIVITY AT THE base of my neck, as if there's a stiff label back there irritating my skin. Whenever it happens, it always means the same thing: trouble. And any time I've ignored it, I've eventually paid for it in one way or another. So over the years, I've learned: when you get the message, kiddo, *pay attention!* Unfortunately, my wedding, as simple as it was supposed to be, had reduced me to a blithering idiot. How people with megadollar budgets and seven-page guest lists do it is beyond me. In other words, I was distracted, and as a result, wasn't paying attention to The Itch. And I paid for it. Big time. So did others, and I have only myself to blame.

I'm still not sure when the prickling began, but I can damned sure mark in red the day I finally realized it was there. December 6. Even then, it took a couple of incidents before I connected the dots. I can be forgiven for not recognizing the first of them that day. After all, it was snowing. If you live in Washington, D.C., you accept the fact that a mere prediction of snow will be greeted with the same degree of panic as an impending nuclear attack. God forbid if the white stuff sneaks up on the city unexpectedly. People drive as if the devil himself is pursuing them, horns and tail a-twitch. And if you're unlucky enough to be a pedestrian, you're on your own, because traffic signals and "Walk" and "Don't Walk" signs become purely decorative to those behind the wheel. Which is why I didn't take it personally when the old tan compact swooshed by close enough for me to warrant checking to see if it had left a streak of rust across my backside.

"Dag, lady." A twenty-something unlocking his car gave me a wide-eyed stare as I reached the sanctuary of the sidewalk. "You all right? She almost cleaned your clock."

I leaned against a lamppost and took stock, my heart skipping double Dutch. "Well, I'm still ticking, so I guess there's no harm done."

At least not physically. I had to admit, however, that the moment I'd spotted the compact barreling down on me, I'd flashed back to the last time I'd found myself a walking target, on that occasion the target of a drunk driver. In trying to get out of his way, I'd collided with a fire hydrant, making mincemeat of my knee and, as a result, my career as a D.C. cop. This time there hadn't been any—time to get out of the way, that is. It was pure luck she'd missed me. Another inch toward her right and I'd have been an inch on the *Washington Post* obit page: Leigh A. Warren, thirty-three, victim of a hit-and-run. Because I knew without a shadow of a doubt that the driver would have kept right on going. Her excuse? Hey, it was snowing!

Turning to look back, I tried to reconstruct the incident. She might not have been able to see me before she'd made that left turn, thanks to a double-parked truck at the end of the block—except that I'd been two-thirds of the way across and should have been visible after she'd rounded the corner. Perhaps I hadn't been walking fast enough for her. Wherever she was going, she was in one hell of a hurry. And I was one lucky duck.

"You sure you're okay?" the twenty-something asked again. "You're shaking. Do you need to sit down? Here." He opened the rear door on his side. "I'm in no hurry."

I focused on him for the first time, surprised and, perhaps because of my years as a cop, immediately suspicious of the offer. He looked harmless enough in his sweats, a gym bag in one hand, and the only expression on his face appeared to be one of genuine concern. I gave myself a mental slap on the wrist. This was no white slaver intent on abducting me and selling me into a life of prostitution or having his way with me himself. In the first place, our skin colors, tinted by our African descendants, nullified white anything, much less slaver, and I was well past the age to qualify as a anybody's pleasure girl. In the second place, as scuzzy as I felt—ratty blue jeans and an even rattier sweater under a well-worn car coat, the only person I could imagine wanting his way with me would be someone being paid to perform a complete makeover.

"I appreciate the offer but I'm fine. Really. And running late. Thanks anyway."

"No problem." He tossed his gym bag in the back and closed his door. "Merry Christmas."

"Same to you," I said, to be polite, and made tracks for Connecticut Avenue. Normally I'm one of those people who loves the holidays and everything that goes with them, but I admit that as I hurried through the late-lunch bunch in Barney's, I was reaching deep for the Christmas spirit.

I spotted Eddie in a booth all the way in the back.

He didn't see me, but from the expression on his face, he and Scrooge were of like minds. Perhaps the raucous office party in high gear a few tables over had gotten to him.

"Greetings of the season," I said as I slid into the booth, just barely avoiding a celebrant gesturing with a full glass in his hand. If I hadn't been watching him, I'd have been wearing his beer in my bra.

"You're late."

Now I'm usually a fairly even-tempered person. And I like Eddie Grimes. I've known him for a long time. He was slated to be Duck's best man, and perhaps under ordinary circumstances I might have cut him a little slack. But my most recent days had involved no ordinary circumstances. Not only was I juggling wedding arrangements for a ceremony that had already been postponed twice, plus the usual chaos that comes with Christmas, but as the future chief of police of Ourland/ Umber Shores, a little Chesapeake Bay community full of my relatives, I was also dealing with all the hoops to be jumped through to set up the Shores' first police force. Considering the trouble I'd gone to to accommodate Eddie's schedule and his "You're late" in greeting, I sat down with mayhem in mind. Unfortunately, the only weapon in reach was the butter knife he was using on a hard roll. Besides, he, as a cop, was carrying, and I, temporarily a former cop, was not.

"Let me tell you something, buster," I said as I shrugged my way out of my coat. "In order to meet you, I had to, one, postpone picking up my wedding outfit and listen to a snotty clerk call my priorities into question. Two," I continued, counting on my fingers, "I had to tear over to Umber Shores this morning instead of this afternoon as originally planned, to fire the idiot wiring the storefront we'll be using for the new police station. One day on the job and he's already damned near burned the place down. And three, to get back here on time from the Shores, I got a speeding ticket, my very first. Plus a half dozen snowflakes drifted down as I crossed the District line from Maryland, which means D.C. traffic has gone into its Chicken Little mode. I just missed being made a statistic in the 'Pedestrian Struck' column. In other words, you are dealing with a black woman with a very bad attitude here. So don't bust my chops about being two minutes and twenty-eight seconds late. Now what the hell was so important that this couldn't wait?"

"Whoa!" Eddie, saucer-eyed, raised his palms in a gesture of surrender. "I'm sorry, okay? Got a lot on my mind. I've ordered a shrimp cocktail for you, but how about I get you something to drink? What'll it be? A Bloody Mary?"

"Yeah, right, so I can get pulled over for driving under the influence too? Thank you, no."

I stopped, closed my eyes, and tried for a calming breath. It wasn't fair to take out my frustration on him. "Sorry, Eddie. It's just that this wedding is driving me nuts. I love Duck, but I'm beginning to wonder if becoming Mrs. Dillon Upshur Kennedy is worth all the aggravation."

"Really?" He hoisted one brow. "Why?" His sour expression was gone, but there was still something not quite right about him, as if he had a burr up his butt. Maybe I could extract it by bringing him up to date on the three-ring circus my wedding threatened to become.

"We start out planning a nice, quiet, early November ceremony in a judge's chamber," I began. "No frills and fuss, just us and our nearest and dearest, a total of eleven people, the person officiating included. Then I find out that not only do I have grandparents, aunts, and, glory be to God, a twin brother, I've got cousins up the wazoo. And honest, I'm not complaining. I feel absolutely blessed. But they want to be there. How could I say no?"

"Guess you couldn't," Eddie agreed, probably not daring to contradict me.

"So scratch the early November date because my grandfather's going in for knee replacement surgery that day. If he postponed it, they wouldn't be able to schedule it until the middle of this month. I couldn't ask him to do that. He'd been in a lot of pain, and if he hadn't wrecked his golf cart trying to catch the bastard who'd mugged me, he wouldn't be going under the knife in the first place. Besides, he wants to walk me down the aisle, and as my grandmother reminded me gently—for her, anyway—I'm the only granddaughter he'll ever have."

"She's got a point."

"As much as I hate to admit her being right about anything, yeah, she has a point. Duck and I figure we've waited this long, what's a few more days, right? Okay, we pick a late November date, then find out my brother's scheduled to be a keynote speaker somewhere and really, really wants to be at the wedding. This time it's Duck who reminds me that—"

"He's the only brother you'll ever have," Eddie finished for me.

"Exactly, so the date for the wedding goes on the to-do list again. And *that's* when Duck's mom and Nunna put their heads together."

"Uh-oh." Eddie paled, sort of, given his dark walnut complexion. As my fiancé's coworker and best friend since childhood, he knew Mrs. Kennedy well. He'd also met Nunna, my foster mother, and could guess what a lethal combination those two could be.

"Uh-oh is right. The only reason I didn't move in with Duck weeks ago is that we both knew they wouldn't say a word but wouldn't really approve. And I love Nunna enough not to want her on my conscience."

"Or Mrs. K. either," Eddie said. "By all means stay off that little old lady's shit list."

"Tell me about it. So the two mamas let it be known— delicately, I'll give them that—that it would make them so much happier if the ceremony were, one, presided over by someone of the cloth instead of a judge or public official, and two, held at a site with at least one stained glass window in it."

Eddie seemed to have relaxed a little. But only a little. "So that's what happened. I wondered. Duck left me a message that the date and place were up for grabs again but I didn't get the details."

"You want details?" I asked, nabbing a roll for myself. "Enter my cousins, first through sixth, seventh, and eighth for all I know. We're talking dozens here. They felt left out. And since it was their idea to take me on to set up the Shores' police force in the first place—"

"You were in a double bind."

"You got it. The last thing I want to do is alienate them."

"Sounds like you'll need to rent RFK Stadium and ask Bishop Crandall to officiate."

I hesitated, since I couldn't remember which denomination the good bishop claimed. "Well, actually, if Duck agrees, it looks like things will work out pretty well. Among those dozens of cousins of mine is a minister of a little church. I just met him today; in fact, he talked me out of killing the idiot electrician. He says he'll be glad to perform the ceremony. From what he described, there's no way we'll be able to squeeze all those people in his sanctuary, but the overflow will fit in the fellowship hall, which has closed-circuit. And he's available the day after Christmas. That's the only good thing that's happened so far today. Now, I repeat, what's up? You planning some kind of surprise for Duck?"

"That's what I'm here to find out." Eddie scrubbed a paw over his face, and I detected a subtle change in his demeanor. Suddenly we were back to Scrooge and Company. His lips flattened into a straight line, his eyes emanating a chill. He, like my Duck, is a detective with the D.C. Metropolitan Police. He's skinny as a finishing nail, dresses like a *GQ* model, and has been on the force long enough to have seen it all. If what he had to say made him hot under the collar just thinking about it, something must be very wrong indeed.

"Jeez, Eddie, you're scaring me. What's the matter with you?"

He fixed me with a squinty-eyed stare. "The question I've been trying to figure out is, what's the matter with you?"

"Me? You mean besides all the wedding hassles and Christmas and meeting a new cousin every other day and trying to keep an eye on the police station-to-be? Nothing."

"Everything's all right between you and my boy?"

I frowned. Granted, he was near enough to family to be entitled to ask, but why would he? "Everything's fine, honest."

He leaned back, staring a hole in the middle of my forehead. Just as suddenly, he seemed to thaw. The chill in the air dissipated somewhat.

"You know how tight me and the Duck are, right? Like this." He crossed his index and middle fingers. "I watch his back, on and off the job, the same as he watches mine. Understand what I'm saying?"

"Sure." I wondered where this was going.

"Then why the fuck," he asked, so softly I could barely hear him, "are you stepping out on him?"

"Excuse me?" Normally a fairly quiet place, the restaurant was doing its part to contribute to the Christmas spirit by playing songs of the season. One of the speakers was mounted directly above our heads, with The Little Drummer Boy drumming with a vengeance. The members of the office party were singing along, contributing to the decibel level, so I was certain I'd misunderstood Eddie.

"I mean, I know some women feel like they're entitled to a bachelorette party," he said. "But the way I hear it, the only women in the Silver Shaker Saturday night were either hookers or hitched to a date. And the way I hear it, you were shaking your tail with any male who wasn't attached and a few who were. And when you left, you were not alone, if you get my meaning."

My mouth gaped open so long that my tongue dried out. "*What? Me?* Who the hell told you that?"

"You wouldn't recognize the names. The important thing is that they recognized you." His gaze was ice-cold again, his jaws clenched."

"Me? In the Silver Shaker? That . . ." I grappled for an apt description. "That cesspool? And you believed it?"

His head shot forward like a strutting pigeon's. "You telling me you weren't there Saturday night? From around ten until closing?"

I was now steaming. "Listen, buster, the only time

I've been in that place, I was in uniform to help break up a fight. Otherwise I wouldn't be caught dead there, in or out of a coffin. It's a john's supermarket for street-walkers, a pimp's paradise. As for Saturday night, I was at home—I mean, at Janeece's, wrapping Christmas presents." Ever since I'd walked in on a body growing mold in my apartment a couple of months ago, I'd been bunking in my best friend's den across the hall.

"So Janeece will back up your story?"

It takes a lot to make me lose it, but Eddie was three-sixteenths of an inch from succeeding. "Can Janeece confirm my alibi, you mean? Janeece home on a Satur-day night? When pigs fly, so you have only my word on it. If that's not good enough—"

"Did you talk to anyone? On the phone, I mean?"

The waiter exited the kitchen and stopped at our booth, a tray balanced on his fingertips, but whatever appetite I had was long gone.

"Eat the shrimp yourself," I snapped at Eddie, and reached back for my coat. The waiter hesitated, then slid the plates onto the table and beat a hasty retreat. I guess he figured as long as he delivered it, somebody was obligated to pay for it; he didn't care who.

"I'm leaving," I said, wrestling with the lining of the coat's sleeve, which had turned inside out. "I am not a perp you're grilling and don't have to prove anything to you or anybody else. How *dare* you suggest—"

His fingers locked around my left wrist. He might be a skinny little man, but he was a skinny little man with a black belt. He'd kicked butts a lot bigger than mine during his years on the force. In other words, I wasn't going anywhere.

"Chill," he said, holding me until I released the inside-out sleeve. "Just calm down, okay? Look, I'm sorry, it's just that . . ." He hesitated, seemingly at a loss.

"It's just that what? By the way, grab me again and you'll get the business end of this shrimp fork. Jesus, Eddie, I don't get it. You've known me almost ten years. How could you believe that kind of shit about me?"

He sat back, brow lined with a confused frown. "I wouldn't have, if the ones I heard it from weren't guys I consider reliable."

"In other words, brother cops? Who?" I demanded. "The law says I'm entitled to confront my accusers. I may just shoot them while I'm at it."

Eddie waved me off. "No reason you'd know them. But they know Duck—"

"As does eighty percent of the population of the District," I interrupted.

"Yeah, but these guys were at Jensen's wedding where you and Duck were toasted as the next in line to get hitched. You caught the bouquet. There was plenty of time for them to lock onto your face and remember you as the Duck's lady, know what I mean?"

"So?"

"They've been undercover at the Shaker for a couple of weeks, setting up a sting. Evidently hookers aren't the only thing on the menu there. And seeing you—" I scowled, and he held up a hand. "Sorry. Seeing someone they thought was you . . . And not that they thought you were on the market, but it's not the kind of scene they'd expect Duck's intended to be in. So they passed the info along to me on the Q.T. They like Duck, knew we were best buddies and that I'd know how to handle it."

"God," I snarled, "I'd forgotten what pure bliss it is being a member of the good ol' boys' club."

He squirmed, which I, not feeling particularly charitable, enjoyed immensely. "Look, Leigh, I said I'm sorry. I'll get back with those guys, make sure they know it wasn't you. I admit, it didn't feel right. But I got to thinking about how long my boy has been absolutely nuts about you, and every time I turned around, the wedding was being postponed. I didn't want him to get hurt."

"Better me than him, huh?"

He took a breath, then nodded. "Yeah. If those guys were wrong, better you than him."

"And especially, *especially*," I repeated for emphasis, "if they were right. Well, I must say you sure as hell know how to ruin a girl's appetite."

I sat and stewed for a minute, reminding myself that I might have known Duck for nine years, but Eddie had known him going on twenty. They'd grown up together, had gone to the same D.C. schools and college, had gone through the Academy together. They were as close as brothers. So as hot as I was, I couldn't fault Eddie. He loved Duck, had proved it more than once, and had just done it again.

"Okay. Everybody makes mistakes," I said, "but don't think I'm gonna forget this."

He smiled, his first. "In other words, I owe you. Tell you what, I'll pay for lunch."

"Got news for you, buddy. You were going to pay for it anyhow. I'm unemployed, remember? Now, let's eat. The wedding outfit can wait, but if I leave here soon enough, I might be able to get to the travel agent's to pick up our tickets to Hawaii. So. How's the new baby?" A change of subject might get us back on a more familiar footing.

We settled into a far more comfortable rhythm as he

brought me up to date on the chaos surrounding the arrival of his fifth child, since his wife went into labor at Tyson's Corner, a monster shopping mall in Northern Virginia. But the hurt still simmered as I demolished my seafood, plus dessert, the first I'd had in weeks to ensure that I'd fit into the two-piece peau de soie waiting to be picked up at the Bridal Bower. Somehow we made it through the whole meal without the Silver Shaker coming up again.

But I had to wonder who this look-alike might be. Another relative? I'd already met one who could pass for my sister, but knew she'd been at a conference for librarians in Atlanta last weekend. Besides, the Silver Shaker just wasn't her kind of scene. Still, there was a host of distant cousins I had yet to meet. The possibility that one of them might look like me and be a slut to boot did not fill me with familial warmth.

Eddie eyed me curiously as he pressed the remaining crumbs of his German chocolate cake onto his fork. "You've been kinda twitchy ever since you sat down. Got an itch between your shoulder blades or something?"

"Think it's the label in the neck of this sweater," I said. "I keep forgetting to cut it off." Then it occurred to me that I'd been bothered by an itch back there for some time.

Leaning sideways, I peered out, scanning the other diners. The office party was just breaking up, more than a few of them none too steady on their feet as they made their way to the door. Most of the other tables were now empty, the remaining few representing the last gasp of the lunch hour. No one met my gaze or paid the slightest attention to me. Yet the itch persisted. There was no mistake. I felt watched, threatened.

Suddenly, I couldn't sit still a minute longer. I had to get out of here. "Thanks for lunch, Eddie, but I've got to pick up those tickets before it gets too late."

He signaled for the waiter and paid the tab, then leaned in to me and grabbed my hand. "Leigh, are we okay? Seriously. We still friends?"

"Don't be dumb," I said, surprised that he had to ask. "Of course we are. If you'd gone to Duck first, it would be a different story. But you didn't, and I appreciate it. So let's forget it, okay?"

He draped an arm around my shoulder as we left, perhaps to prove to himself that we were still buddies, and we parted outside the restaurant. I watched him as he headed for his car with a confident stride. He was probably the most diminutive cop on the police force, but with none of the small-man swagger and bravado. He was loyal to a fault, I'd give him that, and was damned glad he was Duck's best friend.

Out on the street, Mother Nature had changed her mind about the snow and, apparently, about winter altogether. In the time it had taken us to eat, the temperature had jumped a good ten degrees, almost too warm for my heavy coat. It had also turned into too pleasant a day to go the three long blocks to my car when the travel agency was perhaps a ten-minute stroll in the opposite direction, the Bridal Bower a couple of blocks beyond that. By the time I got the car off the lot and maneuvered the one-way streets driving, I could probably be in and out of Margie's with the tickets in my pocket. And my bum knee, which could sometimes make a trek of any distance feel like a marathon, had been quiet all week. I unbuttoned the coat, decision made. I'd hoof it and eliminate two things off my to-do list.

I headed northwest on Connecticut, setting off at a comfortable pace, which was just as well. Speed walking would be out of the question. Christmas shoppers were out in full force but seemed to be in no hurry to get wherever they were going. I checked my watch, convinced myself I could still make it with time to spare, and relaxed.

I was waiting for the "Walk" signal at Rhode Island Avenue when I felt that annoying prickle at the nape of my neck again. Tightening my hold on my purse, I glanced at the people nearest me. In front of me a pair of teens in school uniforms erupted into squeals about some boy too gorgeous to live. To my left an elderly couple, arms linked, chatted in a language I couldn't identify if you'd paid me. On my right a mother tried to explain the concept of gift giving to a toddler clearly defiant about sharing whatever he carried in his small shopping bag. I couldn't figure out what had set off my internal alarm.

The light changed, and I hurried across ahead of everyone else, feeling a little foolish. But the prickle wouldn't go away. Was I being tailed? I needed a window, one clear enough to check the reflection of those around me without being obvious about it.

I passed a restaurant, its diners too snug up against the glass for my comfort, and finally settled on a dress shop with a solitary headless mannequin, its gown a-glitter with sequins and not a price tag in sight. I took census as the uniformed teens, the elderly couple, and the young woman towing the toddler went past me. I hadn't locked onto the others behind them quite as well, but they all kept going with no sign they had even noticed me. Of more importance, they neither hesitated, went into any of the businesses in the next block, nor stopped to gaze in any windows to wait for me. If it was someone on the other side of the street, I'd never be able to pinpoint them. The walkways were simply too crowded.

Checking the direction from which I'd come probably wasted another couple of minutes. One lone female at the corner dropped a package and smiled in gratitude when a middle-aged gentleman picked it up for her. She crossed when the light changed and turned left onto the side street. He strode past me without a glance. Then came an elderly man pushing a baby carriage full of socks and pantyhose. Weird but not my business and nothing to worry about. Everyone else kept going as well.

Suddenly I was completely alone on this block and felt as if I were in the cross-hairs of a rifle. It was crazy, irrational. But I couldn't ignore it any longer. The tickets at the travel agency and the wedding outfit would have to wait. I turned and practically sprinted back the way I'd come. I was thoroughly spooked. But why?

2

BY THE TIME I FOUND A PARKING SPACE around the corner from my apartment building, I'd almost talked myself into believing that my uneasiness had to be related to this latest change in the wedding plans. Duck might not agree to it. He was becoming fed up with the delays and had said more than once, "Much more of this and we're eloping, babe." I'd call him first thing. Well, second, after I'd gotten rid of the boots. My feet were killing me.

I found a parking space on the side street and on my way to my building kept an eye out for the Reverend Mrs. Hansberry, a recent fixture on our corners. A pail dangling from her arm, she was collecting for presents for needy children in her neighborhood. Pure unadulterated guilt at having more than enough to keep body and soul together had kept me dropping loose change in the pail whenever I saw her. Relieved that she was nowhere in sight, I jogged to the door of my apartment building and lost no time crossing the lobby.

Our Christmas tree was up, being decorated by the residents' special events committee and their extended families, from the looks of it. I was in no mood to help. I smiled, waved, and thanked heaven I wouldn't have to wait on the elevator. It opened immediately.

I stepped off on the fifth floor to be greeted by the sight of a denim-clad rear end: Cholly, our apartment maintenance man, on his hands and knees in front of the door of the apartment I'd vacated some weeks ago, his backside twitching from side to side as he scrubbed a square foot of carpeting. He and his wife, Neva, our building manager, and now the proud residents of 502, had had no qualms about taking ownership after I'd jumped ship. In the first place, Neva, of Amazonian proportions, was great with child, and their former first-floor apartment had only one bedroom. The room I'd used as a den would be perfect for the new baby. In the second place, it would take more than the memory of the corpse I'd found in my kitchen to spook Neva.

"Hell, I didn't know him," she said. "Had no business being in here anyways. The nerve, using our— I mean, your—kitchen to light up marijuana like he was in his own personal smoking lounge or something. Glad it did him in." She was still in a snit over the fact that he had managed to sneak into the building without her seeing him.

Her first-floor unit had been ideal for keeping an eye on the front door and lobby, and for the most part she'd been a gatekeeper extraordinaire. It was the only thing she regretted about moving; she couldn't monitor the comings and goings from up here. Word was she was pestering the management company for a closed-circuit camera outside the front entrance and a monitor to be installed in their new apartment. It would never happen, but I had to give her credit for trying.

Cholly, peering back over his shoulder at me, sat on his haunches and scowled. "Hey, Miz Warren. Sometimes I think I oughta go into the carpet cleaning business."

Someone's dog, no doubt with encouragement, had left a deposit at his door a couple of weeks before. Neva, unable to see her feet and anything else under her protruding midsection, had come out of the apartment and stepped four-square in the pile, leaving it well and truly ground into the nap of the carpet. The odor had been an intermittent problem ever since. And as there were at least nine tenants among the dog-walking set, Cholly had more than a few suspects to choose from.

"Any luck finding the miscreant?" I asked him.

A full set of wrinkles furrowed his brow, denoting confusion. "Miscreant? Never heard of that breed. Besides, most of the dogs in this building are mutts, 'cept for Miz Grady's Shih Tzu. Good name for that little bugger. Couldn't have been him, though. Miz Grady gave him to her daughter way before Halloween. But this here ain't—"

Neva chose that moment to open the door, probably to find out who her husband was talking to. Cholly was no prize but he was her prize, and she watched him like a hawk. Truly an odd couple, Neva hovered around the six-foot mark and flirted with three hundred pounds, fifty more than her nonpregnant state, and Cholly, short and squat, resembled a walnut-hued Danny DeVito with a perpetually puzzled expression. I shuddered to think what their baby would look like.

"Hey, Miz Warren," Neva greeted me. Then, glaring down at him, she propped her fists on her hips and sniffed audibly. "I can still smell it. Told you that cheap cleaning stuff was no good. Swear to God, if I ever find out who did this . . ."

"Cholly," I said, "whatever you're using, it's made things worse. The odor's stronger now than when I left this morning."

"That's 'cause it's fresh," Neva said, scowling. "Somebody did it again, only this time it's cat shit. And this time Cholly stepped in it, not me."

"In my new Nikes, too," he grumbled. "Probably ruined 'em."

"Cat?" That made no sense. The only cat in the building was a memory, a sweet eighteen-year-old tabby who'd been put to sleep during the summer. "Did Bill get a new one?"

"No. He ain't got over putting down Whiskers yet." Neva patted her stomach absentmindedly. "Somebody did this on purpose. Can you imagine? Raiding a litter box and leaving it here just to be mean. That's another reason we need one of them closed-circuit cameras. We gotta nip this in the bud."

"Bud, my foot." Cholly stood up. "This here done bloomed and died. I'd figure one of Miz Harley's grandkids did it, 'cept they're allergic to cats. Dogs too. Can't think of anybody else ornery enough to pull something like this twice."

To be honest, I couldn't either. Granted, Cholly and Neva, as representatives of management and sticklers for the rules when it suited them, could be a pain in the rear on occasion, but they took their positions seriously and looked after the property as if it was their own. Neva especially knew her business along with everyone else's, a fact some tenants found annoying. I wondered if perhaps she might have poked her nose too far into someone's affairs, because this latest trick was an especially nasty one. Exposure to cat feces could put her pregnancy at risk if she came into direct contact with it. I wasn't sure she knew it.

"Well, that's that then," she said, arms akimbo again.

"Management ain't gonna like it, but we gotta get the whole carpet replaced."

"The sooner the better," I said. "Until they do, put our welcome mat over it. It won't help the smell, but it's better than nothing. You didn't handle the stuff yourself, did you, Neva?"

"And risk getting that there toxoplasmosis?" she asked, surprising me. "No way. In fact, maybe I ought to wear one of those mask things until we get the new carpeting. And the welcome mat's a good idea. You sure Miz Holloway won't mind?"

"Positive," I said, making a mental note to buy one to replace Janeece's, since it was her property I was being so generous with. I nudged it across to Cholly, who positioned it in front of their door.

"Looks nice," he pronounced. "Thanks, Miz Warren. By the way, we signed for a couple of deliveries for you."

"Sure did." Neva hurried back into the apartment and returned with two large boxes. "Must be wedding presents. One from Bloomingdale's. Don't know about the other. They ain't heavy, just bulky," she said, placing them in my arms. "Got mail for you too." She disappeared and came back with several envelopes and my *Essence* magazine.

Since my hands were full, she tucked them under my arm, then prodded the sole of her husband's shoe with a wide, bunny-slippered toe. "Get on in here. I need a back rub before you go caulk the tub in two-ten."

Cholly brightened. Clearly either rubbing or caulking was a chore he enjoyed. "Thanks for letting us use this mat, Miz Warren. Uh, gotta go." He tipped the brim of his Pep Boys cap and backed into the apartment with a sheepish grin. I heard Neva giggle and suppressed a surge of envy as he shut the door.

The realization stunned me. Envy? Of Cholly and Neva, for God's sake? The intensity of it not only rattled me, it showed me what bad shape I was in.

I unlocked the door of 503, kicked it shut behind me, and collapsed onto the futon, letting the boxes, mail, and my purse land wherever they happened to. Still swaddled in my coat, I pried my boots off and reached for the phone to call Duck, then hesitated. I had to work my way through an explanation for what I'd experienced out in the hall.

For a second or two back there, I'd have changed places with Cholly and Neva, make what they had mine. Not that I wanted the apartment back; the corpse in the kitchen had soured the place for me in more ways than one. And I didn't particularly envy them the impending birth of their baby. Granted, Duck and I wanted children, and my biological clock seemed to tick louder every month, but we both knew we'd need some time to get used to being mister and missus before taking that big step. What I coveted was Cholly and Neva's stability, their permanence. They were man and wife, their relationship set in concrete, to all appearances happy despite their constant squabbling. They had jobs they loved. And a home.

Then there was me. Not quite married. And even though heading the Shores' police force was in the works, it was still just that. In the works. So I was not quite employed. And weighing twice as heavily, I was homeless, no not-quite about it. As generous as Janeece had been about insisting I share her apartment until the wedding, it was her apartment, not mine. The

fact that my feet weren't propped on the coffee table in
toe-wiggling bliss at being free of my boots was just
one reminder that I was company, and had to be re-
spectful of someone else's property. Putting my feet up
would require moving Janeece's collection of candle
holders. As soon as she walked in, she would nudge
them into exactly the spots they'd been before without
saying a word or even realizing she was doing it.

Not that I was complaining. As apartment mates,
we'd been surprisingly compatible, primarily because
other than the placement of her knickknacks, Janeece
was undemanding and, most of all, rarely here. Between
work, church, and a social life so active that she had to
use a Filofax to keep track, she was always on the run,
which was fine with me. I'd lived alone for years and
had no problem with solitude, which presented a nig-
gling area of concern when I tried to imagine my future
as Duck's wife.

Despite that, I was really looking forward to being
with him on a daily—and nightly—basis. As it was, his
two-bedroom condo was almost home anyway, in fact
technically mine since in a moment of temporary in-
sanity he'd signed it over to me. Yet here I was. Feeling
rootless. And envious. And annoyed that I couldn't put
my feet up.

The hell I couldn't, I decided.

I leaned forward to move the candle holders to one
end of the coffee table, and my mail slid off the futon
onto the floor. I picked them up. Big deal. My Mobil
bill. A credit card lure, thank you, no. An announcement of a sale at Salina's, the second I'd received recently. I wondered how I'd gotten on their mailing list,
especially since I'd never been in the store. It was way

up on Wisconsin Avenue, and I'd have to take out a loan to be able to afford anything hanging on their racks. Again, thank you, no.

The last piece of mail was a plain white envelope addressed in block letters, canceled in D.C. No return address.

Curious, I opened it. A review of *Macbeth*, onstage in Chicago. Why would anyone send this to me?

It occurred to me that a while back I'd received an announcement from one of the local theaters, I couldn't remember which, about a Shakespeare festival. I had tossed it since the beginning dates of the first play in the series were the same ones during which Duck and I were to have been in Hawaii. That had since changed, and was beside the point. Who had sent this and why?

Skimming the review, I saw the light. Appearing as the lady with the soiled hands: Beverly Barlowe, who had lived in the apartment next door in my law school days. God, I hadn't heard from her in years. I guess she wanted me to know that she'd been right to kiss the law good-bye and follow her heart. The critic obviously agreed with her; the review was glowing. Delighted for her, I began to fold the article when I noticed the writing at the bottom. *What could have been, no thanks to you.*

Could have been? What did that mean? She'd hit the big time, would shortly go from Chicago to D.C.'s National Theatre with the touring company before opening on Broadway next month. Bev had a skewed sense of humor, but whatever she meant was zipping right over my head. I slipped the review back into the envelope to keep for Nunna, who had adored Bev but had been scandalized at her dropping out of law school.

I reached for the *Essence* and saw for the first time that it had been thumbed through. *My* magazine! I felt my blood pressure skyrocket. Was nothing sacred? Damn Neva! I stood up and, barefoot, headed for the door, ready to raise a little hell about invasion of privacy. And stopped.

If Neva was reading my magazines, I had only myself to blame. She had had a key to my box for a couple of years to empty it for me whenever I went down home to see Nunna. Besides, with her and Cholly's agreement, I hadn't bothered to file a change of address with the post office, because as managers of the building, they had a special mailbox downstairs and didn't need the one for apartment 502.

Plus Janeece, the catalog queen, usually received so much mail that there'd be no room in her box for mine. And among the contents of my tote bag was the mail I'd pried out of her mailbox as I'd come in, which included her *Ebony* magazine, this week's *Time,* and half a dozen catalogs. There were any number of evenings when I'd get here first, pick up her mail for her, and read her magazines before she got in from work. So I had no right to mount my high horse with Neva.

This was stupid. I was losing it. Enough.

There was nothing I could do about being not quite married, since unless Duck objected, I was committed to using the cousin's church for the ceremony on December 26.

There was little I could do about being not quite employed. My brother, Jon, was dealing with Anne Arundel county to make things official. But there was, by God, something I could do about being homeless.

Just like that, the decision was made. I sat down, picked up the phone, and dialed.

"Kennedy." He sounded busy, distracted. I decided to cut to the chase.

"Duck, me. I'm moving in. Tonight if I can swing it."

My grand announcement was greeted with silence. My stomach shifted south a few degrees. Didn't he want me?

"About damned time," he said, chuckling. "What finally did it for you?"

"I'll tell you later. And before I forget, how would you feel about getting married in Maryland in Arundel Woods A.M.E. Church?"

Silence again. Then, "Don't tell me. Another cousin."

"You guessed it. The Reverend James Shelby Ritch. Details to follow."

"To hell with the details. We're still on for the day after Christmas, right?"

"Right." Relieved at his unspoken agreement, I still hesitated, suddenly unsure of myself. "You don't mind my moving in now? Honestly? I mean—"

"Babe, please."

Hearing patience, impatience, a note of chiding, and a lot of love in those two words, I was on firm ground again. Nunna and Mrs. Kennedy would just have to get used to the idea. Janeece would be disappointed—she enjoyed playing roommates—but she'd understand.

"Will you need any help?" he asked. "I'd come by, but this looks to be a late night. How much stuff do you have left to bring?"

I hadn't thought that far. There was no way I'd be able to carry all my clothes in one trip, but there really was no hurry. It wasn't as if I was being kicked out of here, eviction notice in hand and marshals on my tail. Besides, I would need a farewell session with Janeece, which would involve sharing a few tears and a bottle of white Zinfandel.

"Thanks, hon, I can handle it. I'll bring all I can take

down to the car in one trip tonight. Someone's bound to see me loading it, so I don't dare leave it to come back up for more or it'll be gone and I'll be replacing a window, if not the whole car. There's always tomorrow for the rest of my stuff."

"Smart move. Okay, Scarlett O'Hara." I could hear the smile in his voice. "Hey, speaking of tomorrow, maybe you can do me a favor. Can you hang around until ten to let the cleaning lady in? She left her keys the last time she was there."

I had yet to adjust to the idea of a cleaning lady.

"It occurs to me," I said, approaching the subject warily, "we won't need her any longer. I'll be there to do the cleaning."

"Hmm. Are you sure about that? Neither one of us will be around much. And when we're home, I don't know about you, but housecleaning will be the last thing on my mind."

"We can talk about it later," I said, opting not to push for the moment. "But we should at least warn her so it won't come as a surprise."

"We nothing. You warn her—if you can."

I wondered what that meant. "Be glad to," I said, and hoped I wouldn't regret it. "Well, I'd better go. My supply of boxes is down in Janeece's storage area, so I'd better get to it."

"Great. I'll stop and get some curry chicken from Honan's, so if I'm super-late, nibble on something until I get there. Gotta go. I'll see you at home."

At home. I hung up, feeling grounded and in control of my own fate for the first time in days. That is, until I realized just how much was involved in this spur-of-the-moment move. All the furnishings from my former apartment were already in his, waiting patiently for me to join them. The only things left to go were winter clothes. But for someone who claimed to have little interest in what I wore, I'd managed to keep enough of them to fill Janeece's hall closet. Whether I'd have as many boxes as I'd need was open to question.

I emptied the closet, piled the clothes onto the end of the day bed in the den, the rest on the futon in the living room, and began sorting through them leisurely. If Duck was going to be late getting home, there was no point in hurrying. I considered stopping long enough to make coffee, decided against it. I'd had coffee at lunch, so strong I could still taste it.

I would need a separate box for shoes, one for underwear and jammies. Then there was all the miscellaneous stuff from the bathroom. Seven boxes minimum. No, eight. My bathrobe, so plush it made me resemble a big, fat Easter bunny, would require its own carton.

Then there were the two packages Neva had signed for. I was tempted to open them but shoved temptation aside. It would be more fun to do it when Duck and I were together. I wondered who'd sent them. We'd assured everyone that we already had everything we needed and would not expect gifts. Janeece had suggested we let folks know we'd welcome money, but I couldn't bring myself to do it.

Janeece. I checked the time and wondered when she'd get home. There would be no point in waiting around for her. She might have gone shopping, to the gym, anywhere. Janeece did what she wanted when she wanted, accountable to no one and enjoying it immensely. That would last for another few months before she would begin considering marrying her first husband again. They'd tried it twice, that is, after she had ditched the second husband, who'd turned out to be already married anyway. I wasn't sure I understood my roomie's definition of marital bliss, but that was her problem, not mine.

I thought I heard her at the door and came out of the den to say hi just as the phone rang—a wrong number, but by the time I'd assured the caller that he had not reached Thrifty's Rib House and hung up, she hadn't come in. I opened the door in case she was loaded down. The hall was empty, the only sign of life a glimpse of red as the door to the stairs creaked closed.

It was time to deal with boxes. I answered a call of nature, then went searching for my better slippers. The ones for every day were too ratty to be worn outside the apartment.

I grabbed my keys and my Maglite and took the elevator to the basement, not one of my favorite places. It reminded me of a crypt, the twenty-five-watt bulb outside the storage units far too dim for anyone to see much clearly unless you were an owl.

The elevator stopped at the first floor, which it did whether or not someone there had pushed the call button. The doors wheezed open onto pure chaos. The decorators were in full swing now, bellowing carols off-key while they jockeyed ladders into position and dangled ornaments from the branches of the tree. They'd obviously recruited help from friends as well as family; half of the faces I'd never seen before.

Mr. Stanley, coming in from outside, raised his cane in a gesture for me to hold the elevator.

"Take your time," I called to him above the din of the carolers, and put my back against the rubber stop. "I'm going down, though."

He limped slowly across the lobby, his cane thumping against the marble floor. "Thanks, dearie," he said loudly. "You'll be a while down there. One of the dryers is on the fritz."

"Not a problem," I bellowed back. "I'm heading for the storage units. How's Mrs. Stanley?"

"Middlin'," he said, stepping in. "This cold weather, doncha know."

He rode down with me, pressing the button for his floor as I got off. "You take care, now. Tell Miz Holloway I said hello."

"Will do," I said, suppressing a grin. Janeece, a flirt from the day she was born, was a favorite of all the elderly men in the building.

Relieved to hear one of the washers going in the laundry room at the far end of the hall, I turned left toward the opposite end. At least I wouldn't be alone down here. I hurried toward the storage lockers, anxious to get in and out as soon as I could. Arranged along both sides of the narrow passageway, the cubicles were about five feet wide by nine deep, with solid side and rear walls and fronts of heavy chain metal so the contents were visible—or as visible as the dim bulb in each cell would allow.

The one for my former unit was crammed with blanket and tool boxes, crates full of yarn, and pots of paints and brushes, testimony to Neva's arts and crafts through the years. Janeece's was across from it, jammed with as many clothes racks as she could get in, each groaning under the weight of her summer wardrobe swathed in plastic bags or tissue paper, the odor of moth balls and squares of cedar in assorted pockets pungent and stifling. Monster shoe racks took up most of the floor space, every niche containing a pair of spike-heeled sandals high enough to cause nosebleeds. And not a box in sight. Which meant they were at the very back, behind all those clothes.

I cussed, pocketed the key, and began plotting strategy. I'd have to move at least one of the shoe racks outside to have room to walk. Each housed a dozen pairs and were awkward to handle, but I managed to wrestle the middle rack into the corridor. That freed enough space for me to reach the pull chain for the light. Big wow. If the bulb in the corridor was a twenty-five watt, the ones in each cubicle had to be fifteens. My Maglite would serve for more than moral support.

And any illusion I had about simply squeezing between clothes to get to the rear rapidly bit the dust. I slithered between some rather staid suits to be confronted with a row of full-length, see-through wardrobe bags so stuffed that I couldn't wiggle between them. I wedged one arm past a pair of them and found yet another row of the things. Janeece had managed to fill every inch.

Lifting the wardrobe bags off the rails was out of the question; they were heavy and unwieldly. I'd have to go under them. It was just as well I was still in jeans.

Maglite ablaze, I lowered my backside to the cold concrete floor, rolled under the two rows of wardrobe bags and bang into a single row of cartons, all labeled in Janeece's florid printing. Behind them lining the rear wall were my boxes, folded flat, as pristine as the day I'd lugged them home from the moving company. At least three of her cartons would have to come out so I could crawl in far enough to get a hand on mine.

The first two of hers were no trouble; I slid them forward easily. I hooked a hand around the third and pulled. It not only came out readily, it also came apart. The tape holding the seams of one end disintegrated. The side bulged, bowed, then burst open in spite of the top on it. The contents, old newspaper articles, photographs, and letters, spilled onto the floor.

I swore again, nudged the pile back in, and turned the carton so that the wounded end butted up against one of the others I'd moved. With enough space to maneuver, I had my boxes free in no time, one of which I'd have to sacrifice to replace Janeece's. Taping hers would be a waste of time. She'd filled it too full to begin with; the other sides bulged dangerously as well.

I carried my load to 503. The apartment was still empty. I propped the flats against the end of the futon and went in search of tape. I had just found it on the shelf in the hall closet when I heard the click-click of a key. I peered around the corner, and Janeece burst through the door, Neva behind her.

"See? See?" Neva said. "There she is. Told ya she was here."

Janeece gawked at me, then slammed the door behind her, almost hitting Neva, who'd stepped in, clearly intending to find out why my roomie was so agitated.

"Where the hell have you been?" she demanded. "I've been trying to reach you for hours! Why didn't you call me?"

She towered above me, her French roll fraying around the edges, the tail of her chartreuse silk blouse coming loose from the waist of her short black skirt. This on a woman who always looked as if she was ready for a shoot with a *Vogue* photographer meant she was in a state.

"What do you mean, you've been trying to reach me? I've been here since—when, Neva? A little after four?"

"Thereabouts." Neva moved to the futon and perched on an arm. I winced, but it held. The fact that Janeece didn't even blink was testament to how upset she was.

"Four?" Janeece hurled her ridiculously small Kate Spade purse onto the futon. "Then why didn't you answer the damned phone? Didn't you get my messages?"

I glanced at the cordless, its light blinking steadily. "Janeece, I talked to Duck a little while ago, and there were no messages on that thing. You must have called while I was—"

"You talked to Duck? He's all right?"

"He's fine. Why wouldn't he be?"

"I take it you haven't been in the kitchen."

"Uh—no." I shoved the stack of my jeans and slacks aside. "Sit down, girl. What's got your knickers in a twist?"

She stared down at me, then threw her head back and examined the ceiling. "Swear ta God, I'm gonna kill me somebody." Her gaze swiveled back to me. "Where was he?"

"Duck? At work. Why?"

"Where's the Scotch? I need a drink." She strode into the kitchen.

Neva and I exchanged expressions of alarm. Everyone who knew Janeece well also knew she never imbibed during the week, except on special occasions. She maintained that considering the number of drunks on her father's side of the family, she might be genetically disposed to join their ranks. She usually restricted herself to the occasional snort anywhere from Friday after five to Sunday before six. And she stuck to it.

She returned to the living room and passed the glass in her right hand to Neva and a ragged sheet of paper to me while she got rid of her coat.

I scanned it, barely able to decipher her writing, which bore no resemblance to her usual elegant scrawl. "What's this say? Duck's been in a what?"

Retrieving the glass, she tossed the contents down in one gulp and shuddered, her face in a knot. "Gawd, this is nasty stuff. Okay." She pulled in a deep breath, straining the delicate fabric of her blouse. "I decided to take half a day's leave," she said, pacing the length of the room. "Got here and the phone was ringing off the hook, some woman saying that Duck had been in an accident in Baltimore and—"

"An accident? That's ridiculous. And in Baltimore? What would he be doing in Baltimore?"

"How the hell would I know? Anyway, she said he was being taken to shock trauma and you should come immediately because he was critical."

"Now, that's downright mean," Neva said, wiggling to get more comfortable on the arm of the futon.

"I called your cell phone but you didn't answer, so I left a message. I called your aunt in the Shores, no answer. I couldn't figure out where else you might be, so—"

"It wasn't on," I said. "The battery's low, and I . . . Never mind, go ahead."

"I didn't know what else to do, so I drove into Baltimore. At least someone would be there who knew him. I kept trying to reach you every time I got stuck at a light."

"And of course you couldn't find him," I said.

"Right. I figured maybe I'd gone to the wrong hospital, so I got directions to the one on South Hanover. When I didn't find him there, I got smart and used the Yellow Pages. Have you any idea how many hospitals there are in that city? Finally, I gave up and came home."

"Oh, Janeece." I rose and gave her a bear hug. "I'm so sorry. What else can I say? Duck will be touched that you went all that way to be with him."

"Yeah. Well." She moved from my embrace, looking wrung out. "I'm glad he's all right." Equanimity restored, she spotted the boxes. "What's going on?" Her features drooped. "You're moving out?"

This wasn't quite the way I'd planned to tell her. "It's past time, Janeece. I've imposed on you long enough."

She threw herself into an easy chair. "It hasn't been an imposition. It's been fun. I really hate to see you go. Shit. You know what this means, don't you? I'll have to find somebody and get married again."

"But you'll still stay here, won't you?" Neva asked her. Vacant apartments meant someone new, someone she felt might not be up to her standards.

"One never knows, do one?" Janeece grinned. "Quit worrying, Neva. You couldn't get me out of here with a keg of dynamite. Oh, well. I've got to get to the dry cleaners before it closes. Guess I'd better stop at the liquor store, too. I'm out of white Zinfandel, and we've got to have a farewell drink. Promise you won't leave before I get back."

I promised. She collected her coat and purse and hauled Neva off the arm of the futon. We all left together, Neva to check on the decorating downstairs, Janeece to her weekly run to the cleaners, and me back down to the catacombs.

There were no sounds from the laundry room this time. Nothing unsavory had ever happened down here as far as I knew, but the thought of being alone made me twitchy. I returned to the storage unit, taped a new box together, and set about filling it with the flotsam from Janeece's.

It was like a print version of *This Is Your Life*. Baby pictures, report cards, school photos, family snapshots, tons of them. For the second time today, I wrestled with a bout of envy, and regret that I would never have a cache of memories like this. I'd been orphaned at five when my parents had been killed, victims of arson. The conflagration had eliminated any keepsakes my parents might have collected. I was left with the clothes I was wearing and a few wisps of memories of them. The new family I'd discovered recently made up for a lot, but not entirely. Fighting a pale blue funk, I dug into Janeece's box.

I don't know how long I sat there completely enthralled by the young Janeece, thin as a number two pencil, all arms, legs, and teeth. I didn't read the letters but I'd glanced my way through at least half the box and dozens and dozens of old snapshots and fading Polaroids when I became aware that something had changed down here. It was harder to see. In fact, outside the open door of the cubicle was nothing but pure darkness, the fifteen-watt bulb above my head too weak to throw light beyond the confines of this space. The hall light must have burned out.

I dropped the photo I'd been holding and got up, stiff from being in one position so long. Maglite illuminating my path to the door, I looked out. The entire corridor was pitch black, no light outside the laundry room, no fluorescent glow from its interior or thump-thump from the dryers. Goose bumps rose on my arms, nudged from under my skin by a seismic muscle spasm.

Then I heard it. A sound, just barely audible, not quite a footfall so much as the crunch of grit on concrete from somewhere along the darkened hallway. No doubt about it. I was not alone.

3

STEPPING BACK INTO THE CUBICLE, I REACHED up and turned the light off, wincing at how loud the chain sounded as it moved in the lamp housing. Dreading the result, I doused the Maglite. Darkness seemed to swallow me whole, and in an instant, I was five again, waiting for the monsters that lurked in unlit rooms. Breathing deeply, I gave myself a good talking to. I was an adult, with damned near nine years of experience as a cop. If I was in trouble, it was up to me to get out of it.

It came again, a scrape, a soft squeak somewhere near the elevator and stairwell just beyond it. Definitely someone there trying unsuccessfully not to give themselves away.

My pulse rate had tripled, my heart pounding so hard I was sure it could be detected from the other end of the hall. I had a decision to make: stay or go. Neither option was particularly appealing. I'd be vulnerable either way. If I left I'd be approaching whoever was out there in the dark. But remaining here left me little protection. I couldn't just pull the door closed; Janeece's shoe rack held it open. If I tried to hide, the wardrobe bags might camouflage the top two-thirds of me, but I'd be visible from midcalf on down. Besides, there was no guarantee they wouldn't cave under my weight. The bottom line, however, was that I did not want to be trapped in this little room.

Grateful for my soft-soled slippers, I inched my way toward the door, senses on full alert, flashlight held in position to be used as a weapon. Mentally I rehearsed what parts of the body to aim for. I tested my knee, shifting my weight to my right side. This had been a good day on it so far, all things considered. I'd been neglecting the exercises my physical therapist had recommended. Lord, I vowed silently, get me through this and I swear I'll go back to the gym and—

Suddenly a din erupted, scaring my pants off until I realized what it was. The fire door. Whoever was down here had pushed it open, and it had hit the wall behind it with explosive force. The corridor erupted in a blaze of light streaming toward my end. No twenty-five-watt, this one.

"Police! Slide your weapon outside the door, then follow it with your hands up! Now!!"

Police? Thank God! They'd take care of the intruder. All I had to do was stay the hell out of their way. My bones melted with relief.

"We're not playing games here, lady! Drop your weapon, kick it out hard, all the way across the hall! Then step out slowly, hands above your head!"

Lady? Second thoughts slithered under my moment of gratitude. They couldn't mean me. Could they?

I started to move, then stopped, caution gluing me where I stood. No way was I falling for this. "What district do you work out of? I want to see a badge."

"And I want to see your hands. Lemme see your hands, Valeria. NOW!!"

Valeria? Who the hell . . .?

The ball dropped into the correct hole. Jesus! They thought I was Valeria Preston? The one who'd blown her husband's head to smithereens in a restaurant full of witnesses and had walked out unmolested? Vince Preston had been a cop, and the whole city had been looking for her ever since. With a vengeance. In other words, I could be in deep doo-doo.

"All right, now listen," I called, stooping to send the Maglite skittering into the hallway. "I'm coming out and I'm unarmed. You've got the wrong person. I'm not Valeria Preston. My name in Leigh Warren. I used to be a cop, worked out of the Third District."

"Yeah, right. I wanna see those hands out that door, then you. I'm counting to three, then we're coming in. One. Two."

This was no time to test his knowledge of basic arithmetic. I stuck my hands beyond the cubicle and wiggled my fingers. "No weapon, see?" Stepping out, I raised my arms, blinded by the high-powered light someone held, definitely not the one doing all the yelling.

I sensed movement, then felt myself flattened roughly against the wall, my arms yanked behind my back. Cuffs snared my wrists, and I fought an instant of panic. I'd never imagined how vulnerable one felt cuffed like this.

Beyond me, someone began the Miranda bit. Submitting to a none-too-gentle frisking, I willed myself still and my temper quiescent. One move and I wouldn't live to regret it. Besides, this guy was only doing his duty.

He spun me around to face him. "Oh. Oh, shit," he muttered.

"Oh, shit indeed," I erupted, free to vent my anger now and unable to contain it. "Do I look like Valeria

Preston?" Granted, she was African American and wore her hair cropped like mine, but from her picture and the info in the *Washington Post*, it was obvious that she was several inches shorter than I am. But of more importance, to me anyway, she had an unsightly birthmark under her jaw down onto her neck that he had to see was definitely not on mine.

"Uncuff her," a voice directed from the darkness. "I recognize her. Pass the word back up the line that this is a false alarm, somebody's idea of a joke. Whoever that somebody is is in big trouble with the department."

Perhaps they were, I thought, steaming, but not nearly as much as with me.

There was procedure to be followed, so it was a good half hour before they were satisfied that I was who I said I was, my identity confirmed by the powers-that-be, my driver's license, union card, along with the other cop who recognized me, and Neva, more interested in how the uniforms had gotten into the building than by what was happening to me.

"Dammit, that button outside the door is for calling the management in an emergency," she fumed. "Might as well disconnect it for all the good it's doing."

"I want to hear it again," I said to Willard once we were upstairs in 503. In plainclothes, he was evidently the spokesperson for the cadre of uniforms that had filled the basement corridor. "You got an anonymous call saying Preston was hiding out downstairs, armed and dangerous?"

"Someone on a cell phone. We're still trying to trace it but it's probably one of those throwaways. We apologize again, but you've been there. You know we couldn't afford to take any chances."

I grudgingly allowed as how, no, they couldn't.

Willard scowled. "Even a blind man could see there's no resemblance between you and Preston. This was a waste of time and manpower."

"Didn't do my blood pressure any favors either," I grumbled. "What gets me is that the only people who knew I was downstairs were the ones in the lobby decorating the tree. They saw me on the elevator and must have heard me talking to Mr. Stanley. I don't understand why anyone would do this. They're all neighbors," I protested.

"Not all of 'em," Neva reminded me. "Miz Donovan's son was there, him and his daughters, and Mr. Bean's family. And Gracie Poole invited all them women from her arts and crafts group. They made most of the ornaments."

"How many outsiders are we talking about here?" Willard asked.

Neva's frown deepened, her lips pursed. "Not sure. A couple of dozen or more. Gracie's bunch is probably in her apartment, three-seventeen, for hot chocolate and cookies if you'd like to talk to them."

"Oh, I do. I definitely do." Willard pushed himself to his feet with effort. Sit in Janeece's living room chair and your butt is scant inches off the floor.

He cast a jaundiced eye in my direction. "You don't have a beef with one of your neighbors, do you?"

"Good Lord, no!"

"Our residents are quality people," Neva came to their defense. "Teachers, social workers, and the like. And retirees. We all get along like one big family."

That was a bit of overstatement, if not an outright lie, but now was no time to quibble, so I kept my mouth closed.

"Well, someone in that lobby had to make that call to us," Willard said, "someone who saw you on the elevator because she described what you're wearing right down to the slippers."

"Definitely a she?" I asked.

"Oh, yeah. The question is whether or not this was an honest mistake, and my gut says it wasn't. Looks to me as if someone thought they'd have a little fun at your expense. Only it was at the city's expense too. I'll follow up on this, talk to the ladies in—" He squinted at his notebook.

"Three-seventeen," Neva supplied.

"Thanks. And, Mrs. Burns, if you'll make a list of the residents you remember seeing down there. One of my men will stop by for it. I doubt anyone will admit to anything, but whoever it is needs to know how seriously the department takes false reports. Well, enjoy the rest of your evening."

"Oh, thanks loads," I said, and opened the door for him. "Will you let me know what you find out?"

He hesitated. "Maybe. Guess it wouldn't do any harm if you took a look at the list Mrs. Burns makes, see if it rings any bells. We'll get one from this Ms. Poole, too, make some comparisons. That's all for now." With a brief excuse for a smile, he was gone.

Perched on the arm of the futon again, Neva eyed me. "You all right? You looked kinda shaky for a while."

"I'm fine. Mad, though, so mad I could spit. And if Willard's coming back, my plans for tonight are shot. This was supposed to be my first night at Duck's."

"There's always tomorrow night. I wouldn't put it off any longer than that, if I were you. That Mr. Duck's a stone hunk," she said, her grin suggestive of what she'd like to do to him or, perhaps, with him given the chance.

She stood up and massaged her back. "Miz Holloway's gonna miss you, though."

"Likewise. She's been a good friend. She'll hate having missed all the excitement."

I'd barely finished the sentence when we heard her key in the door. "Who was that just left here?," she asked, balancing dry cleaning and a bag from Lexxon's Wine and Spirits. "You having gentlemen callers in behind my back? And Duck's?"

Neva chuckled and got up. "Reckon she could have done without this one. Miz Warren," she said, on her way to the door. "You need to think real hard about who you've pissed off. Seems to me with two dirty tricks in one day, somebody's tryin' to tell you something. Y'all have a good evening." And she was gone.

"Two dirty tricks?" Janeece demanded. "What's she talking about? What did I miss?"

Uh-oh. I should have told Willard about the call Janeece had intercepted earlier. I'd fill him in when he came back with the list.

I jerked my head toward the easy chair. "I think you'd better open the Zinfandel and sit down for this one."

4

"RUN ALL THAT BY ME AGAIN," DUCK SAID THE next morning, his brow furrowed with concentration. I had no illusions that the bizarre narrative explaining why I hadn't arrived the night before might be the sole reason for the ridges lining his forehead at the moment. Not that he hadn't been listening, but somewhere on the bottom of his cereal bowl, hidden by an ocean of milk, was an errant raisin he was determined to find. Fortunately, he had the kind of mind that could compartmentalize easily, so it didn't bother me that he appeared to be paying more attention to the raisin chase than to the misadventures that had delayed my spending my first night as a permanent resident in the condo. Duck loves raisins, but again, fortunately, I was confident that he loved me more. Really.

I began again with the prank call that had sent Janeece scrambling all over Baltimore, then the incident in the basement.

"So," Duck said, giving up and draining the milk in one swallow, "first the bogus call about my alleged accident, then the one to the department while you were down in the storage room."

"Isn't that what I just said?" I asked, wondering if the raisin had won the battle for his attention after all.

He got up to put the bowl in the dishwasher. "You were definitely the target, not Janeece. I'm thinking that whoever called and got her really thought you'd be home to answer the phone, and when you weren't, assumed that Janeece would be able to find you with no trouble. The caller had to know you'd try to track me down at work first before you'd take off for Baltimore. But—" He leaned back against the sink, arms across his chest. "That assumes she knows you as more than a passing acquaintance. Perhaps she doesn't. Perhaps she thought you'd do exactly what Janeece did: go off half-cocked. But what was the point? Simply to jerk your chain?"

I wasn't ready to pose the only possibility that had occurred to me in the middle of the night. I was fairly certain how it would be received, so I chickened out and kept my mouth shut.

"As for siccing the cops on you, that's the one that worries me. It could have backfired. Unless, again, she figured that since you'd been a cop, you'd know how to react so you wouldn't get yourself shot—assuming she knows you were in uniform for eight years. You say the senior man's name was Willard? I'll give him a call, see what he's found out."

"If anything," I said, momentarily distracted. I'm a leg woman. Wearing only a pair of briefs and T-shirt, Duck stood barefoot, ankles crossed, presenting one long line of smooth, yummy, brown, well-muscled thighs and calves. He'd make a great model for Jockeys or BVDs, especially with that nice round butt and . . .

I yanked myself back to the subject at hand. "He left to question some of the people decorating the tree, but face it, what with heightened security and all these days, the department doesn't have the time or man-power to waste on a prank caller."

"Oh, they'll take it seriously, all right. Think of the number of cops they sent."

"I'd just as soon not," I said, with a shudder. All those uniforms, their weapons aimed at me. I'd be dreaming about that for a while.

"Can you think of anyone who'd go to such lengths to shake you up? Someone at one of the districts you were assigned to maybe? Think male *and* female. She might be some joker's girlfriend he's asked to help. Because we've both worked with a lot of practical jokers, but the women in the department don't tend to go in for the kind of juvenile behavior the guys enjoy. Smelly cheese in the bottom of a locker, swiping a dude's lunch while his back is turned, that's the kind of stupid stunt we pull on each other. But this has a really nasty feel to it. You sure you haven't crossed someone here recently? You may not have meant to, but—"

"No, I haven't. Honestly." I pulled up short, something he'd said opening up possibilities that hadn't oc-curred to me. They rapidly escalated to probabilities. "Oh, my God."

"What?" Duck glanced at his watch, then sat down, straddling a chair backward. "You remember some-thing?"

"Realized something. The dog and cat turds."

"Say what?" He lowered his head, gazing up at me, as if over his reading glasses.

"Someone left a pile of dog poop in front of Cholly and Neva's a while back and some cat poop yesterday. It wasn't for them, it was meant for me! Whoever did it didn't know I'd moved out."

"Until sometime yesterday," Duck amended, "or they wouldn't have known to call Janeece's."

"Right. That rules out the residents; they can probably give you the precise date I carried my clothes across the hall. Which means it has to be an outsider, perhaps someone in Gracie Poole's group. They're members of her arts and crafts classes at the Seniors' Center and were in and out of the lobby all day, plus hitting all the floors to collect ornaments from people—"

"A perfect opportunity to leave the cat crap."

"Poor Neva and Cholly. I don't know if I have the guts to tell them. I guess it's just as well I'm moving out so they don't ask me to."

"Hey, none of this is your fault, at least as far as you know."

I waved that away as irrelevant, still trying to work out a plausible scenario. "If this woman helping with the tree just happened, intentionally, of course, to mention my name, sooner or later someone was bound to tell her I've been bunking with Janeece."

Duck smiled, got up, and planted a kiss on the top of my head. "Smart girl. That's it, then. So we find out who was in the Poole woman's group and go from there. Come on. I've got to get dressed."

I grabbed a banana from the counter and followed him into the bedroom. I still wasn't used to seeing my bed in here, in fact, got a small jolt every time I saw my furniture in this condo. But of all the items that had been moved from my apartment to Duck's, the bed seemed as if it belonged here the most. It looked at home, the head-and footboard with their unfussy, clean lines. Like Duck, I realized, who had helped me pick it out back in the spring. We had similar tastes, and on the few occasions we'd been in furniture stores, had always gravitated toward the simple and uncluttered—Scandinavian or Shaker or, like the bed, mission style.

I patted the pillows to say hello, then stretched out on my stomach to watch Duck get dressed, something I love to do. Truth is, I love to watch him do anything, love the way he moves, like a well-toned athlete, smooth, with a masculine grace.

Funny thing about Dillon Upshur Kennedy. At first glance there's nothing remarkable about him. He's your basic black brother, average height and weight, average looks. Round face, skin the color of Hershey's (with almonds, my favorite), and dark eyes with obscenely long lashes. What gets you is that he always appears to be smiling, something about the curve of his lips, I guess.

And he has a way of looking at you that gives you the impression he's glad to see you and whatever you have to say is important to him. He makes you want to be his friend, which probably accounts for how easily he's managed to get bad guys to confess. Got a hard case who refuses to talk? Call Duck. The local jails are populated with criminals who spilled their guts to him, yet still yell his name and wave whenever they see him there. In spite of the fact that he was instrumental to their being there, they like him. Go figure.

As for his effect on women, it can be devastating and something I decided I'd just as soon not think about at the moment.

He disappeared into the walk-in closet and came out with a gray shirt and charcoal slacks on hangers. "There's plenty of space for your clothes in there," he said. "In case you missed it, that's a broad hint."

"It was? Duh! I hope you've enjoyed all that room to yourself because that's over. But wait a minute, honey."

My mind had skittered back to the previous subject. "All the women Gracie had working with her on the tree are seniors. You know how dopey I am about old ladies. I'd probably love them even if Nunna hadn't drummed 'respect your elders' into me. No way would I do anything to antagonize one. And frankly, I can't imagine an old lady making those calls."

Duck snorted in derision as he grabbed a pair of black socks from a dresser drawer and perched on the side of the bed to put them on. "Inside every old lady is a young one, babe. You know how I feel about the b-word, but if one of those old biddies was a bitch thirty years ago, chances are she hasn't changed."

I found myself resisting the whole notion. It simply didn't feel right. "Tell you what," I said, undoing the buttons on his shirt for him. "Check in with Willard when you have a chance, and I'll do some fishing around with Gracie Poole, no pun intended."

Duck rolled his eyes at that and extended a hand for his shirt. "Deal. Let's hope that whoever she is, she's shot her wad. What are you up to today?"

I hadn't made my to-do list yet, so I had to wing it. "Pick up our tickets to Hawaii, swing by the Bridal Bower for my wedding outfit, check to see if my laptop's been repaired, buy a doormat for Janeece, for a start."

"You gonna be able to hang around to let Clarissa in?"

It took me a moment to switch gears, primarily because it was the first time I'd heard her name. I was also intrigued by the fact that he felt free to call her that instead of Miss or Mrs. Whatever. That was one of the reasons women of all ages fell for him like a ton of bricks. He was always unfailingly polite and never used their first names without permission.

"I'll be here. Just how old is this Clarissa person?"

Buttoning, he appeared to think about it. "Got me. Thirty-five, maybe forty. With her kind of face, it's hard to tell."

"And just what kind of face is that?"

He smirked and patted me on the fanny. "What's the matter, babe? Jealous? Well, you should be. I like her." The smirk segued into a grin. "I mean, I really like her. Man, can she cook!"

For the first time, I was genuinely concerned. It wasn't so much that Duck loved to eat as his delight and appreciation of the process of preparing a meal. He had flirted with bankruptcy to stock his kitchen with Calphalon cookware, his most prized possessions. He'd given them to his sister, Vanessa, when he'd taken off back in August to search for his missing father. Once the search was over and he realized he wouldn't be spending the rest of his life in jail for patricide, he'd taken them back. Vanessa hadn't spoken to him for a week afterward. In other words, Duck loved to cook, and the only danger I sensed when it came to competition from other women was from some female in an apron with a box of recipes from her mama.

"Clarissa has cooked for you?" I asked.

"Man, she makes a mean jambalaya." He was enjoying himself immensely. "Never tasted anything like it."

Eyes narrowed, I sat up. "Well, be sure you tell her what you want for your last meal by her because she won't be cooking for you much longer."

He gave an exaggerated sigh and reached for his slacks. "Oh, well. For you, I'll give her up. But don't forget, you've got to tell her."

"No problem. And since you've had so much fun at

my expense, I'll also tell her you'll give her a month's severance pay."

He slid his feet into the slacks. "Babe, she's worth it. Gotta tell you, if we weren't engaged—"

I grabbed a pillow and whacked him with it, whereupon he snatched it from me, wrestled me onto my back, and kissed me.

Duck's a dynamite kisser, the kind who makes your toes curl. I forgot Clarissa, dedicated myself to the task at hand, literally, since his slacks were around his ankles, and, in the process, made him sorry that he had less than ten minutes to hit the door or be late for work.

He finally left, and I set about filling up the empty clothes pole in the walk-in closet. In my hurry to get here in time to have breakfast with him, I'd managed to bring only two boxes with me. They didn't make much of a dent, but it was a start.

I wandered into the living room looking for something to do until this Clarissa person arrived. There were a couple of hours to fill. I debated running back to Janeece's to bring another load of boxes, but it was rush hour. Not a good idea. I might not make it back in time. She might not wait, and I wanted to meet this woman in the worst way and begin the process of eliminating her from our lives.

I glanced around and wondered why I wasn't as content at being surrounded by my own furniture as I thought I should be. The condos in this building, like the building itself, had all the personality of a shoe box. No decorative features, like molding or chair rails, no ceiling lights except in the kitchen. Sick of all-white walls, Duck had at least painted, a soft green in the living room and guest room, a medium blue in the master bedroom and bath, and a sunny yellow in the kitchen.

That was the end of it. Except for his bookshelves, he had had no qualms about getting rid of his belongings to make room for mine, since his had come from a combination of yard sales and Goodwill. He'd done wonders with the little he'd had, and I missed a few of them.

But ever since his family had been evicted when he was a kid and he'd watched people swipe practically everything they'd owned off the curb, he swore he never wanted to become attached to anything he couldn't walk away from and not look back. That didn't apply to his cookware, of course, and except for his desk, which I'd asked him to keep, he'd cleaned out this place in the space of four hours the day the movers were to arrive with the contents of my apartment.

So now the sofa, coffee and end tables, lamps, easy chairs and étagère, everything was mine. I'd left the arrangement to Duck, who had a flair for decorating I envied. Still, there was something not right about this room. Perhaps if I shifted both easy chairs to right angles of the sofa with an end table between them . . .

I rolled up the braided oval rug to get it out of the way and began moving things around. Periodically I get an itch to shove a piece from this corner to that, and before I know it, the whole room's been changed. I knew Duck wouldn't mind; he was under the impression it was part and parcel of PMS, and I'd never disabused him of the notion. Men can be so dumb about some things, thank God.

I moved the étagère, then wrestled the couch into a different place. Still not satisfied, I tried another configuration. And another.

I'm not sure how many I had tried when I heard the knock at the door. Stunned, I checked the time. Nine fifty-five! I'd been shoving furniture this way and that for two hours.

I groaned, dismayed at meeting this woman who had her tentacles wrapped around Duck's heart when I was now sweaty, disheveled, and probably smelled like a polecat.

"Just a minute," I called and pulled the neck of my sweater out to get a whiff of my underarms. It wasn't too bad. Perhaps if I kept some distance between us she wouldn't pass out.

Adjusting the sweater, I crossed to the door and, after wrestling with the deadbolt, opened it. "Hello. I'm—"

"Dillon's Leigh, of course."

"It's nice to meet you," I said, moving out of the way. "I've heard a lot about you from Duck."

She peered at me curiously. "Uh . . . I've heard a lot about you, too. Look just like your picture. Only I thought you were taller. Oh, there they are!" Waddling in, she grabbed a set of keys from Duck's desk, leaving a sizable brown grocery bag in their place. "Don't know where my head is these days. Speaking of which, I wish I had the nerve to wear my hair like yours. When did you get it cut?"

"Day before yesterday." I smoothed my edges, dismayed. If she had to ask, I must still have that just-plucked chicken look.

"Sorry, darlin', I've gotta come out of these shoes." She plopped herself down on the sofa, shedding her coat to reveal a deep purple sweatsuit. Evidently her shoes weren't the only things that pinched. Wincing, she tugged off her earrings, bright, dangling mini-chandeliers, then massaged her earlobes with gusto. She leaned over to loosen her laces, puffing a little, and I gave serious consideration to killing Duck.

Clarissa was perhaps five feet tall and as wide as she was high. Light-skinned with a hint of olive, she had a moon face and full cheeks, her complexion as clear and smooth as a baby's. Bright, hazel eyes squinted myopically from beneath reddish-brown brows a couple of shades darker than a head full of Shirley Temple curls generously streaked with gray and held off her face by a yellow plastic headband. She was sixty-plus if she was a day, in other words, almost an old lady. And an eccentric one, considering the number of colors she wore. The effect was blinding. I liked her already, just as Duck had known I would.

"Things are different in here," she said, toeing off each shoe. "Nice. What happened to the rug?"

"Over there in the corner so I could move stuff around."

She cut her eyes at me in a semisquint and smiled. "PMS, huh? Used to hit me and Sister the same way. What will you put on the shelves of the étagère? It's awfully pretty to stand there empty."

She had a point. Perhaps filling it up might give me the quality I kept feeling was missing from the room, whatever that was. "There's a whole box of things, knickknacks and stuff. If I can find it, I'll unpack it."

Three horizontal lines zipped across her forehead. "That's yours?"

"Everything in here is, except for the desk."

She nodded. "That explains it. I didn't think this room looked like him. Not that I can see it all that good today."

It was my turn to frown. "Why not?"

"It's Sister's turn with the eyeglasses because she's driving today. I took the Metro. Can't see boo without them. Shoot, we're both so nearsighted that . . . Uh-oh."

Her mouth turned down at the corners. "That wasn't what you meant by your 'why not.'" She sighed. "Me and my big mouth. Sister always says I talk too much."

"You haven't said anything wrong," I assured her. "The room hasn't felt right to me, and I haven't been able to figure out what the problem is. That's why I've been moving things around."

She hoisted a brow. "You're sure you don't mind me meddling? I mean, sometimes folks want your opinion, but only if it matches theirs. That's Sister, for one."

"I'm sure. Feel free." I propped one butt cheek on a corner of Duck's desk to wait. I didn't have long.

"Understand," Clarissa began, "you've got nice things and I can tell you've taken good care of them. But it looks like an old folks' room, child. I had a sofa like this when I first got married—high back and these big round arms—and I'm no spring chicken. And these mahogany end tables. What do you call that? Louis the Something? Or French something? It's not just that these things don't look like Dillon, unless I miss my guess, they don't much look like you either." Her eyes narrowed. "Bet they came from your mama's house. Am I right?"

"My lord." Flabbergasted, I dropped onto the desk chair. "Of course. I couldn't figure it out. I've had this stuff for ages. Some of it comes from down home but—"

"Down home? Where's that?"

"Sunrise, North Carolina."

"Sunrise? Sister and I, we're from Rocky Mount, but I never heard of Sunrise."

"Most folks haven't. It's in the mountains. Anyway, when I moved into my apartment, I was trying for the same feel as the house I grew up in. But it's my foster mom's taste, not mine. Or Duck's. And he never said a word."

"He wouldn't. That Dillon's a sweet boy. Well, let me get up off of here, put that lot in the refrigerator, and get to work. I always start with the bathroom. Makes you appreciate having room to move around when you come out."

It took a couple of pushes on the cushions on each side before she made it up, but once on her pudgy feet, she moved with a speed that surprised me. She snatched the big grocery sack off the desk and headed for the kitchen. If that was her lunch, no wonder she had a weight problem. Whatever was in it, it smelled damned good, though.

I stayed put for at least fifteen minutes, trying to figure out how to resolve the problem with the furniture. The chintz, the old-fashioned lamps. No doubt about it, it had to go. Well, most of it, anyway. There was nothing wrong with trying for eclectic. I'd talk to Duck about it tonight, see if he thought our savings could survive the big chomp it would take to refurnish.

The glass-shelved étagère could stay, another piece we'd picked out together. The least I could do was fill it with my knickknacks.

I massaged my knee for a moment. All the furniture arranging had put more stress on it than it liked. I'd be paying for it the rest of the day. And night. Poor Duck. Our first night living together and I'd be reeking of Ben-Gay.

His guest room, which he'd used as a workroom during his ceramics and pottery period, contained the remainder of the items moved from my apartment, most packed in boxes stacked against one wall. I squeezed my way around my little desk and two kitchen chairs, grateful that Duck had been smart enough to put all the cartons marked "Fragile" on the top layer. The one I needed was also labeled "My Babies," since it contained my collection of crystal owls and dolphins. I might have overdone it with the Magic Marker, but there was no doubt as to what was in what.

I found it easily enough, bless Duck, moved it from a stack and set it on my desk to get a better grip when a subconscious nudge from somewhere prodded me to examine those stacks again. It took me a couple of seconds before the reason surfaced. The last time I was in here, the boxes had been stacked like stairs, one lone carton on the left end, two next to it, then three, then four, etc. Now the configuration was one, two, three, four and four. A box was missing.

In search of it, I slithered around my den furniture and the chest of drawers we planned to leave in here. No box. Duck, in one of his cooking moods, had asked me which one contained the wok he'd given me in hopes I'd fall enough in love with stir-fry to use it. Perhaps he'd unpacked the whole thing. But no, there it was. "Pots, Pans, Wok" printed clearly on the two sides I could see. So which one was missing?

Knickknacks forgotten, I went in search of the errant carton, Clarissa's tuneless humming from the bathroom grating on my nerves. Nothing in the kitchen or shallow pantry. I didn't bother with the bedroom; I knew it wasn't in the closet. Where else could he have put it?

"Oops." Clarissa, a pair of sheets draped over one arm, caromed off me as she exited the bathroom. "Hope you don't need to use the facility for a few minutes. Floor's wet. I declare, I don't know why Dillon bothers to keep me on. This place is always as clean as an operating room. But then, after y'all get married, you probably won't. Need me, I mean." A wistful expression softened her features. She resembled an elderly baby.

I couldn't do it, damn Duck's butt. He'd known it too.

"Duck is genetically disposed to be neat," I said. "I, however, am not. I'm a clutterer from way back. After a month of my being here, you'll probably demand a raise."

She smiled so sweetly I felt like hugging her. "I'm glad. Not about the raise; he's already paying me too much, considering how little there's been to do. It's just a joy to work for him. He's such a nice child. Sister just loves him." She clamped her lips together, as if afraid she'd said too much again.

"Your sister's met him?"

"In passing. The thing is, he reminds me of my boy. He's crossed over now, killed in a construction accident. Likes to eat, just like my Shelton did. Your Dillon, I mean. I made some barbecue last night. Brought some for lunch and a couple of helpings for him."

Mention barbecue and I begin to drool, mentally. It must have shown.

"You cotton to barbecue? Not the Texas kind," she added. "Nothing against it, but I prefer the way they make it in North Carolina where you take the pork and—"

"Don't, please. All I had for breakfast was a corn muffin and a banana."

"You poor child! Why don't I warm you a little barbecue soon's I finish in the bedroom? I brought rolls and everything."

I couldn't have said no if you'd paid me, even though, truth be told, the only reason I hadn't eaten more for breakfast was because I'd been a little queasy. Perhaps the three-fire-alarm chili and Zinfandel Janeece and I had feted with last night hadn't been the best combination.

"By the way, Duck hasn't stored one of my boxes in the linen closet, has he?" I peered past her into the bathroom.

"No, ma'am," she said, shaking her head. "Nothing in there but sheets and towels and the like. Can't find your knickknacks?"

"I found them all right but a box is missing and I can't imagine where he might have put it."

"It's bound to be around here somewhere," she said, with a pat of assurance on my arm. "Let me go change these sheets and dust so I can feed you. Shouldn't take me two shakes."

Suddenly, her left hip began to trill "America the Beautiful." She grinned at my surprise and dug into her pocket, pulling out a tiny cellular phone. "Just my way of waving the flag," she said and flipped open its top. "What, Sister? I'm busy." Executing a perfect about-face, she hurried into the bedroom.

I left her to it and went back into the kitchen. I hadn't checked under the cabinets. I knew which ones contained the holy Calphalon. No point in looking there. No room. The others were empty, waiting for my assortment of cooking utensils. Frustrated, I grabbed the tea kettle, filled it, and put it on to boil, then just in case I should have enough for two, stuck my head in the bedroom door.

Clarissa, smoothing the bottom sheet with one hand as she circumnavigated the bed, barked into the phone.

"No, ma'am, I will not sub for Geneva Ladyslipper to-night. You know what she's got her students reading? *War and Peace,* for Lord's sake! I agree they ought to be introduced to the classics, but Tolstoy? They aren't ready for that. What's wrong with Hemingway or O. Henry?" Spotting me, she blinked. "Hold on a minute. Need something, sugar?"

"Sorry to interrupt," I said. "I just wanted to know if you'd like a cup of tea."

"That would be nice. I'll be done shortly. Sister, I've got to go or I'll never finish this bed."

Back in the kitchen, I found the tin of tea bags, the conversation from the other room drifting across the hall.

"Yes, she's as nice as can be and looks just like her picture. She likes to shove furniture around, just like you. Even moved the sofa. You wouldn't think some-body as little as she is could even budge it."

I glanced down. Granted, I'd lost some weight over the last month, worrying that my backside would strain the seams of that blasted wedding suit Janeece had talked me into buying. But "little" is not a term I'd ever associate with my one hundred and thirty-something pounds. Even my height wouldn't qualify. I was five-six, and that's average in anyone's book.

Determined not to eavesdrop, I returned to the guest room. I had to figure out which box was missing or go nuts. Rifling my desk, I found the detailed list I'd made of what was in what. It was supposed to make un-packing simpler. The boxes were numbered as well as labeled, most on all four sides. One or two near the bot-tom, of course, were not, their marks facing the wall or the one adjacent.

After checking off the numbers of those I could see,

I grabbed the top layer of the first stack, moved them to the floor to get to those on the bottom, in the process dropping one. Fortunately, it wasn't marked "Fragile."

Clarissa appeared in the doorway. "What was that? Are you all right?" She still held the phone to her ear. Evidently her conversations with her sister amounted to telethons.

"Fine. Just lost my grip on this boy," I said, nudging it aside. "Trying to figure out which one is missing." I waved the list.

"Nothing serious," Clarissa pronounced into the phone and backed out. "Trying to solve the mystery of a missing box. She's so organized, just like you. Has a list of the things."

I turned the bottom one around, checked off its number.

"Ask her what?" Her voice drifted back down the hall, and when she didn't return to ask me whatever, I tuned out.

At the end of the exercise, the only one left unchecked was the carton with the contents of my desk drawers. Granted, I wouldn't need them any time soon, but it was the principle of the thing.

It occurred to me that I should check the tea kettle. I hadn't heard the whistle, but it was past time that the water should have come to a boil.

I found Clarissa in the kitchen, the table set for two with plates, flatware, and all. "Sit yourself down," she ordered. "The barbecue's in the microwave. I was just waiting until you finished." Punching in the time, she pushed start and stood back to make certain it would. "Um, how'd you and your list make out?"

I explained the problem. "I'll give Duck a call later. Maybe he put it in the storage room off the balcony.

Can't imagine why he would, but it's the only place left to look. I don't have the key or I'd do it now. By God, if he took that box to the Dumpster with the stuff of his he threw out, I'll sue his pants off. All my financial records are in it."

Clarissa stiffened, then turned to watch the window of the microwave as if she could see what was going on under the lid of the bowl. "So it's just one box? And you're sure it's not back at your place? Or still in your car or something?"

"Positive. It was in that room the last time I was here two weeks ago. I think I'll have Lemon Zinger." I got up and poured the water in both cups since Clarissa seemed to be determined to babysit the barbecue. "I couldn't help overhearing some of your conversation with your sister." She stiffened again, and I rushed to explain. "When I came to ask you whether you wanted tea. You've been a teacher? Clarissa? What's wrong?"

She hadn't moved but her olive complexion had paled a couple of tints. A pudgy hand covered her mouth, and she turned away.

"Uh . . . I'm not feeling very well. I've . . . I've got to go." She rushed out of the kitchen.

I followed her to the living room and watched, concerned, as she wrestled her shoes onto her feet. She pulled on her coat and grabbed her purse, her hands trembling.

"Is there something I can do to help?" I asked. "Would you like a ride home?"

"No. No, thank you," she said, bustling to the door. "Tell Dillon he won't have to pay me for today. Maybe I can come back tomorrow. I . . . I'm sorry, I just . . ." She gave up on whatever she'd intended to say and turned to fumble with the deadbolts.

"Here," I said, coming to her rescue. "I'm sorry you aren't feeling well. It was nice meeting you."

Her hazel eyes widened, and she emitted a sound somewhere between a moan and a whimper. "Yes. Yes. Nice to meet you too." She practically ran to the elevator. She pushed the call button, then, not waiting, shook her head and took the stairs.

I stood in the doorway, wondering. Perhaps I shouldn't have asked about her having been a teacher, although I couldn't imagine why. I rewound my mental tape, trying to figure out what I'd said wrong. One thing I was sure of. Clarissa wasn't sick. Something I'd said had pushed her button, the one marked "Panic."

5

"YOU SURE YOU WOULDN'T LIKE A LITTLE pick-me-up in your tea?"

Gracie Poole hovered over me, a bottle of Jim Beam in one hand, a delicate cup and saucer in the other. My stomach was still feeling iffy, but I'd had to agree to have some Constant Comment since it seemed so important to her. Now that I saw that she used more than sugar, cream, and/or lemon in hers, I understood now why she'd been so insistent. And it wasn't even noon! I'd known Gracie for several years and never suspected that any of the empty liquor bottles I saw going out with the trash on Tuesdays were hers.

"No, thank you, Gracie. It's a little early for me."

"Oh, well. *Chacun à son goût.*" She sat down opposite me, a butler's tray coffee table between us, and poured a splash of the bourbon into her cup.

I found myself a little disoriented by her apartment. The floor plan was a duplicate of my old unit, but that's where the similarity ended. Our building was itself a senior citizen, built in the forties by someone trying to harken back to an even earlier day when high ceilings, deep-set windows, fireplaces with marble surrounds and mantels, and hardwood floors were de rigueur. Gracie had taught art history for forty years, and her love of the Old Masters formed the basis of her decor. Prints of Rembrandt, Leonardo da Vinci, Degas, Toulouse-Lautrec, van Gogh, you name it, filled her walls ceiling to floor in frames that had probably cost more than the prints. Miniatures of well-known statuary served as her knickknacks, although in my opinion the six-foot-tall replica of Michaelangelo's *David* in the corner was a bit much, certainly more masculinity than would be good for my libido.

Fortunately, Gracie's living room furniture, while ornate, with gracefully curved arms and legs, was a dark wood upholstered in a neutral fabric, leaving all the prints and the thick Oriental area rugs to supply color in the room. Even her draperies, which swept to the floor under matching pelmets, and must have cost a mint, were a pristine snow-white. The effect was stunning and I liked it immensely. The only other contribution to color was her complexion, a delicate pink that matched the rosebuds on her cups and saucers.

"Gracie, you have to have the most beautiful apartment in the building," I said, with genuine admiration.

"Well, it's home." She patted her lips with a white linen napkin before folding it neatly across her lap. It seemed to disappear, since the pleated caftan she wore was also white. "Now. You're interested in the members of my little class who were here yesterday."

"Yes. You can understand why."

"Of course, Leigh. I'm so sorry about what happened to you. You must have been terrified. Lord knows the sight of all those policemen bursting into the lobby terrified us. It took a whole bottle of my Jim Beam to calm everyone down. But I'm sorry, I'm not comfortable giving you the list I gave to the policeman. It's one thing to give it to him since he asked for it in his official capacity. But you're no longer a member of the police force, so I simply can't. Privacy issues, you understand. But I can assure you, none of my students would do anything so vicious."

"You know all of them well?" I asked, disappointed but determined. More than one way to skin a cat.

"Well enough. Most of them have been with me since I started teaching at the Seniors' Center, and that's been six years. Some come and go because of their health, a few have died, but there's still a nucleus of a good dozen that are regulars."

"So no one new?"

"In my class? No, but as I told the nice young man last night—such a gentleman—several of my students did not come alone. I won't use their last names, but for instance, Willa's sister, Mary, came with her because Willa doesn't drive any longer. Ina and Phyllis invited friends. I did tell them they were welcome to do that. What I'm saying is that there were a number of faces I didn't recognize. I'm past the age where I remember names of people I'm meeting for the first time, so I couldn't add those to the list. But some of the students were still here when the officer came up, and they supplied those names they knew. I gave the detective a list of the ones who had left and a description of whoever came with them."

"And all the unfamiliar faces were accounted for? As far as who they came with, I mean."

"Well, no, I wouldn't say that." Gazing into the middle distance, she tapped the rim of her cup in thought. "There was the man in the Santa hat. He was a stranger to me, but he had a conversation with Neva, so I assume she knows him. And a teenager, a lovely girl. Georgia Keith. You can understand why I'd remember her name, so close to that of one of my idols. The granddaughter of someone on the fifth floor, according to Phyllis. They were untangling tinsel together. Phyllis is good with young people. Oh, yes, and the woman with the lovely accent. Jamaican, I think. I'm not sure how she was connected to anyone. Perhaps a friend of the Winstons."

That would be easy enough for me to follow up. Libby Winston and I had become cozy over loads of laundry, and I knew all my fifth-floor neighbors well, so I could track down whoever Georgia Keith belonged to.

An hour and a half later, the only person I'd managed to identify was the man in the Santa hat.

"Al?" Neva's broad face beamed. "He's Cholly's brother-in-law, the only one in his family I can tolerate. Lord, they're snooty. Al's a minister, teaches at Howard's School of Religion."

I'd checked on him out of curiosity more than anything else.

None of the neighbors on my floor who were at home laid claim to the teenager. I'd have to catch the others once they came in from work. Which meant calling them, I reminded myself. By this evening, I'd be in Southwest D.C. at the condo, not here.

I returned to Janeece's, set about finishing the rest of the packing, and was trying to find the end of the tape on the roll when the phone rang. My morning had been interrupted by two wrong numbers and one heavy breather, so I admit I answered with an attitude. "Yes?"

"Good afternoon, Leigh. I must say you do sound out of sorts."

Oops. "Grandmother! Hello!" I curled up on the futon, wondering how long it would take me to get used to having grandparents. I cleared my throat, realizing it felt a bit prickly. "I'm sorry. I was losing a fight with a roll of packing tape. How are you?"

"Quite well, thank you." Elizabeth Ritch was, if nothing else, proper, as my Nunna would say. "I won't keep you, dear. Is there any possibility you could come to see me sometime today? It's quite important and really shouldn't be put off any longer."

"Is something wrong?" Two trips to Ourland/Umber Shores in two days? We're talking eighty-something miles round trip and fifty minutes each way in non–rush hour traffic. I really didn't feel up to it, in fact was feeling worse by the minute. I was definitely coming down with something.

"No, nothing's wrong," my grandmother was saying. "In fact, it might be something to your advantage. Wayne and I had planned to inform you before your wedding, but as it's been postponed twice already, he and I felt it might be best if we take care of this matter now. Of course, if you're too busy . . ."

It's time I admit that my paternal grandmother and I got off on the wrong foot the first time we met. I hadn't particularly appreciated her high-handed manner, and she didn't like me, period. A truce had been declared since then, but I still had to count to ten occasionally and accept the fact that she was not and never would be a warm fuzzy like Nunna and Duck's mom.

"I am busy, Grandmother, but I'll try to get there before the day's over. I just can't tell you what time."

"That doesn't matter. I won't speak for Wayne—his sessions with the physical therapist seemed to last all hours—but I'll be here. Thank you, dear. You won't regret it. I look forward to seeing you. Good-bye."

I replaced the phone, bent over forehead to knees, and moaned, then sighed and sat up. She was, after all, family, something I'd longed for since I was five. Family meant obligations. It was time to count my blessings.

I got up and returned to my labors, but only managed to get two boxes packed when I had to accept the fact that I had indeed overdone it with all the furniture shoving this morning. Not only did my knee ache, everything did. The Constant Comment I'd had with Gracie hadn't done me any good either. Any kind of tea with little under my belt tends to leave me feeling queasy.

Or perhaps I should have eaten more of Clarissa's barbecue, but once she'd left, I'd tasted only a couple of forks of it. It had been every bit as good as it smelled, but I simply hadn't wanted any more and had put it back in the refrigerator. Now my stomach bubbled. This did not bode well. I downed a couple of Tums and stretched out in the den, my makeshift bedroom.

I didn't even realize I'd been asleep when I was awakened by Janeece-type sounds in the apartment. I rolled over, checked the clock. Three-fifteen? It was awfully early for her to be home.

"Janeece?" Getting up was a struggle. And the room seemed much cooler than earlier. Shivering, I opened the door of the den and stuck my head out. "You decide to take another half day off?"

The living room was empty but her coat lay half on, half off the futon, her purse upside down in front of it on the floor. She must have been in hurry because she

KILLER CHAMELEON ◆ 71

was usually a damned sight more careful about her clothes, especially her Burberry.

"Janeece?"

The toilet flushed, explanation enough. While I waited for her, I checked the thermostat. Seventy, its normal winter setting. Perhaps the heat was off in the whole building. Still fully clothed, I felt chilled to the bone. I jacked it up to seventy-five to see if it would come on.

A groan from behind me made me spin in my tracks. Janeece leaned in the door of her bedroom, her usual rich bronze complexion more like charcoal-gray. "Hey, roomie," she said, wiping her mouth with a facecloth. "Better keep your distance. I am one sick puppy, probably picked up the bug that's making the rounds in my office."

I heard the thermostat click and a whoosh of heated air from the vent washed over me. "Too late, home girl. I think I've got it, too. Or it might have been the chili. Whichever, it looks like we're in this together."

She came in and slumped into the easy chair. "God, I'm so sorry, Leigh. I'm pretty sure it wasn't the chili. I was feeling kind of icky yesterday, but what with all that running around in Baltimore, I had other things to worry about. Now I've given it to you."

We commiserated with each other, comparing aches and pains until nausea sent her scurrying to the bathroom again. I didn't really feel queasy so much as empty and preferring to stay that way—which sounded like a smart idea.

Once she was done, I found the thermometer, determined that my temperature was inching toward 102 degrees, and counted myself lucky that I hadn't packed any sleepwear yet. I filled a carafe of water for Janeece, who was back in the john again, and left it on her nightstand. I filled a thermos for myself, put on pajamas, and went back to bed.

It was dark outside when the dream in which I was knocking on Duck's door with all my worldly possessions in hand segued into reality. Someone was pounding at ours. I grabbed my robe, slid into my slippers, and hurried to answer it. The fact that Janeece hadn't budged meant she had to be in bad shape. Normally she answered doors and phones as if she knew Mr. Right was calling and didn't have time to waste.

Duck was about to knock on Neva's door when I opened ours, his expression a cross between anger and anxiety. One look at me and the anger was gone.

"Aw, babe, you're sick?"

I nodded, tempted to belabor him with a list of my ailments: sore throat, temperature, et al., but decided against it. It would take too much energy.

"I thought maybe you'd changed your mind about moving in and were too chicken to tell me," he said, shutting the door behind him. "Let's get you back to bed."

"Sorry," I croaked, surprised at how hoarse I'd become. "I should have called but I fell asleep. And I'm contagious, Duck. So's Janeece. I think she's sicker than I am. You should leave."

"Bull." He peeled me out of my robe, sat me on the side of the bed, and removed my slippers. "I'm immune. I never get sick." It had been years since he'd last had a cold or the flu so I didn't bother to argue. He looked particularly hale and hearty at the moment. The man exuded health. I wanted to snarl at him.

He palmed my forehead and pronounced me feverish, asked if I'd eaten, what if any medication I'd taken, and in general lifted my spirits and made me downright soppy. He cared.

"You just relax," he ordered. "Dr. Duck will take care of you. Janeece too. Where's your key? I'm going out for supplies."

I wasn't certain what his definition of supplies might be but didn't care either. The fact that he was coming back was all that mattered. Normally when I'm sick, which isn't often, I want to be left alone to wallow in my misery. The fact that I found myself welcoming his company showed me just how much he meant to me.

He went to check on Janeece, left the apartment, and returned a while later laden down with cough syrup, zinc lozenges, tissues, hot soup from my favorite restaurant, ginger ale and crackers to soothe my roommate's tummy, and a single red rose in a bud vase for each of us. If my cousin the minister were in hailing distance, I'd marry Duck on the spot in my jammies and with a tissue stuck up my nose.

He'd also brought my laptop. "Picked it up from the shop on my way home from work," he said, plugging it in and connecting the phone cable to the wall jack beside my bed. "It'll give you something to play with until you feel better." He disappeared for a moment and returned hefting one of the easy chairs from the living room.

"What are you doing?" I asked, the mug of soup warming my hands.

"Making sure I'm gonna be comfortable. If I've got to sleep sitting up, it ain't gonna be on that director's chair there."

"You're staying? All night?"

"Of course. Gotta take care of my sweetie." He settled in the chair and arranged his face with a beatific smile. I melted inside, and it had nothing to do with the hot soup or my temperature.

He'd brought paperwork with him, so I finished the soup, popped a cough drop in my mouth, and powered up the laptop. It had been in the shop for two weeks, so I knew I'd have a hundred e-mails to delete about Viagra, weight loss products, mortgages, and miracle potions to increase my penis size. I was wrong; there were only seventy-one of them.

"You got any interest in these?" I asked, angling the monitor so he could see them.

"Dunno," he answered. "You think I need them?" His eyes began to smolder.

I knew that look, and he knew I knew that look. Considering the effect it had on me most of the time, one of these days I'd probably be able to blame it for however many children we had running around.

"Reckon not," I said hurriedly. Being horny was one thing, horny and contagious quite another.

I deleted the offending messages and settled back to open the rest. A series of messages sent daily for the last ten days made me growl, since they appeared to be to me from me. It wasn't the first time, always someone hawking something with a "click here" at the bottom. I highly resented the misuse of my name. And one a day? There was no attachment so I opened the earliest of them.

It was short and simple: *Dear Bitch, I HATE you!* No signature, no link to click. I rubbed at the nape of my neck. The itch was back.

Closing the message, I opened the next day's, a variation on a theme. *Dear Bitch, I HATE you intensely!* The remainder were repeats, each with a different adverb and a slightly larger font. The message dated three days ago went further, adding, *I intend to make your life as miserable as you've made mine. That should give you something to think about.* The next day's: *Clever, wasn't it?* The one after that: *I've just begun!* The last of them, today's date: *Did you enjoy last night? Were you afraid? Wet your pants, maybe? Get used to it.* The font was enormous, only one or two words to a line. This woman was crazy.

"Duck." He glanced up from the booklet he was reading. "Mark your page and take a look at these." I placed the laptop across his thighs. "Start with the earliest date and go from there." I watched as he read each one, his posture becoming more and more rigid.

When he was done, he sat back, his focus in the middle distance. "This is one lunatic son of a bitch. Willard needs to see them. Forward them to him with a note of explanation. To me too. I want the department shrink to see them."

"I'll forward them to Plato too." My fingers were crossed under the blanket; Duck had decidedly mixed feelings about Plato dePriest, a lunatic of another sort who laid claim to every phobia in the medical encyclopedia. He was also a genius and knew more detours around firewalls, passwords, and computer databases than anyone on the globe. He'd been instrumental in helping me find my Ourland/Umber Shores family and considered me a friend. He didn't have many, by his own choice.

"You figure he can trace these back to the sender," Duck said.

I nodded. "Each comes from a different dot com or whatever. If anyone can do it, Plato can."

"Okay. In the meantime, did you find out anything about the people decorating the tree last night?"

I filled him in on my conversation with Gracie and the two females unaccounted for.

He passed the laptop back to me, his expression grim. "Libby Winston is the one from Jamaica, right? The one I met outside the day we were going to see Dr. Ritch?"

"Oh, jeez." I'd forgotten I had told my grandmother I'd come out to see her and my grandfather. I'd have to call them. "Yes, that was Libby. Why?"

"I'm going to talk to her, see if she knows who the woman with the accent was. What's her apartment number?"

I gave it to him along with Mr. Trotter's in case he or his granddaughter knew anything about Gracie's Georgia Keith. I doubted Georgia had had anything to do with any of this but would consider it unfinished business if we didn't check.

"Gracie Poole's in three-seventeen," I added. "Since you're official, she might tell you more than she told me. I'll call her and let her know you're coming."

"Good idea." He got up and probably without thinking, leaned down and kissed me on the forehead. "Be back shortly."

By the time he returned an hour later, I had made my apologies to my grandmother, had received an update on how my granddad was doing with his new knee, and had promised on the head of my firstborn child that I'd come to see her as soon as humanly possible. I'd also left a phone message for Plato to expect the forwarded e-mails, with a request that he see if he could track them to their sources.

I heard the key in the door and levered myself to a sitting position. Duck came into the den with a thermal mug and a plate, its contents covered with a napkin. "Cookies from Ms. Poole, and some Jamaican concoction for colds from Ms. Winston," he said, placing them on the bookcase that served as a nightstand. "They told me to tell you and Janeece to call them if you need anything. Nice ladies. Ms. Poole's apartment is something else. Speaking of which."

He sat down, and I detected cookie crumbs on his sweater. "I like the way you rearranged things. Looks better. By the way, how did you and Clarissa get along?" I could see that it was killing him not to smile.

"Just fine. I like her. You lied to me about her age. I'll get you for that. And we need to talk about our furniture, but it can wait. What did you find out?"

He scooted down in the chair, legs extended. "A lot of nothing, on the face of it. First, Mr. Trotter said he'd never heard of a Georgia Keith. His granddaughter and any friend of hers he might know are on a class field trip to New York. Ms. Winston claims she has no idea who the visitor with the accent might be. She didn't ask any of her family or friends to come help decorate the tree; in fact doesn't remember even mentioning it to anyone. As for Ms. Poole, you were right; the badge did the trick. She gave me the names of all the class members who came and the friends whose names she remembered. She also gave me phone numbers, but I'll talk to Willard before doing anything with them. I don't want him to feel I'm trespassing on his territory or implying that he isn't doing his job."

I sighed, considered eating a cookie, and settled on a zinc drop instead. "Well, at least we've eliminated a couple of avenues. I'm not sure it's worth it to pursue the identity of the teenager, although when I think about it, the stunts with the dog and cat poop are pretty juvenile. And for all we know, she might have been with the woman with the accent."

Duck shook his head. "According to Ms. Poole, our Jamaican lady arrived shortly after the main group and stayed about an hour. The kid didn't show up until later. But they might have been related. Ms. Poole said there was a superficial resemblance."

"Oh, terrific," I grumbled. "Now what?"

"For you, nothing except getting better. I'll check on Janeece, then make some hot chocolate. Or would you rather try Ms. Winston's potion? She says it won't take much; I understand it's heavy on the rum."

I poured half of it into the cap of my thermos and sniffed, a waste of effort since I couldn't have smelled a skunk parked on my pillow. "Worth a try," I said. I took a swallow, fortunately a little one. A second later the top of my head blew off.

"Mercy!"

In an instant, my sinuses cleared and my nose began streaming. I grabbed a tissue. "This stuff is stronger than Chinese mustard!"

Duck's grin matched that of an imp of Satan's. "She said it would either kill you or cure you. You're supposed to drink it down, cover up, and prepare to sweat. I'll take the rest of it in to Janeece. I want to see that blanket all the way to your chin when I get back."

"Yes, sir," I said, my eyes watering. If this stuff drained all other superfluous fluids as rapidly as it had my eyes and nose, by tomorrow I'd be five pounds lighter and dehydrated.

I don't know how long Duck was gone. By the time he returned, I was as high as a Georgia pine and too sleepy to do anything other than throw a foolish smile in his general direction. That was it. I was gone.

When I awoke the next morning, so was he. He'd left a note saying he was heading home to change and go to work, and he'd check on me later.

I heard sounds of stirring, and Janeece opened the door, as bright-eyed and bushy-tailed as a squirrel with a cache of newly discovered acorns. Dressed for work, she was the picture of the professional woman in a navy suit, pale blue scooped-neck blouse, and heels high enough to give anyone else vertigo.

"Hi! Hope you feel better," she said. "That stuff Liz sent did it for me. You need anything before I go?"

"Uh . . . no." I sat up. "You're really okay?"

"Yeah. One of those twenty-four-hour viruses, I guess. Tell Duck we're even. Staying the night was above and beyond the call of duty. He was so sweet, talking me to sleep. Marry the man, roomie, because if you don't, I will. See ya." She wiggled fingers at me and left.

I took stock. I did feel better, also completely wrung out. Only then did I remember two events of the previous night or perhaps the early hours of the morning. The first was waking up soaked to the skin and Duck helping me change pajamas, after which he'd also changed my damp sheets. The second thing I remembered caused momentary paralysis as I started to get up—I had roused enough to see Duck on the phone and reporting afterward: "Plato says that each of the e-mail messages was sent from a different computer. He tracked a lot of them to public libraries in D.C. and northern Virginia."

"That's all?" I remember responding.

"That's as far as he's gotten. One thing's for sure, babe. He agrees with me that this woman is nuts and we've got to start taking this business seriously."

6

I SPENT THAT DAY TRYING TO DRUM UP ENOUGH
energy to do something productive and failed. Duck
phoned to see how I was feeling, and, at his suggestion
I began a journal of sorts, laying out everything that
had happened so far with times and dates.

"We're assuming that the dirty tricks began with
that first deposit outside your old apartment," he said,
"but just in case, try to remember anything out of the
ordinary for the last, say, couple of months."

I was so wiped out that I couldn't think straight. I
managed to get the list done between naps, but could
not guarantee it was all-inclusive. The phone was a nuisance, one wrong number, three hang-ups, and a call
from Salina's letting me know that some new Mephistos had arrived. I had no idea what Mephistos were but
thanked her for the information, since if I'd blown her
off, I'd have had a guilty conscience and Nunna's voice
in my ear. *Those folks are only earning their keep, honey,
so be polite.*

By six, I threw in the towel, called Duck and told
him to go home tonight, put my grandparents off one
more day, and went to bed for good. I awoke the next
morning a match for Janeece's Little Mary Sunshine
persona. I felt like me again. After a breakfast worthy

of a long-distance hauler, I was good to go, determined
to finish the move to Duck's or die trying. I caught him
at work to tell him so.

"You do sound better," he said. "But don't overdo.
I want you in tiptop shape tonight."

"Oh? Why?"

He lowered his voice, practically whispering. "Because I plan to jump your bones, that's why. We're gonna
make the Kama Sutra look like a Girl Scout's manual in
comparison. And before I forget, two things. I moved
your car off the street last night. It's parked by the basement door so you won't have far to go to load up. And
Helena Campion called you."

"You're kidding." Another country unheard from
for years. We moved in different circles now that she'd
joined one of the most high-powered legal firms in D.C.
"You mean I slept through her call the other night?"

"No, she was trying to reach you at my place, thought
we'd gotten married last month. She didn't get an answer there so she called here yesterday and asked me to
give you the message. She's throwing a get-together for
somebody called Bev the Beaver. She said you'd know
who she meant."

I whooped with laughter. "I do. She's an actress
friend of ours. When and where?"

"Tomorrow evening, seven o'clock at Helena's. I have
her new address. Evidently she's moved since the last
time you saw her."

I could just bet she had. The dump we'd lived in dur-
ing law school was far behind and below her now.
"Okay. I'll put it on my calendar. Go do some work.
I've got packing to finish. See ya tonight."

"You most certainly will," he purred, and it was
hang up or burst into flames. Kama Sutra, huh?

I took my time filling the last few boxes, even managing to put aside a few things to take to the Salvation Army. I had just sealed the last box when someone knocked at the door. I opened it and suppressed a groan. Just what I needed: Tank and Tina.

"SO, WHAT CAN WE DO TO HELP?" Tank, real name Bernard Younts, to which he rarely answered, stood in Janeece's living room looking around. "AND WHAT TIME DOES JANEECE GET HOME?"

Tina, his diminutive wife, punched him on the shoulder. "One, you're not talking to your granny and nobody's deaf here," she said, "so keep your voice down. And two," she added, eyes narrowed, "it's none of your damned business what time Janeece gets home. Swear to God, you're absolutely foolish about that woman."

"Maybe a little," Tank admitted, with a sheepish grin. "Just not as foolish as I am about you."

I gazed at the two of them, antenna a-quiver. Not that I wasn't glad to see them; it's just that the timing was a bit suspicious. I detected Duck's fine hand in it somewhere. Both cops with the D.C. Metropolitan Police, Tank and Tina were charter members of Duck's fan club and, as a result, had a rather proprietary and protective attitude about me. At times it could be a nuisance. I'm ashamed to confess that it took me a four-second beat to admit that at the moment, their intrusion and assistance were more than welcome.

"How about helping me get all these boxes down to my car? Tina, if you could babysit the car between loads, that would be great."

"I can carry stuff, too," she said, looking insulted. "I'm as healthy as I've ever been, thank you very much." Tina had recently had a miscarriage, an event that, for the first time, had put a dent in her tough-girl armor.

"Gimme your car keys, Leigh," Tank said. "Where are you parked?"

"Around back."

"Okay. And you, bride of mine, are not lifting any of these boxes, and that's all there is to it." He stacked three together and hefted them easily.

"Don't tell me what to do." Tina whacked him on the shoulder again and glared up at him. Well over a foot and some shorter than Tank's six-four, -five, or -six, depending on whether he was slouching and she was in heels, Tina was the boss, bullying her husband and leading him around by the nose. And he loved it. A chocolate fudge–hued Mr. Clean with the build of a weight lifter, Tank was a gentle giant whose size generally intimidated most people. Not Tina. Her fiery temper was enough to serve as an equalizer. She rarely used it, but just knowing it was simmering down there under that small frame tended to keep him in line.

It had taken me a while to become comfortable around Tina, the only woman who made me conscious of my height and weight. But I knew because I'd asked that Tina was a size two. Two, for God's sake! She was in yellow today, slacks that fit like a second skin and a cable-knit turtleneck sweater that made her deep mahogany complexion seem to glow. In other words, she didn't look like someone who'd come prepared to work.

"I can carry a box down if I want to," she said, scowling, then lifted her chin haughtily. "It just so happens that I don't want to. Come on, you're wasting time."

I placed the key ring on one of Tank's sausage-sized fingers and told him where to find the car. "By the time you get back, I'll have this last box labeled. I sure appreciate this, guys."

"No problem." Tank smiled down at me. "Nothing's too good for Duck's lady."

Tina rolled her eyes, then grinned. "What can I say? He's right. Come on, man."

While they were gone, I wrote "Shoes" on the one remaining box, crammed my robe and slippers into a shopping bag, and patted myself on the back for a job well done. After checking the closet and all the drawers in the little chest in the den, I made one last perusal of the bathroom and found a few things I could simply drop into my purse. I was on my way out of the bathroom when I heard a knock at the door.

Tank came in, his face full of thunderclouds. "Hate to be the bearer of bad news, but somebody's spray-painted your car. You won't be able to see to drive."

"What?"

I swore my way downstairs and out the basement door. The only time a resident could park in back by the Dumpster was when we were loading or unloading something. Unfortunately, this area wasn't visible from the street or the first-floor apartments on the rear, so the painter had had both time and privacy to complete the artwork.

The windshield wore a solid coat of Chinese red. The rear and side windows weren't as bad, depending on your point of view; one word, "BITCH," in capital letters, in a dark blue, along with a single stripe of the same color on the body from front fender to rear. Since the car was white, it might as well been a flag on wheels.

"Oh, my God." I felt as if I'd imploded, everything collapsing to fill the vacuum in my chest.

"Somebody sure as hell doesn't like you," Tina said, testing the stripe with a finger. "Quick-drying, too."

I plopped my backside onto the steps and tried not to cry. "It's ruined. I'll have to get the whole thing repainted. I've only had it two months!"

Tank peered over the hood at his wife. "Think Chet could do anything with this?"

I was too upset to wonder who Chet was. "I can't walk to Ourland. I need my car. What am I gonna do?"

"Hold on a minute." Tina unclipped a tiny cell phone from her belt and began punching numbers.

"Wonder if this stuff would come off with a razor blade," Tank said, scraping at a window with a fingernail. "Just might, depending on what kind of paint it is."

Getting up, I tried the same stunt on the driver's side window. A bit of blue collected under the nail of my middle finger. I kept scratching and managed to remove one whole letter. There was hope yet.

Tina had moved away from us and was talking a mile a minute. "I don't want to hear it," she said, I assumed to the mysterious Chet. "Come and tow it to your garage as soon as we've finished with the police report."

Another police report in less than seventy-two hours. I wondered if that was a record. The only consolation was that it was doubtful any of the cops of the other evening would show up again today. Different shifts.

"We've got running around to do," Tina was saying, "so we'll drop by later to get an estimate. Don't give me any lip, now, boy. This is Duck's lady we're talking about here."

Those must have been the magic words because she snapped a nod, a pleased smile rimming her lips, and disconnected.

"All set. Chet—he's my brother—will see what he can do. He works at a car dealer and does detailing on the side. He'll get to work on it tonight and let us know how long he thinks it'll take. By the way, we put your boxes in the Explorer. Looks like we'll be able to fit the rest of them in it too."

"So now we wait for the District's finest," I said, disheartened. "There goes the rest of the afternoon."

"Nope, they're on their way now. I called them while I was waiting for you to come down. Y'all had much of a problem with vandalism in this neighborhood?"

I allowed as how as far as I knew, there'd been none. Besides, there was no doubt of something personal about this. The prankster had been at it again. But until I figured out who she was, there was probably no way to prove it one way or another.

I wondered how much the paint removal would cost me, especially if Chet had no luck with the stripes. There was also the question as to how my auto insurance might be affected. They'd written off my old car, in which I'd had an argument with a tree while searching for Duck back in October. Duck, who swore he knew a mechanic who could work miracles, had left it with him for a month, wanting it in decent enough shape to donate to one of his pet organizations that trained dropouts to be certified mechanics. The Chevy was parked in a dark corner of the garage under his building but had no tags, so I couldn't touch it. Which meant I was stuck with Tank and Tina for the immediate future.

"How is it," I asked, an hour later as we crammed the last box into the Explorer, "that you two are both off work today?"

Tank, opening a rear door for me, shrugged. "Pure luck. Last time this happened has to be a year ago."

"Then there must be other things y'all want to do. I don't want to spoil your day off together."

Tina hopped into the passenger seat, dug into her purse, and began filing nails long enough to be considered lethal weapons. Looking back over her shoulder, she cut me a look that let me know she wasn't fooled. I would not be getting rid of them.

"We didn't have anything special planned. Might as well hang out with you."

"How about Christmas shopping?" I asked, fishing for a suggestion that might get them off my tail. Thanks to Duck, I'd had previous experience with these two as babysitters. They took it seriously. I might need a ride, but I didn't think I needed bodyguards, at least not yet.

"Finished all our Christmas shopping way before Thanksgiving," Tina said. "Gifts are all wrapped, tree's up. Nothing else to be done. Besides, the Duck said you've been sick and could use some help. We're helping whether you like it or not. So get over it."

Tank folded himself behind the wheel. "Pay her no mind, Leigh. She didn't have her Wheaties this morning."

"Or my ham and eggs and potatoes. Damned refrigerator died and everything spoiled. We just came from Sears and bought the biggest one they stock. Let's move it. We've got to get those boxes over to Duck's."

I gave myself a good talking-to as we made our way from Northwest to Southwest D.C. It had always been so difficult for me to ask for and accept help. Even if Duck hadn't suggested it, I knew that Tank and Tina would have rolled up their sleeves to do anything that needed doing. And realistically speaking, without my car I'd have been up a creek today without them. The least I could do was to be gracious about it.

"You two are lifesavers and I really do appreciate this," I said, as we got out in the underground garage of Duck's building. "I'd have been in one hell of a mess without you."

Tank pulled three boxes from the back and maneuvered them into his arms. "Glad to help."

I found I could manage two boxes, and Tina grabbed the big shopping bag in which my robe and slippers were crammed.

"I hear you've met my auntie," she said, as we stepped on the elevator.

"Your auntie?"

"Clarissa. She's actually a great-aunt of a second cousin or something. I'm the one who steered Duck to my family's cleaning company. It was a good match. He loves her."

I was trying to formulate a response when the elevator jerked to a stop at the first floor and Mrs. Luby, a neighbor of Duck's, got on. A member of what he'd tagged the Gang of Four, she was the reigning queen of a quartet of elderly ladies who camped out in the lobby to watch the soaps together and meddle with whoever came in and out.

"More things?" she asked. "Well, you're smart to bring only a few at a time." She eyed Tank and smiled flirtatiously. "And just who is this?" She and Janeece might be generations apart, but they were sisters under the skin.

"My husband." Tina managed a dangerously sweet smile in return. Mrs. Luby might be shifting gears toward eighty but she was still a woman, and Tina didn't take kindly to females, no matter what age, moving in on her territory.

"Detective and Sergeant Younts," I said, "this is Mrs. Luby, one of Duck's favorite people. She lives across the hall."

"Ma'am," Tank said, nodding his head in greeting. He scowled at Tina, who, after a moment's hesitation, shook Mrs. Luby's hand.

"Pleased to meet you," she murmured.

"Likewise. How much more do you have coming?" Mrs. Luby asked me. "I wouldn't think there'd be enough room over there."

"This is almost the last of it, thank heaven. How are the grandbabies?" I regretted the question almost immediately, since Mrs. Luby was known to wax ad nauseam about them.

"They've got the chicken pox, every last one of them," she said, as the elevator door opened. "I just hope they'll be done scratching by Christmas. Y'all will have to pardon me but I've got to hurry. Time to take my pill. You all have a good day." She hurried toward her door, a vision in Barbie-doll pink, from the fancy comb in her hair to her ballet flats. Mrs. Luby believed in monochrome, the more intense the better.

"Clarissa was here the day before yesterday," I said, as we neared Duck's door. "I didn't realize she was a relative of yours."

"One of my favorites," Tina said, "and Aunt Sister, of course."

"Wonder if she made anything for Duck." Tank waited while I dealt with the deadbolt. "Man, that lady can cook."

"She brought barbecue," I said, "but Duck has probably wiped it out."

The apartment was empty. The refrigerator, however, was not. Tank deposited the boxes in the guest room, returned to the Explorer for the two remaining, then made short work of the last of the barbecue. I wasn't hungry, and Tina declared that she'd hold out for pizza. The two of us camped out in the living room while Tank ate.

"So," Tina said, "what's with this trouble you've been having? Why did Duck send us to keep an eye on you?"

My heart sank. I had hoped he'd simply asked them to help me with the last of the things to be moved. If he'd put them on guard duty, the rest of my day really was shot. They'd stick to me like lint on wool.

"Duck may be overreacting," I began. "It's not such a big deal that I need bodyguards."

Tank moved his chair close enough to the door that he could peek around the corner from the kitchen.

I ran down the list of pranks, omitting editorial comments to facilitate an objective opinion from them. Granted, the call that had sicced the cops on me had been over the top, but the deposits outside Neva and Cholly's door and the one about Duck having an accident, although malicious, were, for the most part, harmless. The e-mail was unnerving and a nuisance, but when it came right down to it, all I had to do was hit the delete key.

"Well, hell," Tina said, her elfin features uncharacteristically solemn. "I don't like the sounds of this. Add the damage to your car and you've got to figure some female is going to an awful lot of trouble to make your life miserable. You're sure you haven't made an enemy recently?"

"Positive. Shoot, girl, I haven't had time. I've been

too busy with Christmas and keeping an eye on the renovations of the police station in Umber Shores and trying to get myself married."

"I thought the place was called Ourland," Tina said.

"Well, it is, on the east side of town. Blame it on a long-standing family feud. I'll explain later."

"Maybe it didn't happen recently," Tank said, mid-chew. "Whoever you crossed, I mean. Think back."

"I have. I still come up empty. It may sound like I'm a goody two-shoes, but I try to be nice to everybody. I really do. I try to treat everyone with respect. Always have, even when I was in uniform."

"Much more of this," Tina grumbled, "and I'm gonna throw up. The fact remains, some woman's pissed at you. She made a big mistake, getting the cops involved, and should realize it by now. Let's hope that the paint job, assuming she did it, is her swan song. So. What's next on your agenda for the day?"

So indeed. Tina might think the pranks were history, but she obviously intended to fulfill her contract with Duck to hold my hand for the rest of the afternoon.

It was pick-and-choose time. The Bridal Bower. Hmm. I'd left the peau de soie for minor alterations, which meant I'd need to try it on, just in case. With the undies I'd put on this morning in mind now, I scratched the bridal shop. I could imagine their expressions at seeing my well-worn old faithfuls. It would make more sense to go decked out in the ridiculously fancy ones I'd wear on the big day.

Instead, I explained my need to get to the travel agency to pick up the tickets to Hawaii. "They're closing early today for the office Christmas party. And I hate to impose, but I need to run over to Ourland to see my grandparents. Don't know what's up, but my grandmother was kind of insistent, and I promised I'd come today."

"Let's hit it then," Tank said, downing the last of the barbecue. "We'll stop and get pizza first. This was just an appetizer."

"Goody." Tina hopped up and grabbed her coat. She lived to eat, not the other way around.

The sign on the door of Graystone Travel announced that the agency was closed, and I indulged in some sotto voce swearing before I detected movement in the back behind a translucent panel. Taking a chance, I rapped on the glass and crossed my fingers. A second later, a familiar face peered around the panel. Margie, still here, thank God, but lacking her usual smile of recognition. She hesitated for a second, then strode to the door.

A former cop who had decided the stress wasn't worth it, Margie was a substantial woman, taller than average, with shoulders like a linebacker. She had intimidated any number of juvenile offenders in her day and seemed to assume much the same attitude as she unlocked the door and stood there, blocking the way. "Yes?"

"Sorry I'm late, okay?" I said, guessing that she was miffed at me for showing up after hours. "Car trouble. But it's not three yet. I thought you weren't closing until three."

"No reason to hang around," she said, not moving. "Everyone slated to pick up tickets has been here and gone. If you've got new travel dates, you'll have to wait until tomorrow. We've signed off for the day."

"Come on, Margie," I said. "I appreciate the trouble you've gone to to reschedule us twice, but it couldn't be helped. December twenty-sixth is it, so just give me the tickets and you can go on to your party."

Her eyes narrowed a trifle. "What do you mean, the twenty-sixth is it? You called and canceled. I don't mind telling you—"

"Wait a minute. Just hold it," I said. "What do *you* mean, I called and canceled? The wedding's set for the day after Christmas and we're leaving for Hawaii that evening come hell or high water."

Margie stared me down, literally, for several seconds, then jerked her head for me to come in. She locked the door, then led me back to her station behind the panel. Dropping into her chair, she pulled a folder from the shelves attached to the wall behind her, opened it, and skimmed a pink "While You Were Out" message slip across the desk toward me.

I caught it, turned it right side up, and felt my jaw and innards spasm. In flowery letters, the kind with little circles above the i's, someone had written last Wednesday's date, ten-twenty A.M. as the time, Lee Warren as the caller, and "Honeymoon trip is off, she'll be in touch," as the message.

"Margie," I said, lowering myself into a visitor's chair, "I didn't make this call."

She was clearly insulted, her features rigid. "Dolly Cranston may look like an airhead but when it comes to taking messages, she gets them right."

"And I'm here to tell you that this time," I said, with a death grip on my temper, "she got it wrong. I didn't make this call. Dammit, Margie, I know how much of a pain in the butt these arrangements have been for you. And each time they've had to be changed, as much as I dreaded it, I've come in and talked to you personally. It was the least I could do. I did not make this call.

Someone's been pulling practical jokes on me and, dammit, this looks like another one."

For the first time, a measure of uncertainty peeked from beneath her hard shell. "She did say you weren't specific about the date you and Duck were to have left, only that I should cancel it. And I did. Figured you two had had a fight or something."

I squeezed my eyes shut for a moment, and massaged my temples. I felt sick, nausea roiling in my midsection. All our plans down the toilet.

I pulled myself together. First things first. "Any chance we could still get those reservations?"

She snorted. "You jest. Christmas in Hawaii is usually sold out weeks in advance, airlines and hotels. I moved heaven and earth to get that last date for you. I might be able to get you on a flight to the West Coast but you'd have to swim from there and honeymoon on the beach because I can guarantee you, there's nothing available left, at least no place fit for human habitation."

"How many toes would I have to kiss to ask you to at least check?" I ventured.

"Thanks all the same but I've got a husband who takes care of that for me." She made a face and sighed. "All right, I'll see what I can do, but it'll have to wait until after the party today. A couple of corporate clients are invited and I've got to be there to welcome them and kiss their toes if I want to stay in business. I'll give you a call tomorrow morning at the latest." Rising, she removed her purse and coat from the coat tree in the corner and turned off her desk lamp. "Sorry about all this, Leigh, but we had no way of knowing." She hustled me out, said a hurried good-bye, and disappeared into the passing crowd.

Tank and Tina were parked around the corner. I

wasn't quite ready to face them yet. Taking advantage of the niche afforded by the recessed doorway, I fished in my purse for my cell phone.

Surprise, surprise, Duck answered, and on the first ring.

"Kennedy," he announced.

Hearing his voice brought me close to tears. "Duck, I'm outside. Graystone. She's done it again, called here last week and had them cancel all our reservations for Hawaii."

"WHAT?" His usual baritone soared into coloratura range.

"You heard me. Margie was plenty pissed until she realized I was serious about not having canceled anything. She says she'll do the best she can to find a flight and hotel for us but she's not hopeful." I dreaded doing it, but it was time to bite the bullet. "Duck, I hate to ask, but is there any way one of your former girlfriends might be doing this?"

The ensuing silence made me wonder if I'd struck a nerve. He had had quite a reputation as lady-killer in the earlier years of our acquaintance, allegedly unwarranted. "Duck? You still there?"

"Oh, yeah, still here and trying to decide who I'm more pissed at, you for asking that question, or whoever made that call. How the hell did she know what our plans were? I mean, she might have lucked up on someone who'd tell her we were going to Hawaii, but how could she know which travel agency we used? When did all this happen again?"

"Last Wednesday. And somebody spray-painted my car. It's a mess. Tina's brother does detailing and will see if he can remove it, so Tank's playing chauffeur. I'm sorry, Duck. I'm just so mad I could spit. What'll we do if Hawaii's a bust?"

"Keep it down, dammit," he yelled at his coworkers, inflicting considerable damage to my right ear. "Sorry, babe. Look, push comes to shove, there are plenty of other places we can go—the Caribbean, maybe. We'll talk tonight. Don't sweat it. At least we had cancellation insurance so we won't lose that much—I hope. Everything will work out okay. I haven't caught up with Willard yet but I'll damned sure keep trying. This shit has to stop. Look, honey, gotta go. See you tonight."

He had disconnected before I could say good-bye. At least he hadn't flipped his lid, leaving that to me, I guess. It was just as well someone was keeping a cool head. I sure as hell wasn't.

I trotted around the corner and found Tank and Tina playing kissy-face. I gave them a couple of minutes, then couldn't take it any longer.

"Sorry to interrupt," I said, climbing into the back-seat, "but it's too cold to stand out here and watch."

Tina unglued herself from her husband's shirtfront, looking more than pleased with herself. "Just as well you came back now or there'd have been no turning back. You get the tickets?"

I wasn't ready to talk about it yet. "No. Long story. Let's go get your pizza. I'll tell you then."

Tank said, "Uh-oh. I smell trouble. How about Paisan's, Tina?"

Her expression made it plain that he had hit the jack-pot. Tank zipped through Northwest D.C. to just in-side the District line.

We'd settled into a booth and were scanning a menu packed with four pages of different kinds of pizza and pasta when my cell phone rang. It was Margie, the murmur of voices in the background and yet again, wherever she was, the Drummer Boy on the Muzak.

"Leigh? I left a message on Janeece's machine, but thought I'd better try your cellular too."

My pulse rate tripled. "Don't tell me. You'll be able to get us to Hawaii after all?"

Tank and Tina looked up with interest.

"No, no. I just got to this stupid party. I cornered Dolly about the message she'd left and it turns out I misunderstood one thing."

"What?" I couldn't see how it mattered.

"She apologized for not making it clear. It wasn't a call, Leigh. She says you came in and canceled the trip yourself."

Numb with shock, I counted to five. "Again, no, I didn't, Margie. But thanks for letting me know." Without a good-bye, I hung up.

"What?" Tina demanded. "What's going on?"

Somehow, I managed to relay this latest foul-up of my life.

"That," Tina said, slamming a small fist on the table, "does it. She's gone too far this time. We're not gonna take this. She's messing with our Duck's money!"

7

WE WERE HALFWAY TO THE SHORES BEFORE
Tina's fuse finally burned itself out. Tank's eyes had met
mine in his rearview mirror, his message telegraphed
across his broad open features: just wait; eventually
she'll shut up. By the time she did, the silence in the
Explorer was so welcome, neither Tank nor I opened
our mouths, except for his sigh of relief. All I could
think was: ditto.

Other than that, I was incapable of thought. My
brain had the consistency of lumpy oatmeal. Who the
hell was this woman? What could I have done to her to
warrant this kind of maliciousness?

Tina turned around in her seat as far as her seat belt
would allow and demanded, "Well, what are you gonna
do?"

I fought the temptation to remind her that, contrary
to the accusation implicit in her tone, as far as I could
determine, this whole business was not my fault. I had
done nothing to deserve it. Rather than waste breath
in defense, I took the direct route.

"I'm doing all I can for the time being, Tina, trying to
figure out who the hell this woman is. I'm assuming
she was in the lobby of my building Monday, helping
to decorate the tree, an outsider, one of two. What's

puzzling is that none of my neighbors who were there has mentioned any resemblance between this woman— or girl—and me. Yet she must, to have fooled the receptionist at the travel agency. I've been in there several times. They all know what I look like."

Saying that triggered a connection that hadn't occurred to me before: the woman who'd walked into that travel agency and the one whooping it up at the Silver Shaker. One and the same? I wasn't sure. Eddie said that the cops there to set up a sting had thought it was me because they remembered me from Jensen's wedding, not because the woman had identified herself as Leigh Warren. If she had, Eddie would have said so. And the woman could not have known that a few of the nightclub's patrons were boys in blue, much less boys in blue who knew me. Coincidence, pure and simple.

Then why did it smell so much like rotten fish?

Once again I wondered if it might be a cousin. Tracy, my aunt's daughter, and I were enough alike to be sisters. I'd only known her a matter of weeks but had no doubt that she had nothing to do with any of this. We had clicked immediately, a blood bond formed over plates of cheeseburgers and French fries.

Ourland, however, was chockablock with cousins I had yet to meet. And I had been responsible for the death of my father's first cousin, a man so consumed with jealousy and hatred of my dad that he'd been willing to kill my father and mother years ago, then try for me and my brother. I'd had no choice and had acted in self-defense. But he'd been a man well thought of in town. Perhaps someone was exacting revenge. I'd have to ask around, find out if there was yet another relative who looked like me and Tracy.

"Hey!" Tina snapped her fingers toward me. "You still in there?"

"Do you mind?" I asked, annoyed at having my train of thought derailed. "I was thinking. Okay, I've narrowed down the number of unfamiliar faces in the lobby to a teenager named Georgia Keith and a woman with a West Indian accent."

"Well, I know Ted Willard," Tank said, zipping with panache past a sixteen-wheeler. "He'll have checked to see if there was anything distinguishable about the voice of the woman who called. If he didn't mention an accent, it probably wasn't your Jamaican lady."

"Duck talked to Libby Tuesday evening," I said. "She had no idea who it was."

Tina gave me a penetrating stare. "So if you eliminate those two, where do you go from there?"

It burned my butt to admit that I didn't have a backup road map in mind. "Perhaps a cousin," I ventured. "I've already met one who could pass for my sister. She's definitely out, but God knows there are a whole crop of them I haven't met yet. Make the next exit, Tank, then watch for the first turn on your right. It's the back way into town but it's quicker."

"Gotcha." He sped up, scared the bejesus out of a man in a battered pickup, and me, then zipped down the off ramp. I closed my eyes. Tank drove as if in hot pursuit of a stolen auto, and my nerves were frayed enough already.

I didn't dare even peek until he said, "Hot damn! It's been a long time since this baby got to do some off-road maneuvering." He hit a pothole in the long-neglected two-lane road, and Tina went flying toward the roof of the Explorer.

She squealed and, once no longer airborne, hauled off

and whacked her husband on the shoulder with enough muscle behind it to make me wince in sympathy.

"Slow down," she said, teeth gritted. "And next time, Leigh, we go in the front way."

I doubted there'd be another occasion for them to make the trip to the Shores, front way or back. Tank and Tina were big-city denizens. Native Washingtonians, they eschewed the suburbs except for the occasional restaurant. Tina, especially, looked down her pert little nose at anyone who lived more than a mile or two beyond the city limits, considering them too chicken to live in the District. What she'd make of Ourland/Umber Shores challenged the imagination, especially after a mile and three-quarters on a rutted road that should have been condemned long since.

"Sorry, Tina," I said. "I promise, we'll be there soon. Tank, take it in second and stay off the shoulders or you'll be listing worse than the *Titanic*."

"Yes'm, Miz Daisy." He grinned and downshifted, clearly enjoying himself, zigzagging to avoid the craters in the pavement until we began to pass the industrial section, ancient warehouses that must have been empty for years, their sidings bleeding rust.

"Jesus," Tina said, staring gloomily out the windows. "This is where you're gonna work?"

"I'll have to check, but I don't think the Shores extend this far."

"Can't tell you how happy I am for you," she grumbled.

I decided to shut up. Something told me that she was just beginning to realize how far she was from what she considered civilization. Probably nothing I could say would improve her disposition.

Which was a shame, because it was a beautiful,

atypical December day, the temperature inching toward the mid-fifties, with the sky a shade of blue you'd love to paint a room. Once past the warehouse graveyard, there were few opportunities to see it until we'd cleared the section where trees older than Moses arched branches, still in full leaf in spite of the season, over the road to form a dimly lit tunnel. Then, in an instant, we were in open air again, and directly in front of us was an expanse of warm gray water that seemed to stretch into infinity.

Tina sat up straight and leaned forward. "Holy shit. That's the bay?"

The road came to an end at a cul-de-sac. Well beyond it, the incoming tide caressed the shoreline, which consisted of rich, umber-hued sand pockmarked with wispy stalks of grass that swayed gently in the breeze. A parade of wooden piers of varying lengths jutted from the shore, a few fat gulls standing sentry on the railings.

"Stop, Tank. I want to get out." Tina wrestled with her seat belt.

"What for?" He slowed and pulled onto a paved section on the right, the excuse for a parking lot protecting two sides of the ramshackle house that camouflaged the Ourland Eatery, the best restaurant in the area. Thank God none of the aromas of Mary Castle's cooking wafted toward us or we'd be eating again.

Tina threw open her door and scrambled out. Slowly she made her way onto the sand, walking as if testing her weight on it. The water was perhaps thirty yards ahead, the first pier a good ten yards beyond that.

Tank cut the engine and got out, but remained standing against the open door of the Explorer, his expression quizzical. Reaching back, he opened the rear door for me. I unbuckled and joined him for a second, then followed Tina onto the sand.

"This really is the bay?" she asked softly. "I mean, not a river or something?"

Belatedly I realized that this might be her first time seeing the Chesapeake. "This is it, Tina. But just a tiny section of it. It runs the length of the state."

"And that's the Bay Bridge way down there?" she asked, pointing. Barely visible at this distance, the umpteen-mile-long bridge wore a ghostly quality, as if you blinked hard it might disappear.

"Yup. Pretty, isn't it?"

She took it all in, seemingly mesmerized, before glancing toward her left, where the roofs of the houses that backed up onto the sand peeked from among surrounding trees. "People live there? All the time?"

"Most of them. See that street?" I nodded toward the only one branching off the cul-de-sac on our left. "That's North Star Road. All the property on this side is Ourland. On the other side, it's called Umber Shores."

"Why?"

"I had an aunt who was killed way before I was born, and her death caused a big multifamily feud. East side versus west, actually. The ones on the west decided they didn't want to have anything to do with anybody in Ourland, so they changed the name to Umber Shores. Everybody's kissed and made up just recently, and now they're trying to decide what to do about the names. There's a lot of history to Ourland, so no one really wants to give it up, but they also like the fact that Umber Shores is a perfect description of the area. I figure they'll work it out sooner or later."

"And *this* is where you'll be working."

"Yup. Lord knows when, the way things are going."

Tina, squinting across the bay, moved farther toward the water, stopping just beyond the point where it lapped against the shore. "Is that land over there?"

"The Eastern Shore. You know—Cambridge, Salisbury, Ocean City."

"Oh."

My phone jiggled. Janeece.

"Hey, roomie, gotta make this short. I just ran into Gracie. She told me to tell you that one of her students remembered that the woman with the accent was named Nell Gwynn. She's already called the cop you talked to but I wanted you to know."

"Thanks, Janeece. I'll try to pop in tomorrow and thank her."

"Do that. She's a sweetie. Gotta go. Later, gator." Click. She was gone.

Nell Gwynn. I'd heard the name somewhere before. Where?

"Hey," Tank called, "y'all gonna stay there all day or what? It's gonna be dark by the time we start back."

"So what?" Tina responded over her shoulder. "It's not like we've got anything special planned this evening."

"Well, I," he responded, sounding peeved, "thought we did."

Tina threw up her hands in defeat. "Swear to God, you'd think he never gets any nookie. Guess we'd better get moving. Where are we going?"

Back in the SUV, I directed them to my grandparents' house. I'm not sure which impressed Tina more, the gate to the compound—"Just like in *The Godfather*!" she said, wide-eyed—the fact that my father's family members lived beyond it, or that a good many of the houses were those she'd spotted from the shore. Most perched on brick pillars tall enough to protect a home during a flood, some high enough to afford covered parking spaces. Stand out in the street, look under the house, and one had an unobstructed view of the Chesapeake. So did the houses across the street, each positioned at a point between the ones that backed onto the bay.

"These folks have boats?" she asked.

"Some do, but most don't. A good many are retirees who live here year round, the others only during the summer or weekends."

"And they're all your relatives?"

"In one way or another. You want to talk about cousins fifth and sixth removed? Knock on any door."

"Jesus," she whispered.

I wasn't sure whether she thought that was good or bad and decided it might be better not to ask.

Ritch Road homes ran the gamut from old clapboard edifices and modest ranches, through redwood A-frames and sturdy stucco two-stories. All had decks or porches, almost all with a swing or hooks for hammocks. The lots were rife with trees older than the town itself, lending an air of permanence.

I pointed out my brother's house, and that of an aunt I had yet to meet, described by various cousins on my mother's side as having a whimsical nature.

"Bullshit," my brother had confided. "The truth is, Aunt Beth's nuttier than a bar of peanut brittle."

The white clapboard home of my grandparents anchored the end of the road, its three stories stacked like a wedding cake, each with its own wraparound porch, and a widow's walk skirting the roof. It gleamed in the late afternoon sun, the effect blinding against the muted gray of the Chesapeake beyond it. The lawn, in winter hues of muted greens and browns, was immaculate, not a dead leaf in sight in spite of the oaks and fir trees nestled around the house.

"Fair warning," I said, as we climbed the steps to the porch, "the first floor is a museum, literally. There are things in here that date from the town's founding in nineteen-oh-one. I don't know how long this visit with my grandmother will take, so feel free to wander through all the rooms."

I pulled a lever beside the front door and heard the distant jingle of a bell, noting the candles and wreaths of holly in each window. My grandmother must have been waiting because the door opened almost immediately. She stood, hand on the knob, her pale brown eyes regarding me coolly. Elizabeth Ritch was barely five feet tall, yet somehow managed to tower above us all, even Tank, something about her snow-white hair and erect posture lending her a regal air.

"Leigh. You're better. Good. Thank you for coming. And you've brought friends. I thought I made it clear that we would be discussing business."

Actually, she hadn't, and any other day I might have reacted differently. But it wasn't any other day, and she'd pissed me off.

"Grandmother, I'd like you to meet Bernard and Tina Younts. Tank." I turned to him, hoping he realized that under no circumstances could I continue to call him Bernard or, God forbid, Bernie. "Tank, Tina, this is my grandmother, Mrs. Ritch. Tank and Tina are members of the D.C. Metropolitan Police Department *and* Duck's and my close friends. They are also our financial and legal advisers, so there should be no problem with their sitting in, don't you agree?"

I sensed, rather than actually saw, Tank's start of

surprise. Tina, cool as ever, didn't bat an eye and reached to shake my grandmother's hand. Tank followed suit, his big mitt swallowing Elizabeth's. Hey, they were cops, which took care of the legal, and with luck, they'd be instrumental in my getting a good price for the removal of the paint on my car. So I'd stretched it a bit. Sue me. As I said, I was pissed at her high-handed manner.

"Then of course they're welcome," she said stiffly, a patch of pink rising in her cheeks.

"What a terrific room," Tina said, her eyes widening. "Oh, Tank, look at the decorations!"

Ritch Manor was ready for the holidays, a monster tree in the corner. Strung with popcorn, candy canes, and baubles that were clearly from another era, it was unlit, with candles perched on the branches. I hoped they were only for effect. This place was a tinderbox, a first-class fire hazard. Toys, obviously homemade and, from the looks of them, thrice my age, were clustered around the base of the tree. It was like an old-fashioned Christmas card.

"The room looks lovely, Grandmother." I could try for graciousness, even if she couldn't.

"I'll let Amalie know. It's her handiwork, too much for me now. If you'll follow me, we'll go up to—"

She was interrupted by a squeal from Tina, her eyes glued to the front corner on our right. "Tank, look! A potbellied stove!"

My grandmother, who I admit I tended to think of as Elizabeth, as opposed to Grandmother, Gran, or any other affectionate variation, eyed Tina with surprise. "I'm pleased that you recognized it. Most your age have never seen a potbellied stove."

"I used to spend summers on my great-aunt's farm in Virginia," Tina said, making a bead for the corner. "She had one of these in her living room, a Klondike or something to do with Alaska, and another in the kitchen." She dropped to her knees and opened its door. "Oh, it's wonderful!"

I looked at Tank, who shrugged. Elizabeth missed our reactions, since she had followed Tina to the stove. "This came from Grandfather Ritch's home, built in 1902. We have most of its contents, as well as items from other Ourland homes of that era. Would you— and your husband, of course—be interested in seeing them?"

Tina, still on her knees, looked up at Elizabeth as if she'd been offered the crown jewels. "Oh, could we?" This was no act, a Tina I'd never seen before.

I gave Tank a quick jab in the ribs and he came to life. "Only if you can spare the time, Mrs. Ritch. If you'd prefer to get on with the subject of the meeting, Tina and I could come back another day."

Elizabeth beamed at them, glowing with pleasure, yet another first for me. She was usually cool as a cucumber, a pickled one at that. Her sister, Ruth, or my cousin Amalie normally conducted the tours through the museum, and I'd gotten the impression that my grandmother considered the whole business a nuisance. It bugged me that I'd been wrong.

We covered the whole of the first floor, including nooks and crannies not normally open to tour groups, thanks to Tina's obvious appreciation of Ourland's antiques. Between homemade furniture, Franklin stoves, pie chests, vintage kitchen utensils, telephones, gramophones, spinning wheels, butter churns, you name it,

Tina appeared to be in her own personal Garden of Eden.

"Did you know she liked antiques?" I asked Tank sotto voce as we made our way through the second of the two kitchens on display.

"I knew she liked them, just didn't know she was ape-shit over them. The thing that gets me is that it sounds like she knows what she's talking about. I mean, I wouldn't be able to figure out what half of this stuff was used for but she's actually naming them." His chest swelled as he watched her. "But that's my Tina. She's always surprising me."

That made two of us. I knew that she was taking college courses and that she was good at her job, but not much more. When I'd met her back in October, she'd given me the impression that she'd spent her early years on D.C.'s meaner streets and could mix it up with the best of them. She was definitely smart, and on her way up the promotional ladder. But I was beginning to wonder about her tough-girl persona.

"Well, that's the lot," Elizabeth said finally. "I've enjoyed this immensely, Christina."

It was my turn to stiffen with surprise. Christina?

Tina squeezed my grandmother's arm. "I have too. This place is wonderful. I'll have to bring my mom to see all this. She'd love it."

"You're welcome any time," Elizabeth said with such warmth, I felt a pinch of jealousy. She'd never spoken to me in that tone. "Well, I was hoping that Wayne might get here before now. He's still at the physical therapist's. Those two get to talking shop and go on for hours. There's no point in our waiting for him. Let's retire to his office."

My curiosity ratcheted up a couple of notches. If we

were to use Granddad's office, this was serious business indeed.

One of the first-floor nooks masked an elevator but my grandmother walked us up two flights of steps instead, her gait far more sprightly than mine. She flipped the switch to turn on the lights as we entered Granddad's sanctuary, its paneled walls and massive desk reminding me of the last time I'd been here searching for the Silver Star awarded my father. The room smelled like old books, of which there were plenty, the majority of them medical tomes.

Tank squinted at a framed document on the wall just inside the door. "Leigh, your granddaddy's a doctor?"

Elizabeth answered for me. "An obstetrician, retired now, although you'd never know it considering the number of calls he still gets. He's delivered practically every child born in the area. I think he lost count after twenty-five hundred."

She skirted the desk and sat down in the big leather chair behind it, its size reducing her to childlike dimensions. I doubted her feet reached the floor.

"Have a seat. Bernard, if you'll please move chairs for yourself and Christina closer to the desk."

"Yes, ma'am." He'd winced when she'd used his name but didn't object. I saw the corners of Tina's lips twitch.

Once we were all seated, Elizabeth gazed at the solitary folder on the desk and cleared her throat. She hesitated, and I got the distinct impression that she felt awkward about whatever was coming.

"This," she said, tapping the folder with a slender index finger, "is the last will and testament of . . . my half-brother, Roosevelt Lawrence. It seems he died in September but we weren't notified until a month ago."

She squirmed a little, and I suddenly realized the source of her discomfort. When I was searching for my father's family I had jotted down all the names on the family tree displayed in the Ourland town hall. There had been no Roosevelt Lawrence dangling from any branch anywhere. I would have remembered.

"I'm sorry, Grandmother," I said. "It must be difficult to lose a sibling." It was the best I could do, especially considering that her sister, Ruth, was terminally ill too.

She glanced up at me, her lids lowered. "You're being very diplomatic, and I appreciate it. The truth is, my father had a dalliance, shall we call it, during the First World War. He was in the army, and Roosevelt's mother lived in the town in which he was stationed. Roosevelt—named after Theodore, of course—was almost ten years old before we found out about him. When his mother died and there was no other family, he came to live with us until he was old enough to enlist himself. He made a career of the army, retired and lived out his remaining years in Virginia."

"I see," I said, even though I didn't.

She folded her hands, index fingers touching, like "here's the church, here's the steeple," and gnawed on her bottom lip for a moment.

"We didn't see much of Roosevelt after he left Ourland, which was just as well, since he was . . . well, a bit of a rake. He'd pop up unannounced every couple of years with a different lady friend, stay for a short period, then disappear. So I'm not hypocritical enough to say that I'm devastated by his death."

"Understandable." I still couldn't figure out what this had to do with me.

She must have sensed it. "I'll get to the point. Your

great-grandfather felt the same obligation to Roosevelt as he did to his other children. As a result, Father purchased a lot for him, and during one of Roosevelt's abbreviated visits, he had a house built on it. Roosevelt had no children, in fact, never married. Which means his property reverts to the family. Wayne and I would like to give it to you."

I should have seen it coming a couple of sentences before, but for some reason, I didn't. "You . . . you want to give me a house?"

Elizabeth's questioning gaze raked my features. "Is there a problem? I realize that you've also inherited your mother's lot, but as you and Dillon will be newlyweds, I assume it will be a few years before you'11 be able to afford putting a house on it. Besides, if you accept, you'll have a home base here as well as in Washington. Once you're working here, I'm certain there'll be nights you won't feel like making that long drive back to town. This solves that problem. You don't want it?"

Tina leaned over and swatted me. "Are you crazy? Take it, girl! As your financial adviser, I'm advising you to take it."

"It's free and clear of any encumbrances, if you're worried about that," Elizabeth said, in concern. "There are the taxes, of course, and utilities and the usual upkeep that comes with a house this close to water—"

Tina edged forward in her chair. "It's one of the ones that backs onto the bay?"

Elizabeth blinked. "Well, no, it's across the street, but one can clearly see the bay from the decks."

"Decks, plural?" Tina scooted farther toward the edge, in grave danger of winding up fanny on floor. She turned and glared at me. "Take it, girl. What's the matter with you?"

"Nothing. I'm . . . I mean, I'm just shocked. It's so generous of you, Grandmother. And unexpected."

"Generosity has nothing to do with it," she snapped. "You'd be doing us a favor. If you don't accept, we'll have to turn over the property to the Ourland Trust. Only relatives of founding families are allowed to own property inside the nineteen-oh-two town limits," she said for Tank's and Tina's benefit. Mine too, since I'd gotten the impression that ownership of property extended to the whole town.

"The trust would put Roosevelt's house up for auction," she continued, her patrician features molded in lines of displeasure, "and then the squabbling would start over which Ourland family should get it. They'd be outbidding one another, the property would probably be sold for an outrageous price, and the losers wouldn't speak to the winners for the next decade. Thanks to you, the town's just getting over the feud that divided us for thirty-some years, and it's been wonderful, just like the old days. I'd like to see it stay that way. As a member of an Ourland family, and a representative of the law, it's your double obligation to see that the peace is kept."

I'd have to give Elizabeth credit for the most creative argument for home ownership I'd ever heard. Regardless, I wasn't sure Duck and I could afford it. Any residence within spitting distance of the Chesapeake had to bring a smile to the face of the state treasurer. You paid for the view in more ways than one.

"I'll have to discuss it with Duck," I said, my head still spinning. "If he agrees, I'll accept, Grandmother."

"He'll agree." Tank nodded sagely. "Duck's no dummy."

Elizabeth slid the folder across to me. "Wayne

computed everything he thought you'd need to know to make an intelligent decision—how much the taxes and utilities have run for the last five years, seasonal maintenance, the rents."

"Rents?" Tina and I asked in chorus. What was she offering me, a rooming house?

"Didn't I say? That's how Roosevelt made it pay for itself. Here, child. Go see for yourself. It's unoccupied." Opening the lap drawer, she extracted a set of keys on a small black key retainer. "I think the longer one is for the upper unit."

"Upper unit?" Tina and I again. Work out a dance routine and we could cut a video.

My grandmother stood. Clearly the meeting was over. "Four-ten Ritch Road. It's fully furnished, so of course the contents are a part of the estate as well." Her nose twitched with distaste. "Feel free to do what you wish with them."

It sounded to me as if Elizabeth considered the property mine already and its appointments undeserving of further description, as if Great-uncle Roosevelt had caught a sale at the equivalent of a Dollar Store.

"One thing at a time, Grandmother," I said, and she stiffened. I doubt she was used to hearing "no." "I'll need a few days to go over Granddad's figures with Duck. He'll want to see it, of course, and I'm not sure of his next day off. But you have my word you'll have our decision as soon as we can manage it."

She was not happy and made no effort to hide it. "Well, do the best you can. Bernard, Christina, do come again." Sweeping around the desk, she took their arms and escorted them from the room. Me she left to my own devices.

"Man, she's something else, isn't she?" Tina said, as we closed the front door behind us. "I can see why you two butted heads when you met. She's used to getting her own way. But, jeez, Leigh, a house! And one that pays for itself? What could be better?"

I wasn't sure. I could hear Nunna's voice in my ear advising me not to look a gift horse in the mouth, but something, I couldn't pinpoint what, made me cautious. Elizabeth's reason for wanting me to accept Roosevelt's house made perfect sense to anyone who knew Ourland's history. Still, something about this didn't feel right.

It was almost dark now, that soft, shadowy period after the sun's just dropped below the horizon. With the demise of day, the temperature had plummeted, the breeze off the water contributing to the chill in the air. I shivered and buttoned my coat. Winters on the water had to be colder than in town. I'd have to invest in some thermal underwear. I shuddered again, remembering the snuggies I'd hated as a child.

"There's got to be a fortune in antiques in there," Tina said, as we went down the steps. "Hope they've got a good security system."

I snorted. "They do. Nothing but first-class for my grandmother. Sorry Granddad wasn't here. He's an absolute doll. And you'll have to meet my Aunt Ruth. She's —"

"Goddammit!" Tank roared, his long legs narrowing the distance between us and the SUV. "Just goddamn!"

"Tank!" Tina hurried toward him. "Lower your voice! What's the matter with you?"

"What's the matter with me?" he asked, performing an about-face to confront her. "What's the matter with your eyes? Look at the tires, woman!"

The floodlights at the corners of my grandparents' house illuminated the parking circle out front just well enough for us to see. All four of the Explorer's tires were as flat as crêpes.

8

TANK WAS STEAMING AND I COULDN'T BLAME him. Silently, he circled the vehicle, checking each tire with my Maglite. I sat down on the bottom step, dismayed.

Tina dropped down beside me and wrapped an arm around my waist. "Come on, it'll be okay. It's not your fault."

"I'm so sorry," I said for the tenth time. "I'll pay for everything."

Tank stood up and brushed the grit from his knees. "Stop kicking yourself, Leigh. All the son of a bitch did was let the air out. Who do you know that drives an old tan compact? And I do mean old, an early model Honda."

The question seemed to come out of left field, yanking me out of my self-imposed misery. "Uh . . . Eddie Grimes but he traded it in last year. I can't think of anyone else." A distant bell tinkled somewhere deep in my gray matter, but I was too distracted to figure out the reason. "Why?"

"I think we had a tail," he said, leaning against the passenger door and gazing off into the darkness.

"A tail?" Tina stood up, fists propped on her

nonexistent hips. "And you didn't say anything or try to lose them?"

"I wasn't sure at the time. Probably wouldn't have noticed it at all, except back there where we got off the Beltway, the Honda was in the wrong lane and cut in front of a Jag to move over. Missed hitting it by a whisker. I spotted it again at the next exit, then again on Route Four, but once we turned onto the road with all the potholes, I didn't see it again and we were going slow enough that I wouldn't have missed anyone behind us. I figured I was being paranoid."

"Well, did you at least notice the license plate, Mr. D.C. detective?" Tina demanded, hopping off the step.

"Maryland, but that's all. Thought it was probably someone who lived out here somewhere."

"What about the driver?" I asked, moving down to join them.

"Black, medium complexion, short gray hair, so it could have been a male or a female. I just couldn't tell."

"Well, that helps a hell of a lot," Tina grumbled. "So now what?"

"Oh! Wait a sec." My mental gears had finally engaged, and I sat down again to search in my purse for my address book. "I've got a cousin who owns a service station here. I just hope it's still open."

"It's not all that late." Tank checked his watch, the kind that looked like it did everything except scour toilets. "Not even six."

Shows you how subjective time can be. I would have sworn it was more like ten. I found the telephone number and used my cell phone, praying that it wasn't W. Two's poker night. It wasn't.

"You're at the manor?" my cousin bellowed in

my ear, the whine of a lug wrench almost drowning him out.

"Parked out front, an Explorer. Someone's let the air out of all four tires."

"Sounds like Grady's boys are back in town. It's the sort of thing they'd do for fun. Y'all are in for a wait, though. Gotta finish what I'm working on. That'll give you time for a nice visit with the grands."

I'd had enough of the one grand for the night. "I've already seen her. Tell you what: we'll be at Four-ten Ritch Road. That okay with you guys?" I asked Tank and Tina.

Tina bobbed her head with enthusiastic approval. Tank shrugged. His attitude toward life seemed to be if it was all right with her, it was all right with him.

"Rosie's place?" my cousin said. "Well, well, well. Okay, see ya there."

"Thanks so much, W. Two. We're saved," I said, as I disconnected. "But he'll be a while, so let's go see this house. It can't be that far away."

"Your cousin's name is W. Two?" Tank asked, as we set off in the direction we had come.

"Short for Wayne Walter Ritch. Every other male around here is a Wayne after my grandfather, or a Warren. Add members of the family whose last name is R-I-C-H and it makes for a lot of confusion. By the way," I added, "W. Two mentioned local boys who have a reputation for letting air out of tires. So maybe we jumped the gun."

"Yeah. Maybe," Tank said, without conviction. He didn't believe it any more than I did.

"Ooh. How pretty." Tina pointed down the street. Now that it was dark, Christmas lights were on along Ritch Road, white electric candles glowing softly in the windows of practically every home. No outdoor displays, not a single Santa, reindeer, or lawn decoration. I wondered if there was a neighborhood covenant stipulating what was acceptable inside the gates and what was not. Probably.

"Oh, Tankie!" Tina stopped in her tracks, head thrown back. Above us a clear, cloudless heaven was strewn with points of lights that set the standard for the twinkle of the Christmas candles. "I've never seen the sky look like this!"

"Too much competition from city lights," I said, nudging her into step again. "Growing up in Sunrise spoiled me. Nunna and I used to sit on the back steps and watch the moon and stars move across the sky. Sometimes I miss that, a lot."

Tank chuckled. "Duck always said you're a country girl at heart. This is four-eighteen. We're getting close."

"Should be the fourth from here," I said, squinting into the darkness, but trees between adjacent residences would block our view of it even in daylight. "It'll probably be the only one with no decorations."

I was mistaken. Neither of Roosevelt's neighbors, four-oh-eight or four-twelve, was lit. One, I knew, was occupied only on weekends. I wasn't sure about the other. Taken together, the three houses amounted to a black hole, a "bah, humbug" in the face of all the Christmas spirit in the vicinity. Four-ten, set farther back than its neighbors, was barely visible from where we stood.

"Maglite," I urged Tank, who still had mine. He flipped the switch and aimed it at the house.

My mouth dropped open. I'd been expecting something small, perhaps one among a number of decades-old cottages on Ritch, with rough-hewn clapboard and screened porches. The yellow beam of the flashlight played across the railing of a very broad deck and beyond it an expanse of plate glass surrounded by redwood siding. I had wondered about this house each time I'd passed it.

"Come on," I said, grabbing Tina's hand.

We had been walking in the middle of the street, since there were no sidewalks on Ritch and traffic almost nonexistent. Twin driveways edged by holly bushes enclosed the lot, a feature that had always puzzled me. We turned onto the closest along the right side of the house. I couldn't see much of the lawn but it seemed to be in good shape. At least it wasn't smothered under a blanket of leaves.

"Man, you need night goggles around here," Tank said as we halted at a bank of steps. The house loomed above us, its outline barely distinguishable from the inky blackness surrounding us. I tripped over a stone or something, and Tank steadied me, a hand on my elbow. "Give me the keys. I'll go open the door and find the lights. No point in all of us stumbling around in the dark."

I fished the keys from the coat pocket, my thumb inadvertently fitting into a depression on the small plastic key retainer as I pulled them out. Immediately, lights flared from beneath the house and each corner of its exterior.

"Oops!" Tank exclaimed, hand shielding his eyes. "We must have set off a motion sensor or something."

"I think it was this." I extended the key ring. "It's a remote. Why didn't my grandmother say so?"

"Probably didn't know. Will you look at this place!" Squinting, he started up the steps, Tina dogging his heels. As I hadn't moved, he asked, "You coming?"

"In a minute, okay?" This was the closest I'd been to it, and I wanted to see it from the bottom up.

Like most, it was elevated, and although I couldn't see it, I realized that the driveway must circle the rear because not only had Roosevelt paved under the house, he had marked off four spaces for cars, two labeled "Unit One," the others "Unit Two." A bank of steps, also reached from the rear, scaled the left side of the house.

I came out from under and backed up a little to get a good look so I could describe it for Duck. A redwood square, two stories, a deck around each floor, the railings leaning outward at an angle. Vertical blinds behind plate-glass windows across the entire front of each level. Redwood timbers framing an A-shaped roof. All in all, it was completely different from its neighbors, yet seemed perfectly at home tucked back among a grove of fir trees on one side and some variety of oaks and birches on the other. And definitely not your typical rooming house.

I climbed the steps to join Tank and Tina, who was hopping from one foot to the other.

"Need a bathroom?" I asked.

"No." Her eyes gleamed in the light above the door. "Just excited, is all. Can we go in now?"

"Why not? Tank, do your thing."

He tried a couple of keys and finally found the right one. Nudging the door open, he groped the wall inside, and lights came on.

"Oh, my God," Tina said, sighing.

Given my grandmother's pained expression when she'd mentioned the furnishings, I'm not sure what I expected, certainly not what greeted us. A wagon wheel chandelier illuminated a great room, its walls swathed in panels of light oak, the sofa and easy chairs straight out of *Country Living* with a dab of chintz here, a small floral print there, the occasional tables a pleasant mixture of dark and light woods. The planked oak floors were relieved by braided and rag rugs of assorted sizes. A rocking chair and spinning wheel in a front corner contributed a final, homey touch.

On our right, a well-appointed kitchen occupied an L-shaped niche in a rear corner, its cabinets of dark oak with glass front panels. An old-fashioned sideboard separated the kitchen from the great room and dining area nestled behind a massive open hearth in the center, complete with cast-iron hooks on which to hang pots.

Next to the kitchen a hallway led to a utility room at the rear on the left. On the right was the guest room with twin beds, a mahogany chifforobe and dresser, sturdy and old-fashioned. In the bathroom, Uncle Roosevelt had installed a vintage toilet with overhead water tank and chain and a claw-footed tub.

Upstairs in a loft running the length of the house front to back was the master bedroom, its main feature a patchwork quilt–covered sleigh bed so high that there were step stools on each side of it. A wall-to-wall closet behind shuttered doors was roomy enough for a complete year's wardrobe, floor-to-ceiling drawers in one end substituting for a dresser. The master bath was a twin of the one downstairs, the tub practically deep enough to swim in. The only concession to the contemporary were the plush carpeting in the loft and the vertical blinds at the wall of windows on the front.

"It reminds me of Aunt Freda's house on the farm," Tina said wistfully. "Especially the bed. I always needed a boost to get in it at night. And I just love the tubs. They're almost long enough for you, Tank."

"Yeah, I guess they are," he responded, watching her warily. "Let's take a look at the upstairs."

We went out, rounded the rear, and took the steps to the second unit. Tank found the right key on the first try, unlocked the door, and hit the light switch.

It was my turn. "Oh, my God."

Either Roosevelt Lawrence had plowed every cent he'd saved into this house or he had a hell of a lot of expendable cash. Up here I was reminded of Gracie Poole's apartment with the contents updated by seventy-five or so years—white walls decorated with enormous abstract paintings, splashes of vibrant colors that challenged the imagination. Highly polished hardwood floors dotted with thick Oriental rugs, a massive see-through stone fireplace dead center of the great room. Contemporary sectional furnishings, simple, upholstered in white, occasional tables of teak that smacked of Scandinavian design.

The kitchen cabinets had solid doors rather than glass, the countertop beneath them a warm, smooth granite cradling a pair of stainless-steel sinks. Up here a butcher-block island separated the kitchen from the great room and the dining area.

Upstairs in the loft, which could be closed off by a wall of sliding shuttered doors, the reason for my grandmother's sniff of disdain became clear, and I dissolved with laughter.

Tina's reaction? "Holy shit!"

"Looks like good ol' Uncle Roosevelt was a player," Tank said, his grin so wide it practically wrapped around his head.

The master bedroom was, so to speak, a chamber of sinful pleasures or pleasureful sins, take your pick. Mirror on the ceiling above a heart-shaped bed plumped with heart-shaped pillows, another mirrored expanse behind it with a shelf lined with bottles of scented massage oils and lotions. If you didn't like your reflection in either of the mirrors, you could look through the skylights flanking the mirror overhead.

A dozen shallow niches resembling shadow boxes were cut into the wall on either side of the bed, each with a frosted snifter containing a candle. Satin drapery camouflaged a door opening onto the outside, to a diminutive platform and steps down to the second-floor deck. The master bath, with mirrors on the walls and ceiling, starred a toilet, bidet, glassed-in shower stall with nozzles on three sides, and glory be to God and all His angels, a Jacuzzi.

I could sense Tank and Tina watching me, waiting for my reaction. The truth was, I was speechless. Elizabeth was right. I had no idea what the market value of this place might be, but I could certainly envision fisticuffs on the front lawn to claim ownership.

"So, what do you think?" Tank asked finally.

"It's incredible. Let's face it, the bed is downright tacky. Makes me wonder how many women Uncle Rosie played honeymoon with over the years. But the house itself doesn't feel like a vacation home, a place for weekends or the occasional stay."

Tina bobbed her head as we went back down to the great room. "Can you imagine anyone renting out a place this nice? You are gonna take it, aren't you? I mean, you'd be a first-class dumb ass not to."

"I need to think. You two make yourself comfortable."

I opened the blinds wide enough to access the center glass pane, unlocked it, and stepped out onto the deck. As my grandmother had mentioned, I was treated to a view of the bay between the two houses across the street. It would be the same from the deck of the lower floor. This, along with the master bath, sold me. I might even sign over my mother's lot to the Ourland Trust. If Duck didn't like this house, I'd spend the rest of my life a single woman right here. Well, not really, but I'd damned sure be tempted.

It was cold as hell out now, but wanting a private conversation, I closed the sliding door and used my cell phone to call the man in question. To my surprise, he was at home.

I plunged right in. "Duck, how would you feel about having a house in Ourland?"

"Is that where you are?" he asked.

"Yeah, with Tank and Tina. You didn't answer my question."

A chair scraped. He was in the kitchen. "What's the big deal? We talked about putting one on your mom's lot, didn't we?"

"Yes, but I'm talking about now, one already built. On Ritch Road. With a view of the Chesapeake."

Silence hummed at me for an eternity. I stopped breathing. Then, "How about you explain?"

I ran it down for him, described the house as best I could and held my breath again.

"You're talking about the place about, oh, three houses east of your brother's on the other side of the street? Redwood, wraparound decks? Double driveway and lots of holly bushes?"

Why was I surprised that he remembered it? "Yes, that one. I have all the information on it, cost of taxes, utilities, upkeep, etcetera, which, according to Elizabeth, was more than covered by renting it out. Uncle Roosevelt only used it himself for short stints every few years."

I closed my eyes and crossed my fingers. I'd save praying for later. "Maybe you can take a look at it on your next day off. I'm just letting you know that if you're interested, it's available."

"You want it, don't you?" A smile warmed his voice.

No point in hedging. "Yes."

"Then I guess I'd better come see it, don't you think?"

"Now?" I gasped. "I mean, tonight?"

"Might as well. Traffic should have let up some by now. I'll be there in, say, forty minutes."

"Duck, I absolutely love you," I said, and meant it.

He chuckled. "Almost as much as you love the house? I'm touched. Hey, tell Tina to call Clarissa. She's misplaced her sister and seems to think Tina might know where she is. See you shortly."

He hung up, and I danced a little jig. The fact that he remembered the house and hadn't said no immediately was a good sign. And this really would solve a problem for me. Aunt Frances, my mother's oldest sister, had offered me free room and board whenever I needed to stay once I started on the job. I could even have the room my mom had shared with her baby sister. So far I hadn't figured a diplomatic way to turn her down. There was a lot of history in her home, and I still had a lot to learn about my mother's years growing up there. But I wanted to absorb all that at my own pace without Aunt Frances hovering in the background.

I also wanted to cook and eat when I felt like it, leave dirty clothes lying around if I was too tired to make it to the hamper, parade around in the altogether if the spirit moved me. I needed my own space, one I could share with Duck, of course. Now I might have it.

There had been a lot of changes in my life in the last eighteen months. Duck had gone from best friend to fiancé. I was no longer one hundred percent, my knee tacked together like a jigsaw puzzle, forcing me to leave a job I loved rather than settle for desk duty. I was no longer the orphan I thought I was; I had family coming out of my ears. And whereas I'd always considered Sunrise as the "down home" I returned to as often as I could, my attitude about Ourland/Umber Shores was gradually changing.

I'd considered it charming and interesting at first, a nice place to get away for a weekend if I was so inclined. Once I had been asked to set up their police force, it became a community in which I'd be working and staying overnight when necessary. Sometime within the last hour or so, however, another change had begun, the thought that this little town might become home with a capital H. There was a lot to be said for it, a lot that appealed to me, surprising since I had come to love the District so much. Yet for the first time I realized that I really wouldn't miss it that much. In its own way Ourland was much closer to Sunrise, where my heart would always be.

I sensed the same brand of small-town intimacy and caring here as had nurtured me there. Ourland/Umber Shores, or whatever the residents finally decided to call it, could become my hometown, my permanent haven.

I could only hope that Duck would eventually see it the same way, but I had good reason to be concerned. He had D.C. in his blood, was proud to say that he was a native because there weren't all that many in the city; practically everyone was from somewhere else. Now I wanted to be somewhere else—here. I also wanted Duck and was terrified that I couldn't have both.

I opened the sliding door and stuck my head in,

interrupting what appeared to be a very weighty discussion in the kitchen.

"Hey, y'all, Duck's coming out. Tina, he says to call Clarissa. She's lost track of her sister."

"Oh, Lord, those two." Tina, perched on a counter, hopped down, and reached for her handbag.

"Leigh, all right if I use the john?" Tank asked, with a measure of anxiety.

"As opposed to taking a whiz off the deck? Just be sure and leave a tip for the bathroom attendant."

He gave me the finger and Tina a pat on the fanny as he left the kitchen.

I closed the door again and returned to the railing. From here the length of Ritch Road was a fairyland, the Christmas lights a-twinkle. Due to the way my grandparents' house was sited at the end of the street, I could see it clearly. A new element had been added since we'd left, a five-pointed star on the roof so brightly lit that I wondered if Elizabeth was expecting a visit from the Magi. Evidently whatever covenants might exist did not pertain to the royal family. Or if they did, Elizabeth Ritch ignored them.

I gave myself a mental slap on the wrist. My grandmother was so unlike my foster mother that on occasion she could make my teeth itch. If Nunna was salt of the earth, Elizabeth was more like owner of the salt company and the sod on which it sat, at least in attitude. I was certain I'd come to love her eventually, if I lived long enough.

An engine growled, disrupting my train of thought. A tow truck crept along—W. Two, mindful of the ten-mile-an-hour speed limit. He slowed, rolled down his window, and waved.

"Hey, Leigh. This shouldn't take long. I'll stop on my way back."

I returned his wave, and he inched on toward my grandparents'.

I spent a few minutes listening to the sibilant whisper of the water, and was making an about-face to go back in when something out of place caught my attention: blinking yellow lights from a car on the shoulder just outside the gates of the compound. Less than two months ago that gate would have been closed and locked, affording entry only to those who lived on this side of it. The first time I'd come to Ourland, I'd climbed the fence to get in and had found myself at the business end of a shotgun wielded by my great-aunt Ruth, Elizabeth's sister. Those days were gone and everyone had access now. Perhaps someone had had car trouble, and the gate was as far as they'd made it. At least they were in walking distance of home.

A second vehicle turned onto Ritch from North Star Road and approached the gate, its headlights throwing the car on the shoulder in stark relief. I stiffened, my nape a-prickle. It was beige or tan, I couldn't tell which, an older model Honda. The odds that it might be the vehicle Tank thought had been tailing us could not be ignored.

I opened the sliding door. Tina was still on the phone. "Where's Tank?" I mouthed.

"Just a minute. Aunt Clar." She pressed the tiny phone against her breast. "He's still on the john. All that sausage on the second pizza. Better than Ex-Lax. I warned him," she added self-righteously, then returned to the phone. "Now calm down, Auntie Clar."

Opting not to wait for Tank or for Tina to finish giving aid and comfort to Clarissa, I closed the door and sprinted around to the steps. There were perhaps eight houses between here and the gate. If someone was in the car, there was no way I could approach it without being seen once I'd passed next door with no lights. So be it. If the driver was just another cousin who'd run out of gas, I'd feel foolish but at least I'd know for certain. Deep down inside, however, I doubted this was one of my relatives. Family might get on my nerves now and then, but none had made the nape of my neck itch.

Once on the street, I crossed to walk facing oncoming traffic, should there be any. The crunch of my shoes on the film of sand dusting the tarmac seemed as if it could be heard a mile away. The next good rain would wash it off but by the following day it would be back, blown onto land by the faintest breeze. Whether anyone could hear me or not, I had to stay on the pavement. The Honda was parked on the right shoulder, and if I could keep the fat brick pillar housing the gate between me and whoever was in the driver's seat, I might be able to avoid being visible until the last minute. Besides, considering the temperature, the car windows were probably up, muting exterior noises. The hazard lights flared rhythmically, painting the area around it in intermittent flashes of old gold.

Treading as lightly as I could, I neared the gate, surprised to detect the sound of the engine. At the entry to the compound, I hesitated, my back against the brick pillar. Directly across from me, the Dutch doors of the small gatehouse were closed and shuttered. I could still remember Aunt Ruth, an elderly Kewpie doll, waiting to confront the intruder—me—the remnants of a peanut butter sandwich between her teeth, the shotgun in her hands. I wished for her now. I'd have felt a lot more confident with her as backup.

Taking a deep breath, I darted around the open gate. Almost immediately the hazard lights went off, leaving the surroundings pitch-black. The sound of the engine changed as the driver shifted gears. Ever so slowly, the Honda inched toward me. I gaped at it, my back against the brick pillar. Did she—in my mind the driver was definitely a female, even though I couldn't see her—did she really intend to hit me? And are you, I asked myself, going to be dumb enough to stand here and let her do it?

Before I'd had a chance to make a decision, the gears changed again and she began backing up, first along the shoulder, the rear end angling onto the softer ground beyond it. I felt my muscles go slack with relief. With any luck, her back tires would become mired, at least temporarily. Energized by a sudden injection of pure, senseless rage, I ran toward the Honda. It didn't occur to me to wonder what the hell I'd do once I'd caught up with it.

I never found out. She shifted, gunned the engine, and pulled forward, the sound of debris under the wheels spraying the undergrowth as it lurched onto the tarmac. She executed a wide U-turn and sped away toward North Star Road. At the intersection, she turned left without pausing, earning a blast from the horn of someone who had the right of way.

"Damn!" The oath seemed swallowed up by the darkness. I turned back, walking in the middle of the road this time, drained of adrenaline, which seemed to be leaking out through my shoes. I was certain that I'd almost confronted my nemesis.

I stopped and looked back, a memory sneaking up on me. Was the car that had almost hit me on Monday a Honda? I wasn't sure. A compact, yes. Old, yes. Coincidence? Yeah, right.

Tank and Tina stood on the deck, watching my approach.

"Where'd you go?" Tank called down.

I waited until I'd climbed the steps to the second level before responding.

"You were right, Tank. The Honda was parked outside the gate with the flashers on. I tried to sneak up on it. Yeah, I know, stupid, especially since it looked for a second like she intended to hit me. Or maybe she just wanted to scare me, I'm not sure. Anyway, she finally made a U-turn and burned rubber hightailing it away from there without headlights. Almost creamed a car out on North Star."

"So you didn't get a look at her?" Tina asked.

"No. And it bugs me that she knows about this town." An unwelcome thought slithered through my mind. I had just returned from Ourland when that compact had nearly run me down on Monday. Had she followed me here that day? The very idea made my blood boil. "I won't have her causing havoc out here. I won't."

Tank slipped an arm around my shoulder and walked me inside. "I understand how you feel, Leigh, but how do you plan to stop her?"

"I don't know yet," I admitted. "But I will. I've got to."

9
—

"I HAVE A THEORY ABOUT WHO SHE MIGHT BE," I said later as we waited for Duck in the first-floor unit. I wanted him to see it first.

Tank had spent the last half hour reading me the riot act for not having waited for him. That was followed by a minor spat, Tina taking umbrage at the implication that she couldn't have offered as much support as he could have. I sat it out, accustomed to their short-lived squabbles. It was simply the way they related to each other.

I decided to end it. For all I knew, they'd forgotten I was there.

"Look, y'all, we don't have much time. I'd like to run my theory by you before Duck gets here."

"Oh. Yeah. Sorry. Bet I know what you're thinking." Tina eyed me with speculation. "It's probably the same idea I've been tossing around."

"What?" Tank took our coats and draped them over the divan. We settled around the old dining room table. "Spill it."

"One of the Duck's old girlfriends," Tina said, elbow on the table, chin cupped in her hand. "Am I right?"

I nodded. "I suggested that to Duck and he didn't like it at all. But it's a definite possibility."

Tank scrubbed one side of his nose and slouched in his chair. "I'm not sure about that. I've known the man a long time and he was never a player like a lot of guys. Popular with the ladies, sure, and never at a loss for a date. But I don't remember him getting serious about any of them, and the kind of dude he is, he'd have been right up front with them from the git-go."

"Well, hell, Tankie," Tina said, with a scowl, "that doesn't mean they didn't fall for him anyway. I know for a fact that Jennifer Cowley's nose was wide open for the Duck, right up to the time she married Ike. She wasn't the only one. This may be someone who went ass over teakettle over the Duck and wants to get back at the one he's ass over teakettle about."

" 'Hell hath no fury' and all that," Tank offered. "I guess it's possible. Wonder if there's anything to eat in those cabinets." He got up and began to investigate.

Tina looked exasperated, then focused on me again. "So we're on the same page?"

"Evidently. Except wouldn't it make more sense for her to take out her revenge on Duck?"

"She did," Tina said. "She messed up his honeymoon plans."

"They were my honeymoon plans too," I reminded her. "And it's me she's been stalking, so to speak. Well, one thing at a time. I'll let him concentrate on the house tonight and hit him with my theory about the old girl-friend again tomorrow."

Tank found a box of Cheez-Its so old that Tina maintained she could have hatched and given birth to a couple of babies since its sell-by date. He nibbled on them, pronounced them edible, and began dispatching them one by one while we tried to list all the women Duck had dated over the years. By the time we heard his car turn into the driveway, we had dredged up sixteen names, some of whom I knew personally, but only one Tina thought resembled me. Her name rang no bells with me.

"Similar coloring and build," she said. "You wouldn't pass for sisters but she does make me think of you. Wonder if that might have been the reason the Duck dated them in the first place. Stand-ins for you, know what I mean?"

I thought it was pretty farfetched, but face it, when it comes to men and how they think, anything's possible.

"Gimme that," I whispered to Tina when I heard Duck pull under the house. She'd been doing the writing. She tore the sheet from her notepad and I stuffed it in a pocket, then ran out to the deck to wait for him.

"Duck? Up here," I called, hearing his door slam. "The first floor, stairs on the right."

He appeared and stood looking up at me. "What's with the labels on the parking spaces?"

"Come on up. You'll see."

He climbed the steps, gaze riveted on my face, an amused smile on his. When he reached the landing, he wrapped his arms around me, and the next thing I knew I was being well and thoroughly smooched. I even forgot about the house, the list, and everything else for the moment. Man, that man can kiss!

He released me. "That's just to show you how much I miss you during the day."

I went into complete meltdown inside. Why had it taken me so long to realize how much I loved Dillon Kennedy? Not that I regretted the days we'd spent as very close friends, but the nights could have been a hell of a lot more interesting.

"All right, babe, time for the tour. By the way, where's the Explorer?"

"In front of my grandparents'," I said, deciding not to ruin the mood by telling him about the tires. I'd also exacted a promise from Tank and Tina not to mention my encounter with the Honda, knowing Duck would blow his lid. Looping an arm through his, I led him toward the front. "Let's go in this way."

There was a method to my madness. The moon had made an appearance, its beams gilding the tips of the whitecaps of the bay; otherwise it would have been invisible. Duck stopped at the railing overlooking the yard, gazed out across the water, then up and down the street. Between the Christmas candles, the glistening Chesapeake, and the incredible night sky, he had to be impressed.

"Quite a view," he said, nodding approval. "Inside, babe. You're shivering."

I slid open the center pane and separated the vertical blinds for him.

Neither Tank nor Tina had moved. "Hey, Duck," they said in chorus, an idiotic grin lighting Tank's Mr. Clean visage. Talk about open hero worship.

"Hey, yourselves." Duck strode to the table, leaned over, and pecked Tina on the cheek. "How are you feeling, little T.?"

"Middlin'. Isn't this the neatest place?"

"Don't know yet. Let's see." Sliding his coat off, he turned in a circle, his eyes taking in everything as he pivoted.

I removed the coat from his hand and folded it over

my arm, needing something to hold on to. "Look around. I'm thirsty."

I finally draped his coat across a chair, found a tumbler, and drank two glasses of water while he circumnavigated the main room. He stopped to peer at all the antique reproductions and wall decorations, closely examined the kitchen, opening each and every cabinet, upper and lower, never saying a word. Tank and Tina remained at the table, displaying crossed fingers whenever Duck wasn't looking. As for me, my stomach had turned into a butterfly farm, and the poor things were drowning in all that water I'd had.

He peeked into the guest room, laughed uproariously after pulling the chain of the water closet, and spent an inordinate amount of time in the back hall before reappearing. "Nice," he said, leaning against the wall. "Whoever built this meant it to last."

"My great-uncle Roosevelt," I said. "A half-great, actually. Turns out Great-granddad's eye wandered, at least once."

"Happens in the best of families. Only thing is, why hide the staircase?"

"Huh?" Tank, Tina, and I in unison, of course.

"You didn't see it? Come back here."

We followed him to the rear of the hall and into the utility room. Adjacent to the washer/dryer combination were ceiling-to-knee-high shelves. Tucked under one of the shelves in the adjoining wall was a semicircular metal plate with a hole. Duck stuck a finger in it and pulled. A pocket door slid onto darkness.

"This locks," Duck said, "but you've got to know how. Hold on." He groped the wall until he'd found a light switch. A narrow staircase, just as he'd indicated.

Flabbergasted, we followed him up. At the top was the door into the utility room of the upper unit.

"How'd you know about this?" I asked.

"I didn't. I just wondered why all but one shelf had one-by-three anchors. I looked to see what was holding it up and spotted the faceplate on the lock. Jensen's got a lock like that on the door of his gun closet."

"I'll be damned," Tank said. "Sneaky, but smart."

We'd left the lights on up here and now it was my turn to cross my fingers. This floor was much more to Duck's taste.

Bypassing the bathroom and guest room, which were serviceable but also boringly pedestrian, he headed toward the front and stopped dead at the entrance to the great room.

"Wow," he said softly.

Tina, second in line, turned to me and Tank and pumped her fist in a silent "Yes!"

I pointed toward the sectionals, and the three of us plopped down on them while Duck gave a repeat performance of the one he'd made downstairs. I swear he didn't miss a thing, going over every piece of furniture, every painting, rug, cabinet, appliance, faucet, as if he was expected to pay for them and had no intention of being cheated.

He took the steps to the loft, stopped at the top, and looked down at us. "You're kidding."

"Keep looking," I said, hoping the bedroom wouldn't foul up the works.

He opened the closet doors and began to hum. "Practically a walk-in." He tested the drawers, took one out and checked the construction. He stepped outside onto the tiny balcony, examined the lock on the door, closed it. He stooped and fingered the wall-to-wall carpet. Then he went into the master bath, and I held my breath.

I heard a low whistle of admiration, the toilet flush, the bidet swish, water run in the his-and-hers wash-basins, cabinet doors under them open and close, the spray from the shower, the gurgle of water in the Jacuzzi. Finally, nothing.

Tina looked as if she might scream with impatience. I gulped in a deep breath, my body reacting to having been oxygen deprived from the moment Duck had walked up into the bathroom.

He came out, leaned over, elbows resting on the railing. "The bed's gotta go. When do we move in?"

There ensued a good five minutes of shouting, squealing, back-pounding, hugging, and kissing, in which I took little part. I couldn't. Too shocked to move, I just sat there. It wasn't that he had agreed that we should accept the house, he'd said "When do we move in?" the word of note being "move." I wasn't sure how to interpret it.

"What's the problem, babe?" Duck asked, pulling me to my feet. "It's what you wanted, isn't it?"

"Yes, but . . ." I tried to figure out how to phrase it to find out what I needed to know. "I guess you surprised me. I thought you might argue that two households was a bit much since we—"

He pressed a finger to my lips, silencing me. "Not two households. One. This one. This floor. We'll rent the lower."

"We'll take it!" Tina bellowed.

Tank ogled her. "Say what?"

She rounded on him, chin raised, eyes narrowed.

"I want to rent it. I like it out here. What's the problem, Chuckles? We can afford it."

For the second time in less than five minutes, I was rendered speechless. Part of my brain considered it a dynamite idea, the other part warned me about familiarity breeding contempt.

"I—I don't know what to say," I admitted.

"She's right," Duck said. "Ourland's a nice town, and this is a terrific house. But another reason I say let's go for it immediately is that I want you out of reach of your she-devil. At least I know that you'll be safe here."

Tank, Tina, and I exchanged a pointed glance.

"What?" Duck demanded, immediately suspicious.

We were saved from having to respond by a bell. The door. W. Two.

After the "how're ya doings" and "glad to meet you's," he got down to business. "The SUV's in the driveway down there. Who gets the bill? I only charged for a one-way tow."

"Dead battery?" Duck asked, amused.

Tank scowled at him. "No. Someone let the air out of the tires while we were inside talking to Mrs. Ritch."

Duck's brows flipped in surprise. "You're kidding."

"And it wasn't Grady's boys." W. Two looked from one to the other. "Turns out they don't get home from college until the nineteenth."

"Well, hell." Tank shrugged in defeat. "Might as well tell him. We think Leigh's mystery woman tailed us out here," he said, digging in his back pocket for his billfold.

"Put that away." Duck, veins throbbing in his temples, removed his own and handed over a credit card. W. Two, clearly sensing trouble of some sort, made short work of the transaction. "What's this about y'all being tailed?"

"Some woman's been making a nuisance of herself," I said. "Tank saw an old model Honda behind us most of the way here."

"And Leigh went out there to try to talk to her," Tina chimed in, spilling the rest of the beans, "and almost got herself hit."

I glared at Tina.

Duck glared at me.

"The Honda that was parked outside the gate?" W. Two asked. "What's that old biddy got against you?"

That got our attention. "You saw her?" Tank demanded. "Close up?"

"Well, yeah, on my way to get the Explorer. I mean, she's sitting out there with her blinkers on and I'm driving a tow truck. You figure I'm gonna pass up potential business? She said she was fine, just waiting to meet someone, and she appreciated my checking."

"What did she look like, W. Two?" I asked.

"Black, older than me, say in her sixties from all the gray hair. Shorter than yours, Leigh. Hell, shorter than mine. About your color, maybe a tad lighter; it was hard to tell. That's the best I can do."

This was ridiculous. How could I have aggravated someone this woman's age without knowing it? "Did she have an accent? West Indian, perhaps?"

"Nope, sounded like a regular American to me."

Scratch Nell Gwynn.

He promised to call me if he remembered anything else, and left.

"All right, let's hear it," Duck said, closing the door. "From the top." To say his jaws were tight would be an understatement.

We were repeating the story for the second time for him when my cell phone burped. I glanced at my watch. It was past nine. If someone was calling this late on my cellular, something must be wrong.

"Leigh, where are you?" Janeece, sounding slightly frazzled.

"Ourland. What's up?"

"The police were here looking for you."

"Willard? He found out who made the call?"

"These guys didn't know anything about that. They wouldn't tell me what they wanted, either. We're talking some tight-lipped sons of a gun, Leigh, dead serious. They gave me a number to call if I heard from you."

I repeated it, committing it to memory. "Thanks, hon. Got big news but it can wait until tomorrow. Go back to bed."

Duck didn't recognize the number but to my surprise, suggested that I wait and call once we were back in D.C. "If it's trouble, we'll deal with it when we get there."

"We've got to go." Tank pulled Tina to her feet. "I'm on the early shift, and my sweetpea here has a doctor's appointment in the A.M."

Tina rubbed her tummy. "Just making sure everything's back to normal down here. Hell, we forgot all about Chet and your car, Leigh. I'll have him call you first thing tomorrow. My shift ends at four if you need me to take you somewhere."

We agreed to wait and see what Chet had to say and decide from there.

The two T's departed. Duck and I weren't far behind, but they lost us once we reached the highway. I settled back in Duck's oil-guzzling clunker, relieved to be alone with him. As much as I liked Tank and

Tina, they had a way of sapping my energy. Somehow they seemed to take up more room than most, used up more oxygen or something. Which did not bode well if they were to be weekend neighbors. Which also brought me back to the subject of the house.

Duck's ready acceptance of it struck me as something to be examined more closely, in spite of his initial declaration that he wanted me out of reach of the she-devil. He was a home boy in the most literal sense. He loved D.C. Besides, members of the District's police force were required to live there. So his wanting to move was inexplicable.

"Duck, about the house. I want it, yes; it'll give me a home base while I'm working there, a local address in case there's a county residency requirement. But moving lock, stock, and barrel never entered my mind because you can't. Your job, remember?"

He reached over and gave my thigh a squeeze. "Don't sweat it, babe. It would solve a lot of problems for me. I've been thinking about making a change, and tonight may help me get off the pot."

"A change?" This was new. It was also unsettling in that he'd never mentioned it before. "What kind?"

He slowed to let a low-slung sports car cut in front of us. "I'm considering leaving the job."

"*What?*" I couldn't have been more surprised if he'd told me he was going into a monastery.

"It's a long story. Let's just say that September eleventh made me begin to wonder about the value of my contribution to the District, to the country, for that matter. And before you say it, I know I'm too old to join the service."

Well, I wouldn't have said it, even though I was thinking it.

"I've been nosing around, trying to get a feel for what else I could do. There are a couple of opportunities out there—well, more than a couple, actually. And somehow, word got out that I might be open to making a move, I still haven't figured out how. All of a sudden, I'm being courted by federal investigative agencies *and* private industry. And I'm definitely interested. It would mean more money, and that's nice, but it would also mean making a bigger contribution, a bigger difference. And that's important to me."

I let him talk. Even though I had never imagined him as other than a detective with the D.C. police, I'd sensed a certain level of frustration but considered it an occupational hazard. Everyone in the department became frustrated at some point. Most got over it. Those who didn't left. It never occurred to me that my Duck would join the latter.

"I haven't been ready to talk about it," he explained, "because I wasn't sure how you'd react. I remember the big deal it was to you when I made detective."

I removed his right hand from the steering wheel and kissed the back of it. "Duck, I wouldn't care if you wanted to run away and join the circus as long as you took me with you."

"Really?" he asked, an impish gleam in his eyes. "I mean, I'd love to be one of those clowns that climbs out of one of those little bitty . . . Oh-oh."

I'd been so engrossed in our conversation that I didn't realize we were pulling into his underground garage. Turning to see what had interrupted his ridiculous train of thought, I saw a cluster of uniforms and plainclothes types milling about in the far corner near my old Chevy. A cruiser idled about a third of the way from the entrance, chase lights ablaze. Not only was it blocking several others if they wanted to leave, it was also in our way.

"Looks like trouble for sure." Duck slowed, shifted into reverse. Turning to look back over his shoulder, he said, "Guess I'll have to park on the street tonight."

"There he is!" A lanky, middle-aged man in green hospital scrubs separated from the crowd and pointed toward us.

All heads swiveled in our direction. Two of the uniforms began trotting toward us, arms outstretched in the universal signal for "Halt," one of them reaching for his service revolver in the process.

"What the hell?" Duck shifted into park and lowered his window. Sticking his head out, he called, "Hey, guys, what's going on? Adams, is that you?"

The stockier of the two slowed to a walk, shading his eyes against the overhead lighting. "Duck?" He waved for his companion to relax. "I didn't know you lived here."

"I didn't know you'd been transferred to this district," Duck said, getting out.

I released my seat belt and scrambled out, too. "Hey, has something happened to my car?" I grabbed my purse and hurried toward the gathering. "What's going on?"

A pair of plainclothes moved toward me, their expressions slammed close, official masks in place. "You're Ms. Warren? Leigh Warren? We've been looking for you."

"Evans, Thackery," Duck said, in greeting. Stopping beside me, he draped an arm around my shoulder. "Don't tell me somebody tried to heist this thing. It can be driven, but it'll cut out on you in no time. Did you catch the bastard?"

Their faces relaxed a bit but they still wore an air of caution. "Bastardess," one responded. "Female. Mr. Grandison here saw her trying to hide behind it and started over to investigate. She spotted him and hauled ass."

"Had she broken into it?" I asked, wondering about my sudden possessiveness over a car I no longer owned.

"She didn't need to," Evans said, watching me. "When's the last time you drove it?"

"Uh—sometime in October. I hit a tree and . . ." They didn't need the details. "It's been in the shop. You had it towed back in here when, Duck? About ten days ago, right?"

"And an old pro like you would never leave the keys in the ignition, right, Kennedy?"

"You're kidding." Duck stepped to the front passenger side and looked in, then back at me. "They've been hanging on the pegboard in the kitchen. How . . .? You and Clarissa are the only ones who've been up there."

"Clarissa?" Thackery prompted.

"Cleaning lady." Duck shook his head. "She would have no reason to take them, and I can't imagine her giving them to someone else. She knew it still needed work and was risky to drive. Someone must have broken into my unit, dammit." He turned on his heel, heading for the elevator.

Thackery cleared his throat and Duck stopped, looking back over his shoulder.

"It's not quite that simple, Kennedy. We're waiting for forensics and someone from the coroner's office." Eyes still glued on us, he reached down and lifted the lid of the trunk.

The odor hit me first, one I wasn't likely to forget. It was faint but memorable under any circumstances, and my stomach lurched. Cradled inside the trunk on top of the spare, assorted tools, a defunct flashlight, and a ratty old blanket, Clarissa lay curled in a fetal pose staring into nothing, well and truly dead.

10

"OH, NO. GOD, NO. CLARISSA." DUCK, ANGUISH mangling his features, moved as if to reach in and touch her, but caught himself. "How the hell did she wind up in the trunk?"

"This is your cleaning lady?" Thackery asked, his face thawing a little. "We could use a positive identification. No purse in there, unless she's lying on it. We don't want to move her before forensics shows up."

"Her name is Clarissa Farrell. But . . . but I just talked to her," Duck said, then flushed, undoubtedly realizing how many times he'd heard the same after breaking the news of someone's demise.

"When?" Evans demanded. "Tonight?"

Duck turned to me. "Seven-thirty, somewhere around there, you think?" Evans frowned and glanced at Thackery, an exchange Duck missed. "She called me looking for Tank and Tina," he continued, "thought they might have stopped by. I was just about to phone Leigh, since I'd asked them to drop in on her, when she called."

"She knows Younts?" Evans asked Duck, not me.

"Clarissa's a relative of Tank's wife," I said. "Lord, Tina's gonna have a fit. Should I call her?"

Duck shook his head, his gaze riveted on the body.

"Clarissa cleaned my toilet, changed my sheets. It's my obligation." He reached for his cell phone and started back toward his car.

I stepped closer to mine and peered in. "I don't see any signs of trauma. Wonder what . . ." Frowning, I knelt at the back bumper. Something wasn't right. "Duck, wait a minute," I called.

"What?" He turned around, the pain on his face making me flinch.

"Just . . . just don't call yet."

"Something we should know?" Evans asked, coming up behind me.

I shook him off, signaled for him to wait. "Let me borrow your flashlight." He placed it in my hand, a whopper compared to mine. Holding my breath, I leaned in and played the beam along the still figure from head to toe.

Horn-rimmed glasses lay at an angle across her nose. Lividity had set in, just barely visible on her left cheek and leg because of her position. But by the time I'd reached her feet, I was sure. "Duck, this isn't Clarissa."

"What the hell!" Evans and Thackery glared at me, then at him, as if we'd pulled something over on them.

Duck bounded back to the car. "What do you mean, it isn't Clarissa? Wait. Her sister, maybe? But they weren't twins." He stared in. "Were they?"

"Must have been. But look, her ears are pierced. Clarissa's weren't. The day I stayed to let her in, the first thing she did was yank off her earrings and massage her earlobes because the earrings pinched."

"I guess I never noticed. Are you sure, babe?"

"You don't yank earrings off pierced ears, Duck. And Clarissa had . . . has," I amended stubbornly, "fat feet. This woman's are delicate in comparison. And her hair isn't as brassy."

He stooped, examining her with narrowed eyes. Finally he rose. "You're right. Thank God. I never met her, so I didn't realize . . . Poor Clarissa. This will kill her."

I could have pointed out that it was a poor choice of words but kept my mouth shut because I might also have blurted out the fact that he had just fibbed. I was trying to figure out what to do about it when Thackery derailed the effort.

"So what's her name?" he demanded.

Duck shrugged. "I don't know. All I ever heard Clarissa call her was Sister."

"And Tina called her Aunt Sister," I added. "She can fill you in on whatever you need to know. She talked to Clarissa after Duck did."

"How do you know?" Evans challenged me.

This man was beginning to annoy me. "It goes like this: Clarissa called Duck asking if Tina was there. Duck knew Tina was with me, but before he had a chance to call me, I called him. He told me to tell Tina to call Clarissa. I told Tina. Tina called Clarissa. That clear enough?" He reddened. I didn't care.

Duck, perhaps sensing the possibility of fireworks, stepped in. "Look, let me get Tina. They should be home by now. And unless you guys object, she'll probably want to tell Clarissa herself."

"First things first," Evans said, taking charge again. "Ask Mrs. Younts to come so we can get a positive ID once and for all. If she wants to bring her aunt, so much the better. Adams, find out what's keeping the damn techs and whoever's coming from the medical examiner."

Grandison cleared his throat since it was obvious we'd forgotten he was there. "Can I go now? I'm sorry about the lady and all, but I've gotta get to work."

Thackery didn't even look up. "One of you guys move the cruiser so he can get out, then check in with your dispatcher. No point in your hanging around here any longer. Mr. Grandison, we'll need you to come in sometime tomorrow to make a formal statement, the earlier the better."

Grandison mumbled agreement, climbed into a late-model Volvo, and followed the cruiser out.

Duck went back to his car again and sat in the front seat to call Tina.

In the meantime, Evans leaned against the fender of a nearby Taurus. "Mind accounting for your movements today, Ms. Warren?"

I didn't particularly appreciate the suspicion underlying the question, but there was no point in antagonizing him any further. After all, it was my car. And who knows how long the body had been there. December temperatures would have slowed decomposition. Further speculation was futile. I might as well answer the question.

"I was home until late morning—"

"Alone?"

"Yes, packing."

"You're going somewhere?" Thackery asked, reaching for his notepad.

"I'm moving in with Duck; we're getting married the day after Christmas. Tank and Tina arrived around noon, perhaps a little before. They went down to pack my car for me, but someone had spray-painted the windshield. You can check; I filed a report with the police."

They both scribbled, then waited expectantly.

"Tank and Tina and I got back here around two, I guess. We took boxes upstairs and stayed less than an hour."

"The three of you. How many trips did you make to get everything upstairs?" Thackery asked.

"Just one."

"And you didn't come back down again, then go back up?"

It was a puzzling question. "There was no need to. Why?"

"You noticed nothing unusual about this car earlier?" Evans asked, before his partner could respond. "When you three arrived?"

"I doubt I even looked in this direction. All I had on my mind was getting my boxes upstairs."

Thackery's face was unreadable. "And the three of you left here at what time?"

"About two-thirty, two-forty. I needed to get to Connecticut Avenue by three—"

"Because . . .?" said Thackery.

"I was supposed to pick up some tickets from our travel agent because she was closing early." I hesitated, decided to skip the gist of my conversation with Margie. "From there, we stopped and ate lunch."

"We? You and the Yountses?"

"Right. At Paisan's. From there we drove to Ourland—"

Evans frowned. "Where's that?"

I was trying to describe it in relation to Annapolis when Duck returned and stationed himself at my side. Without interrupting, he took my hand and squeezed it. I wasn't certain whether it was a signal or a gesture of support. He looked like the one who needed it;

evidently the conversation with Tina had been rough. I squeezed back.

"That's where we were coming from when we arrived here," I finished.

"Hmm." Evans scanned his notes, then gazed in thought at poor Sister. "And yesterday?"

"What about it?" I wasn't being obstreperous, just somewhere else mentally, remembering Clarissa and Sister on the phone the day before yesterday, the impression I'd gotten about how close they were.

He looked as if he might skewer me to the concrete walls. "Your movements. Where were you?"

"At home, all day, recovering from a virus."

"Alone?"

Praying for patience, I closed my eyes and nodded. "Alone."

Duck's radar finally picked up on the nuances. He draped an arm around my shoulder and said, "There's a problem?"

Evans's sharp gaze shifted to him. "I'd say so, since one of your neighbors . . ." He flipped backward a page. "An Evangeline Luby reports seeing Ms. Warren on the elevator with your cleaning lady—or perhaps this one—"

"Her name's Claudia." Duck's voice was hard. "Claudia Hitchcock. And they were twins." Pencils went into action again. "Let's back up and start from the beginning. How'd this all come down? Who called it in? And why did you open the trunk to begin with?"

There seemed a slight change of attitude in Evans and Thackery, as if they remembered that they were not dealing with the ordinary John Q. Public.

Evans removed his rear end from the Taurus and stood erect, as if reporting to a superior. Perhaps he was;

no one had mentioned his rank. He referred to his
trusty notepad and cleared his throat.

"Grandison called it in at twenty thirty-two. Uniforms responded, a suspicious circumstances. Grandison was waiting for them, said he'd witnessed a woman
hiding beside this car. She realized he'd seen her and
took off running. They checked the car, found the keys
in the ignition. Grandison said he'd seen you working
on it, so one of the uniforms went up and knocked at
your door but of course got no answer."

"Any description of the woman?" Duck asked with
studied casualness.

"No. The light's pretty dim over here, lots of shadows.
And she was fast, according to Grandison, too fast for
him to consider going after her."

Duck, arms folded, nodded. "Okay. Sorry, didn't
mean to get you off track. No answer at my door. Then
what?"

"Music, from the trunk."

"No kidding? Interesting," Duck said dryly, "since
I'd removed the radio."

"They noticed. The fact remains that 'America the
Beautiful' was playing in the trunk."

"Claudia's cell phone," I blurted, remembering
Clarissa's. Matching tunes. It figured.

"Right. It kept sounding off, so one of the uniforms
popped the trunk. After seeing what . . . who was in it,
they called us."

That was all well and good, but I wanted to get back
to Mrs. Luby and what she said she'd seen.

Evidently Duck was on the same track. "How is it
you talked to my neighbor again?"

It was Thackery's turn. "Grandison suggested we
check with her. I take it she has a reputation for knowing

everyone's comings and goings. We tried your unit again, then knocked on her door. We identified ourselves, and she told us she'd heard you leave. By that time we had traced the vehicle identification number of the Chevy and knew Ms. Warren was listed as the most recent owner, so we asked Mrs. Luby if she knew her. You, I mean," he amended, a tacit apology for talking about me as if I weren't there. "She said she was in the lobby this afternoon when the elevator door opened. She said that you, Ms. Warren, were on the elevator with the cleaning lady. You were carrying a box."

"No way," I said. "Didn't happen. What time was this?"

He examined his notes. "Between noon and twelve-thirty. She said the twelve o'clock news was on."

"I was home labeling cartons. Or out back trying to scratch the damned paint off my car windows. Tank and Tina will verify what happened when."

I didn't understand it. How could Mrs. Luby make such a mistake? She knew me and had for a couple of years at least. Unless . . .

"Clarissa didn't mention being here today," Duck said, clearly puzzled. "She'd have no reason to be. She'd just cleaned the day before yesterday."

I had to intervene. "She didn't finish, Duck. I assumed she'd told you. She wasn't feeling well and left early." Now was not the time to tell him I was pretty sure something I'd said might have upset her.

"Well, it'll be simple to clear up when we talk to her. As for the woman with the box . . ."

"That *bitch!*" I erupted, realizing the implications of the earlier sighting by Mrs. Luby. "She's been in your apartment, Duck. The box she was carrying. It must have been the one I was looking for."

"Huh?" He squinted at me.

I reminded him of the missing carton, watching as his eyes darkened with rage. "It all makes sense now. She must have shown up on a day Clarissa was there, some time over the last two weeks. So *that's* what she meant." Puzzle pieces had begun to interlock.

"Which 'she'? You mean, Clarissa?"

"Yes. She said, 'You look just like your picture today,' as if I didn't before. And she asked me when I'd gotten my hair cut."

Duck shook his head. "You've left me."

Evans and Thackery were probably as puzzled but were doing a good job of trying not to show it. They simply watched, two pairs of eyes darting back and forth between us.

"That's why she seemed surprised when I said I was pleased to meet her," I went on, as much for myself as for him. "As far as she was concerned, we'd met before. Except," I added, "that doesn't quite scan. Oh, my God."

"Yes?" From the expression on Evans's face, something told me he used those piercing gray eyes as a means of intimidation. I had news for him; they weren't working on me.

"It wasn't Clarissa, it was Claudia," I said, hoping they'd be able to follow me. "Before, I mean, whatever day the she-devil showed up here. I'm sure the twins must have had a good reason for pulling a switch, but that had to be what happened. Clarissa was reacting to her sister's description of me. If Clarissa had been there that day, she would have reminded me that I'd taken the box right off the bat. She mentioned the box to her sister on the phone while I was searching for it. Claudia must have told her I'd been there and had taken it. But in the kitchen a while later, Clarissa seemed distracted, worried. Then I mentioned that the box had been in the guest room the last time I was here two weeks ago. That's when she must have realized that her sister had screwed up and the woman who'd taken the box couldn't have been me. Understand?"

"All right." Thackery snapped his notepad closed. "I give. What the hell is going on here?"

I dreaded having to explain. It was all so bizarre. Fortunately a stay of execution arrived in the person of the crime scene technicians and a medical type, all stepping over one another in an intricate ballet as each went about his assigned task.

Duck found an unmarked space for his car near the entrance and we sat on the hood watching, with no further discussion of the interloper. The least we could do for Claudia was to make her the focus of our attention, since we'd pretty much ignored her for the last quarter hour or so.

The medical examiner had just finished when the Explorer barreled into the garage. Seeing us parked off to the side, Tank pulled up beside us.

Tina was out before he'd come to a halt. "Is it her? Aunt Sister?" She seemed to have aged since I'd seen her an hour ago.

"We think so. Evans," Duck called. The detective glanced over his shoulder, saw the new arrivals and, after a word to Thackery, made his way over to us, his brow wearing a puzzled frown.

He shook Tank's hand then turned to Tina. "You're Mrs. Younts? I remember you now, but I thought your name was Jones."

"Maiden name," Tina responded, her eyes glued on the trunk of the Chevy. "I want to see her. Now."

"Of course. It's not bad, no blood or anything."

"Not bad? She's dead. How could it be any worse?" She walked away. Evans, after an apologetic shrug, followed her. Tank was last in the procession, catching up with Tina in time to slide his arm around her shoulders as she halted at the trunk.

She nodded almost immediately. "It's her. Aunt Sister. Claudia Jean Hitchcock." Jerking free of Tank's embrace, she spun around. "What the *hell* is she doing in the trunk of your car, Leigh?" she yelled. "You had to say the magic word, didn't you? This is your fault, dammit!"

She might as well have cold-cocked me. Magic word? What was she talking about?

"Be cool." Duck pulled me closer and murmured in my ear. "She's upset. Let her get it out of her system."

As hard as it was, I managed to nod agreement. I had thought that Eddie's suspicion that I might have been stepping out on Duck had hurt. In comparison to this, it was a pinprick. Tina blamed me. I had no idea why.

I slid off the hood and climbed into the passenger side, closing the door. I groped until I found the correct lever, reclined the seat back as far as it would go and shut my eyes. I wanted to cry so badly that it hurt almost worse than Tina's accusation. Instead, I got mad.

There was no proof yet but I was certain my doppelganger had to be smack in the middle of this. It was one thing to be the target of her acrimony and dirty tricks, and bad enough that in getting at me she'd also drawn blood from Duck; he'd wanted to see Hawaii for as long as I could remember. We'd get there one day. But there'd be no "one day" for Claudia, or for Claudia and Clarissa as twins. The she-devil had severed that unique connection, perhaps mine with Tank and Tina as well. That remained to be seen.

But in her pursuit for revenge for whatever she felt I'd done to her, Ms. Witch had grievously wounded others, people I cared about. An innocent woman was dead. And until the time of death could be established and my alibi confirmed, I was number one in the investigation's bull's-eye. Leigh Ann Warren. Murder suspect.

11

I REALLY THOUGHT THINGS WERE ABOUT AS bad as they could get. Then the elevator door opened and who peeks out? Mrs. Luby and Clarissa.

I practically fell out of the car, hurrying to waylay them. Fortunately, Duck, who'd returned to the Chevy to talk to Evans and Thackery, spotted the two in time and hurried toward them, getting there a few steps ahead of me. I'd lost track of Tank and Tina; they were nowhere in sight.

Apparently Duck's neighbor had been in bed, or on the way. Filmy orange pajama bottoms peeked from beneath a calf-length robe. Her high-heeled mules matched the pajamas; her night cap, the robe. Clarissa, however, in no way resembled the person I'd met earlier in the week. The trim navy pantsuit and tailored yellow blouse under the black chesterfield coat made her the prototype of the professional woman fresh from a day at the office. And no dangling chandeliers from her earlobes this time; she wore small, gold clip-ons shaped like hearts.

"See? I told you they were probably still down here," Mrs. Luby said, escorting Clarissa off the elevator.

"Clarissa." Duck took her arm, turning her so that

her view of the activity in the corner was blocked. "You were looking for me?"

"Well, yes. I know it's late but I simply couldn't put it off any longer. Hello, Ms. Warren. I . . . I'm glad you're here too." She couldn't seem to meet our gazes, hers skittering about like a hummingbird, never lighting on any one place. Her cherub's face wore more seams tonight. "I owe you both an apology. I—we, that is, deceived you."

"You and your twin." Duck's voice was gentle, non-judgmental.

"Yes. We meant no harm. I mean, it wasn't the kind of prank we used to—" She stopped, taking him in for the first time. "How did you know we were twins? Oh. Tina told you? It's just as well."

Mrs. Luby, who'd been waiting for the elevator to return, abandoned it and edged closer, eyes bright with curiosity.

"I woke up sick that day, you see, a migraine, and I didn't want to disappoint you. So Sister said she'd come in my place, do your apartment for me. Only . . . only—" She couldn't seem to finish.

"Only a woman showed up who said she was me," I volunteered, "and took a box when she left, the one I was looking for the day before yesterday, and a set of keys from the pegboard in the kitchen."

"Sister told you!" In an instant she was transformed, the fretful ridges disappearing from her forehead, her animated demeanor returning. "Oh, I'm so relieved. And so sorry. I'd have said something, but I couldn't make heads or tails of what had happened while I had her on the phone. Sister gets muddled a lot these days, mixes things up. But then you said you hadn't been here in two weeks and I knew I had to get home and talk to her, find out exactly what she'd done. We decided we had to 'fess up, then let you take us in."

"Take you in?" Duck asked.

We'd gained quite an audience. Evans and Thackery had eased up behind us, I wasn't sure when, and Mrs. Luby had edged closer still.

"The woman was a thief." Clarissa quivered with indignation. "She stole Ms. Warren's property, and we were accomplices. But I wanted to square things between us first. I hadn't finished your apartment, and since today's the day I normally do it, I came as usual. Sister was supposed to pick me up because I had a class to teach at the Literacy Center this evening and I'd have to rush home to change. Then afterward we were going to call you, ask if we could drop by so we could confess that we'd allowed an impostor into your apartment. Only Sister forgot she was to come and get me, and I had to take a cab home. I've been trying to track her down ever since."

Duck drew in a deep breath and looked back at Thackery and Evans who, after a second, nodded, leaving the hated task to him.

He slipped an arm around her shoulder. "I'm sorry, Clarissa, but I have bad news—about your sister."

Her eyes widened, alarm scrubbing all color from her face. "What's she done now?"

"It looks like she did come to pick you up today. It also appears that she ran into the woman who had fooled her before. We aren't sure what happened, but . . . I'm sorry, Clarissa. There's no easy way to say it. Your sister is dead."

There was a moment of pained silence as we waited for her reaction. It was not what we expected. She burst into laughter, the sound echoing hollowly against the concrete walls.

"Oh, Dillon, don't be ridiculous. Just because I can't find her doesn't mean anything. Claudia's never where she's supposed to be and when she is, more often than not, she's late. She'll turn up."

"She already has," Duck said. "That's what I'm trying to tell you. She's probably been here since sometime this afternoon."

"Dillon." Clarissa pulled herself to her full height, a no-nonsense-brooked expression across her face. "Enough is enough. Claudia is not dead. She couldn't be. We're twins. I'd know."

Duck's eyes met mine. He shrugged, defeated. "Find Tina," he said. "Come with me, honey." Arm still around her shoulder, he escorted her through the group.

"Where are we going?" The first traces of fear lent a tremor to her voice.

I squeezed past Thackery, relieved at having a legitimate excuse to escape. The Explorer hadn't moved but was vacant. Surprised to see the ubiquitous yellow tape stretched across the entrance, I ducked under it and was stopped outside by a youngster in uniform.

"Sorry, ma'am, but no one's supposed to leave."

"I'm not going anywhere. I'm looking for the couple who came in the Explorer. Really tall, bald dude with a woman a third his size."

"Oh." He jerked his head toward the street where a cruiser blocked the driveway into the garage. Tank stood, his back against the passenger door, Tina in his arms, her face buried against his chest.

I counted to ten, then approached them slowly. "Tina, Clarissa's in there. She'll need you."

She spun around. Her face, illuminated by a nearby streetlight, glistened with tears. "Auntie Clar? Here? Oh, Lord!" She sprinted toward the garage and zipped under the tape.

Tank watched her go, then gazed down at me. "You okay, Leigh?"

"To tell the truth, I've been better. And poor Clarissa."

"Yeah. This is gonna be rough for her. Look, what Tina said in there, she didn't really mean it. Well, she meant it, just not the way it came out. I'll let her explain. Who called Clarissa?" he asked, moving away from the cruiser.

"Nobody. It's a long story, and a big mess." We stopped just outside the entrance while I repeated the story Clarissa had told us.

"Terrific." Tank scrubbed at his bald pate. "Now on top of losing her twin, Clar will have to deal with feeling guilty for letting Claudia stand in for her. She really shouldn't have. Claudia is . . . was a lot of things but she damned sure wasn't reliable anymore. Then there's Tina, who's feeling guilty for referring Clar to Duck to begin with and for yelling at you. They're long on guilt, the whole family. This is not gonna be fun. Come on."

I ducked under the tape again. Tank stepped over it.

While a pair of technicians scoured the surrounding area for clues, others were packing up, the medical examiner, removing his gloves as he huddled with the plainclothes crew and Duck. A pair of men were about to remove Claudia, the body bag ready and waiting. Tina and Clarissa, heads together, sat in the backseat of the cruiser blocking the entrance at the opposite end of the garage.

Duck beckoned for us. "A curious development," he said, speaking softly. "She may have died of natural causes. I repeat, may have."

"In the trunk of my car?" I asked, incredulous.

He gestured for me to keep my voice down. "There's not a mark on her. The examiner can't be sure at this stage but wonders if she might have had an asthma attack. She has an inhaler in her pocket. Or she died of fright. Clarissa says she was severely claustrophobic."

"Jesus." Tank glanced toward the Chevy and winced. "That would do it for her. It's another reason Tina's so upset, Leigh. She says Claudia fell into an abandoned well when she was a kid on that farm Tina mentioned to your grandmother. They didn't find her for hours. She's been terrified of the dark and small spaces ever since. And along with asthma, she had a dicey heart and a million other medical problems. She just might have freaked out in that trunk and from there—" He broke off, leaving the rest to our imaginations.

"Better tell the M.E.," Duck suggested. "They'll still open her up, but it may simplify things for them."

"Yeah. I reckon," Tank said, clearly not relishing the task. He strode away and pulled the medical examiner to one side.

Other movement caught my eye, and I turned to see Mrs. Luby trying to snag our attention. Duck left to see what she wanted, and after an agitated exchange with his neighbor, wiggled a finger for me.

"Something else wrong?" I asked.

"Oh, Leigh, I'm so sorry." One of Mrs. Luby's chins quivered with anxiety. "I didn't know, you see. It was just a glance, but I really did think it was you. I didn't mean to get you in trouble with the police."

I squeezed her hand, which was icy cold. She shivered, her flimsy nightwear offering little protection against the December chill. "It'll all be straightened out eventually. I've got witnesses to my whereabouts, at least for most of the day, so I'm covered. But they—and I, for that matter—will need as detailed a description as you can give us of the woman on the elevator. It would be helpful if you could jot down what you remember while it's still fairly fresh."

"Yes, of course. I'll do that." Her head bobbed with each word. "In fact, right now. I'll slip it under your door, Dillon."

"A good idea." He leaned down and gave her a peck on the cheek. "Now, you'd better skedaddle. A man can only stand so much, and those flimsy pajamas of yours are testing my self-control."

"You dog," I whispered as the elevator door closed.

He managed a tight smile. "She's a good old soul. I'll miss her."

That startled me. I'd completely forgotten about the house and our earlier conversation. There was a good deal of hashing over to do yet it would have to wait. There was still the question of how Claudia Hitchcock had wound up dead in the trunk of my car.

"Well, that's quite a story," Thackery said later, pinching the bridge of his nose as if we'd given him one hell of a headache.

We had retired to Duck's apartment, where coffee was now percolating, the aroma beginning to waft from the kitchen into the living room. There were only seven of us, all in various stages of collapse, but the atmosphere was so heavy that it felt as if there were three times as many in the room. Tina sat on the couch with Clarissa glued to her side, their fingers locked together in Tina's lap. Clarissa seemed to have shrunk, as if all vital fluids had been siphoned out of her. She emanated pain; it radiated from her in waves like an outgoing tide. There was room for another rear end on the couch, but with everyone's tacit agreement, we left it to them. Tank perched on Duck's rolling desk chair, leaving the two easy chairs for Thackery and Evans. I'd maneuvered my desk chair in from the guest room, and Duck straddled one from the kitchen.

"And you have no idea who this woman might be," Evans said, for the first time addressing me as if he'd deleted me from his list of suspects.

"None." I was so tired of talking about it, of wondering and worrying about what this hellion might do next.

"What about someone you arrested or testified against? You were in uniform long enough to have made more than a few women unhappy."

The prospect was enough to boggle the mind. "I guess it's a possibility. But most of the females I brought in were streetwalkers. They weren't bothered at all. For them, being arrested was an occupational hazard. There were a few shoplifters, a few assault and batteries."

"Catfights?" Evans asked dryly.

"Essentially." I decided to ignore the chauvinistic dig. I wasn't sure he even realized it was one. "A few were domestic, oddly enough, wives beating up on their husbands. As for testifying, I can count those cases on one hand. Two of them walked—lack of evidence. A third got thirty days, and the fourth is behind bars for the duration."

"Hmm. Except for the lifer, doesn't seem to be much to get het up over."

The coffee smelled as if it was ready, so I retreated to the kitchen to hide my dismay at having the most fulfilling years of my life reduced to a series of petty incidents. At least that's how it had sounded.

It had not included, however, the number of people I had helped, I reminded myself, those who'd simply needed the sight of a uniform to prove that someone cared, or a warm body to talk to. It had not included the ones an inch from trouble who I'd convinced to try another way. It was those faces I remembered most, those moments I prized the most. To me the arrests were an occasional necessity because the truth was I hadn't had to take someone in all that often. What I'd valued most was being of help, and no one could ever take that away from me.

My scales in balance again, I filled a tray with cups and saucers, sugar and creamer, ready to play hostess and face the continuation of the inquisition.

Duck caught me as I was about to leave the kitchen. "You okay?" he asked softly. He stroked my cheek with the back of his knuckles. "You looked like you were about to slide into a navy-blue funk back there. Evans didn't mean to belittle your record, babe. He's concentrating on the negative because it's the logical thing to do."

I felt my eyes begin to sting and blinked them dry. Trust Duck to sense how Evans's slant on things had affected me.

"I'm fine, now. Just needed to regain some perspective. Why don't you bring the coffeepot. And something to put under it."

"Yes, ma'am." Leaning in, he rewarded me with a peck at the corner of my mouth. "We'll get through this, babe. Together."

I pecked him back, no other response required.

Evans continued his train of thought as if I'd hadn't left the room. "We'll request a search on your arrest record, look to see if there's anything you might have forgotten. People out there are so crazy these days, you might have simply stepped on her toe accidentally."

"Well, hell, I'd have apologized," I protested.

"You might not have sounded sincere." He extended his cup.

Thackery eyed the coffee service with the attitude of a drowning man being thrown a lifesaver. "Christ, that smells good. Decent java, for a change. Not sure my system can take it. Black for me, please."

Clarissa shook her head. "None for me. I won't sleep, as it is." She sniffed behind a tissue and sat up straight. "When can I have Sister's body? I have to make arrangements, take her down home. We have plots there." She had turned some kind of emotional corner, at least for the time being.

"If you're planning a local service, you might want to consider a memorial." Evans's features seemed to have thawed considerably, whether because of the coffee or sympathy for Clarissa was open to debate. "We'll do what we can, but the way things are backed up at the, uh, medical examiner's, they may not get to your sister until next week. We'll let you know as soon as it's completed, of course."

"I'll help you, Auntie Clar." It was the first time Tina had spoken. "Whatever you need done."

I was pouring for Tank when someone knocked.

"Probably Mrs. Luby," Duck said, coming in with napkins, which I'd forgotten.

"I'll get it." Tank opened the door for her. "Ma'am," he said, stepping back to let her in. She had abandoned the shorter robe for a lilac one of full length, its top button missing.

She pulled its collar closed with one hand, several sheets of paper clutched in the other. "I wrote down the description like you said. And made enough copies for everyone." She distributed them, reminding me of a teacher passing out test papers. "I called Zenia and asked what she remembered, but she only got a quick glimpse before the elevator door closed."

"Typed." Surprised, Evans set his cup down and fished for reading glasses.

"Printed," Mrs. Luby corrected him. "I did it on my computer, so I can give it to you on a floppy, if you prefer."

Scrutinizing her with new respect, he seemed to consider it. "No, this will do for now. But don't erase the file, in case something else comes to mind."

Duck, remembering his manners, offered her coffee, but she declined. "It'll destroy my beauty sleep. I'd best get back across the hall. Clarissa, I'm so sorry. You let me know if there's anything I can do."

I could tell she'd have paid cash money to stay, but with no invitation forthcoming, she left with a smile of regret.

Her contribution took center stage for the next few minutes. She'd employed an unorthodox method to describe the person she'd seen.

Height: a little taller than Leigh, I think.
Weight and build: a little heavier, but not by much.

Perhaps broader across the shoulders. At least that's the way her coat made her look.

Age: thirties, early to mid–.

Complexion: lighter than Leigh. At the time I thought it was because of the lighting in the elevator.

Eyes: too far away to tell. They didn't impress me as any different than Leigh's.

Hair: dark, curly, and short but longer than Leigh's. I hadn't seen Leigh in a while, assumed she'd decided to let it grow.

Wearing: white car coat with hood. Could not see what kind of top under the coat because of the box. Jeans, tall boots, perhaps riding boots.

Comment: she looked enough like Leigh for me to assume it was her. The fact that I assumed the woman with her was Clarissa may have influenced my view.

"A sharp lady, your Mrs. Luby. And that reminds me." Evans peered at me over his lenses. "There was a cardboard box in the trunk behind the . . . behind Ms. Hitchcock. We've already dusted the car for prints but we didn't see the box until we'd removed the body. We'd like to take it in to see if there are any prints on the tape. It looks as if it's been opened and resealed."

Rage ripped at my composure. Another corner of my life invaded, in this instance all my bills, receipts, tax records. The damage she could do . . .

Pulling my thoughts back into line, I responded to Evans.

"We may get lucky. I used good packing tape. If she tried peeling it free, hoping she could just press it back into place, she found out that wouldn't work. She would have to use fresh tape."

Clarissa must have changed her mind because she

removed the last cup from the tray and filled it with a steady hand. There was a studied calm about her now, as if she held herself together with pure force of will. Clearing her throat, she took the floor with a manner of someone accustomed to it.

"Listening to everything everyone has said, it sounds to me as if this woman may have only superficial resemblance to Ms. Warren. The only person to see her who knows Ms. Warren well is Mrs. Luby, from a distance at that, and only for a moment. She admits she assumed it was Ms. Warren—"

"Leigh, please," I interrupted, tired of the formality.

She gave me a trace of her usual cherubic smile. "Leigh it is, then. Then there's the receptionist at the travel agency. The only face she'd lock in on would be someone who comes in frequently. You said you'd been in twice?"

"Three times. The first time to tell her where we wanted to go and when, then twice more to change the dates. Come to think of it, Dolly wasn't there the second and third times. So she only saw me once, long enough to show me back to Margie's cubicle."

"Then you understand what I mean. Unless she's the kind who remembers faces, she'd have only a vague picture of you. And Sister . . ." She paused, blinked, swallowed. "Sister said that picture of you in the bedroom wasn't a very good one because it didn't look much like you."

"In comparison to the other woman," Thackery said, pouring himself a second cup of coffee.

"It was the hair, you see. In the picture, it's the same length as she's wearing it now. The woman Claudia saw wore her hair longer."

"The one that puzzles me," Duck said, hunkering down backward in his chair, "is the incident in the Silver Shaker." He was still simmering about that, incensed that I hadn't mentioned it before tonight and wouldn't have, if only to keep Eddie out of it. But Claudia's death changed things.

"We're talking about professionals here, trained officers," he continued. "If it's the same woman and they mistook her for Leigh, then she must bear a fairly close resemblance to her."

Tank imitated Clarissa's method to get our attention by clearing his throat. "And yet none of Leigh's neighbors decorating the tree mentioned it. They've known her long enough that they'd have said something to somebody. I suggest we don't get hung up on appearance and stick to what we know."

"There is no 'we.'" Evans drained his cup and stood up. "I appreciate the fact that you three, sorry, you four," he amended, nodding at me, "are professionals, and involved in one way or the other, but leave the investigating to us. If this woman is responsible for the death of Ms. Hitchcock, we won't rest until we've found her."

"And if she isn't?" Duck's voice was soft. "Directly responsible, that is?"

Evans's eyes became that flinty gray again. "It's still our job, our case. Willard's working the prank call. As for the vandalism to Ms. Warren's car, I'll make sure he gets the word. He may be able to tie both events together. Otherwise, you know the drill, all of you. Stay out of it and let the ones assigned to it do their jobs. You ready, Thackery?"

Five minutes later, with business cards distributed

and telephone numbers exchanged in case they needed to get in touch with us, they finally left. A good deal of tension left with them. It seemed easier to breathe.

Everyone sat back but seemed hesitant to speak. I hadn't said it, and it was past time.

"Clarissa, I can't tell you how sorry I am."

She sat up straight, managed a ghost of a smile. "Thank you. I wish you and Claudia had met. She'd have liked you."

There was another heavy, gloom-filled silence. Finally Duck rose, spinning his chair around.

"All right, listen up. Clarissa, you just became family. Leigh and I can't replace your twin but we'll do everything we can to support you and see things right."

She blinked, dabbed at her nose, and nodded. "You're a good man, Dillon. Thank you."

He wasn't finished. Eyes narrowed, he turned his attention to me. "I know you, Leigh Warren. Nothing those guys said makes a difference to you; you're gonna keep poking and prying to find this woman. I'm going on record here to say I'm gonna be poking and prying along with you."

"Me, too," Tina spoke up, to no one in particular. She couldn't seem to look anyone in the face, especially me.

Tank nodded. "Count me in."

Clarissa's eyes welled. "I know you're doing it for me and Sister—well, partly, anyway. And I really appreciate it, but I don't want any of you to risk your jobs. Sister wouldn't want it either. You heard what they said."

"We heard them loud and clear," Duck said. "And

we don't care. We're gonna get this woman off the street. And if Thack and Evans don't want our help . . ." He looked at me. I knew precisely what he was thinking.

"To hell with them," I finished for him.

12

IT WAS STILL INKY-DARK WHEN DUCK KISSED me awake. "Rise and shine, babe. Breakfast is ready. Everyone's waiting for you."

I rolled over and willed the face of the clock into focus. Six-ten. "Why so early?" He smelled of soap and aftershave and, in fact, was already dressed. My brain cleared, his last statement finally registering. "What do you mean, everyone's waiting? Who's here?"

"Tank and Tina. Move it, sleepyhead. We've got things to discuss." He yanked the covers to the foot of the bed and handed me his robe.

I made do with minimum ablutions and toothpaste, pulled a rake through my hair, and managed to get to the kitchen just as Tina yelled, "Hey, I'm eating whether you're here or not!"

"I'm here, I'm here," I said, tripping over the hem of Duck's robe in my hurry.

"Morning," she muttered, in my general direction. She still hadn't looked at me in the eye since her outburst of the night before. If this was to continue, it would be a long morning.

One good look at the spread on the table, however, made me willing to put up with anything: a platter of crisp bacon, another of fluffy scrambled eggs half a foot high, and a third of fried apples, a breakfast favorite of mine that Nunna fixed every Sunday the Lord sent.

"Good grief, Duck, what time did you start cooking?"

"I didn't." Pulling a chair out for me, he jerked his head toward Tina. "She did. Even brought everything with her."

Tank grabbed the plate of bacon. "Had me shopping for brown eggs at five o'damn clock in the morning. Have you any idea how hard it is to find a store open that early? And they had to be brown, too. Only African-American eggs for Tina J. Younts."

"Oh, shut your yap." She took the plate from him, forked three strips for herself, four for him, and passed it to me. "I don't care what anybody says, they just taste better."

The bacon looked ready for an ad in a magazine, lean, straight, and crisp. "Lord, Tina, you did yourself proud."

That elicited a pained smile. "It was the least I could do." She got up, grabbed the coffeepot, began filling cups, but put it down before she'd finished. "I owe you an apology, Leigh. Well, two, actually."

"Two?"

Nodding, she continued serving the coffee. "You have to understand. Aunt Sister was losing it, but none of us could bring ourselves to admit it. To be truthful, we were taking the easy way out because getting her to a doctor was like bathing a cat. It wasn't just that she was forgetful; I mean, you expect that at their ages—"

"How old are they?" Duck interrupted, helping himself to eggs.

"Seventy-four."

"Seventy—" He halted, midscoop. "You're kidding. Why were they still working?"

"Because they wanted to. Neat n' Tidy is a family business started by my grandmother's sisters. Practically all of us have worked for it at one time or another, and Aunt Sis especially loved putting things right, she called it. After Auntie Clar retired from teaching full-time, she started helping out with her twin's clients because it was getting too much for her. But I have to be honest, Aunt Sis was always one sheet short of a linen set. She could clean her ass off but that's the only thing she could be trusted to do perfectly. Her head was always somewhere else."

"Get to the point, honey," Tank said, shoveling sugar into his coffee. "You've got to be at the doctor's by eight."

She made a face at him and sat down. So far she hadn't eaten a thing, which meant she was more upset than I'd realized. Anything bad enough to come between Tina and a plate of food had to be on a par with Armageddon.

"What I'm trying to say," she continued, "is that when I talked to Auntie Clar on the phone out at your new house, she told me that Aunt Sis had screwed up somehow, that it had something to do with you and a box. The problem was, she wouldn't explain, said they wanted to talk to Duck about it first because it had happened here. Then they intended to tell you, Leigh, and they were terrified you were gonna sue them over it."

"Sue them?" I put my fork down. "Over a stupid box? What would make them think that?"

"According to Auntie Clar, you said you would."

"How could I, when I didn't even know what had

happened to it? I . . ." Then I remembered running off at the mouth, something about suing Duck's pants off. "Oh, no," I said, groaning, and explained. "I was kidding. I'm planning to marry the man, for pete's sake. How could Clarissa think I'd actually sue him?"

Tina sighed. "Because she did. Auntie Clar, that is, years ago. She got left at the altar and sued the dude for breach of promise. Won, too."

"Holy shit." Duck shook his head. "Who'd have thought it?"

"They did." Tank gestured toward his wife with his fork. "Her people have this thing about the justice system: if somebody does you wrong, sue 'em. They're regulars in small claims court. Go to a family reunion and sooner or later you'll hear that Cousin So-and-So's suit is scheduled for whenever and Great-uncle Doozy-whatsis finally decided to settle."

"You make it sound like it's a hobby," Tina grumbled. "It's not. They've never had a suit dismissed as being capricious, so lay off my folks. What was I saying?" she asked, then remembered. "Oh, yeah. I owe you an apology, Leigh, for not saying anything after I got off the phone with Auntie Clar, but she made me promise. Then when I saw Aunt Sis curled up in the trunk of your car and the box behind her, I figured she'd done something dumb just to avoid winding up in court. You didn't deserve what I said then and I'm sorry again, I really am."

"Tina." I nudged her plate closer to her. "Apologies accepted. Now eat."

"Honest?" Her expression was comically pitiable.

"Honest. Your eggs are getting cold."

"Women," Tank muttered, his mouth full. Tina

whapped him on the back of the head with a pot holder. He grinned, she smiled with relief, and all was right with the world again.

Except for the clink of cutlery against china and the ccasional crunch of bacon, the kitchen was silent while we got down to business and, oh, the fried apples were to die for.

Once we'd finished, I started up to clear the table, but Duck forestalled the effort.

"Let 'em wait. We've got stuff to discuss, then I've got to get out of here. The whole point in my getting up early was to go in before my shift and see what I can find out."

"About . . .?" I asked.

"We have to get this woman for Clarissa and Claudia, and you. So I need to see if Willard's gotten anywhere, for a start. I wish I knew him. It would make things simpler."

"Let me do it," Tank volunteered. "We go back a ways."

"Great. They'll have dusted the Chevy and the box, so I'll check to see if we got lucky with prints. Then I'll tackle Marty, see if there's anything in the system that'll help. If I take her a carton of Newports, maybe she'll give me a printout of your arrest record."

Marty. Martha Makrow Jensen, twenty-year veteran with the D.C. Metropolitan Police and expert at massaging the department's computers to find out anything one wanted to know. She was almost as good as Plato dePriest, someone on my list of people to see today.

Tina pecked crumbs off the plate that had held the toast. "I'm kind of in a bind. I've got the doctor this morning and court this afternoon, which I'd forgotten. And after work, I promised I'd take Auntie Clar shopping for a dress to bury Aunt Sis in, so I won't be able to drive you around, but not to worry. Chet's letting you use his car until he's finished getting the paint off yours."

Either she had one helluva secret she could use as blackmail or his car was a dog. "That's awfully nice of him, Tina. What does he drive?"

"A Vette."

"As in Corvette?" Duck asked, brows flapping like a flag in the wind. He'd kill for a Corvette.

"Yup." Her smile was sweet, belying the devilish glint in her eyes. "Loves the thing like it's his firstborn child, and a surefire way to see that he gets your car back to you in record time. Says he'll drop the Corvette off about nine."

"I'm speechless. Thanks, Tina. And don't even ask," I warned Duck. I could see his wheels turning, trying to figure a way to get me to trade wheels with his oil-burner.

It was time to broach the subject I'd avoided. If nothing else, it would take his mind off the Corvette. "There's one more avenue I have to pursue if I'm to eliminate possibilities, and that's women you've dated, Duck."

Thunderheads gathered in his eyes, the kind pregnant with cloud-to-ground lightning. "Anyone particular in mind?"

"Ilene Quarles," Tina said, elbow on table, chin on fist.

She must have struck a chord because his expression became one of speculation.

"Touché. She did make a real pest of herself. Only thing is, she couldn't pass for Leigh in a month of Sundays."

"Damn. You're right." She nudged my foot under the table, confirming my suspicion that she had tossed that name into the hat to take the heat off me and at least make him consider the possibility. "How about Dana Underdown or Selena What's-her-name? They sorta look like Leigh, sort of."

I felt Duck's gaze and found him scrutinizing me as if for the first time. It was a little creepy, making me sympathize with specimens under a microscope.

He nodded, slowly. "More than sort of. Guess I was working my way toward you even back then, babe. Okay, I'll track them down and check 'em out."

I wasn't sure I was particularly happy about that, but it made sense. He knew them; I didn't.

"What's on your plate today, babe?" he asked.

"Enough to keep me busy for a week." I ticked them off on my fingers. "I need to eliminate the teenager and Nell Gwynn once and for all, even if it means contacting every member of Gracie's class. Those two had to have been invited by somebody. There's Plato dePriest to see, and Dolly at Graystone. I want her to take a good look at me and give me similarities and differences with the woman she saw." That took care of three fingers. "I've got to file a change of address at the post office, buy Janeece a welcome mat, and I still haven't picked up my suit for the wedding. That's for starters. Then there's Ourland and the police station to check on. And Elizabeth—I mean, Grandmother—is waiting for an answer about the house. Oh, and Tracy should be back from her conference in Atlanta."

"Who's Tracy?" Tina asked.

"A cousin who could pass for my sister. She'll be able to tell me if there's any other female in the family who's our age and looks like us. It's a reach, but I'd be stupid not to check."

Duck tapped me on the forearm. "Why not ask your mom's sisters? They'd know."

"Because they want to make a bridal gown for me. I don't want to hurt their feelings, and I'm running out of ways to say no. This family thing's a lot more complicated than I expected."

Suddenly Tank whacked the table with a hammy fist, making the dishes jump. "Speaking of families, I just remembered something."

His wife gazed at him sidewise. "This had better be good."

"It is. Think back, Tee. Remember a certain juvenile who got picked up during a raid of Helle's Hole a few years back, the one you helped out?"

I frowned. "A juvenile? You're kidding." Helle's Hole. Strippers. Lap dancing.

Tina's jaw hung slack, her eyes the size of the toast plate. "My God. I'd forgotten that. She'd gone on a dare with some college-age friends, used someone else's ID. Once she admitted who she was, I recognized her last name, realized she'd simply gotten in over her head, and called her dad to come get her."

"In other words," Duck said, pouring the last of his coffee into the sink, "someone owes you. And that would be . . .?"

She shot him a smug smile. "My lips are sealed. Let's just say that there's a distinct possibility Aunt Sis's autopsy may be performed before the day's over." She hopped up, placed her dish on the counter. "Move it, Tankie. Places to go, people to see."

The leisurely breakfast was over. Ten minutes later, they were gone.

I checked the time. It was still a little early for making calls, except, I reminded myself, all the women on the list Gracie had given Duck were retired and probably at home.

I cleaned the kitchen, then myself, enjoying the invigorating sting of Duck's fancy dual-head shower, almost worth marrying him for, even if he'd been a loser. I dressed, opting for fancy undies, my better slacks, a silk blouse, and a good blazer, with the snobs at the Bridal Bower in mind. At eight-fifteen I got on the phone and, as I'd suspected, woke only one person on Gracie's list. All the others sounded bright-eyed, bushy-tailed, and more than willing to indulge in a rehash of the decorating, caroling, invasion by the police, and grilling that had ended their evening. None admitted knowing Georgia Keith or Nell Gwynn. Two, however, assumed that they'd been related.

"A similarity, doncha know," a Mrs. Williams told me. "The shape of the face, more than anything else. Must be some Caucasian in the young lady's family, though. Long, straight hair halfway down her back. The one my age with the charming accent, she wore hers in a short Afro like, gray all over. Very attractive."

Short gray hair like the driver of the compact?

A Miss Cobey, however, wasn't quite as complimentary. "Too much foundation for a woman her age. I used to sell Mary Kay, so I notice that kind of thing. No reason for all that makeup either. I mean, it wasn't a dressy occasion, we were decorating a tree, for God's sake. And she had quite good skin underneath all that goop. I told her she was ruining her pores lathering it on with a trowel like that. I had hoped she might have taken the hint when she left to go to the bathroom, since it would have been a good opportunity to wipe some of it off, but she didn't. She'll learn."

"Whose bathroom did she use?" I asked, paying attention for the first time. There was no public restroom in the building.

"I don't know, I'm sure. She got on the elevator, so I assumed she went to someone's apartment."

Damn. Eight apartments on each of five floors. It would take me a couple of days, if not longer, to catch everyone. I could just hear myself: "I'm sorry to bother you, but did you let a lady with a Jamaican accent use your bathroom on Monday?"

Figuring I'd get other calls out of the way while I had the time, I caught Tracy as she was about to leave for work as a branch manager of one of the county's libraries.

"Hi, cuz," she trilled. How could anyone sound so chirpy this early? "When are you coming out? It's been a while since we had a girly session over a plate of fries."

"Soon," I promised. "I'll make this fast. You know the family. Is there anyone else who looks like us, enough to pass for you or me if someone didn't know us well?"

"Well, that's one hell of a question, cousin. Let me think." I heard the tap-tap of a fingernail, but it didn't take her long. "In a word, no. Not even close. What's going on?"

"Long story and you don't have time. Perhaps this weekend. Thanks, Tracy. Tell your mom I said hi." I hung up before she could ask more questions.

Next was Elizabeth, who sounded delighted that we would accept the house. I put her on my list of weekend visits and phoned Plato next or, rather, his voice mail, which meant he either was in the john or didn't feel like being bothered. There was no question that he was home. Agoraphobic, he only left his sanctuary under pain of death. I left a message that I'd call him later and just might stop by. It paid to warn him or he'd ignore the doorbell.

Someone knocked at nine on the dot, and I opened the door to a masculine version of Tina a foot taller in height and a lot less talkative. With a minimum of words he informed me that my car would be ready tomorrow, the next day at the latest, that there was a LoJack installed in the Corvette and alarms up the wazoo, but regardless, he'd just as soon I not park it in a neighborhood where it was guaranteed someone would try to steal it. He showed me how to work the remote, dropped the keys in my hand, and left looking as if he was losing his only friend in the world. Once I saw it, I understood why.

Turquoise, long, and low-slung, it was parked in someone's reserved slot, the reason perfectly clear; it was the only space open with a light directly above it. No dark corners for this baby. Not only could you not miss it, you'd be clearly visible if you tried to steal it.

I got in it and prayed that mine would be ready tomorrow. My knee, unused to having to bend at such an acute angle in order for me to sit, snarled at me. This turquoise beauty was so low, I might as well have been sitting on the ground. I wondered if I'd be able to get out without a hoist of some kind. Then I started the engine and forgot any misgivings I had. This thing had Power with a capital P!

I headed for the Bridal Bower to get that out of the way first, and during a stop at a traffic light a couple of blocks from the store, used the wait to dig the Bridal Bower receipt out of my purse. And didn't find it. An annoyed blast of a horn from a cab alerted me that the light had changed, so I interrupted the search and continued it at the next stop. And still couldn't find it.

Irritated, I turned onto a side street, eased into the vacant space beside a fire hydrant and, with emergency blinkers on, emptied the contents of the damned bag onto the passenger seat. I'm always amazed at the amount of pure junk I wind up carrying, but the receipt from Bridal Bower was definitely not among it.

What could I have done with it? I squinched my eyes tight, trying to think. Janeece had dragged me to the shop kicking and screaming back in October. No way was I getting married in white satin or organdy fluff. That's not my style. Besides, to wear white anything would be a travesty, since Duck and I had known each other—and that's in the biblical sense—for over a year. Last but not least, anything in the shop had to be six times more than I was prepared to shell out. It was in a high-rent district and I was already paying rent, at my insistence, to Janeece. But she's six-feet-plus with Georgia mule in her veins and wouldn't take no for an answer.

"Dammit, it's your wedding, Leigh. Whether it's your first or fifth, you should at least get gussied up for it. Now, come on."

I had eventually settled on an unfussy ecru suit with a mandarin collar and straight skirt, the only decorative elements a bit of embroidery around the sleeves and the bottom of the jacket. It didn't help that I looked fantastic in it. Still, I could use it again on dressy occasions, the only thing that salved my conscience and wallet, along with the fact that it was on sale. And I'd insisted on paying for it myself, since Nunna, a retiree and recently married herself, really couldn't afford it.

I'd left it for minor alterations, shortening the sleeves a bit and lengthening the hem in the back since my ample rear end tended to hike it up back there.

I'd squeezed the receipt into my wallet, but I remembered taking it out at Duck's and sitting at his desk a couple of weeks before to tally up how much I'd spent on Christmas and the wedding to that point. I could swear I had put it back but honestly couldn't remember doing it or seeing it since. Still, I might not need it. I had enough ID to prove who I was, and the credit card I'd used.

I parked in the lot behind the shop, hauled myself out of the car with every bit as much trouble as I'd anticipated, set the fancy alarms, and hurried inside, bells tinkling "Here Comes the Bride" announcing my entry. Flocked satin lined the walls and covered the lounge chairs, and bouquets of lilies of the valley and baby's breath draped the doors, windows, and mirrors. A white baby grand, complete with candelabra, was parked in a corner. The only thing missing was Liberace.

The fitter, a tiny, ageless woman with the exotic features of the Orient and straight pins between her lips, stuck her head from between the curtains separating the fitting rooms and stock from the front. She gestured for me to wait, and a few seconds later a statuesque blond flirting with middle age swept into the room, a plastic smile in place. "Yes? I'm Monica. How may I help you?"

"I'm Leigh Warren. I left a suit for alterations," I said. "I'm a couple of days late; I was supposed to pick it up on Monday but had to postpone coming in that day."

She nodded. "I remember the call. Is there a problem with it?"

"With what?"

"The fit. If there is, we'll do what we can, of course, but you really should have tried it on before taking it."

A chill slithered down my back. "Don't tell me. It's gone? Someone picked it up?"

Something filtered into her eyes, a certain wariness. "Yes, on . . . Just a minute." She strode away, disappeared into the corridor to the fitting rooms, and returned almost immediately, a pink fabric-covered file box in her hands. The Asian lady stuck her head out of the curtain, watching.

"Here we are," Monica said, her relief palpable as she removed a card from the box. "Picked up early yesterday. 'Customer declined final fitting.' Is something wrong? I'm a little at a loss here."

"Join the club," I said, the chill replaced by white-hot lava. "I'm at a loss of three hundred twenty-nine dollars and ninety-nine cents and the suit I'm supposed to wear at my wedding. A woman claiming to be me has been making my life hell, and she's obviously done it again. She picked up the suit, not me. Just damn it!"

"I told her!" The fitter burst through the curtains. "I told Catherine something wasn't right. I may not recognize a face every time, but I remember busts and waists and hips, and the woman who came for the ecru was the wrong shape."

Monica paled, but stood her ground. "I'm so sorry. We've never had anything happen like this before. But Catherine would have had no reason to doubt this other person. She had a receipt."

Which she'd swiped from Duck's desk in the living room. My suit was gone, and there was nothing I could do about it.

I turned, and my legs gave out. Rather than winding up on the floor, I plopped down on one of the brocade love seats. I had to think.

Monica and the fitter watched me anxiously. After a moment, I decided to fall back on the tried-and-true and dug out my notepad.

"Anna, isn't it?" I asked, belatedly remembering the fitter's name. "Describe her for me, please. You may be able to give me details the average person couldn't."

She fingered the scissors hanging from a cord of the belt of her trim black dress. "Taller than you are, short-waisted, probably a thirteen, and broader through the hips. Her skin was a different color, a bit lighter. But, Monica . . ." She turned, glancing back at the taller woman. "We can do better than describe her."

It took the clerk a moment to catch her drift, her confusion contributing a frown and crow's-feet that hadn't been visible before.

"Oh! Of course! Do you have a few minutes, Ms. Warren?"

"However long you need." I wasn't sure what was what, but they clearly had something up their respective sleeves, and I was in no shape to go anywhere.

They retired to the inner sanctum again, Anna practically running to keep up with Monica. I used the time to pull myself together and jot down the fitter's unorthodox description to compare with Mrs. Luby's and Dolly's at the travel agency, my next stop. I was debating where to go after Graystone's when my cell phone burped. To my surprise, it was Eddie Grimes.

"You ratted on me," he said, without preamble.

"I had to. Did Duck tell you what's been happening? She's stolen my wedding outfit, Eddie," I blurted, unable to contain my anger any longer, "marched in the Bridal Bower and out with my damned suit. She had the receipt, and the only place she could have gotten it was from Duck's apartment."

"Jesus! This broad's a real con artist. Listen, let me talk to the guys who told me about the Silver Shaker look-alike, see if there's anything they know that might help. It may not have been the same woman at all, but it couldn't hurt to ask. They're supposed to be trained observers, right? Hold on a minute, can you?" The line went blank. Damn all hold buttons.

I'd been waiting for a decade before Monica and Anna swept through the curtains to the fitting rooms, their smiles reminding me of well-fed cats. Anna planted herself in front of me and handed me a business-sized envelope, the baby's breath insignia of the shop embossed on its corner. "For you. Maybe it'll help make up for . . . the mix-up."

Inside the envelope were two underexposed photographs, one of a woman entering the store, the second of her at the circular counter in the center of the floor, the face in profile.

I looked up in search of a camera and wasn't surprised at not having noticed it. Above the curtained door in the center of one of the flocked blossoms of the wallpaper, a tiny red light blinked. There were, in fact, several of them, one near each corner. They looked like jewels, part of the decor.

"Very clever," I said.

"You'd be surprised," Monica said, one brow arched, "how often someone tries to pull a switch on us by changing a price tag or walking out with a veil under their skirt. Will the photos help? We enlarged them as much as we could. You're lucky you came in so soon or it would have been recorded over."

I had wanted to wait until I was outside to take a good look at the woman I was coming to hate with a searing passion, but realized that would cheat these two out of what little reward they would get for their efforts. Crossing to the counter, I placed the photos side by side. And wondered what was wrong with people's eyes. As far as I was concerned, she looked nothing like me at all.

"Thank you so much." I extended a hand to them both. "This will help enormously."

"Hey!" Eddie's yell from the love seat reminded me that I'd been on hold. I sprinted for the phone.

"Hey. Sorry. Are we done?" I asked.

"Yeah, for now. I wanted to check to see if any of those guys were working this shift and where. Got lucky; two of them are. They're on their way in from court, so maybe I'll have something to tell you before the day's over."

"Keep them there," I said. "I'm on my way. I got lucky too, thanks to a couple of smart thinkers here at the Bridal Bower. She screwed up, Eddie, and now I have *her* face."

13

I WAS TOO CLOSE TO GRAYSTONE'S NOT TO STOP so I zipped around several blocks and lucked out on a parking space across the street from the travel agency. Didn't even have to feed the meter; there was more than enough time left on it. The face of my nemesis in my pocket, an open spot within a few yards of my destination, and a half hour on the parking meter? Hey, things were looking up! Buoyed by this turn of fortune and a decent break in traffic, I jaywalked across the avenue, feeling better than I had in days. Granted that wasn't saying much, but you take what you can get.

I recognized the willowy blonde with the curly hair and no hips immediately. Dolly, sans jacket and absolutely stunning in a coral knit dress that fit her like a coat of paint, stood at the curb in front of Graystone's in animated conversation with a tanned hunk of masculinity in a UPS uniform. He took the package she extended to him, his expression making it clear he could eat her alive without benefit of knife and fork. She shooed him across the avenue to his truck, double-parked on the other side, then saw me approaching.

Her first reaction was to turn the color of a sheet of

twenty-weight bond, her second to lose control of the bottom third of her face. Her eyes, a robin's egg–blue, widened.

"*You're* Ms. Warren! I remember you now. Oh, I'm so sorry about my mistake. But I just realized why I assumed the other woman was you. It's your walk!"

"My walk."

"You have a very distinctive stride," she said, her cheeks flushing with excitement. "I'm a runway model, part-time, of course, and one of the things they yell at us about is our walk, so I notice other people's. Some sort of stroll or lope, some slam down on their heels or bounce up onto their toes with a lot of head-bobbing. Your stride is smooth and energetic and long, as if you have places to go and look forward to getting there. Your head doesn't move at all and you've got dynamite posture. It makes you seem taller than you really are."

I can't say it was the first time I'd heard this or variations on the theme. It was one of the reasons I made such an effort to walk without a limp, even on days when my knee was raising hell. Duck claimed he loved to watch me, coming and going, and my Aunt Frances said she'd have recognized me as her sister's child because I walked just like my mom.

"And this other woman?" I asked, guiding Dolly back inside the store. Just looking at her without a coat made me shiver.

"She had the same walk. I could see her from my desk, coming across the street like you did just now, and I knew I'd seen that arm-swinging stride before. Then when she said she had come to cancel the reservations for the Kennedys' trip to Hawaii, I remembered you'd been in a while ago, put the two things together, and just assumed she was the same person. Does that make sense?"

Unfortunately, it did. "Is this the woman?" I showed her the photos.

"Yes! It's funny. Now that I see these I realize you don't look that much alike, feature for feature. You're just similar in type, close to the same coloring, same shaped face and eyes, close to the same height and build, similar hairstyle. But the walk's what fooled me. I'm really sorry."

I told her to forget it since there was nothing to be gained by stringing her up by her bra. I asked about Margie, hoping there'd be good news in regard to reservations for our honeymoon. No such luck. Margie wouldn't be in for another hour and, as far as Dolly knew, was still working on it.

Deciding I'd be wasting valuable time by waiting around, I left and this time crossed at the light. At the Corvette, I folded myself into it and headed for South-east Washington.

I'd left a message for Duck about the pictures—to which he hadn't responded—and blessed my luck again when I spotted him outside the Sixth District substation in conversation with a kid in a Boy Scout uniform. I spot-ted a space around the corner, eased into it and reached him just as the scout was leaving.

No "hello," no "hi, cutie." "Where's the Corvette?" he asked, glancing up and down the block.

"Never mind the Vette," I said. "I left a message for you. Look what I've got."

I waved the photos under his nose and he grabbed them.

"This is the woman? Terrific, babe! Where'd you get them?"

"She walked into the Bridal Bower yesterday with the receipt for my suit. They caught her on their hidden cameras and made these copies for me." I swallowed around the lump in my throat, determined not to cry.

He must have sensed how close to the edge I was and folded me in his arms. He still smelled good, fresh, soapy, and woodsy, as if he'd just stepped out of the shower.

"I'm sorry, Leigh. She's really hitting you where it hurts, isn't she?"

"Duck, she got the receipt from your apartment. I'd left it on the desk in the living room."

He stiffened, leaned back, and looked down at me, Mount Vesuvius rising in his eyes. "You're sure?"

"Yes." I reminded him of the day I'd been going over expenses, knowing he'd remember since we were both nude at the time. "She must have lifted it the same day she took the box."

"And the keys to the Chevy. I guess I really should have removed that miniature license tag on the key ring. I'm sorry, babe. It led her right to it. I'm just glad I didn't have an extra set of keys to the place on that pegboard."

Letting me go, he focused on the two blow-ups. "How the hell could anybody mistake her for you?" he demanded. "She's not even pretty!"

I could have kissed him but there were too many guys in uniform coming and going. "That's the sweetest thing you've ever said to me. Thank you. The receptionist at Graystone said she walks like me and that's what fooled her. The fitter at the Bridal Bower realized it wasn't the same person she'd altered the suit for but since the woman had the damned receipt, there was nothing they could do but give it to her."

"Well, in a way this makes me feel better," he said,

still scrutinizing the shots. "I don't know her. There is something familiar about her but I sure as hell never dated her. Look, babe, I'm running late. Get Eddie to make copies of these, enough for Tank and Tina too. And you might want to show these to Ms. Poole, see if she remembers seeing her at all."

I hadn't thought that far but agreed it was a good idea. "I'm on my way to see Eddie. He's rounded up a couple of the guys who were in the Silver Shaker, so they can take a look at these, since I've got them."

"Yeah, I've already chewed him out for believing it was you." He leaned down and kissed me, obviously less concerned than I was about his image as the consummate professional. "Good luck. Keep me posted. I'll see you later. Gotta go."

I watched as he hopped into the car and pulled into traffic. It occurred to me that running into him had been a stroke of luck for him too. He could scratch finding the two old girlfriends off his list.

I found Eddie squinting at a monitor over the rim of the biggest thermal mug I'd ever seen.

"Want some coffee?" he asked, after we'd dispensed with the amenities. On the surface, he was his usual model of sartorial splendor—blinding white shirt, not a wrinkle in sight, navy and blue striped tie, navy slacks with a crease so sharp you could slit your wrists on them. His jacket, which matched the blue in his tie, hugged the back of another chair.

In spirit, however, he seemed to be dragging, Samsonite luggage under his eyes.

"No, thanks." Squad room coffee could be used to strip paint. "You okay? Nunna would say you look kind of peaked."

"No sleep. The kids are sick. We were up all night with them. So, let's see the pictures."

I passed them over and waited while he switched glasses and stared at the photos with narrowed eyes. Behind us, a scuffle broke out, a hefty woman objecting, as far as I could determine, to her arrest on charges of prostitution, maintaining that she'd been giving the man she was with a freebie. He was, she allowed, a gentleman.

Eddie seemed oblivious. "These were taken in the shop?" he asked.

I went through my tale of woe again and added the saga of the canceled reservations and the woman's involvement in Claudia's death.

"Yeah, Duck told me. This is way more serious than I thought." Deep ridges lined Eddie's forehead. "And you have no idea why she's pulling these stunts?"

"None. I thought for a while she might be one of Duck's old flames out for revenge, but I ran into him outside. He doesn't know her."

"Me neither, but there is something familiar about her." He stared at the face a little longer, then shook his head. "Can't put my finger on it. Don't worry, it'll come. Let's find Marshall and Billings."

Eddie was right; I had never met these two but remembered them from Jensen's wedding, only because Marshall reminded me of Tom Selleck and Billings was a clone of Donald Trump. They looked me over openly and grinned.

"A dead ringer for the woman we saw," Billings announced. "Lady, you've got a twin walking around out there."

I swallowed my disappointment. "Then you won't

recognize this woman," I said, and handed them the blow-ups.

"Uh-oh." Marshall grimaced, peering over the other's shoulder. He looked up at me, down at the photos, then up and down again. "It is her, Bill. Look at the profile. That's where we made our mistake. From the side, you two are a lot alike. And from where we were sitting, that's pretty much all we saw, her profile."

"I'm not sure," Billings said, clearly undecided. "What about when she was up dancing?"

"Well, I don't know about you but between that strapless dress and the moves she was making out on that dance floor, I wasn't paying all that much attention to her face then." He flushed. "I'm sorry, but it's the truth."

"Did she at any point tell anyone her name was Leigh Warren?" I asked.

"We wouldn't know." Marshall glanced at Billings for confirmation. "We were in the corner, too far away to hear anything she said. She was just part of the scenery. We were watching the bartender, at least most of the time. That's why we were there."

"What it is," Billings said, giving the snapshots back to me, "is one of those cases where two people look alike when you see them separately but not when they're together. Know what I mean?" he asked me, his face intent.

I acknowledged that I did, remembering a pair of fraternal twins in Sunrise who fit that description to a T.

"We're really sorry." Marshall tucked his cap under his arm. "I hope we didn't cause any trouble between you and Duck. It was an honest mistake."

"Forget it. And thanks, both of you."

"Yes, ma'am," they said together and headed toward the locker room.

"Well, that was certainly enlightening," Eddie grumbled, as I trailed him back to his desk.

"It really was. What they said made perfect sense and it explains how she's gotten away with things. Besides, there's no proof that she gave my name, and she couldn't have known there would be cops on the scene."

Eddie slouched in his chair and extended a hand for the photos again. He stared at them intently. "I still say I've seen her somewhere, and it's gonna drive me nuts until I figure out where."

He made copies for me and kept a set for himself. "You watch your step," he advised as we parted. "Marilyn and I want you and Duck to be Pat's godparents—"

I squealed, surprising both of us, him because he wasn't expecting it and me because I'd never imagined myself as a squealer. "You do? Honest? Oh, Eddie I'd be honored."

"That's all well and good, but I want you honored and in one piece. So you take care of yourself, hear?"

I floated out of there. Me, a godmother. Now, all I had to do was stay sane so I could enjoy it. That meant getting this woman off my back once and for all.

It occurred to me that I should check on Clarissa, but had no idea where she lived. I darted back into the station, borrowed a phone book from a harried desk sergeant and found her listed on Holly Street in Northwest Washington—in other words, not that far from where I'd lived for almost ten years.

It was one of those old, white clapboard houses, two-stories, black shutters at the windows, and surrounded with azaleas that would enrich the small yard with color come spring. There was an aura of permanence about the whole block, the sidewalks lined with trees that probably predated the houses they would shade in summer. This was truly representative of the heart of the city, the one rarely seen by tourists. There were hundreds of such old neighborhoods where residents had lived and thrived for decades in quiet stability, far from the monuments and white marble institutes of government and the hordes alighting from chartered buses at the Mall. Yet the most the public ever saw on TV and in newspapers were the recognizable symbols of government and memorials or the seedier areas of the city where crime and poverty thrived. A shame, and a disservice to the rest.

Once on Clarissa's front porch, I hesitated. From the number of voices clearly audible even through the closed door, it was apparent she had a houseful already. I might be intruding, especially if they were all family.

Turning to leave, I was halted when I heard the door open.

"Come to pay your respects?" a voice boomed. "Don't go. Clar, more company!"

I swiveled around to meet the welcoming smile of a ginger-haired man wearing the collar of the clergy and facial features that marked him as a blood relative of the twins. Freckles dotted his nose and cheeks like paint spatters, and a slight gap between his two front teeth gave him a boyish look, despite the fact that he had to be at least middle-aged or beyond.

Clarissa ducked under the arm holding the door open, her frazzled expression dissolving when she saw me. "Ms. Warren! Leigh! How nice of you! Please, come in and meet everyone."

I don't know if the reverend picked up on it but I distinctly caught the desperation in Clarissa's "please."

"I can only stay a minute," I lied, feeling no guilt at all once I was inside. If the house had had rafters, there'd have been people hanging from them. The place was jammed, all ages, all sizes, all colors, all identifiable as from either Tina's side of the family or Clarissa's. The reverend, it turned out, was her brother. Considering the occasion for their coming together, they were a darned cheerful bunch. And after all the introductions, the only name I could remember and match to a face was the reverend, whose name, oddly enough, was Lee.

Clarissa hustled me into the kitchen where several preschoolers sat around the table mangling peanut butter and jelly sandwiches, a couple of grandmotherly types watching and wiping mouths and hands. The latter glanced up long enough to smile and say, "Pleased to meet you," before returning to their charges.

"Coffee?" Clarissa opened an overhead cabinet, one eye on the gathering behind her. "Please," she said softly, as she reached for a cup. "Get me out of here."

I managed to swallow my surprise. "Are you sure?"

"If you don't, I'm gonna kill somebody," she whispered. "Or myself. Please!"

"You've got it." I had no idea what I'd do with her, but I recognized a plea to escape when I heard it. "I came to take you to the station house so you can sign your statement," I said, loudly enough for anyone in the vicinity to hear. "Did you forget?"

Her eyes rounded comically. "My goodness, I certainly did. Give me a minute and I'll get my coat."

It took us a good fifteen minutes more to get out of

there, during which Clarissa was called upon to swear that there was no reason for anyone else to come with us and that it made more sense for me to take her, since as a former member of the force, I knew the ins and outs of what would be required of her.

Once in the Corvette, all restraints were off. Clarissa broke down, blubbering into a lace-edged handkerchief. I got us away from there before someone might look out and see her, drove to the end of the block, and pulled over. I dug a pack of Kleenex from my purse. There was no way that dainty hanky would be enough for the job.

"I'm so sorry," she said, sniffling and wiping some minutes later, "and so grateful, Ms. Warren."

"If you don't start calling me Leigh, I'm gonna make a U-turn and take you right back home."

She shot a teary smile at me. "Leigh. Don't misunderstand. They're my family and I love them, but not en masse, unless it's a reunion. It's all that cheerfulness. We truly believe that death is simply a transition from one stage of life to another and that even though Claudia's left this plane, she's still around, watching over me. So there's no reason for a lot of gloom and doom. But I'll miss her, dammit, and I can't pretend I won't."

"I'm sure they don't expect you to. They're probably all putting on brave faces, thinking they're helping you."

"I know." She demolished another tissue and squared her shoulders. "You can take me back if you want to. I didn't mean to interfere with your day."

Dumping her would definitely simplify matters, but I couldn't do it. She looked so brave in her bright red coat and dangling onyx earrings.

"Tell you what. How about hanging out with me for a while? I'm still trying to track down the woman who"—I took a breath, trying to compose a tactful way of referring to the witch who might have been responsible for her twin's death—"who's been masquerading as me." I went on to describe the Bridal Bower farce.

"Oh, Leigh." Clarissa placed a consoling hand on my shoulder. "I'm so sorry. What an awful person this woman must be. And how awful for you. Your wedding dress, of all things."

It occurred to me that as hard as I'd tried to avoid it, I'd have to give in and let the aunts in the Shores make my outfit. The problem would be convincing them to keep it simple. And considering how little time there was between now and the day after Christmas, I'd better get it over with and tell them.

"Is there anywhere you need to go?" I asked Clarissa. "Have you contacted a mortuary?"

"No need to. One of the cousins back there runs a funeral home. He'll handle everything, memorial service and arranging to take Sister back home, and Tina's taking me shopping this evening." For a moment I thought she might break down again, but she hoisted her chin and sighed. "That's part of the problem. I don't have anything to do to distract me and keep me from thinking about poor Sister and how afraid she must have been closed up in all that darkness."

It was my turn for the consoling pat on the arm. Lord knows I couldn't think of anything of comfort to say. We still didn't know whether Claudia had been alive or dead before winding up in the trunk. Either way, she hadn't climbed in of her own free will. Heat simmered between my eyes. The urge to kill was taking on a whole new meaning.

"So where are we going?" Clarissa asked. I had the distinct impression she'd known what I was thinking.

"My old apartment building. There are a couple of people I need to see."

"Shall I wait in the car?"

"It's too cold for that, and I can't guarantee how long I'll be. Besides, I think you'd enjoy meeting Gracie Poole."

I'd said it as a means of assuring Clarissa that I had no qualms about taking her along. As things worked out, I'd been right on target. The two hit it off immediately, thanks to Gracie's decor.

"My Lord, it's enough to make a body swoon," Clarissa declared, hands clasped as in prayer. "All these lovely prints and things. Is it all right if I just look around while you two talk?"

Gracie, flamboyant in a flowing caftan, flushed with pleasure. "Help yourself. I'm so pleased you like them. Let's adjourn to the kitchen, Leigh. We can chat while I make tea for us all. You will take tea, Clarissa?"

"What?" Seemingly mesmerized by a copy of Gainsborough's Blue Boy, she tossed over her shoulder. "Oh, yes, I'd be delighted."

Gracie's kitchen, the same layout as mine, was another gallery in miniature. Small, framed prints of Picasso, Matisse, Klee, Pollock filled every square foot of available wall space. I found the effect claustrophobic, but reminded myself it wasn't my kitchen.

She put the kettle on and set out cups and saucers. "Willa called to tell me she'd talked to you this morning. Was she of any help?"

"I got more detailed descriptions of Georgia and your Ms. Gwynn." I related the puzzle about the latter's use of a bathroom.

"Not mine," Gracie said, shaking her head firmly and dislodging a long white tendril in the process, "although she could have if she had asked. Oh, dear, I just remembered I'm all out of English Breakfast."

I assured her that Clarissa would enjoy whatever was available. "Do you mind if I pass on the tea and leave her with you while I go up and talk to Neva? Oh, and would you take a look at these?" I placed the photos on the table. I doubted that Gracie had seen my nemesis, but it couldn't hurt to check.

She abandoned the tea service and sat down, digging a pair of spectacles from the pocket of the caftan. "Who is this, now?"

"The woman who's been causing me so much trouble. Perhaps she has some connection to your Georgia Keith and Nell Gwynn."

Gracie peered at the pictures, grabbed a napkin, polished her glasses, then examined the photos again. She frowned.

"She definitely wasn't one of the ones helping with the tree," she said. "But I could swear I've seen her before, Leigh. Perhaps at the Seniors' Center. I'll have to think about it."

I ground my teeth in frustration. Everyone seemed to be of the opinion they'd seen this woman before. Why the hell couldn't they remember where?

I took my leave as soon as I could, secure in the knowledge that I wouldn't be missed. Once Gracie discovered that Clarissa had actually met Picasso, I knew it wouldn't matter how long I'd be gone.

Upstairs Neva's snarl when she jerked open the door metamorphosed into a smile of pure relief. "Sorry. I thought you were Mr. Hopkins. He's been down here twice today, griping about his thermostat. He's the one who broke the damned thing. Come on in."

It was even more disorienting being in my old unit than it had been in Gracie's. It was the first time I'd crossed the threshold since moving out, and it looked and felt completely different than it had during the years I'd occupied it. Neva and Cholly were into kitsch in a big way, Neva's arts and crafts a major element of the decor.

She hauled me into the den, now a nursery, to show me the cradle she'd cleaned and painted, and the assortment of baby paraphernalia she'd acquired. Mobiles dangled from the ceiling, making me dizzy. Otherwise, the effect was charming, with teddy bears and rainbows decorating the walls.

"It's lovely," I said, realizing she was waiting for my reaction. "This is gonna be one happy baby."

She turned in a circle, her expression wistful. "I sure hope so. It's likely to be the only one we'll ever have. I'm no spring chicken, you know?"

I wasn't certain how I should respond to that so I guided her gently toward the purpose of my visit.

"The bitch stole your wedding dress?" Neva's righteous indignation was fulfilling. It made me feel infinitely better that someone else, especially a female, understood what I felt.

"I'd kill her, that's what I'd do," Neva said. "Kick her ass good and proper, bloody her up some, and then, whack! Let her have it."

"A tempting thought, but I have to catch her first. I want to ask a favor. The lady with the Jamaican accent I've been trying to find, it turns out her name is Nell Gwynn and she had to use the bathroom while she was here helping with the decorations. I figure she wouldn't knock on a stranger's door and ask if she could use the john. So if I can find out who let her use theirs, I'll be able to track her down. I don't have time to canvass everyone in this building, so—"

"Want me to do it? Be glad to. I'll start right after dinner. Practically everybody will be home by then. And I'll call you at Mr. Duck's and let you know what I've found out."

"You're a good friend, Neva," I said, marveling that I could say this without reservation, considering all the years I considered her a pain in the butt. "Oh, and take a look at these. This is Madam X." Once again, I removed the photos from my pocket and passed them over.

Neva held them up, her eyes widening as if it helped her to see more clearly. "Wait a minute." She stomped into the kitchen and returned with a monster magnifying glass, using it to get a closer look. "Well, shit, I've seen her, even talked to her."

I couldn't believe it. "You have? Where?"

"Across the street on the corner. She's been there for I don't know how long, several weeks, anyway."

"You mean, she's homeless?" That made no sense.

"No. Working, for the city, she said. I asked her. I mean, she'd been standing over there with a clipboard all hours of the day and I couldn't stand it no longer. So the next time I had to go over to the cleaners, I asked her what she was doing. She said something about a traffic survey, counting the number of cars turning left from the side street onto Georgia. I figured maybe they were finally gonna break down and put some left-turn signals up. Only thing is, she was doing a piss-poor job. I never saw her paying one bit of attention to no cars nowhere and there wasn't nothing on that piece of paper on her clipboard but doodles." She looked down at me from her lofty six feet. "So that means . . ."

"That the woman has been watching me, stalking me for God knows how long!"

14

I BOLTED OUT OF NEVA'S APARTMENT, IGNORED the elevator for the stairs, and was peering out of the lobby door not sixty seconds later. The building is U-shaped, the entrance to it recessed and too far back to see the corner. Which I knew, of course, but had reacted first, thought second.

Back up to the fifth floor again, to Janeece's, this time. Thank God she'd insisted I keep a key. I knocked, then went in and hurried to her bedroom windows, almost launching myself straight through them, since evidently Janeece had gone through an eeny-meeny-miney-mo this morning, trying to decide which shoes to wear to work. She'd left them out and I tripped over several. I nudged them aside and plastered my nose against the pane, the corner in plain view. She wasn't there.

I swore, rearranged the shoes, and left the apartment, fuming at the thought of that woman watching me come and go. And she had to have been in the lobby at some point on Monday night during the decorating. How else would she have known that I was on my way to the basement, specifically to the storage units?

Someone had to have seen her. But I wasn't sure there was any urgency to confirm that now. She'd obviously followed someone in. Any resident entering the building would assume she was one of the decorating crowd, or perhaps she had said as much. And she could have stepped outside to use a cell phone and call the police, then simply walk away—or more likely stand on the corner and watch the excitement. It made sense. I could tell Neva not to bother trying to find out whose bathroom Nell Gwynn had used.

She was waiting for me, snatching her door open before I'd barely finished the first knock. "Was she there? Did you catch the bitch?" Good old Neva, harboring no compunction about labeling the woman precisely what I longed to.

"No such luck. But it explains a few things." I laid out my thinking about the prank call to the police. "The only snag is the timing of the earlier incident, the call about Duck's bogus accident. Why do it if she knew I wasn't here to answer the phone?"

"Maybe she didn't. She might have gotten out there after you'd left."

"She'd have seen that my car was gone," I argued. "And that paint job proves she knows it when she sees it."

"So what?" Neva lowered herself onto her sofa. "How often do you manage to find a parking space out front? Your car could be anywhere, around the corner on one of the side streets. And don't forget, Mr. Jolly and Libby Winston have cars just like yours. If she saw one of them, she mighta thought it was yours and you were home."

I suspected that Ms. X probably had my tag numbers tattooed on her butt and could pick out my car in a lot of a hundred, but didn't bother to say so. I had to confirm my initial suspicions about something first.

There are definite advantages to having worked for the city. I knew where to call. After several minutes on hold, and one surly "Why do you want to know?" I had the proof I needed.

"Whoever the hell she is," I informed Neva, "she's not doing a traffic survey, so don't hold your breath waiting for any new left-turn signals."

"Shit." Her lips pursed in a pout. Then she sat up. "Hey, what do I care? We don't have a car. So now what?"

I let the question simmer for a while before answering. "If she's been out on that corner for any length of time, it's a cinch she talked to other people. As much fuss as Roland makes about the homeless loitering in front of his dry cleaners, I bet he went out to ask her what she was doing. If she was smart, and, as much as I hate to admit it, she is, she might even have gotten friendly with him and his help so she could step out of the wind occasionally."

"Or use the john."

"Good point," I said, making for the door. "Only one way to find out."

Roland Roundtree had new teeth and flashed them at me as I approached the counter. "Ms. Warren! Haven't seen you in a while." He frowned. "We don't have anything of yours, do we? You picked up your trench coat. I remember distinctly."

"No, thanks to you, all my winter clothes are clean as a whistle. I came in to say good-bye. I've moved in with my fiancé. He lives in Southwest."

"Aww, we'll miss you." He seemed genuinely aggrieved. "You've been a good customer. I really appreciate your business all these years."

"You earned it. While I'm here," I said, hoping I

sounded a lot more casual than I felt, "I wanted to ask you about the woman who's been doing the traffic survey."

"Miss Bernard? What about her?" He stopped, his mouth dropping open. "I'll be jiggered! That's who she reminded me of. You! Are y'all related?"

"Could be," I fibbed. "I just recently discovered a whole wing of my family in the area. Neva mentioned she resembled me, so I'm hoping to track her down and find out if she's one of the cousins I haven't met yet. Did she give you a first name?"

"She probably did," he said, "but I don't remember it. A cousin. Isn't that something? She was nice as she could be, even ran over to Fred's a couple of times to get coffee for me and Geneva. We even let her use our . . . uh, facility once, if you know what I mean."

Neva would be pleased to hear she'd been right on target.

"Can you think of anything else about her that might be helpful? Did she sound local or from somewhere else? Did you ever see her car?"

"No, sorry. Never saw a car, and she talked like everybody else hereabouts. Wish I could help."

"You have. You gave me her name, which is more than I had when I came in."

"I'd ask Geneva about her first name, but she just left for the other store. Hey, maybe the lady preacher can help you. Not that I saw them talking or anything. This corner was Miss Bernard's and the preacher staked her claim on the other three but maybe they came to some sort of agreement, know what I'm saying?"

A customer came in loaded down with a pair of comforters, so I took advantage of it, said good-bye, and left to check with the folks in Fred's Grill and the liquor store. They'd served her coffee but nothing else, and she had never introduced herself, as far as they remembered.

"Maybe she's a vegetarian," Fred's sister said, and shook her head at the thought.

Yeah, and a teetotaler, I thought grumpily. I scanned the block as I left but saw no sign of the Reverend Hansberry. Perhaps she'd moved on to a neighborhood with more generous residents.

I was waiting to cross at the light when a young woman rounded the corner opposite me and my brain yelled, "Hello!"

She wore a black ankle-length coat with a hood and bright red boots with platform heels. What captured my attention, however, was her hair, a long, straight ponytail anchored atop her head and cascading in a dark fall damned near to her waist. Remembering the description Mrs. Williams had given me of the teenager, I took off running, to hell with the light.

She was nearing the walkway of my building when I reached her. Coming up behind her, I tapped her on the shoulder. "Excuse me, is your name Georgia Keith?"

Startled, she turned quickly and stared at me. Her eyes, intensely black and almond shaped, suggested a touch of Asia or perhaps Polynesia. "Uh, yes, ma'am. I'm Georgia. Do I know you?" She had a little-girl voice, soft, filled with shyness and southern fried chicken.

"No, we haven't met. I'm Leigh Warren. Do you mind if I ask if you were in that building Monday, helping to decorate the Christmas tree?"

She flinched. "Oh, Lord. Yes, ma'am, and I'm sorry, I really am. I know the sign on the door says 'No Soliciting' but this lady was goin' in and had her arms full and didn't realize that some of her Christmas stuff was about to spill out of one of her shopping bags. I asked if I couldn't help her carry something and I did and when another lady in the lobby came and opened the door for her, I went in with her. Then when I saw the tree and everybody having fun and all, I, like, decided the magazines I was selling could wait and I sorta joined in. I never asked anyone if they wanted a subscription, honest. So I wasn't really soliciting."

I could swear she hadn't taken a breath once, it came at me so fast. She watched me, a plea written across her face. Obviously she'd caught hell from building managers before.

"Don't worry, I have no interest in lodging a complaint or anything. How long were you in there?"

Her shoulders hunched. "A couple of hours, maybe. Why?"

"Were you there when the police arrived?"

Her mouth and eyes went round with panic. "Somebody called the police on me?"

"No, Georgia. It was about something else. So you weren't there?"

"No, ma'am. Lord, if I had been, I'd have wet my pants."

I had to smile, since I'd been in danger of doing the same thing back there for a moment or two.

"Okay, one last thing and I'll let you go. Do you remember seeing this woman while you were there?" I held up the photos.

She leaned forward, frowning as she looked from one to the other. "No, ma'am. Of course, there was a lot of comin' and goin' but I don't remember her."

Shit. "Well, thanks," I said, sliding them back into my pocket. "Sorry. I didn't mean to hold you up."

"Oh, I don't mind. To tell the truth," she said, the

corners of her mouth turning down, "I *hate* this job. Come Christmas, these people can take it and shove it. In fact, I've had enough doors slammed in my face today. I'm going home. It was nice meeting you."

"Same here. Be careful."

"Yes, ma'am, I sure will." She smiled, turned, and wobbled back the way she'd come, none too steady on those ridiculous heels.

Well, scratch Georgia Keith. I'd always considered her a loose end to begin with, so it was a relief to be able to weave her into the fabric of that awful day.

It was time to round up Clarissa, which turned out to be quite a chore. In my absence, she and Gracie had become bosom buddies, and I could swear I detected a hint of Jim Beam on her breath. I had to promise to bring her again before Gracie would let either of us leave.

"I can't thank you enough for introducing us," Clarissa bubbled, once we were back in the Corvette. "You can take me home now. Gracie was like a dose of tonic, she cheered me up so. All that lovely artwork. She's invited me to join her still-life class."

"Good idea," I managed to squeeze in.

"I used to paint when I was younger. I wasn't very good but I was painting to feed my soul, not my wallet— which is just as well or I'd have starved to death long since. I'm going to enroll in her class, did I tell you?"

Yes, definitely Jim Beam. I let her chatter on. There was no reason to stop her, even though I had more than enough to think about and could have used the silence.

I dropped her at her house, allowing her to talk me out of parking and walking her to her door, since she seemed steady enough on her feet.

"I'm fine, now, honestly, dear. I can face that mob, out-smile every one of them and almost mean it. You will keep in touch, won't you, Leigh?"

"You can count on it. And not just because of the unfinished business with your sister. You'll let me know about the memorial service?"

Her glowing face dimmed, but just for a second. "Of course. Drive carefully, now." She waggled her fingers in farewell, then marched up the steps from the sidewalk to her yard. She waggled again from there, mounted her front steps, and disappeared inside.

I did a repeat of the maneuver I'd used while she'd gotten the tears out of her system, driving to the end of the block and pulling over. I had to take stock, check my list, decide what to do next.

Bernard. The name didn't ring any bells. My initial excitement faded. She had probably lied about it, given Roland her dog's name, or something. Back to the list. Post office, Plato's, the Ourland police station. The last would have to wait until tomorrow. I could see the aunts about the wedding dress and kill two birds with one stone. Bile surged for a moment. I had done a good job of talking myself into liking that Bridal Bower suit. I wanted my damned suit!

You're old enough not to let your wants hurt you, Nunna's voice whispered in my ear. *Take care of the things you can do something about, and forget the rest.*

Well, hell, I mused. That was the problem. At this point, there wasn't much I could do about anything. Except see Plato dePriest, my hacker genius, a consultant now to unnamed government agencies, charged with trying to break into as many of their shielded Web sites and databases as he could. They'd used good sense, for once, opting to put him on the payroll for doing what he'd been doing just for fun—invading their files and leaving his e-mail address, in case they had any questions about how he'd done it. Suffice it to say, Plato is not your garden-variety hacker.

I crawled my way toward Georgetown, cussing traffic, roadwork, and a fender bender or two, all for nothing. I practically bloodied my knuckles knocking on his door. No answer. That was worrisome. Plato considered me one of the few friends he had and had never turned me away before.

I wasn't sure what to do. Even if I called the police, they in turn would have to call the bomb squad or a safecracker to get past his front door. The unnamed government agencies had seen to it that Plato's residence was as secure as Fort Knox. Was he sick? Or dead in there, surrounded by his phalanx of computers?

I finally gave up and left. Somewhere in my files was a number he'd given me for emergencies. I hoped I could find it before I'd have to start dressing for the party for my actress friend, Bev.

The trip from Georgetown back to Southwest ate up what little goof-off time I had left. I parked the Corvette in an unreserved spot in the garage and crossed my fingers that it was close enough to one of the overhead lights that the Bernard woman might think twice before cutting loose with any more spray paint.

Upstairs, I indulged in a quick shower, then raided the closet, wondering just how much of an occasion this party was going to be. It didn't matter; I still hadn't unpacked any fancy duds, so casually dressy would have to do. I yanked the raspberry peachskin pantsuit off its hanger, found my black T-straps and pantyhose, claret-colored bra and panties, and began dressing.

I was still seminude when I remembered precisely where Plato's in-case-of-emergency number was in my files: in the box in the trunk of the Chevy, which, in turn, was in the possession of the D.C. Metropolitan Police Department. Dammit! But I couldn't get Plato off my mind.

I finished dressing; made a light pass with blusher, eye liner, and lipstick; draped a skein of gold chains around my neck and put studs in my lobes; checked the full-length mirror; and pronounced myself middlin' decent.

I was weeding out essentials to transfer to a smaller black bag and had just stuck Bev's Chicago review in it to get it autographed for Nunna when a key rattled in the deadbolt.

"Honey, I'm home," Duck called, and chuckled at how clever he was. I heard the door close, the locks engage, and a second later he stuck his head into the bedroom and whistled. "You look great. You know, I'm gonna like having you around on a permanent basis. The whole place smells like Cashmere Mist."

Face it, you've got to love a man who remembers the name of the scent you wear.

"Ready to go? How 'bout I run you over to Helena's?" Leaning against the doorsill, he was trying his damnedest to appear casual.

I wasn't fooled. "Sorry, love, but I'd rather drive myself. That way I can leave when I want. Tell you what, I'll come home by ten at the latest. I'll call you, and you can come down and take us for a spin."

His smile of delight reduced him to a ten-year-old being presented with a new skateboard. "It's a deal. How did your day go after I saw you?" He came in, sat on the end of the bed.

This is what I would relish about our being under one roof: rehashing the events that had transpired since we'd last seen each other. My recital didn't take long, but at least I could pass along the news about Ms. Bernard, traffic surveyor.

"For how long?" Duck asked, clearly unhappy knowing she'd been under our noses all the time.

"Neva couldn't pin it down but she's sure for several weeks."

He lay back and propped himself on one elbow, thinking. "What time does the dry cleaner close? If Roland's wife knows Bernard's first name, I could check it against your arrest record. Even if she lied about her name, chances are she used one with the same initials."

It was a good idea. "They're open until nine on Fridays. There's a receipt on the plastic bag over the trench coat in the closet, if you need the phone number. One more thing: Plato didn't answer his door, and the emergency number he gave me was in the box in the trunk of the Chevy. Any way you could convince someone to dig it out and give it to you? I'm really worried about him."

Duck's decidedly mixed feelings about Plato de-Priest showed in his hesitation, but he finally nodded. "I'll try. You're probably worrying for nothing. Knowing him, he's squirreled back there in his computer room with earphones on, listening to the Grateful Dead. Any news from Tank or Tina?"

I had forgotten about them, and he added them to his list of things to do until I returned with the Corvette. I kissed him good-bye, reminded him that he had Helena's number if he needed to reach me, and hit the road.

Helena Campion, the hostess for Bev's party, lived on one of the side streets edging Rock Creek Park, the city's piece of paradise, our own version of Central Park. I scouted for a parking space, uncertain whether I should chance leaving the Corvette on the street or block Helena's driveway. This was one of the District's toniest neighborhoods, but the thought of coming out and finding the Vette gone sent chills down my spine.

A woman came out of a house two doors beyond Helena's and bounded down her steps. She got into a Beemer and in one smooth maneuver eased away from the curb and sped off. I pulled up, craning to see if there was enough room for the Vette. It looked manageable, just barely. It took a couple of tries but I finally got it in, relieved no one was watching. Duck would have hooted his head off.

I pried myself out, locked up, and started back when a late-model Town Car stopped in front of Helena's. A handsome hunk in a dark suit left the driver's seat, strode around behind the Lincoln, and opened the rear door. A white pants leg appeared, then another. "Leigh?"

I stopped at the foot of the steps and waited. With no idea who else Helena had invited, I couldn't be certain who had called my name. "Yes?"

"Leigh!" Beverly Barlowe bounded from the backseat, resplendent in white slacks and a fuzzy white turtleneck sweater. She grabbed me and began jumping up and down, almost suffocating me in all that angora and necessitating my hopping up and down with her or get stomped on. "Gawd, girl, it's so good to see you! How the hell are ya?"

I hugged her back, delighted to find that she hadn't

changed. She was the same effusive, loud, zaftig, occasionally profane screwball she'd been back in law school. "I'm fine, Beev. How long has it been?"

"Shit, don't ask. I don't acknowledge anything that reminds me I'm over thirty. You called me Beev! It's so good to hear that again. Hey, gorgeous," she called over her shoulder, "hand me my coat, will ya? Thanks for the ride. I'll call when I'm ready to go back."

She accepted the full-length fur he pulled from the backseat, draping it carelessly across her arm. He gave her an amused smile and mock salute, then got back in the car.

Bev watched him go and sighed. "Not only married but with four kids. Oh, well. Come on," she said, looping her free arm around mine. "Jesus Christ, will you look at all these steps! That's Helena, still playing Queen of the Mountain after all these years. Hey, Campy, we're here!" she bellowed. This was one actress who never needed amplification onstage.

The door opened and three heads peered out: Helena, Debra Anastasio, and Mary Ellen Flaherty. Helena shouted, Debbie squealed, and Mary Ellen shrieked, a ritual begun one night when we were all three sheets to the wind and they were spoofing the way in which the members of their college sororities greeted one another. Bev and I had never joined one and had simply contributed to the cacophony by laughing our heads off.

"Y'all remembered," Bev said now, tearing up, a talent of hers. Bev could bawl her head off at the drop of a derby. "Oh, it's so good to see y'all."

"Somebody find the damned Kleenex," Helena said, pulling us indoors. "Let's all have a good cry and then we can get down to some serious merrymaking."

"Manischewitz?" Bev demanded, glaring at Helena nose to nose.

"Manischewitz." Debbie, standing behind Helena, held up the bottle so Bev could see it.

"Awwww." Bev dropped the mink on the floor, folding Helena in her arms, tears streaming down her face. Debra moved in, draping her arms around the two of them.

"Group hug, group hug!" Mary Ellen joined them, yanking me into the mass of bodies. "The Bitches of Brandywine Hall, together again!"

I'd forgotten the appellation our study group had been given by the lone male who had assumed he would be the leader and found the position usurped by Helena. He'd considered it a slur. We adopted it as a title complete with sweatshirts with the name silk-screened across the front. He never quite got over it and eventually dropped out.

"Enough," Helena announced, and ducked out from under all the arms. "Let's eat, drink, and be merry."

Thus the party proceeded, after the obligatory tour through the house, which was a darned sight larger than it looked from the street. Forty-five hundred square feet of hardwood floors, ten-foot ceilings, contemporary Italian furniture, a sauna, hot tub, exercise room, and small indoor pool. In other words, money. Helena had done herself proud.

We settled in her family room, plopping down on the floor around a coffee table as big as my bathroom, our backsides cushioned by a thick jewel-toned Persian rug. The table fairly groaned under the weight of a dozen varieties of hors d'oeuvres and an assortment of wines and soft drink bottles. It was much the way we'd spent any number of weekends, sitting on the floor while we demolished tons of carryout food and argued about the law.

The years had been kind to my old friends. They wore maturity well. Helena was still bony and angular but far more polished now, the hard edges that had once put people off buffed with the best sandpaper money could buy. Mary Ellen was as drop-dead gorgeous as I remembered, a red-haired, green-eyed beauty, smarter by half than everyone else around the table and with no patience for those who judged books by their covers. Debra, on the other hand, was usually written off as plain when one first met her. Her hair was a veritable mane, dark and unruly, her brows thick over pale blue-gray eyes. In a crowd she was easily missed, especially since she was quiet and rarely indulged in idle chitchat. Put her in a courtroom however, and she was someone you'd never recognize as the same person, and you damned sure wouldn't forget her afterward. She could be passionate in her defense of her clients, with a way with language that bordered on the poetic. She rarely lost a case.

Then there was Bev, who could have modeled for the Old Masters. There was a lot more of her than was fashionable. She was, in a word, voluptuous, with an hourglass figure that had been compared to Mae West's in a number of reviews. With a porcelain complexion under a smooth cap of thick blond curls, she also had something of the Kewpie doll about her. And, as Helena was wont to say, she could act her ass off. Onstage, she could appear frail or lithesome, mousy or flamboyant.

She'd gone into law school to please her father, who considered trodding the boards an unsuitable occupation for a woman able to trace her ancestry back to those arriving at Plymouth Rock. Bev had stuck it out for a year and a half before phoning her dad and telling him to stuff it. From there it was Yale Drama School, a stint at Actors Studio, summer theater, theater in the sticks, off-Broadway, you name it, paying her dues. She wasn't a household name yet, but was certainly well known by those who counted.

We stuffed our faces, rehashing the old days and bringing one another up to date. Bev entertained us with the foibles of members of the repertory company, of a Romeo who loved garlic, a Hamlet with a case of poison ivy.

"Well, I take it everything went okay in Chicago," I said, wiping away tears of laughter. "The reviewer practically frothed at the mouth about you."

"Didn't he though? Here's to him." She downed a mouthful of wine. "How'd you know? You read Chicago papers?"

"Not as a rule. You sent it to me, remember? Where's my purse? I brought the article so you could autograph it for Nunna. She's never forgotten you."

Bev squinted at me nearsightedly. "And I've never forgotten her oatmeal raisin cookies. But, sorry, Leigh, honey, I didn't send anything to anybody. I don't even send reviews to Dad. What made you think it came from me?"

"Wait a sec." I got up, which wasn't easy, and served as a reminder to forgo any more wine. I wound my way back to the living room, found my purse, and returned to the Persian rug.

"Here," I said, unfolding it. "You're telling me you didn't send this?"

"I sure as hell didn't. Lemme borrow your specs, Debbie. I couldn't get up if you paid me."

Debra's reading glasses were hanging around her neck, so she passed them over. "The right side is double strength."

"Whatever." Bev merely glanced at the review, then the writing on the bottom. " 'What could have been, no thanks to you.' What the hell does that mean? I didn't send this, honest Injun, Leigh."

I slumped onto the sofa. "Shit, shit, shit. Her again."

"Her who?" Mary Ellen demanded. "What's going on?"

"Give," Helena ordered. "Maybe we can help. One for all and all for one and the like."

"From the beginning," Debra said, maneuvering into a lotus position. "And don't leave anything out either."

I poured myself a glass of Pepsi and slapped a pillow behind my back. As much as I normally resisted boring others with my problems, there was something nostalgic and comforting about sharing it with these four. We'd done it often enough in law school.

"I'm not sure how long ago it started," I began, since I couldn't remember when the first incident had happened. "Sometime after Halloween and before Thanksgiving."

"So early November," Helena said, getting up. "I'm going to take notes. Don't stop, I can hear." She headed toward the kitchen, returning with a steno pad.

"Okay. I moved out of my apartment about then and have been staying with a good buddy directly across the hall. Someone left a clump of dog poop in front of my old apartment."

Mary Ellen wrinkled her nose. "Ooh. Not nice."

I went on from there, trying to put things in order and to include even the most insignificant detail. "The review came in the mail on Monday." Somehow it seemed like a month ago, so much had happened since.

"Mailed from the main post office here," Bev said, fingering the envelope. "This is the first time I've been back to D.C. since the auditions for the repertory company. Jeez, that was back in the spring."

"And didn't call any of us," Helena said, glaring at her. "So what then, Leigh?"

I described the events of this week, the raving e-mail messages, the circumstances surrounding Claudia's death, and the attempts to track down this pox on my life while she stood on the corner watching and probably laughing her fool head off.

"I still haven't found Nell Gwynn, the West Indian lady, and unless she's in cahoots with this Bernard, I doubt she has anything to do with all this. Although I'd dearly love to know whose bathroom she used out of pure curiosity. But Georgia Keith is definitely out of the picture."

"Georgia Keith?" Bev gazed into the distance, frowning.

"I think Duck is probably right," Mary Ellen said, eyeing the remains in her wineglass. "This woman's no fool. She wouldn't give the man in the dry cleaners her real name, but I'll bet my salary her initials will be the same as whatever alias she's using."

They went off on a tangent, Helena expounding about a case of identity theft she'd handled a couple of years before. I felt a nudge from my bladder and asked for directions to the nearest bathroom, which turned out to be the size of Janeece's apartment. I answered the call of nature, washed with Helena's French hard-milled soap, and was drying my hands when someone knocked.

"Your purse was beeping," Debra said, handing me my cell phone. "Thought it might be Duck."

I didn't recognize the number in the readout but answered as I strolled back toward the others, Debbie trailing me.

"You *bitch!*" a voice screamed in my ear. "You conniving, double-crossing bitch! No wonder you held me up so I couldn't make the audition! You *knew* that fat, whey-faced cow! She looks like a polar bear in all that white. You ruined my chances because you *knew* her! You ruined my career! I'm going to kill you, do you hear me? I'm sorry about the old lady but I'm looking forward to taking care of you!" She disconnected, evidently slamming the phone onto the cradle.

Stunned, I stood in the family room doorway, trying to make sense of what she'd said.

"That was her, wasn't it?" Debra said. "Jesus, I could hear her from here. She's crazy, all right."

"Helena, write down this number," I said, calling it up on the readout, then dialing Duck's cell phone. "Bernard just got me," I said. "She called from . . ." I gestured at Helena.

She jumped up, showing me the notepad, and I repeated the number for Duck. "Can you get someone to trace it for me? She followed me here, Duck. She must have. She mentioned the white outfit Bev's wearing. And I think . . . wait a minute, hon. What, Bev?"

She was bouncing up and down, waving at me. "I just put it together. Nell Gwynn was the name of one of the English kings' mistresses."

"So?"

"She was also an actress, a famous one in her day. Don't you remember Prinny Kline's mom going on about being a Howard Player back in the fifties, and the drama professor who named his dog Nell Gwynn?"

I looked at the ceiling in disgust. That's why the name had seemed familiar. Prinny's mom had been one of the few to encourage Bev to follow her star. How could I have forgotten that?

"And wait!" Bev snapped her fingers. "Georgia Keith. Georgia Keith. Sure! That was the name of a character in *August Flames*, the last play I read for at Arena Stage. Didn't get the part, but Georgia Keith was the main character, a dynamite role."

I was getting a weird sensation in the pit of my stomach, my mental gears beginning to mesh. The memory was faint but was slowly coming into focus. "Duck, were you able to reach Roland's wife?"

"Yeah, I was gonna tell you when you got back. Bernard told them her first name was—"

"Sarah," I cut him off. "Oh, my God! Not Bernard. Bernhardt! She's an actress!"

Bev grinned. "That was the next thing I was gonna say. Bernard, my ass! Salut!" She tossed down the last of her wine.

"Beverly?" Duck asked.

"In spades, and thanks to her, I know who's been dogging me, Duck. I even talked to her. Oh, my God! I remember now. I know who she is!"

15

"THIS IS RIDICULOUS," I GROUSED AS XAVIER, Bev's driver, reached in to help me out of the Town Car in Duck's underground garage.

"Know what?" Duck said, slipping a twenty into Xavier's free hand. "I don't give a damn. We had to get you away from there without that lunatic realizing you were leaving. Thanks, man. And thank Beverly for me, too."

"My pleasure." Xavier took Helena's wig and coat from me, his expression implacable, as if his passengers played this kind of game all the time. He returned to his place behind the wheel, backed up, and aimed for the exit to the street.

"Let's move it," Duck said, hurrying me into the elevator. "Tank and Tina are upstairs."

"What about the Corvette? I feel responsible for it. I can't leave it sitting on Helena's street all night."

"They'll go get it when they leave here. By the way, that call to you was made from a phone outside a gas station on Connecticut, so she wasn't that far away. Gone by the time the squad car got there, of course. But one of the attendants heard her—not what she was saying, just that she was yelling. He figured it was a lovers' quarrel or something."

"Did he get a good look at her?" I asked, as the elevator eased to a stop at his floor.

"No, he was around the side, checking the air in someone's tires."

I cussed. It was incredible how well the woman's luck was holding. I just hoped mine would too. I'd felt like an idiot, sneaking from Helena's garage entrance into the Town Car in an auburn wig and one of her ankle-length Burberry trench coats over my own, hers so long on me I had to hike it up to keep from falling on my face. Bev had come up with the idea and the others had voted for going along with it, including Duck, yelling his two cents at me over the cell phone.

"So who is she?" Tina demanded as soon as we got through the door. "What's the bitch's name?"

"I don't know." I shed my own coat and tossed it over one of the easy chairs. Duck, Mr. Neatnik, took it and hung it in the guest room closet, leaving the door open so he could hear.

"What do you mean, you don't know?" Hands on her hips, Tina glared at me.

"Just what I said. I don't know. I just remember how I met her months ago, that's all. But once I did, remember, I mean, it began to make sense."

"Well, it's about time," she said, throwing herself onto the sofa. "Let's hear it."

Tank came in from the kitchen, greeting me by raising the bottle of beer in his hand. "Hey, Leigh. It finally clicked, did it?" He passed a second beer to Tina and settled himself on the floor, his back against the couch.

"Yeah, finally. I keep wondering if I'd have put it together eventually, but I doubt it. I don't have the right background. Thank God for the Bitches of Brandywine Hall."

"Who?" Tina asked, taking a sip of her husband's beer.

"Old law school friends," Duck supplied, nudging a chair in my direction. "Okay, babe, you've got the floor."

I sat and tried to recapture an event that, at the time it happened, had meant nothing special.

"Remember back in the spring, around the middle of March, I think it was, when there was a gas leak in a house on Sixteenth Street and we had to evacuate everyone in the block and the one behind it?"

Tina looked blank but Tank and Duck nodded. "Oh, yeah," they said together.

"Most everybody working the day shift in that district was assigned to check to see that all the houses and apartments had been vacated and then cordon off the area until the leak had been repaired."

"Guess I must have been in court or something," Tina said. "So?"

"People groused about having to stand out in the cold so long, but they cooperated because the house could have gone up any time. But this one woman kept bugging me every ten minutes. She was really agitated, kept asking how much longer it would be because she had to be somewhere soon. She lived in the area and needed to go home and change and get her car. I explained that no one was allowed behind the sawhorses because it was too dangerous. She'd go away for a few minutes, then back she'd come, pleading for me to let her pass. I told her no; it wasn't safe. I mean, you could smell the gas from where I stood."

"Shoot, you could smell it from Piney Branch Park," Tank said. "That's where I was but damned if I can remember why."

"Yes, well anyway, the next time she asked if she couldn't just get her car. Even if she couldn't change, if she could get her car, she might make it on time. It was her big chance, she kept saying. She'd been working toward this for years, she was perfect for it, just what they were looking for. She might have mentioned an audition, but I'm not sure. I think I assumed it was a job interview or something. I felt sorry for her, I really did, but I couldn't let her through and that's all there was to it. She freaked, began cursing at me, saying I was ruining her life. She was completely out of control, practically frothing at the mouth. By that time, I'd had enough. I told her if she took one step beyond the saw-horses, I'd arrest her. Then one of the other uniforms came over and asked what the trouble was. Maybe being confronted by two of us in uniform convinced her to give up. She stormed off. That was it."

"So what's this about an audition?" Tank drained his bottle.

"It turns out that's where she was going, to open auditions for the Shakespeare repertory tour. Bev mentioned it, and that, along with the review of *Macbeth*, started the wheels turning."

"What review?" Duck asked.

"Look in my bag. I got that earlier this week and assumed Bev had sent it. Then when Bev caught the implications of the names she's been using . . . And to think I actually met her today, dammit!"

Duck looked up from the newspaper article. "Today?"

"One of Gracie's students described her to a T, so when I saw her on the street earlier today, I recognized her as Georgia Keith. I even stopped her and talked to her and she gave me this perfectly convincing story about how she came to be in the lobby on Monday. The thing is, she looked nothing like the photos from the Bridal Bower. I saw no resemblance at all! The woman's a damned chameleon. Gracie's student said there was a possibility that the teenager was related to Nell Gwynn because there was a slight resemblance, but no one else mentioned it. And Miss Colby? No, Cobey. She went on and on about how much foundation Gwynn was wearing, which makes sense now. Stage makeup. But as far as all of them were concerned, they were two different people. She fooled them all. Hell, she fooled me. I even showed her the pictures of herself. She didn't even blink!"

"Are you sure the names aren't a coincidence?" Tina asked.

"All of the names have a connection to the theater. Helena dug out a volume of *Encyclopedia Britannica* and showed me the section on Nell Gwynn. She might have been a king's bit of stuff on the side but she was also the Sarah Bernhardt of her day. I'd never heard of the play that has a Georgia Keith as one of the characters, but Bev auditioned for it at Arena. They mounted a production of it last year. Perhaps our nutcase was in the play, or saw it. Who knows? But everybody knows about Sarah Bernhardt."

"Well, okay, but why go after you?" Duck folded the review and dropped it on the coffee table.

"She said I'd kept her from getting to the auditions because I knew Bev, knew she was trying out, too. Which I didn't, of course. None of us even knew she was in town. Seeing us together in front of Helena's must have driven her over the edge, for her to call me there. By the way, Tina, she said she was sorry about Claudia."

Tina sat up straight. "She admitted it?"

"Only to being sorry about her. Any word on the autopsy yet?"

"Tomorrow." Relaxing again, she scowled. "They were too jammed up today. Oh, and Tankie, tell them what Willard said."

"The day she called the police, she used a cell phone stolen from a Steve Castello, who moved here recently from Florida. The phone still had a Florida area code. It hasn't been used since, so she probably tossed it afterward."

"Terrific," I said, not the least surprised. "But at least there's a better chance of tracking her down now. We know the general area where she lived, at least back in the spring. We know she's an aspiring actress, which means checking local theater groups to see if anyone recognizes her."

Duck leaned forward in his chair, elbows on his knees, and fixed a penetrating gaze on me. "Let's define some terms here, specifically this 'we' you're talking about. It includes Evans and Thackery. They investigate murders, suspicious deaths. And if Bernhardt/Keith/ Gwynn said she was sorry about Claudia, that's proof at the very least that she was there. I've left a message for Thack and Evans, letting them know there have been new developments and you'll fill them in tomorrow."

"Fine." I wasn't looking forward to it, but they did need to know.

"'We' also includes Willard," Duck continued. "He'll need copies of the photographs. This Castello might recognize her. And she's made threats by phone, another black mark against her he'll want to add to his list."

"Eddie made plenty of copies for me."

"Good. Now, as far as the three of us are concerned, Tank will keep in touch with Willard, who evidently appreciates all the help he can get. Tina's riding herd over her contact at the medical examiner's and is also trying to find out what happened to Claudia's car. She obviously drove it here to pick up Clarissa. Our girl may have used it to get away last night. Me, I'll be dogging Evans and Thackery. Thus ends the 'we.' You, my love, are getting the hell out of town."

I looked at him sidewise. "Excuse me?"

"I've packed a bag for you and I'm driving you to Ourland tonight. If we're taking the house, we might as well use it."

Not only did my hackles rise, they stood at attention. "Now, just wait a minute, buster," I began, simmering.

"Hear me out, babe. I should have thought of this last night, but I was more concerned about how Clarissa was holding up. This crazy woman's done enough. For the moment, let's forget the Hawaii reservations and your suit."

"No," I interrupted. "Let's not."

He held up a hand. "Leigh, it was one thing when she was simply a pain in the butt, but she's crossed the line. She invaded my apartment under false pretenses, removed personal property. She's been stalking you; that's a crime in itself, her e-mail to you may be, too, for all I know. But now a perfectly innocent woman is dead. For all we know, Clarissa may be in danger, too. And that call to you tonight says she's completely out of control now. She's gone way past harassment. I'm taking her threat against you seriously. If I had my druthers, I'd put you on the next flight to Asheville, but I know you'd go kicking and screaming. So Ourland will have to do, and I don't want to hear any argument."

My simmer had escalated to a full, rolling boil. "Who died and made you boss?"

"Claudia," he said quietly.

He had a point but it was beside the point. The other one, I mean.

"I'm not going, Duck. I refuse to run away. If nothing else, I owe it to Claudia and Clarissa to stick it out and put an end to this reign of terror. As far as I'm concerned, the wedding suit is the least she's stolen from me; that's replaceable. She's stolen my name, my identity, my peace of mind. I want it back, all of it."

"Don't think I don't understand that, babe. But how am I gonna concentrate on the job if I'm worrying about whether you're okay, whether you're safe?"

I stood up. "Seems to me we've been down this road before. If I remember correctly, it's the same argument you put to me earlier this year when you backed me into a corner so I'd have no choice but to break our engagement. You couldn't concentrate on the job if you had to worry about me out on the street doing *my* job. I fell for it then. Not this time."

"It's different this time," he said, his hands on my shoulders forcing me to sit again. He got down on one knee. "I'm not trying to break our engagement. I'm trying to protect the life of the woman I love."

Tina and Tank got up. "Uh, we'll leave so you two can talk."

"Sit down," Duck ordered, still focused on me. "I want us married, babe. I want you *alive*! If you were in Ourland—"

"I wouldn't be any better off than I'd be here. She followed us there, remember? If your precious manhood depends on my giving in to you on this, we're in big trouble because I'm not running, Duck. No way, José."

Rising, he glared down at me, his temple throbbing. "God protect me from hardheaded women!" He stormed out, went into the bedroom, and slammed the door.

Tina folded her hands in her lap. "Well. I'm not absolutely sure, you understand, but if I had to guess, I'd have to say I think the man's really upset."

I'd never had occasion to sleep on my couch, and after spending the night on it, I swore at the first opportunity, it would be history. I hadn't expected to be able to sleep at all; I couldn't turn my head off, working out how to get the chameleon's real name and what the hell to do once I'd gotten it.

Peeking from behind all the upheaval in my brain was the fight with Duck. It wasn't our first set-to. I just prayed it wouldn't be our last.

The clock above his desk moved like a snail through syrup. The last time I'd looked at it, it was three-twenty. When I woke up, I knew the apartment was empty. Duck was gone. No coffee, no note, no nothing.

"So be it," I said, and consoled myself in the shower.

I was wrapped in a towel, trying to decide what to wear, when the phone rang. I sprinted to answer it, planting my still-damp fanny on Duck's side of the bed.

It was my beloved. "Take this number." No "good morning," "how'd you sleep?" or anything else. I grabbed a pencil and notepad from my everyday purse.

"Yes?" Two could play this game.

He rattled off a number. "DePriest's parents," he said, and hung up.

I spent thirty seconds feeling weepy. It was no fun

having Duck mad at me. I blew the next fifteen railing at myself for wanting to cry, and the fifteen seconds after that trying to adjust to the knowledge that Plato de-Priest had parents. I'd never imagined him as a member of a family. Screwballs like Plato were hatched, not born.

It was an upstate New York number. I checked the clock. Eight-thirteen. Hopefully, they were awake.

The voice that answered the phone sounded alert and full of piss and vinegar. "Meow, the Cat House. Prissy speaking."

Cat House? "Uh, hello. I was trying to reach the de-Priest residence."

"You've got it. Can I help you?" A decidedly feline voice yowled in the background. "Hush, Roger. Mommy's on the phone."

I figured the best course of action was to cut to the chase. "My name in Leigh Warren and I'm—"

"Oh! Our Plato's friend! How nice of you to call. How's he doing this morning? We haven't talked to him yet."

I wondered if I needed to do some pussyfooting of my own. "That's why I'm calling, Mrs. dePriest. I stopped by his house yesterday and he didn't answer. It worried me."

"Oh, you poor thing. I can imagine what you thought. Plato's in George Washington University Hospital. He tripped over some equipment—no doubt you know what his house is like—and broke his leg, quite badly since they've got him in traction. We just left there yesterday, had to get back for the cats. We raise Siamese, and they get so put out when we're away. Please go see him, Leigh. He's got his laptop but I'm sure he'd appreciate seeing a friendly face."

I exhaled a sigh of relief and promised I'd see him as soon as I could. I'd just replaced the receiver when the phone rang again.

It was Bev. "Mornin', sunshine. You up?"

"Up and squeaky clean. Thanks again for the loan of your car and driver."

"Glad to do it. Lookit, darlin', I called a friend who works at Arena Stage and asked about *August Flames*. Only one male in the whole play. There are several roles for women our age and the cast was mostly Equity, but some were local amateurs, so your crazy woman might have been in it. He's pulling the cast photos for me, but has a late-morning appointment downtown. Think you could make it to Arena by eleven?"

I perked up. "You bet." I assumed that Tina had bought the Corvette back here.

Bev gave me her contact's name. "I'd go with you, but we've got a tech rehearsal this morning. I'm at the Marriott at Thirteenth and Pennsylvania so leave me a message, let me know how it went, okay?" Bang! She was gone.

Fifteen minutes later I was dressed and ready to go, with a couple of hours to kill before going over to Arena Stage, which wasn't that far away. I wanted to check the cast photos before seeing Thackery and Evans. With luck, and I admitted I'd need a lot of it, I could present them with a name and a professionally done head shot.

I nibbled on toast and guzzled some orange juice, then decided to change my footwear. My navy tunic and slacks would probably look dressier if I dumped the boots. In the guest room, I unearthed the box marked "Shoes," and removed my black Ferragamos. Properly shod, I was about to leave the room when

I spotted the two boxes Neva had signed for earlier in the week. Assuming they were wedding gifts, I'd wanted Duck and me to open them together. Since I couldn't be sure when we'd be opening anything together now, I got the scissors from the lap drawer of my desk and started snipping tape.

The contents of the smaller box contained a slinky black peignoir, so silky and sheer that wearing it would be next door to being nude. I checked the card. From Janeece. It said, *This ought to prime his pump.* No lie, assuming I ever got to wear it. I returned it to its cushion of tissue paper, and tackled the second box. In it was a smaller one. In that, one smaller still.

I stopped, ice crystals forming in my veins and visions of letter bombs exploding in my head. I checked the outer carton. UPS. Typewritten labels. Return address: M. Smith, a five-digit number on Jeff Davis Highway, Arlington. I knew a Marian Smith and had worked with a Melissa Smith. Melissa had moved, but I wasn't sure it had been to Virginia.

Sitting back on my Ferragamoed heels, I tossed some mental dice. Melissa knew I was getting married. And the box had not been handled with tender loving care since I'd received it; it had been tossed around, had survived a ride in Tank and Tina's Explorer, and hadn't blown up. It was very light, about the same weight as the peignoir, and had arrived before last night's pointed threat on my life. I'd chance it. Carefully.

I exchanged the scissors for a box cutter, slitting the transparent tape carefully. With the flaps now free, I retreated to the kitchen, got the broom, and stationed myself on my knees behind my old rolltop desk. Reaching around it with the broom handle, I nudged the flaps of the box open. No explosion. I could just barely see inside. Newsprint? I poked the interior. Nothing.

Time to bite the bullet, I hoped, not literally. I eased from behind the desk, put the broom aside. Clippings from newspapers. I flipped through them. Reviews of the Shakespeare repertory's performance from every place they'd been since mid-April. And scribbled in the margins of each, *Bitch!* Or *You owe me!* Or *This was supposed to be mine!* And others of that ilk. She'd coveted the roles of Juliet, Regan, Lady Macbeth. And I'd kept her from them.

Belatedly, I thought about fingerprints. Dusting the outer box would be a waste of time, but the inner ones all had a glossy finish. I repacked them and took the box into the living room. An aspiring actress, for God's sake. A crazy, wily aspiring actress who blamed me for missing what she must have considered the audition of her life. She'd obviously hit a dry spell if she was free to stalk me day and night, changing characters with apparent ease.

I passed the full-length mirror on the bathroom door, then backed up a step to gaze at myself. As soon as I left this apartment, I'd be a walking target. She knew what I looked like. But who would she be today? I had no way of knowing. The least I could do, if only to save my own neck, was to make it harder for her. I was no actress, but in my early years with the department, I'd spent more than one night walking the streets, playing the prostitute for unwary johns. I must have been fairly good at it; Vice had more than half a dozen arrests to thank me for. Unfortunately, I wasn't equipped for role playing of any kind now, but I knew where I could get whatever I needed, since it was the same source I'd used back then. Thank God today was Saturday.

I went to the phone, dialed, heard it ring five times, then the answering machine did its thing.

"Janeece," I yelled. "Pick up!"

It worked. "Leigh?" she answered groggily.

"Yes, it's me. I've got a favor to ask."

"Name it." She yawned.

"Bring me all your wigs and every bit of makeup you have. And I mean PDQ. I've got to be out of here by ten forty-five."

I could hear her sitting up. Her bed squeaked.

"You goin' out on the block again?" she asked. "You can't be. You're an engaged woman, betrothed and shit. What kind of games are you playing, girl?"

"Tit for tat, Janeece. Tit for tat."

16

BY THE TIME I LEFT TO MEET BEV'S CONTACT AT Arena Stage, I had eyelashes. I'd always coveted Duck's, which were indecently long for a male, and now I had some too, dark, swoopy things that made me feel as if I was peering from under a pair of awnings. I also had shoulder-length sandy brown braids, D-cup breasts, and, God forbid, hips. I fought like a tigress against the hips, since I already have fanny aplenty, but Janeece insisted that if I was going to play the game, I needed to go whole hog. Which is initially the way I felt under all that padding. But she was right. I bore little surface resemblance to me. Add the two-inch platform shoes with the Kleenex stuck in the toes to make them fit and I wouldn't be walking like me either.

I knew I'd passed muster when Chet showed up with the keys to my car and didn't recognize me when I answered the door.

"Uh," he said, staring at me as if he still wasn't sure of my identity, "you can see a little of the spray paint on the sides but it sorta looks like it came that way new. The only way to get rid of it is to get an all-over paint job."

I thanked him, exchanged his car keys for mine, and

realized that I was still in a bind. I couldn't use my car. It would be a dead giveaway.

"No big deal," Janeece said, cramming yet more tissues down my bra. "I'll drive you over to Arena, and from there to a rental agency."

"Oh, yeah, as if they'll rent me so much as a kiddy car when they see my driver's license and compare it to the bimbo standing on the other side of their counter."

"You do not look like a bimbo," Janeece said, clearly insulted. "You just don't look like you. Tell you what. I'll take the rental and you use mine."

Drive her Cadillac? I was speechless. Nobody drove Janeece's Caddy. Nobody. Not even her assorted husbands. She was making the ultimate sacrifice.

I choked up. "You're a good friend, Janeece."

She ogled me, horrified. "Don't you *dare* cry, girl! That mascara's not waterproof! Come on. You're gonna be late."

As it was, it wouldn't have mattered. Beth's contact was gone but had left the *August Flames* cast photos with a chunky young woman who introduced herself as Sunny. Her name suited her personality.

"You know Beverly Barlowe?" she bubbled. "I saw her in *Lysistrata* when I was in high school. She was absolutely fantastic. Here, have a seat. You wanted to look at these?" She handed over a file of eight-by-ten glossies.

I flipped through them quickly. Lots of females, none even closely resembling the she-devil. I showed Sunny my photos, hoping she might recognize the face.

"Sorry," she said, shaking her head. "This is my first

season here. I'd ask a few old-timers but they're getting ready for the matinee. Your snaps won't copy all that well—they're really grainy—but I could make a set and show them around between performances. I mean, being that you're a friend of Beverly Barlowe and all."

I expressed my appreciation, let her Xerox the photos, left my phone numbers, and returned to the parking lot.

No Caddy. No Janeece.

A blast from a horn announced her approach from Sixth Street just as a reedy man with a Dennis the Menace cowlick jogged toward the theater from the opposite direction.

Waving, he shouted, "Shelly? Long time no see."

I turned and peered at him. "Excuse me?"

He blinked, then flushed as he slowed to a walk. "Sorry. Thought you were someone else. Is this your ride?" He jerked his head toward the Caddy, which had purred up behind me. "Have a nice day." Legs pumping, he backed away and disappeared behind the building.

"Who was that?" Janeece asked as I got in.

"Don't know. He thought I was someone else. Where'd you go?"

"Around the block to see if I spotted anybody tailing us. Any luck in there?"

"Not yet, but the woman I talked to copied my photos and will show them to people who've been there longer than she has. I've just discovered something. Panties for a size ten don't fit over size fourteen hips. I might as well be wearing a thong."

"Deal with it, because you look fab."

"You're enjoying this, aren't you?" I growled. "I'm

sweating under all this stuff. Might as well be having hot flashes. And my feet are killing me."

"Bitch, bitch, bitch," she said, grinning. "Let's go get us some fancy wheels."

She meant it literally, turning into an agency that handled upscale models. I began to sweat even more. I'd intended to reimburse her for the rental, since she was doing it as a favor to me. Fortunately, she decided on the fanciest Mercedes on the lot, at which point she relieved me of all responsibility by insisting on footing the bill. I wasn't about to argue with her.

"Hell, girl, this will be a test drive for me," she said, smiling sheepishly. "I've always wanted a Mercedes, and this will give me a chance to see how it performs. Take good care of my baby," she said, and sped away.

I settled behind the wheel of the Caddy, adjusted the seat and mirrors, and pulled into traffic, driving like a very senior citizen in unfamiliar territory. Gradually I became accustomed to the smoothness and the power, and wondered if I'd ever be satisfied with my own plain-vanilla vehicle again.

Thackery was waiting for me at the First District station, his desk as neat as if the Merry Maids had just left. He didn't recognize me. "Good morning. Can I help you?"

"It's me. Leigh Warren. Sorry about the disguise, but I figured it was one way to prevent our perp following me."

"Jesus," he said, scanning me head to toe. "If it doesn't work, it won't be for lack of trying. Kennedy's message says our girl got in touch with you last night and you've figured out who she is?"

"I figured out where I met her, what she does, and

why she's been after me, but not her name yet. She's an actress and—"

"An actress?" He blanched, eyes widening.

"What's wrong with being an actress?" I asked, curious about his attitude.

He flushed. "Nothing. So how did you meet her?"

I managed a fairly succinct narrative of my encounter with her during the gas leak evacuation, my reunion with Beverly and company, noting the twitch of Thackery's eyebrows when I mentioned Helena and Debra's names, which he obviously recognized. I gave him a verbatim recitation of the telephone call and her threat, as he scribbled furiously on a lined pad.

"She was sorry about the old lady," he repeated. "Which could mean anything, but definitely puts her in the picture. Good. Go on."

I finished with a description of my conversation with her in her teenage persona in front of my building, the connections we'd made with the aliases she'd used thus far, and how adept she must be at what she does.

"No one decorating the tree realized that she and the middle-aged woman with the West Indian accent were one and the same. And I took her at face value. She looked, talked, and acted like a sixteen-year-old. And I feel like a first-class fool. I didn't even recognize her."

He rubbed a finger over his top lip. "Well, at least we have someplace to start. I'll have someone type this up and print it out for you to sign. She's piling up a list of things we can charge her with, but I have to be honest. Whether this belongs to Violent Crimes still depends on the results of the autopsy, and after the deaths in last night's fire, the M.E.'s may not get to Ms. Hitchcock as soon as we hoped."

"What fire?" I asked, feeling very much out of the loop. If I'd been in uniform, I'd know, if only courtesy of station house chitchat.

"A catering company out in far Northeast late last night, definitely arson, perhaps homicide too. A couple of bodies turned up, so far unidentified, at least not formally. But that'll probably take precedence over Ms. Hitchcock. We know who she is."

I felt a pang of sympathy for Clarissa and wondered how this development would affect her plans for a memorial service. Tina wouldn't be pleased either, but she knew the drill. This would definitely come first.

My statement arrived sooner than I expected it and I read it over, corrected a typo, and signed it. Outside, I debated what my next stop should be and decided to go see Plato, wishing I hadn't promised his mother that I would, since considering where I was and where GW University Hospital was, it would take me a year to get there in lunchtime traffic. Now I was obligated.

It only took three-quarters of an hour. It was also the first time I'd been to this hospital since they'd moved into their new digs in 2002. I was impressed and, by the time I found Plato's room on level four, relieved that he had been brought here. It was bright and airy enough to ameliorate his claustrophobia. Knowing him, however, it had probably ramped up his agoraphobia instead. Plato's phobias were legend, genuine, and debilitating.

There was a "No Visitors" sign on his door. Anxiety coursing through my veins, I stared at it, wondering if his condition had worsened since his parents had left.

"Can I help you?"

A sleepy-eyed young man in a white lab coat and a stethoscope around his neck stood at my elbow.

"I'm here to see Mr. dePriest but . . ." I jerked my head toward the sign. Hoping to make him a little more free with information, since it was obvious I wasn't family, I said, "I'm a close friend. How is he?"

"He's got them?" Nurse or doctor, whatever he was, he seemed genuinely suspicious, one brow arching cynically.

"Them what?"

"Friends."

I couldn't help it. I burst into laughter.

"LEIGH? THAT YOU OUT THERE? HELP!" Plato.

Mr. Lab Coat rolled his eyes and pushed the door open for me.

Plato, in the bed nearest the door, was propped on one elbow, his right leg suspended in a metal frame held aloft by yet another frame attached to the head and foot-boards. His curly, dark hair, unkempt at the best of times, was more so than usual. He stared at me. "What's with the braids and stuff? You've gained weight. Never mind. GET ME THE HELL OUT OF HERE!"

"Mr. dePriest." The lab coat had followed me in. "For the hundredth time, you're in a hospital. Please keep your voice down."

"I'm not a cretin," Plato snarled. "I know where I am, a TORTURE CHAMBER!"

"Oh, for God's sake, Plato, can it," I snapped at him. "Just shut the hell up. The man's right. There are sick people up here."

"Don't you think I know that?" He shuddered. "All those germs!"

It was my turn to roll my eyes toward the ceiling. "Thanks," I said to the nurse/doctor. "I can handle him."

"Want a job?" he asked me. He glared at Plato, then left the room.

I shed my coat and draped it over the back of the chair by the bed. The other bed was vacant; I could guess why.

"You're being a pain in the ass, aren't you? Plato, these people are here to help you. It's not their fault you broke your leg. How is it?"

He flopped back, tears in his eyes. "It hurts. How'd you know I was here?"

"I went by your house. You didn't answer, so I called the number you gave me and talked to your mom."

"They left to go feed the damned cats," he grumbled. "I *hate* Siamese cats. Do you know what it's like to have yowling Siamese cats as brothers and sisters? They used to climb me like I was a jungle gym."

"I assume they wouldn't have if they hadn't liked you," I said, hoping he didn't know I hadn't the slightest idea what I was talking about. Cats in general, I know. Siamese, I don't. "Tell me how you broke your leg."

That, at least, diverted him long enough to forget about his fur-bearing brothers and sisters. His fall had happened about as I'd envisioned. Plato had enough computers to open a store. Normally the floor of his workroom was clear so he could scoot from one workstation to another in his rolling chair. But he'd had to move a desktop to make room for a new one, had left the old one on the floor, had forgotten it was there, and had tripped over its monitor.

"Two months I'll have to be in this damned thing," he said mournfully. "I can't be away from my computers for two months, Leigh. I've got my laptop but I'm going nuts here. And I'm sorry, but I fell before I was able to finish tracing your e-mail. What's with that, anyway?"

I'd lost track of how many times I'd gone through it but did it again, in case he saw something the rest of us had missed.

"Sorry I let you down," he said. "I'd already written off the computers in the libraries. Too much traffic. But I might have been able to get somewhere with the church. Perhaps the other places too. A community center, and some sort of private club."

"How could she have gotten permission to use a computer in a church? It's not as if they'd be that accessible."

"You wouldn't think so, would you? Saint Something in Northeast—"

"Saint Something?"

"One of the apostles, and New Gospel in Mitchellville. Don't remember the name of the community center but it was in Columbia. And the private club was in Gaithersburg."

I wrote all that down, even though some of it was a waste of ink. Saint Something certainly was. And Columbia had almost as many community or neighborhood centers as it had people. But Marty had lived in Gaithersburg before she'd married Jensen, so perhaps she could give me a line on the private clubs.

"This woman certainly gets around," I said, seeing no particular pattern in her movement. "New Gospel and Gaithersburg will probably be the easiest for me to check out. I might not be able to pinpoint the exact date she used their computers, but at least I have a time frame to work with."

"Come to think of it," Plato said, shifting his weight awkwardly, "what set her off?"

"I already told you. She missed an audition—"

"That's not what I mean. She missed the audition back in the spring, right? This just started fairly recently. Why? What triggered it? Why'd she wait until now?"

I hadn't thought of that. "Maybe it took her that long to find me. After all, she didn't even—" I stopped, reconstructing my confrontation with her. "Well, duh."

"What?" He pushed the button that controlled his pain medication.

"I was going to say she didn't even know my name, but she did. I gave it to her. When she flipped out, she said she was going to lodge a complaint against me. I was about sick of her by that point, so I told her to be sure and get my name right. I gave it to her, name, rank and badge number. Jeez, what a dunce I am."

"That still doesn't answer the question," Plato insisted, "especially if she's had the information all this time—and that's assuming she remembered it. Why wait until now to get back at you? What triggered it?"

It was a good question. I tossed it around all the way back to the condo, even during the fifteen minutes I spent in Home Depot looking for a welcome mat to replace Janeece's.

I'd have to power up the laptop and check the date of the first message she had sent, I was thinking, as I stopped in the lobby of the building to check Duck's mailbox. It was empty, as was the lobby itself, the TV in the corner, silent. Mrs. Luby and her Gang of Four had other things to do, since there were no soaps on Saturday.

Upstairs in the hall, I wondered why I hadn't had the foresight to leave the welcome mat in Janeece's car. It was heavy, practically cutting off the circulation in the wrist the bag was dangling from, and hampering access to the pocket I needed to reach to get to the door key. I did some juggling, found it and had it in the lock when the whole of the Baltimore Orioles whacked me on the back of the head with every bat they had, and a voice yelled, "Got you!"

17

"OH, JESUS!"

I didn't pass out. There's no way you could see as many stars in as many galaxies as I did if you're unconscious. I did, however, wind up on my fanny on the floor, probably about the time Orion's Belt flashed past, the back of my head throbbing in time with my escalating pulse.

"Oh, Jesus, oh, Lord," someone mumbled again and, after the ringing in my ears lessened a bit, I recognized the voice.

"You hit me." I squinted up at Mrs. Luby, which only added pain behind my eyes to the equation. Her sweat suit was a shriek of carmine red. Thank God she wore no shoes. I'd seen them. They were American Beauty rose.

"I'm so sorry, Leigh." A tenpin-shaped dumbbell rolled across the carpet and stopped at her door as if pointing a finger of blame. "Did I hurt you? I didn't mean to."

"Couldn't prove it by me," I said. "In fact, I get the impression you meant to knock my block off. Congratulations. You just about succeeded. Mind telling me why?"

"I thought you were *her*," she wailed. "Heard you out

here. I looked through the peephole and thought she'd
come back. I wasn't going to let you . . . her, I mean, get
away again. I was exercising, so I just opened my door
and . . ." Reaching down, she helped me to my feet.
"What have you done to yourself? Why in the world
would you want to look like that awful woman?"

The key was still in the door so I opened it, walking
on eggs, and beckoned her in. "Mrs. Luby." Heading
for the couch, I lowered myself onto it slowly, and
stretched out. "When you saw her in the elevator, you
thought she was me. If, as everyone I've talked to today, insists I don't look like me now, how could you
think I look like her?"

"Because I saw her earlier," she protested, closing
the door behind her.

"Today?" I forgot the manic drumbeat in my head
for a moment.

"Yes. That's what I'm trying to tell you! About an
hour ago, I was out on my balcony. You know how I
love watching planes make their approach to the air-
port. I noticed this woman cross the street. I think
she'd just come out of our garage."

"What was she driving?" I sat up. Slowly.

"Nothing. She was walking. Fast. And she reminded
me of you and I thought, Luby, it's that woman again.
I had my binoculars with me to spot the planes so got
a real good look at her. I could see the difference then.
She's bustier and has more hips than you do and she
was wearing dreadlocks, but that didn't fool me. I called
the police but by the time they got here and checked
the garage and nearby streets, she was gone. But she
had on a white coat. That's why I thought you were her
when I saw you from the back. I've never seen you in a
white coat before."

"Remind me to warn you when I wear it again," I said, taking it off. "I've got to find some aspirin. And an ice bag."

"I'll get the ice out for you. I'm so sorry, Leigh. Think you should go to the hospital? You might have a concussion."

"Been there, done that, concussion-wise," I said, rising very, very gingerly. The room rocked for a moment, then settled down. "I'm all right." An exaggeration, if not an outright lie, but I was fairly certain she hadn't done that much damage. Granted, I had a first-class localized headache and a small lump back there, but my memory was intact, my surroundings had ceased all seismic activity, and besides, I'd had enough of hospitals for one day. Thank God for Janeece's wig with all these braids and the cushion they'd provided. It lay on the coffee table looking like a strange, sandy-colored octopus.

Mrs. Luby helped me get comfortable on the sofa again, aspirin down my gullet, an ice bag chilling the goose egg, and my laptop within arm's reach. After another dozen apologies from her and my assurances that I would live, she left and I sat back up—again, slowly—and turned on the laptop. There were new messages from me to me, in other words from the hellion, all of them today's date. The first had been sent a little after midnight, the second at four this morning (didn't the woman ever sleep?), the last a half hour ago.

It was obvious she was still foaming at the mouth when she'd written the first of them. She hadn't even bothered with caps.

you scheming, conniving bitch! i started out meaning to let you know somebody out here didn't think you

*were such hot shit just because you wear a uniform
and a badge, but that was before i saw you hugging
that blond heifer. i told you how important that audition was that day. i had olivia down pat, she was in my
soul! i could have been a lady macbeth and a portia no
one would ever forget! i had studied for almost a year
to be ready to handle any part they gave me! but you
had to make sure that fat sow got into the shakespeare
company instead of me. sisterhood means nothing to
you! she's not even black! now that i see how things
are don't bother replacing that crappy suit you were
going to get married in. i'll make sure your man gets
it back so you can be buried in it. you ruined my life
and i'm going to ruin yours—permanently.*

My headache intensified. This woman needed locking
up. Jail or psychiatric ward, I didn't care. I forwarded
the message to Duck at work, and to both Thackery and
Willard.

The second message was more controlled but no less
menacing. At least the capitals were back.

*You won't see me but I'll see you. And before it's over
you'll see nothing at all. Hope you slept well.*

The third made me smile a little.

*You can't stay in that apartment forever. When you
come out, I'll be waiting.*

So, if she'd been in the vicinity this morning, the
disguise had worked; she hadn't recognized me. But
Mrs. Luby's conk on the head made me think. Granted,
the coat was the deciding factor for her, but if she'd

mistaken me for the loony, then the wig, makeup and padding had had an unintended result. It had never occurred to me that I might now resemble Bitch Bar None. So there was a possibility that the jogger who'd mistaken me for someone named Shelly might have dropped her first name in our laps. And if she'd ever done a show at Arena, the jogger, at least, would recognize her picture immediately.

I checked the answering machine to make sure there was plenty of room for a message, in case Sunny called with good news. I was just turning away when the phone rang. I snatched it up and said, "Hello? Sunny?" before the caller ID registered in my brain. Things were still processing a bit slowly up there.

"I got the e-mail you sent and who's Sonny?" Duck asked, his interpretation of the name as being masculine obvious by his tone.

"S-U-N-N-Y," I spelled it out for him. "Someone I met at Arena this morning. And there's a possibility—a small one, but still a possibility—that our girl's first name is Shelly."

"What makes you think that?" He didn't sound as miffed as he had last night. By the time I'd finished telling him about the mistake by the jogger and the assault-by-Luby, all evidence of his temper were gone.

"Are you all right? Seriously, babe, you may have a concussion. I mean, a barbell? She could have killed you!"

"Well, obviously, she didn't and my head's feeling better. I swear. The barbell probably wasn't all that heavy, just effective. By the way, I stopped to see Plato and he asked a question I hadn't considered before. I met this Shelly—sorry if that turns out not to be her name; it'll do for now. I met her back in the spring, gave her my name, etcetera when she threatened to lodge a complaint. So why'd she wait until the fall to start this war? What lit the fuse?"

He snorted. "As nuts as she is, it might have been anything or nothing. Maybe she's been stewing about it ever since and finally decided to get it out of her system."

Or perhaps the imminent arrival of the Shakespeare repertory company had pushed her toward the edge. She'd obviously kept up with the reviews as they opened around the country. The symbol of a major missed opportunity right here on home territory might have been enough to do it, since she obviously wasn't stable.

"The reason I called," Duck said, interrupting my thoughts, "Jensen brought in the video of the wedding and reception and is showing it in one of the conference rooms. Thought you might like to see it and go out to eat afterward or something."

Ah. I'd finally gleaned the real purpose of the call, a fishing expedition, a way to find out if I was ready to forgive him. His "or something" gave it away. Duck rarely said that unless he was uncertain about the outcome.

This presented a quandary. I had no interest in seeing Jensen's video; I'd been there, the reception had gone on forever, and I had a to-do list to pare down. And a headache. Still . . .

"Okay," I said. "I'm on my way. Oh, and I'm driving Janeece's Cadillac."

"You're WHAT?"

"See you in a half hour or so," I said, and hung up, grinning. Payback. How sweet it was.

* * *

The skies had been sulky this morning but had improved immeasurably since then. Climate in the Washington area was always fickle, rarely sticking to the party line when it came to seasons. Except for three or four days, few and far between at that, there had been no truly cold weather this month or last, despite the anomaly earlier this week when it had snowed for all of seventeen seconds. Granted, the winter solstice was a couple of weeks away, but given the District's history, it would probably be warm enough for shorts that day, just to show who was in charge. I turned on the radio, found an all-news station, which before long announced that the whole area was wallowing in lower-sixties balminess. Fine by me. I hated cold weather.

As I zipped up the Anacostia Freeway toward Minnesota Avenue, I wondered what the temperature was on the Chesapeake. I'd find out tomorrow; the aunts weren't expecting me, but I knew their after-church routine well enough to know when I'd be able to catch them and let them know I'd need their services as a seamstress after all. I would have to be firm with them. No virginal white frou-frou. It promised to be a battle, but one I was determined to win.

I swept down onto Minnesota and headed toward East Capitol, grumbling at how smoothly traffic flowed today. I'd hoped to get to the Sixth District station late enough to avoid having to sit through too much of the videotape so that Duck and I could go on to dinner. Saturday traffic, however, was never as frenetic as during the week, and I arrived at my destination sooner than I'd hoped. And burst into laughter to see my beloved outside, waiting for me. Correction: waiting

264 ◆ CHASSIE WEST

to see the Cadillac. About that I had no illusions. My
spirits lifted. Perhaps we'd be skipping the videotape
after all.

He recognized the car but did a double-take when he
got a good look at me. I'd have loved to forgo the wig
but hadn't dared. The expression on Duck's face left no
doubt what he thought of it as he pointed, gesturing
toward an available parking spot. I managed to get into
it without embarrassing myself, and rolled down the
window.

"Want to drive?" I asked, fluttering my fake lashes at
him.

"You weren't lying. This really is Janeece's. How's
your head? Are you sure you're all right?"

"As all right as I can be in this getup. The aspirin and
ice bag helped. I'm fine or I wouldn't have driven."

He squatted outside my door, taking in the interior,
and whistled in admiration. "So where'd you bury Janeece? She's gotta be dead. There's no way you'd be
behind the wheel of this beauty otherwise."

I relented and confessed to my astonishment when
she'd suggested the arrangement. "She's in hog
heaven test-driving a rented Mercedes, says she's always wanted one. Chet brought mine back, but we figured that since Ms. Shelly Malicious knows it intimately,
so to speak, we'd pull a fast one on her. Looks like it
worked. Duck, do you mind if we skip watching the
video? I'm starving, enough to let you play chauffeur."

"Deal. Unlock the door." His eyes glittered with anticipation. The man was practically drooling.

I got out and he was in before I'd barely cleared the
seat.

"Some chauffeur you are," I said, watching him

move it backward. "Protocol says you're to escort me around to the passenger side and do the honors for me, door-wise."

"Uh-huh." Fiddling with the controls for the mirror, he hadn't heard a word I'd said. Which is why he didn't notice when one of a pair of uniforms striding past stopped and palmed my shoulder. His partner hesitated, then kept going.

"Hey, Mick! How come you didn't call me?" His voice was a low, sultry growl in my ear.

I turned, looked up. Six-two, Latino or Hispanic, and lip-smacking gorgeous. "Excuse me?"

"You were supposed to call me in exchange for the wine in my lap."

"Wine? In your lap?"

A frown wormed its way between glossy black brows. His gaze shifted from me to Duck and back. "Oh. Hey, Duck. Sorry, miss. My mistake. I thought you were someone else."

"Who?" I asked. If this was a repeat of this morning's encounter at Arena Stage, I was taking no chances.

"Yeah, who, Lopez?" Duck echoed me, scowling, the mirrors forgotten.

The officer backed up a step, distinctly uncomfortable now. "Micky something, I don't remember her last name. She accidentally spilled a glass of wine on me at Jensen's wedding reception and—"

"Lopez!" his companion shouted, snatching open the door of a squad car some distance away. "Come on! We've got a ten-fifty PI, East Capitol and Southern!"

"Uh, sorry, gotta go," Lopez said, backpedaling before turning to sprint away. He hopped into the cruiser and it burned rubber moving into traffic, lights flashing, siren climbing the scale.

Ordinarily the news of a traffic accident with personal injury would have evoked a Pavlovian response from me, pulse jumping, a small jolt of adrenaline. My heart rate had certainly revved up several beats per minute but not because of the ten-fifty PI.

I stared at Duck. "No wonder Eddie and Billings and what's-his-name swore they'd seen her somewhere before! She was at the wedding, too!"

"Be damned. Move, babe." I backed up so he could open the door. "We've got to go watch a video."

The lights in the conference room were lowered, the chairs around the big table occupied by a half dozen cops, most in civvies. A few in uniform ringed the wall, their focus the big monitor at the end of the room. This was foreign territory to me. I'd expected it to be a bit more posh. It wasn't and I was a little disappointed.

Jensen, nearest the VCR, a silly smile on his face, watched his image as he clomped his way awkwardly through a waltz with his wife's sister, the maid of honor. Marty's partner was her father, a real smoothie, circling the dance floor with panache.

Duck pulled out a chair for me and I sat down with a nod in response to the assorted greetings. The few who knew me stared for a moment, undoubtedly puzzled by the wig and makeup. Duck moved to Jensen's side and squatted, whispering in his ear. Jensen stiffened, looked at him wide-eyed, whispered something in return, then got up and left the room.

The plainclothes in the next chair moved down one and Duck slipped in beside me. "He's calling Marty," he said softly. "She's got a whole database on diskette, invitees with addresses and what wedding gifts they sent so she could mention them in her thank-you notes.

Jensen's having her shoot it to him via e-mail. He'll print it out for us."

Good old Marty. She and Jensen had been engaged for fifteen years before tying the knot. It's a good thing she'd never met Plato, I reflected, or she'd have been married years ago. She was older than he was by a decade or more but when it came to computers, they'd have had enough of a shared passion to delete any obstacles.

We sat through more dancing and lame jokes by the DJ between songs, then the four-course meal, which played havoc with my empty stomach. The camera made several circuits of the room, moving in for close-ups of the guests, the videographer obviously determined to catch all the attendees at least once. The conference room erupted in guffaws and good-natured insults as they recognized their images on screen. The headcount ebbed and flowed as some left to answer their pagers and others arrived, still in uniform, their shifts just ending.

Duck and I were silent, intent on the faces on the screen as the camera panned back and forth. I squirmed with dismay whenever I spotted myself. Even allowing for the fifteen pounds contributed by the camera, I looked as if I should have skipped the meal. As hungry as I was now, I reconsidered dinner with Duck. This was sheer torture.

The tape ended. I hadn't seen anyone who resembled the photos from the bridal shop. I'd paid particular attention to Lopez when I finally spotted him, but of the women at his table, only two were African American. Perhaps she'd occupied the vacant chair to his right.

Duck got up and pushed the button to rewind the

tape. Most of the company left but a few remained, settling down at the table, saying they'd missed the beginning. We had too, and as much as I dreaded it, we couldn't afford to leave until we'd seen it all.

Marty and Jensen had just been pronounced man and wife when he returned, a sheaf of pages in his hand. Not wanting to disturb the others, Duck and I got up and moved to the rear of the room, our backs against the wall so we could still see the screen.

"Dead end," Jensen said, handing over the pages. "At least as far as who received invitations. Marty says she's sure she didn't invite anyone named Micky—which is probably Michelle—or Shelly, but she might have come with one of the guys. That's why we didn't use place cards. Some of the RSVPs included who they were bringing, some didn't. As long as they indicated how many, we didn't care."

"We didn't spot her in the video," I said, my eyes glued to the monitor where Jensen and Marty were climbing into the rear of a limousine. "At least not yet." I searched the crowd outside the church, but there were so many. Half the force had turned out for this long-awaited wedding.

"Keep your fingers crossed that she does," Duck said, his expression grim. "Otherwise, we contact every male on the list and ask him the name of his guest."

"Sorry, guys." Jensen jammed his hands into his pockets. "Let me know if you think of anything else I can do."

The wedding proceedings had switched to the reception hall, capturing attendees as they entered through the double doors. Duck draped an arm around my shoulder and we watched with increasing frustration through the introduction of the wedding party at the head table, mini speeches, toasts, and the beginning strains of the wedding waltz, which is where Duck and I had come in. No sign of Shelly. He squeezed my shoulder, a signal that we might as well leave. We waved a good-bye to Jensen and threaded our way out into the hall.

"Well, that was a waste of an hour and a half," Duck said, ushering me through the squad room.

"Yes, but think how much tape wound up on the cutting room floor, so to speak. The wedding was at four. We left at eight-something and people were still dancing. Suppose Michelle got edited out."

He slowed, nodded. "You may be right. Let me go back and get the name of the video guy from Jensen. I'll meet you at the car." He hurried away.

I stood for a moment, consumed with nostalgia by the scents, sounds, and controlled chaos of the squad room. Half of the desks were vacant, phones ringing unanswered. Nearest me a woman who was probably a bag lady sat in a visitor's chair waiting for the return of a detective. A group of plainclothes huddled in a far corner, their conversation low and intense. I hadn't realized how much I missed all this, the camaraderie, the sense of doing something of value despite the mental and emotional fatigue, the stress. Heading up the Shores' police force would be a far cry from my days as a part of this organization.

For a third of a second, I wondered if I'd made a mistake severing my ties with the District police department. There were plenty of jobs I could have done, but the bum knee would have confined me to a desk most of the day. I loved the street, moving from one location to another, responding to calls for help. Yet I'd never be able to join a foot pursuit and that pursuit might be instrumental in catching a perp or, God forbid, coming to the aid of a fellow officer. On the District's streets, one was as likely to occur as the other. I couldn't chance failing, not when someone's life might be at risk. No. No mistake. I'd done the right thing.

I left the building and was heading for the Cadillac when a two-fingered whistle from behind me made me look back. Lopez, a streak of dirt across his cheek and a rip in the knee of his pants, trotted toward me.

"Sorry about whistling," he said, closing in on me, "but I couldn't remember your name. I wanted to apologize again. I shouldn't have—"

"It wasn't a problem. What happened to you?" I asked, my curiosity getting the best of me. "I thought it was a traffic accident."

"It was, a hit-and-run, but the driver bailed out a block away. A couple of witnesses caught him and were holding him for us." He chuckled. "It took a bit of convincing to get him to come along quietly. Uh . . ." His face sobered. "I just wanted to check with you about Duck, make sure I didn't piss him off."

"He understood, and I'm glad to see you again. This Micky you thought was me. Duck and I just sat through the videotape. We didn't see her. You're sure she was at Jensen's wedding?"

"Hell, yes. I've got a cleaning bill to prove it. Something startled her as she was pouring the wine and I wound up wearing it."

"She wasn't at your table. Where was she sitting? Who'd she come with?"

"Oh, she wasn't a guest. She was serving."

I felt something implode behind my eyes. No wonder we hadn't seen her.

I grabbed him and planted an eardrum-shattering

kiss on his grimy cheek. "You, Lopez, are my hero." I left him there, dark eyes wide with confusion, as I hurried back into the station house.

I ran headlong into Duck just inside the door. "She wasn't a guest," I said, pulling him out of the way of traffic. "I just ran into Lopez outside. She was with the caterers, a waitress!"

His jaw sagged for a second before he grabbed my hand. "Come on."

We headed back to the conference room double-time, me struggling to keep up with him. Opening the door, he beckoned to Jensen.

Puzzled, Jensen left the rear wall, tripping over the foot of a baby face in uniform as he made his way out. "What's up?"

"The woman we're looking for, Micky, Michelle, whatever, was one of the waitresses. What's the name of the caterers you used?"

"Uh . . . Celebrations. The owner's some friend of—"

"Celebrations?" Duck cut him off. "Off Eastern Avenue? Not the place that burned last night where they found two bodies?"

Jensen ogled him. "You're kidding. I hadn't heard."

Duck looked down at me. He didn't have to say it, I knew what he was thinking. But he said it anyway.

"Aw, shit."

18

I DIDN'T REMEMBER UNTIL WE GOT THERE because it had been years since I'd worked in this district, but Celebrations had been a big, white clapboard house, two-storied, probably a result of the building boom after World War II. Emphasis on "had been." It would never be habitable again. Sunset was approaching but we could see clearly that the only thing remaining was a shell and not a lot of that.

The walls, those left, were bowed. The roof was gone, one whole side of the house no more than an open wound, the interior black and charred. The siding was blistered and warped, windows shattered and gaping. Debris, largely unrecognizable except for a couple of file cabinets, littered the lawn, the air still acrid with the stench of burned wood, furnishings, carpeting. The ubiquitous crime scene tape marking the perimeter of the property made it resemble some sort of obscene gift.

The curious lingered in twos and threes on the sidewalk, subdued, faces mirroring their horror. A police car blocked the driveway, behind it one from the fire department. The only free parking spot was across the street and we jaywalked to get to the other side. Duck lifted the tape for me.

"You sure about this?" I asked.

"My district," he said tersely, as if that was all that was required.

I squatted, knees protesting, and scooted under the yellow ribbon, still a little nervous about it. He had a badge. I didn't. As far as the law was concerned, I was trespassing.

"Hey!" A broad-beamed cop in uniform rounded the house, scowling, the setting sun glinting off his glasses. "You two blind? Get back behind that tape."

"Hey, Masters." Duck smiled affably. "Just nosing around. How long have you been working days?"

"Duck! My man!" They shook hands, did the usual knuckle-to-knuckle nonsense. "Just started last week. Still not used to it either. This your lady? Seems to me I know you."

"Leigh Warren," I said, extending a hand.

"Oh, yeah. You used to work out of the Fourth. Haven't seen you in a while." His body language was now completely relaxed. After all, he was in the company of members of the brotherhood. Evidently Duck considered it prudent to keep to himself that technically, I no longer belonged. I wasn't about to correct him.

"How'd it start?" I asked. "It must have been one hell of a fire."

"Gas leak, they think. Blew furniture and stuff all over the neighborhood. Lucky there aren't any places closer by."

A gas leak. Duck and I exchanged wondering glances. He took my hand and squeezed it. Translation: button up, babe.

"I hear two bodies were found." His arm snaked around my shoulder. "ID them yet?"

"Nah, but most likely a couple of cooks. According to the owners, they had a brunch scheduled for today, so the lady who did most of the baking might have come in early. Their offices were on the second floor and all their records were destroyed. The owners are scrambling to dig up phone numbers for their employees. The last I heard, they had a few left to find."

"Large staff?" Duck asked.

"A dozen or so, mostly part-timers. They did a good business, though. A shame. Y'all excuse me," he said, his attention caught by a white paneled van pulling up behind the fire inspector's. "This here's one of the owners." He moved toward the new arrival with a flat-footed gait.

The man who climbed out of the van was on the short side but solid, with a caramel complexion and, I suspected, a plethora of deeply etched furrows in his face that hadn't been there the night before. His eyes were bloodshot, visible even from where we stood. Shoulders slumping, he hesitated, looking at the ruin his business had become, shook his head, and slammed the door of the van.

"Hey," Duck said, surprise plastered across his features. "I know that dude."

Big wow. The number of people in the District he didn't know would only fill a storefront church.

"Who is he?"

"Give me a minute. I'm working on it."

It took less time than that, thanks to the newcomer, who glanced without interest in our direction, looked away, then back again. "Kennedy?"

"Haskell!" Duck responded, striding toward him. "I didn't know you were back in town. My God, Beanie, this was your place?"

He blinked, his eyes filling. "Yeah. Aw, man, look at it. Just look at it! Goddamn!" He turned away, but Duck, at his side now, pulled the man into his arms. Haskell didn't resist, burying his face against Duck's shoulder. Masters, the cop, looked embarrassed, and retreated. I stayed put, knowing Haskell was in good hands.

In short order he pulled what had to be a linen napkin from a back pocket and wiped his eyes and nose, mumbling apologies. Duck murmured assurances, one arm still grasping Haskell's shoulder.

He looked back at me. "Give me a few minutes, okay, babe?"

I nodded. "Take your time. Unlock the car."

He aimed the remote at the Caddy and I crossed the street and got back in, watching as he and Haskell walked slowly up the driveway toward the charred remains of the house. They talked for a short while, Duck nodding at Haskell's replies, before disappearing in back of the ruin. Masters followed them, lagging far enough behind to give them privacy.

I reclined the seat a little and made myself comfortable with a pencil and notebook, jotting down thoughts, unanswered questions, and potential trails to explore given this new development. Having learned that our girl worked for Celebrations, we would have asked Marty or Jensen to act as a go-between to get the full name and address from the caterers, since I suspected that the owners would be more inclined to give it to the Jensens than to Duck or me.

That was no longer necessary. Duck would find out what we needed to know from Haskell. With his records up in ashes, Haskell might not remember Michelle's address, but he would surely remember her name. From there, Marty would find out where she lived. Like Plato, she could massage a database into giving her the precise moment of conception of Genghis Khan, if it existed anywhere.

I must have nodded off because a rap on the window jarred me awake. The locks released and Duck opened the doors on the driver's side. He was not alone.

"Sorry, babe," he said, getting in. "I didn't think I'd be this long."

Haskell slipped into the backseat. "My fault." He extended a hand. "Jim Haskell. Duck tells me you're The One. Pleased to meet you."

"Leigh Warren," I said, twisting to take his hand. "Likewise."

"I'm sorry about what happened back there. I saw old Duck and I couldn't help it, all the starch went out of my stiff upper lip."

"You're entitled," I assured him. "I'm sorry too. You had a good thing going, if the service at the Jensen wedding was any example. I hope you'll be able to recoup."

He sighed. "It's up to the wife. She worked so hard, put so much of herself into building the business. We'll see. Forget me for the moment. The Duck says one of my former employees has been giving you grief."

"Former?" Was she slipping through our fingers again?

"Oh, yes. I fired her ass. By the way, her name is Michelle Halls, plural. And anything I can do to help, just ask. If it wasn't for Brother Duck here, I'm not sure where I'd be now. He got me into the fraternity, loaned me enough money to pledge. And he kept me going while I was 'on line', hid me when I had a test so I could study without the brothers coming to get me."

"Beanie." Duck slouched under the wheel, looking embarrassed.

"Well, you did. You saved my hide more times than I can count. So how can I help?"

"Tell me about Michelle, for a start," I said.

"She's a very troubled woman. It's almost like she's got multiple personalities, a real sweetheart and charismatic one minute, a bitch on wheels the next. But she was also a dynamite waitress and my best bartender. She could charm anyone she was serving, but behind the kitchen door hard as hell to work with, snotty, talking down to coworkers as if they were beneath her. And untrustworthy. That's what finally did it for me."

"What happened?" I asked.

"People who turn over their kitchens, hell, their homes to us when we cater a dinner or party or whatever, have to be able to trust us, to know we won't abuse the privilege. Michelle broke the rules. She had to go."

"How long ago was that?" I asked.

He thought about it. "I'm not sure. If you'd asked me yesterday, I could have told you. Unfortunately, all my records are toast. We used the second floor for office space."

"Which, by the way, is where the fire may have started, babe," Duck said. "They found a trash can that looks suspicious."

"What about the gas leak?" I asked.

"I still haven't figured that out." Haskell yanked off his cap and scrubbed his fingers through his hair. "Jackie—that's my wife—and I, we had a nightly routine. Before we left, we checked all the burners to make sure they were off. The equipment was new; we'd just upgraded all the cooking surfaces and ovens, had Washington Gas come and check everything out. I'm here to tell you that every last knob was turned to off and there was no smell of gas or anything."

"Maybe one of the cooks turned it on," I ventured.

"They hadn't arrived, weren't coming in until six. The only people in the place before six would be the cleaners, and the kitchen wasn't their responsibility, just the second floor and the reception area on the first. Now they're dead." Heat flared in his eyes. "They were good people, hardworking. They didn't deserve this. Jackie's with their families now. We're gonna foot the bill for their funerals. In fact, one of them is . . . was a distant relation of Michelle's, a third or fourth cousin or something."

Which meant I had to erase one of the images that had slithered through my mind when we'd first arrived: Michelle skulking around inside Celebrations and for whatever reason, turning the knob on the oven and blowing the place to hell and gone. With a cousin right upstairs? That made it seem less likely. But then what did I know? My dad's cousin had killed him and my mom. So who was I to guess at the dynamics in Michelle's family?

"But Michelle definitely served at Jensen's wedding, right?" Duck asked.

"Yeah. That was one of her bad days. She was fine the first hour or so, then somebody must have done something or said something, I don't know. Anyhow, it rubbed her the wrong way. She couldn't seem to keep her mind on what she was supposed to be doing, spilled things, snapped at a guest. I had to pull her off the serving floor, keep her in the kitchen."

I processed that information and jumped, right or

wrong, to my own conclusion. "She saw me at the wedding! She couldn't have missed me, Duck, not after the way everyone toasted us and with Marty walking over and plopping her bouquet in my hands. Michelle must have remembered me, remembered how we met."

Duck swiveled in his seat. "That might have done it, lit her fuse. A fine actress—that's obviously how she sees herself—yet there she was, serving drinks and hors d'oeuvres."

Now that I thought of it, she was in a white uniform that day on Sixteenth Street. Oh, yeah, there was Plato's trigger all right. Seeing me at the wedding.

"Well, to give her credit," Haskell was saying, "according to my wife, Michelle is very talented. She went to a couple of her plays, sort of felt obligated to support her as a member of our staff, I guess. Jackie said you could have knocked her over with a feather, the woman's that good."

I'd already seen proof of that. "Do you remember where she lives?"

"Lord, no. She used to have a room in a house on Sixteenth, but got herself kicked out. She worked for us for a year and a half and had to move three times that I know of. Guess she was as hard to live with as she was to work with. But the job was perfect for her because she could work around auditions and plays she was in. If she hadn't been so good behind a bar, I'd have let her go long since. But once I caught her on a client's computer, I had no choice."

My gaze locked with Duck's. "How'd that happen?" I asked.

"Oh, yeah, babe, listen to this." Duck swiveled around, his back against the door.

"We were catering a fiftieth anniversary party at a place in Gaithersburg. Everything was going smooth as silk, folks having a good time. I notice Michelle's missing, figure she's in the john. I go to knock on the door to tell her to make it snappy because it's time to serve dessert. I pass the door of the manager's office and there's Michelle plunking away on his computer! Her ass was grass, gone. I let her stay until the party was over so she'd have a ride back here but that was the end of it."

I flipped through my notes. "Haskell—"

"Beanie," he corrected me with a sheepish grin. "Around my frat brothers, I prefer Beanie."

"You got it. Did you cater a party or anything at New Gospel in Mitchellville?"

"A wedding reception. Three hundred guests, hors d'oeuvres, Cornish hen with wild rice and baby peas," he recited. "Why?"

"I hate to tell you, but she used their computer, too, and one in some church here in the District. Saint—"

"Dammit!" Haskell exploded. "Ours too. I kept blaming Jackie, thought she'd left it on. Oh, my God. How'd you know?"

"She sent me hate e-mail, that's how, and a friend traced them for me." Which made me wonder if Michelle might have used the Celebrations computer to send the last three messages. If the cleaners had arrived before she could leave, would she have resorted to setting a fire to cause a diversion?

"Leigh, I'm so sorry." Haskell reached over the console to squeeze my arm. "I had no idea. Look, I'd better get back over there. The fire inspector's bound to wrap things up soon; it's getting too dark to see. Duck has my number. If there's anything else I can do, let me know. Duck, my brother, thanks for the shoulder. Keep in touch." He opened the door.

"Count on it," Duck said, getting out. They embraced again, went through the complicated handshake deal, and Haskell bounded back across the street, his steps slowing the closer he got to his ruined business.

"A nice guy," I said. "How'd he get the nickname?"

"Beans were all he could afford to eat back then. He put himself through college working as a fry cook. Once he moved into the frat house, he took over the kitchen. Swear to God, he could fix beans seven days a week and they'd never taste the same twice."

"And now his business is in ashes. Duck, I'm going to feel lower than snake shit if Michelle had anything to do with this. I'm already feeling guilty about Claudia. If I hadn't been so pigheaded about not letting Michelle go get her damned car that day—"

"Cut the bullshit." Duck reached over, squeezed my thigh. "What if you'd let her through and the block had gone up? You were doing your job. If she wasn't such a nutcase, she'd realize that."

"But she is and she doesn't. So what do we do now?"

"Nothing. Now that Beanie knows what's been going on, he'll ask the family of the cleaners if they know where Michelle is living now."

If he remembered. Under the circumstances, he just might forget. The end of this nightmare had seemed so near for a moment.

Duck's pager went off as we pulled into traffic. He checked it and swore. "That's Cap's number. Guess I'd better get back. Sorry about dinner, babe."

The apology was unnecessary. I knew how it worked. Duck reported to Captain Ray Moon, so when Cap Moon called you, you went.

"I'll survive," I said. "Maybe we can go out to dinner tomorrow night."

Speeding through a yellow light, he yanked one of my braids. "It's a deal. Where are you going now?"

"I don't know. I need to grab a sandwich or something and sit down and think." For some reason I had the feeling that I was rapidly running out of time.

We rode the rest of the way in silence, dealing with our own thoughts, Duck tempting fate a couple of times in his hurry to respond to Cap Moon's summons.

He screeched to a halt in front of the Sixth, and grabbed me for a quick kiss before scrambling out. "I'll make sure Evans and Thackery get the message about the name. You stay out of trouble," he warned me. "And lose the makeup and braids. They make me feel like I'm cheating on you." He sprinted for the entrance and was gone.

I got out and took his place behind the wheel, then sat there thinking until I realized I was double-parked. I drove around, trying to work out my next move. Waiting for Haskell to get an address for Michelle was impractical. He had too many other issues on his plate. There had to be things I could do in tandem with Thackery and Evans, or, if necessary, alone to find her.

By the time I skirted the Capitol, I'd decided on the sweet and simple. And tedious. It meant settling down with a phone. And perhaps a few slices of Heavenly Ham on sourdough bread with lettuce, tomato, and mayo. No perhaps about it. Thank God Duck was a firm believer in keeping the refrigerator stocked. It was just as well. I hated shopping in general and grocery shopping in particular.

"Home, James," I muttered, and searched until I found a radio station playing Christmas carols. Michelle had tried to ruin my wedding. I'd be damned if I'd let her ruin Christmas for me, too.

Back in Southwest again, I circled the block a couple of times checking for her tan compact, but didn't see it. I checked the underground garage. No elderly Honda. The coast looked clear.

Bypassing the elevator, I took the stairs, removing my shoes halfway up. Duck would have to check for any mail. I was not up to facing the Gang of Four in this getup, even though Mrs. Luby had probably told them about our earlier meeting.

Wig discarded and sandwich made, I brought the District's phone book into the kitchen and planted myself at the kitchen table. Humming with pleasure as I demolished my late lunch, I flipped through the white pages to the Hallses and moaned. For some idiotic reason, I'd assumed there wouldn't be all that many since Hall singular was much more common. Feeling masochistic, I counted them. Seventeen of them. No Michelle Halls, of course. Sighing, I began to dial, trying the M. Halls first, just in case. If she'd had a phone recently, perhaps there was a referral to her new number.

Nix. Several no answers, a couple of voice mails and answering machines. I left messages and went back to the A's.

All things considered, I lucked out. I hit pay dirt with the twelfth Halls on Alabama Avenue, Southeast.

The phone was answered by a juvenile, whether male or female I couldn't tell.

"I'm trying to reach Michelle," I said, jaded by now and anticipating a "No Michelle here" at best or an oath followed by a dial tone. I got neither.

"Shelly don't live here anymore."

I sat up, almost dropping the glass of water in my hand. "Uh, do you know how I can reach her?"

"Uh-uh. Ma!" he/she yelled in my ear. "Somebody's looking for Shelly! It's a lady."

There was an unintelligible response from some distance away.

"I already told her. She—"

"Look, honey," I interrupted, "may I speak to your mother?"

"Okay. Ma, she wants you!" The phone was dropped, the sound assaulting my eardrum.

A muffled oath from a clearly annoyed woman filtered through the line, then heavy footsteps.

"Yes? My son told you the truth. Shelly doesn't live here any more, so I'm sorry if she's late paying you but—"

"Oh, it's nothing like that," I said, hurrying to assure her. "I just need to get in touch with her, but I lost track of her after she left Celebrations. Is there a phone number or an address where I can reach her?"

"What do you mean, she left Celebrations? She quit that job?"

Obviously this branch of the family hadn't heard about the fire. "Yes, a few weeks ago. Do you—"

"I swear to God!" If she'd been annoyed before, she was well beyond that now. "I don't know what's the matter with that fool girl! Have you talked to her recently?"

"Well, yes, I have," I responded, relieved to be able to answer truthfully. "Just last night. But it was a short conversation and I didn't get a chance to ask her for a phone number. I'm sorry to bother you, but it occurred to me I might be able to get it from you."

She snorted. "Are you kidding? We haven't heard from her in months and don't know where she's living now. You'd think she'd try to keep in touch with family but no, not Shelly. We're not good enough for her, don't understand the creative temperament, whatever the hell that is. Don't get me wrong, miss, we love Shelly but it's hard work. I already got two jobs, I don't need me another one. You see what I'm saying?"

I hadn't expected her to be so forthcoming but there was no mistaking her exasperation. This warranted a fishing expedition.

"I understand completely. Michelle can be ... difficult."

"Difficult? That's a nice way to put it. Have you known her long?"

"Well, since spring. March, I think."

"That's probably longer than most folks put up with her. I mean, as smart as she is and what does she want to be? An actress. How many black women you know make any kind of living as an actress? Even if she's talented, and I hear she is, there's still things like rent and gas and food. Them things take money, you see what I'm saying? I wasn't asking for much, way less than I'd charge a stranger for room and board, but I've got kids to feed and upkeep on this place. It ain't much but it's all I've got. She had to go."

The light dawned. This woman was on the defensive, running on out of guilt.

"We've got to pinch pennies and there she is, burning lights all night studying her lines, she called it, even when she wasn't in a play or anything. Taking showers two and three times a day, running up my water and utilities bills. When she hit my baby for poking around in the makeup kit she left in the bathroom, well, that was it. Nobody hits my young'uns but me. She had to go."

"I'd have reacted the same way," I assured her, wondering how much more I could learn without giving myself away. "I have to be honest, Ms. Halls. I worry about her. The last time I talked to her she didn't sound quite . . . well, rational."

She grunted. "What's your name again?"

I didn't point out that she hadn't asked before and I certainly hadn't volunteered it. "Ann Warren." So I left off the "Leigh." Sue me.

"Well, Miss Warren, if you're trying to find a polite way to say Shelly sounded crazy, don't bother. She is, always has been. Came by it honestly; her mother was just as batty. The family's done all we can by her, both sides. Counseling, therapy, medications. She'll start out keeping the appointments and taking the pills and then stop. Says there's nothing wrong with her, so what can we do? She's a grown woman. Look, Miss Warren, I've got to get a load out of the dryer before it wrinkles up. I wish I could help you but I can't. For all I know, Shelly may be living out of her car, she's done it before instead of a shelter where at least she'd have a proper bed. The only other place she might be is that cheap hotel she checks into when she's between places to live."

"A hotel? Do you know which one?" The District has its share of flophouses, but I couldn't imagine anyone staying in them voluntarily.

"I don't remember. It's got a funny name. Made me think of a bird singing. Whatever it's called, it's one of her old stomping grounds. If you catch up with her, ask her to call her folks, let us know she's alive, okay?"

"I'll do that. Thanks for talking to me."

"Any time," she said and hung up.

A hotel named after a singing bird? I grabbed the Yellow Pages. There were dozens of hotels listed, not just those in the District but in suburban Maryland and northern Virginia as well. Most could be eliminated at a glance since by no stretch of the imagination could they remind anyone of a bird, singing or not. And I doubted Michelle would go too far afield. She'd probably stay within the city limits.

The A's yielded nothing, neither did the B's. In fact the whole alphabet seemed to be a washout. Only two came close, but I knew the Phoenix Park and the Swann House. It wasn't likely Michelle would be able to afford either of them.

I started at the beginning again, becoming more and more frustrated. The place might not even exist any longer. And if she avoided the District's shelters, I was sunk.

At the T's again, my finger hesitated. The Trilby? I was fairly certain a trilby was a hat but someone who didn't know . . .

My pulse accelerated. I could almost envision the place. A cross between a hooker's rent-by-the-hour and a last resort, the next stop being a grate on a street somewhere, the Trilby had practically been a nightly stop when I'd worked out of the Fourth District. Fistfights were routine, along with overdoses. If Michelle had been reduced to the Trilby, she was indeed near the end of her rope.

I wondered if I'd be wasting my time calling there; keeping up with its transient population had to be a daunting task. Still, it couldn't hurt to try.

"Trilby-Hotel-how-can-I-direct-your-call?" All one word from a distinctly uninterested voice.

Fingers crossed, I said, "Michelle Halls in three-oh-four, please."

There was a pause. "It's two-oh-five, not three-oh-four. Hold, please."

Flabbergasted, I dropped the phone. I'd found her.

19

I WAS STILL GLOATING, MY HAND ON THE phone when it rang, and I jumped two feet, my first thought being, *Dammit, it's her!* I answered with a snarl. "Yeah?"

"Jeez, babe, what put the burr up your butt? And who have you been talking to? I've been trying to get you for an hour."

"Duck! I found her!"

"Who, honey?"

"Michelle. She's at the Trilby Hotel. I even have her room number, two-oh-five."

"Good work, babe. Beauty and brains. I'm a lucky man. Call Evans and Thackery and let them know. By the way, I just got off the phone with Beanie. The fire did start on the second floor, something smoldering in a trash can. And before you say it, it wasn't a cigarette. The cleaners didn't smoke. It gets more interesting. They found a front panel of one of the ovens. It had been blown into the backyard. One knob was turned all the way to the highest setting. They'll be checking to see if there are any prints that don't belong on it. Look, that's not why I called. Shields and I have to make a quick trip to Seattle."

"Washington?"

"Gotta pick up Valeria Preston. How's that for irony? Turns out she has a stepsister who lives in the suburbs and she's been hiding out there since she shot Vince. The stepfamily had no idea she was wanted. The fool woman ran a red light with a joint burning in the ashtray, can you believe it? That's how they got her."

I sulked for a couple of seconds. Of our two nights under the same roof, we'd slept through the first and I'd spent the second on the couch. We were overdue for some togetherness. But this was his job, and Preston had eluded D.C. for a long time.

"Do you need me to pack a bag for you?" I asked. Might as well get into a wifely mode now.

"Already have one here ready to go. You know me, always prepared. I just wanted you to know I wouldn't be home tonight. With luck, I'll be back by tomorrow night. At worst we'll have to take a red-eye. I'll keep you posted. Gotta run, babe. Stay out of trouble. Love ya."

He was gone before I could respond, wise of him since I'd have asked what the hell he meant, stay out of trouble. It was the second time he'd said that.

I dug out Thackery's card and called him, still preferring to talk to him rather than Evans. Not that it mattered; neither was in. Feeling cheated, I left a message regarding Michelle's current whereabouts and did the same for Willard.

At loose ends and feeling appropriately bereft, I divested myself of all the stuffing, putting it in a trash bag for safekeeping, since I'd probably have to use it again if I went out. Next came all the glop on my face, although I couldn't bring myself to get rid of the awnings quite yet. My own lashes were short and stubby, and I'd spent my whole life envious of Duck and everyone else with long ones. I *liked* the way I looked with them. And heck, I'd be alone on this Saturday night. Who else would see them?

I was out of sorts, fidgety, or, as Nunna would say, suffering from a case of the move-arounds. I couldn't sit still, needed something to do. I turned on the television and stumbled onto one of my favorites, *A Christmas Story*, which kept me occupied for a while. By the time it ended and Ralphie had his Red Ryder BB gun, I had a bee in my bonnet: I wanted a Christmas tree.

There'd been no decorations up at Janeece's; she stuck to her family's tradition of waiting until Christmas Eve to put up a tree. I usually went slightly nuts, decking my halls with tree plus greenery, mistletoe, a crêche, ceramic Santas, stockings hung from a snowflake-sprayed windowsill, the whole bit, a holdover of my Christmases in Nunna's loving care.

The subject of decorating hadn't come up with Duck; we'd been preoccupied with other things. Even though we'd be going somewhere the day after Christmas, I could at least enjoy symbols of the season until we left. Considering all the chaos I'd lived through, especially this week, reminders of what this season represented would be more than welcome. I hoped Duck wouldn't mind.

My four-foot Douglas fir had a box of its own in the guest room, all the decorations in another. Energized, I dug them out, cleared a lamp table to use as a base, and began putting the tree together. Padding around in my underwear singing carols at the top of my voice, I had the lights strung and had started unpacking the ornaments and icicles when the phone rang yet again. This time I had the good sense to wait and check the caller ID before answering.

"Me," Tina said. She sounded odd, as if her nose was stopped up. I could swear she'd been crying, which boggled the mind. Tina and tears seemed mutually exclusive.

Guilt filtered through my head. I should have called her with the latest news. "Tina, guess what. We got her!"

"What do you mean, you got her? They picked her up?"

"No, no. We know her name now. And—"

"What is it?"

"Michelle Halls, with an S. We got her name from the owner of the firm that catered Jensen's wedding. She served at Jensen's wedding, Tina."

"What? *What?*" she screeched in my ear. "She was walking around in the same room with us for three hours?"

"Yes, but she hadn't done anything then. I think she saw me and remembered how we'd met. It set her off. After I got home tonight I went through the phone book and called all the Hallses and lucked out on someone in her family. She told me where Michelle might be. Turns out she's at the Trilby Hotel. I called and sure enough, she's registered. Room two-oh-five. I left a message for Thackery and Evans, so they'll probably pull her in tomorrow."

"That's not good enough, dammit. She doesn't deserve another single night of freedom. Her ass needs to be behind bars *now*! Not tomorrow, not the next day. *Now!* I'm not waiting. I'll talk to you later."

"Wait a minute, Tina." A bead of sweat trickled down my spine. "What do you mean, you're not waiting?"

"I'm a cop, right? Cops arrest people. That's what we do. I gotta go." She did, leaving me gaping at a phone with no one on the other end.

I had my finger poised to try to get her back when it rang, startling me. I didn't recognize the number in the caller ID display but answered anyway. "Yes?"

"Leigh," Tank said loudly, voices yelling in the background, "do me a favor, okay? Talk to Tina, calm her down. She's really upset. Her contact at the medical examiner called her, probably on the Q.T., and told her Miss Claudia died of anaphylactic shock. She had allergies up the wazoo and evidently the bitch exposed her to something that killed her. Tina freaked."

"Oh, my God. I didn't know. Tank, she just called me. I told her we'd finally found the woman's name and where she's staying. Tina's on her way there."

"Shit, shit, shit!! Leigh, you've got to stop her. She's mad and when Tina gets mad . . ."

"I think she just intends to pick her up and bring her in. At least that's the impression I got."

"That may be what she told you, but there's no guarantee that if she gets her hands on this woman, she won't lose it. She was very protective of Miss Claudia because she was such a dingbat. Please, Leigh, go after her. I'd do it but I can't leave here. Things look like they're about to get out of hand and I've gotta get off this phone. Stop her, Leigh. Please."

"Okay. I'll try. Stay safe, Tank."

I slammed down the receiver and scrambled to get some clothes on. There was no time to restuff myself; the wig would have to do. I secured it on my head; grabbed my coat, purse, and keys; and hot-footed it out of there.

December chill or no, the usual Saturday evening foot traffic was out and about along the Fourteenth Street corridor. I barreled toward U Street, marveling at the impact the Metro stop had made on the area that had remained a blight for so long after the riots in 1968. The neighborhood still wasn't quite the vibrant soul of the community it used to be, at least according to the old-timers, but its revitalization was on its way. The scars were healing.

I worked my way over to Tenth, wondering belatedly where to risk parking Janeece's Caddy. If it wound up with so much as a scratch, our friendship would be history.

I needn't have worried. Pelrose Street, an afterthought between Ninth and Tenth and almost impossible to find on a District map, was completely blocked off, cruisers slewed in the intersections, chase lights painting swaths of color across the faces of nearby rowhouses and apartment buildings. I backed into a vacant spot one car removed from the corner and got out, joining a clutch of neighbors huddled near the rear of the closest police car.

"What's going on?" I asked.

"Drug raid in the Trilby," someone responded. "Second one this month. Don't know why they don't close the place down. At least there was no gunfire this time."

I tried to locate the speaker but couldn't. "Did they evacuate the place?" I asked.

"Dunno. Sometimes they do, sometimes they don't."

I moved to the far corner to get a better view of the hotel, at the other end of the block. It was even seedier than I remembered, most lights in the sign above the entrance missing, duct tape decorating a number of windows, screens escaping their frames. At some point in its history, its brick facade had been painted white. It had long since begun to peel, the exterior fairly scabrous now.

It appeared that the excitement was almost over. A police van was leaving. People who'd been sitting on their front steps to watch stood and stretched before retreating behind their barred front doors. Groups huddled all along the block began to stir, a diverse crowd that appeared to include a number of the homeless, if the assortment of shopping carts overflowing with trash bags was any clue.

There weren't many cars along the street. I checked for the Explorer but didn't see it. If Tina had driven her own car, I was stumped since I couldn't remember what model it was; I'd only seen it once and that had been a while ago. I didn't see her either, but as small as she was, she would be practically invisible in a crowd of more than five or six regular-sized adults.

I ambled toward the hotel, keeping to the other side of the street, to take a visual census of various groupings. I still didn't see her. It didn't matter. She saw me.

"Holy shit," she said from behind me. "Who are you supposed to be?"

I whirled around, more than a little perturbed that she'd managed to sneak up on me. "Anybody but me, only it turns out that I look like Michelle in this get-up. Tank sent me after you. You didn't tell me you'd gotten the results of the autopsy."

"You didn't tell me you'd found out the bitch's name until I called you," she said, her eyes glittering dangerously. "So we're even."

I had to concede that point. "I take it you haven't seen her."

"I was about to ring the bell—you can't just walk in there—when I saw the cruisers pull into the intersections. As soon as Jamie Crowder got out of one of them, I knew what was up. Nothing I could do but get the hell out of the way and wait. I hadn't counted on that."

"It's just as well," I said. "Look, Tina, there's nothing you can do here. Michelle hasn't been charged with anything yet, at least as far as we know. Taking her in would be jumping the gun. Let's go home and let Evans and Thackery, or Willard for that matter, do their jobs."

"She's a fucking murderer," Tina said, with heat. "And she knows it. You think she's gonna sit around with her thumbs up her ass waiting for them to come get her? Or that I'm gonna hang around with my thumb up mine and watch her go underground? Not gonna happen. She killed Aunt Sis! I'm not gonna let her get away with it!" She spun away and marched toward the door of the Trilby.

"Damn it, Tina!" I trotted after her and caught up with her as she reached for the doorbell.

The door opened before she had the chance, and a cop in uniform stepped out, in the middle of a conversation with a grizzled man in a shiny black suit.

"—should be done in that room in a few hours," the cop was saying. "Sorry about the lock, but they should have opened up when we knocked. Jones," he greeted Tina. "Long time no see. How's Tank?"

"Hanging in," she said with a tight grin and squeezed past him.

"Back already, Ms. Halls?" Mr. Shiny Suit held the door open for me and stepped outside to join the cop.

Tina turned around and stared at me. "He thought you were Michelle? Hot damn!" She grabbed my sleeve. "Come on. We'll take the stairs."

"And do what?" I hissed at her as she tugged me across the lobby. Fortunately, the front desk was unattended. "I'm not going to hang around while you pick her lock, if that's what you've got in mind."

"Oh, hush! All I'm gonna do is knock on her door, see if she's in. If she isn't, I'll look for a place to squat until she gets back. I remember lots of nooks and crannies. Jesus, this place stinks!"

She meant the stairwell, and I'd have agreed but thought it more prudent to keep my mouth shut and hold my breath as long as I could, not an easy feat when you're climbing steps. The walls looked diseased, with suspicious stains in the corners of the landings. The lighter ones were urine. I decided not to think about the darker ones.

Tina pulled open the fire door of the second floor and peeked up and down the hall. "All clear. Let's move it."

I was torn between towing her back down the stairs or leaving her to her own devices. Before I'd made up my mind, she was knocking on 205. I stayed put, waiting to see if Michelle answered. If she did, I'd decide what to do from there. Nothing would give me greater pleasure than confronting her and, given the slightest excuse, punching her lights out. It would almost be worth a charge of assault and battery.

My luck held, or Michelle's did, depending on your point of view. She didn't answer.

"Psst." Tina beckoned frantically. "Come on! We can hole up in the room where the ice machine used to be."

I'd been in the Trilby a number of times, responding to fights or noisy guests, but was nowhere as knowledgeable as Tina about its floor plans. "How come you know this place so intimately?" I asked as I joined her in front of 205.

I got a shadow of her more usual impish grin. "I used to work Vice, spent a lot of hours in these rooms as bait. It's just around here," she said, jerking her head toward the juncture of the L-shaped wing.

The words were barely out of her mouth when a housekeeper rounded the corner pushing a linen-laden cart and muttering under her breath. "Damned cops gonna leave a mess and who's supposed to clean it up? Me, that's who. As if I ain't got—" She looked up, saw us, and frowned. "You done locked yourself out again? Girl, you are hopeless." She trudged toward us, pulling an enormous key ring from the pocket of her apron.

"Oh," I said, realizing her mistake. "Sorry, but I'm not—" Tina stomped on my arch. "Ow!" I hopped away. "Dammit, Tina!"

"Sorry," she said, glibly, as I limped to the opposite wall. I leaned against it, using one hand for balance, flexing my foot, wiggling my toes. She'd gotten me good.

"What was going on with all the police out there?" Tina asked the housekeeper, so she wouldn't focus on me, I assume. The woman seemed tired and frazzled at all the to-do. The light level in the hall was low, but given one good look at me, she'd see that I was not Michelle.

"Damned druggies," she grumbled, unlocking the door. "They get in a room and shoot up or smoke that crack stuff or pot, stink up everything, make a mess. Somebody will tell security and security calls the cops, and by the time it's all over, the room's even a bigger mess. Oh!" I looked up just as Tina slipped a bill into the woman's hand. "No need for that, but I thank you. Y'all have a good evening." She shuffled back to her cart.

Tina reached over and snatched me into the room.

I turned around immediately and retreated to the hall. "No," I said. "Do the words 'illegal search and seizure' mean anything to you, Tina? Or 'trespassing'?"

She set her jaw. "Just chill, will you? I'm not gonna touch a thing, just look around. Jesus, what a pig she is."

That was an understatement. The room itself was nothing to write home about, assuming you had a home. Stained walls seemed to be part of the Trilby's decor. The drapery drooped, some of the hooks missing. I couldn't describe the color of the carpeting for love or money, and the queen-sized bed sagged in the middle like a spavined horse.

A dresser served as a TV stand, its top marred by scratches and rings left by years of water glasses. A single chair and a desk completed the furnishings. The room smelled of smoke and mildew.

Michelle's contribution to the sad scene was chaos. Clothes and shoes were strewn everywhere, across the bed, the chair, the dresser. A pair of suitcases sat open in the corner, more clothing spilling out of them. There was a closet behind the door but perhaps there were no hangers. I couldn't see into the bathroom and was grateful for small favors.

The only sign of order was the books lined up along one end of the desk, a stack of three-ring binders and scraps of paper in the middle, and the array of theatrical makeup on the other end. A hatbox sat under the window, a long, ebony braid sneaking from beneath the top like a snake escaping confinement. The Georgia Keith wig, perhaps?

Tina, working her way around the room, hands clasped behind her back, focused on several well-stuffed shopping bags atop the pillows on the bed. "Our girl's been spending money." Her brows hitched in surprise as she read the name printed on the bags. "Salina's? I can't afford Salina's. How can she?"

I didn't respond, knowing how well voices reverberated in hallways. The housekeeper might come back at any moment.

Tina continued her tour, nudging shoes and boots out of her way. "Wigs," she said, indicating the hatbox. She perused the titles of Michelle's mini-library. "Plays, textbooks on acting." Moving on to the binders, she wiggled her fingers. "Boy, I'd love to open those."

"Tina, that's enough. Come on!" I didn't like this at all.

"I'm coming," she said, waving me off as she peered at the pile of papers on top of the binders. "Jesus Christ! This is a receipt. She paid two twenty-nine ninety-nine for a sweater! Can you imagine? I—" She stopped, emitted a sound somewhere between a shriek and a hiccup. "Leigh, your name is on this!"

"What?" I stepped over the threshold.

"This receipt's from Salina's. She charged the sweater. Looks like the store's card instead of a bank card. She signed your name."

Illegal entry or not—and there was still some debate about that—I had to see this for myself. I joined Tina at the desk. There it was, Leigh A. Warren on the signature line. She'd used whatever information she'd needed from the box containing my tax records, receipts kept for items under warranty, personal stuff. No wonder I'd been receiving sales brochures from Salina's.

Clever girl, our Michelle. She'd been smart enough not to apply for a Visa or MasterCard in my name. That would have required a wait to receive it in the mail. With no permanent address, that would be a problem for her. But a credit card from a store was a different matter, especially during a sales promotion the day after Thanksgiving when merchandise could be bought at a discount if one opened an account on the spot.

And a false ID, driver's license or whatever, would be easy enough for her to obtain. We'd closed down open markets for them a number of times, only to have them set up business in the next block. How many other stores had she hit?

Rage bubbled in my veins. I'd been so careful of my use of credit over the years. Michelle could have destroyed my credit rating in a matter of days. She was now a felon in more ways than one. Unfortunately, I'd have to use other means to prove it. I couldn't take the receipt. It would place us in this room.

"All right, Tina, you stay if you want, but I'm out of here," I said, turning to leave. My glance swept past the pile on her bed, shopping bags, boxes. I stopped, finding one of them heartbreakingly familiar, the pink and white logo of the Bridal Bower angled across the sides. My wedding outfit. And I couldn't touch it. I mean, I could, but I couldn't. I wasn't supposed to be here. I wanted to scream.

I stalked back out into the hall. "I'll deal with this, believe me. She's on her way to jail, but I have no intention of going with her."

I left Tina, mad as hell at Michelle for what she'd done, mad at seeing that box and being unable to take it. I was just as angry at myself and Tina for sinking to Michelle's level by pulling the same trick she had in gaining entry to Duck's apartment under false pretenses. Michelle had taken advantage of Claudia. We'd done no less to the housekeeper. I felt dirty and angry and conflicted. Perhaps I didn't deserve to be a cop.

I'd reached the sidewalk before Tina caught up with me. I strode toward Ninth and the Cadillac, relieved to see that the cruiser was still there. That lessened the chances that someone would risk tampering with Janeece's baby.

"Where are you going?" Tina asked, walking

double-time to keep up with me, my legs, gimpy knee notwithstanding, being considerably longer than hers.

"Home to take a bath because I feel so damned dirty. Then I'm gonna hunt up the info on the credit bureaus and hope they're available twenty-four seven. God, Tina!" I stopped, wheeling to face her. "We had no business up there! We're cops! Employed or not, I'm still one in my blood. It was wrong, illegal! I saw the box from Bridal Bower back there, big as life on her bed, and I couldn't just grab it and bring it with me. Why? Because it would have been illegal!"

She nodded, looked away. "I know. I saw it and was hoping you wouldn't. I'm sorry. I've never done anything like this before, I swear. It's just that after I found out about Aunt Sis, how she died . . ." She swallowed, her eyes filling. If she was faking, she was damned good at it.

"Did you take that receipt?" She shook her head. "Did you touch anything after I left?"

"No. And I used my elbow on the doorknob to pull it closed. I want her, Leigh, so bad I can taste it. I—"

I grabbed her arm. "Shut up and look." Approaching on foot from Tenth were two familiar figures: Evans and Thackery heading for the Trilby. "We've got to get away from here." I started for the car again.

"Why?" Tina demanded, tugging at my sleeve. "Let's go back and— "

"And what? Tell them we just happened to be in the neighborhood? Where's your car?"

"On Tenth, near T Street."

"I'll drive you," I said, hustling her toward the intersection.

The uniform in the cruiser eyed us with suspicion as we hurried past. My heart executed a somersault when

KILLER CHAMELEON ◆ 303

he opened the door and got out. "Hey, Jones, is that you?"

"Oh, hell!" Tina muttered. She slowed, then detoured to greet him. "Yeah, it's me. How's it going, Bucky?"

I left her to deal with him, hoping she'd come up with a credible reason for being in the area.

The Cadillac seemed to be untouched but I checked all sides, just in case. And since Tina would be looking for my car, I leaned against the passenger door to wait for her.

The conversation lasted far longer than I thought necessary, but she finally backed away from him and turned to see where I'd parked.

"What did you tell him?" I asked, unlocking the doors.

"That I have a relative who lives in the area. It's not a lie; Uncle Boo's house is a couple of blocks away. This is new," she announced, smoothing the leather seat. "Don't tell me you went out and bought this because of the spray paint on the other one."

"Janeece's," I said, getting in, "so Michelle wouldn't be able to tell when I was coming or going. Call your husband and let him know there'll be no warrant out for you for assault and battery. I strongly suggest that's all you tell him too."

She winced and buckled up. "Right. I'm really sorry, okay?"

Her conversation with Tank lasted long enough for me to work my way over to Tenth. Her car, a black Taurus, had evidently been protected by the same circumstances mine had; two cruisers were double-parked midway on the block, there on business unrelated to the raid on the Trilby.

Tina apologized again and got out. I stayed put until

she was in the Taurus and pulling into traffic. From that point, she was on her own, and I plotted my route back to Southwest D.C., stopping once to fill up in case Janeece wanted her car back tomorrow, and again at a supermarket to pick up some fruit, creamer for coffee, and snack food.

The phone was ringing as I unlocked the door of the condo. I hurried to answer it, momentarily brought up short at the sight of the Christmas tree. I'd forgotten all about it. It felt as if I'd been gone for days. And the message light on the answering machine was blinking, but that would have to wait.

"Ms. Warren?" It took me a moment before I attached the name to the voice. Evans.

"Yes. Did you get my message?" I asked disingenuously, and feeling like two cents.

"I did. I'd appreciate knowing how you came by the information you left for us." He didn't sound all that appreciative.

I launched into my explanation, beginning with running into Lopez outside the Sixth District station, through my tromp through the Hallses in the phone book.

"I see." Evans's tone was still dry. "And it didn't occur to you to simply pass along the information about Ms. Halls's possible whereabouts and leave it to us to track her down."

Peeling out of my coat, I tried to figure out why he sounded so pissed off. "No, I guess it didn't. I was so excited that I simply took a chance and called the Trilby Hotel. Why? What difference does it make?"

"Well, for your edification, Ms. Halls has definitely been implicated in the death of Ms. Hitchcock. Thack and I went to bring her in, but she wasn't there. Narcotics pulled a raid tonight. Thack's trying to pin down the time they cleared the building because the manager and one of the cleaning ladies saw her after that."

I crossed my fingers. "Oh?"

"Yeah. Her room was enlightening. It looks like she's engaged in some identity theft along with everything else, so she's now committed a federal crime. I'll fill you in on that later."

"Please do," I said, hoping my sarcasm hadn't bled through.

"Anyway, sometime between our setting up surveillance at both entrances to wait for her, she returned to her room. There's a possibility she was in the building all the time. Thack went back in to ask the house dick a question. The desk clerk heard us talking about her and said she had gone by the front desk not long before. He was working a split shift and had just come back to work. When he mentioned to her that he'd taken a call for her earlier, she took off upstairs like a cat with its tail on fire, as the desk clerk so wittily put it. We checked her room again and she'd definitely been there."

"How do you know?"

"There were things missing we'd seen the first time security let us in, that's how. My point is, if you had left it to us, we might have caught her. But because you called, now she knows someone has tracked her down. I warned you to let us do our jobs, Ms. Warren. I'm repeating it now. Any more interference from you and I'll haul you in for obstruction of justice. Am I clear?"

"Perfectly," I said and slammed down the phone.

I wasn't fooled. Granted, I'd made a mistake calling the Trilby, which, thank God, was the only infringement he was aware of, at least for the moment. But he was also pissed because she'd been right on the premises and had managed to give them the slip.

I took little comfort in that. Michelle was still out there. And until she was behind bars, my troubles weren't over, not by a long shot.

20

I ADMIT TO GREETING SUNDAY MORNING IN A less than positive frame of mind, perhaps because the previous night had been such a downer. After my chewing out by Evans, I'd checked the messages on the answering machine. There were two, the first from Duck.

Hi, babe, and where are you, I wonder? Just letting you know that I probably won't be home until Tuesday. Preston has a bug, one of those twenty-four-hour viruses—sound familiar? Anyway, we can't leave until she's over it. I'll make it up to you. Talk to you tomorrow. Love ya.

I growled, erased it, and went on to the second message.

Hi, Ms. Warren, this is Sunny. At Arena? Sorry I couldn't get back to you sooner. About the lady in the pictures you left, her name is Shelly Halls and she was the understudy for the role of Georgia Keith in last season's production of August Flames, *only she got kicked out of the cast because they think she doctored the coffee of the actress playing the role so she could go on instead. It didn't work because Celia got her stom-*

ach pumped and made it back in time. Hope that helps.
Say hello to Beverly Barlowe for me. Tell her I'm a big
fan. Bye.

The information was superfluous but, if nothing
else, reinforced the lengths to which Michelle would
go to get what she wanted. And she was out there
somewhere plotting her next move, her goal: to get rid
of me for keeping her from the audition that she was
certain would have been her big break. Given her single-
mindedness, I was not encouraged.

I was still in jammies, face yet unwashed and toothbrush in my mouth when I heard the kind of knock on
the door that did not bode well. I can't explain it but
there's something about the sound that's different
when it's a cop on the other side of the door.

I slithered to the peephole and groaned. Evans and
Thackery. I yelled at them to hold their horses and let
them wait until I'd gotten rid of the toothbrush, pulled
on a robe, and scrunched my hair into a semblance of
order.

"Sorry to disturb you so early," Evans said, coming
in. I didn't believe him for a minute.

"Nice tree." Thackery scrutinized it as if he'd never
seen one before.

"It isn't finished," I said, gesturing for them to sit.
"I'd offer coffee but—"

"No, thanks. This won't take long, but we wanted to
give you the word personally." Evans perched on the
edge of the couch, leaving the impression that a relaxed
position would be inappropriate. "We got Halls's prints
off a glass the housekeeper had just removed from her
room at the Trilby. They match a set on the trunk of
your old car, and on one of the knobs on an oven—"

"At Celebrations?" I blurted. "So she *was* there!"

"Yes. By the way, the cell phone she's been using was stolen from one of Celebrations' waiters weeks ago. But she's wanted for murder and arson now. The thing is, Ms. Warren, after last night she knows we're after her."

"You already told me that," I said, irritated that he felt he had to rub salt into my wounds.

"It bears repeating. She's a cold-blooded killer even though Ms. Hitchcock's death may have been unintentional; turns out she was allergic to latex."

"Latex? Like in gloves?"

"Among other things. Evidently it's a cumulative thing. In her case, it was probably a result of her years working with her family's cleaning service. She wore one of those bracelets with a warning on it but Halls didn't notice it, and she obviously wore gloves because there was cornstarch and latex particles on the victim's scarf. Looks like she might have been gagged with it and inhaled the particles, which caused anaphylactic shock. Without immediate treatment, she was a goner."

My God. Poor Claudia.

"But the two poor working stiffs at Celebrations, pardon the pun, were already dead when the place went up, one from blunt-force trauma, the other from multiple stab wounds."

Wow. She'd do that to a cousin?

"The rest," Thackery took over for Evans, "the smoldering rags in the wastebaskets and the gas, was an attempt to cover her tracks. She assumed the bodies would be so badly burned that the fire and explosion would camouflage the cause of death. It might have if they hadn't been blown into the backyard."

That didn't make sense to me, given the second

floor's charred interior. "But the offices were gutted."

"In spades," Evans said, dryly. "She left one wastebasket smoldering upstairs and a second one somewhere in the kitchen. The one downstairs triggered the explosion once the gas had been on long enough and in the process, blew the contents of the wastebasket upstairs through the ceiling."

"Which ignited the insulation," Thackery clarified. "But by then, the bodies of the cleaners were already outside."

"Lordy." I slumped in my chair, imagining the horror of it.

They let me do that for a moment, before revealing the main reason for this wake-up call.

"Now, Ms. Warren." Evans sat up even straighter and fixed me with a stern gaze. "I repeat, we're dealing with a cold-blooded killer, one with nothing to lose. And your experience as a cop notwithstanding, we're officially warning you to butt out and let us do our jobs. We'll even go so far, unofficially, as to ask you to make yourself scarce. Go somewhere, the farther away the better."

"Excuse me?" I wondered if Duck had put them up to this.

Thackery leaned forward for emphasis, elbows on his knees, big hands clasped. I was surprised to notice that he was a nail chewer. "We don't have the manpower to give you round-the-clock protection; our resources are spread about as thin as they can get. Increasing patrols through the area is possible but probably not all that effective, since we can never be sure what Halls looks like at any given time. So it would be a load off our shoulders if you'd go underground. Someone mentioned you have family in North Carolina."

There was no point in wondering who that someone might be. Duck was in for it.

"I do have family there," I said, "but you forget, Michelle's been through that box of my personal papers, which includes cards and letters from my foster mother. No way will I expose her to Michelle's lunacy by going down home. And before I forget, do you mind explaining that little gem you dropped into the conversation with me last night, the one where you used identity theft and federal crime in the same sentence? I assume you weren't referring to such mundane capers as her posing as me in order to steal my wedding suit and cancel our honeymoon reservations."

He grimaced, but he'd muddied the waters himself. It was obvious he considered this element of the case a nuisance. His focus was the homicides. So he told me what I already knew, that Michelle had had a field day in Salina's at my expense, along with a couple of other stores at which she'd opened accounts. I had started working on that last night, courtesy of the Web. Following through was at the top of my list of things to do.

I expressed appropriate outrage to cover the fact that I'd known about it already, then responded to the purpose of their visit. The whole business had kept me awake until the murky hours of the morning, even without knowing for certain that Michelle was a murderer. Some time between then and now, I had come to a decision.

"Gentlemen," I said, giving them the benefit of the doubt, "you have every right to tell me to butt out, and I'm sorry if my call to the Trilby tossed a monkey-wrench into the works. Now I'd appreciate it if you'd look at it from my point of view."

They finally sat back, both their expressions acutely

wary, as if there was a snake somewhere, ready to strike.

"In the process of doing what was my job at the time, protecting and defending, so to speak, I set off a chain of incidents for which, no matter what I tell myself or anyone else says, I feel responsible. Those incidents include the deaths of three people I never met. But I've seen the impact of those deaths on the owner of Celebrations, and on Clarissa, someone I've come to like very much. The bottom line is that I'm the cause and I'm the one Michelle Halls is after. The easier it is for her to get to me, the sooner you'll catch her."

They jerked upright again, as if yanked by a single set of puppet strings. "Now, just wait a minute," Thackery began.

"Let me finish. I have a couple of chores to take care of which will get me out of your hair for today. I have to go out and I'll wear a damned wig and the makeup, etcetera, so if she's around she won't recognize me. It worked yesterday; there's no reason it won't work again today. But today is it. Effective tomorrow, no more wigs, no more disguises. I'm going to make myself as accessible as I can be. I *want* her to make her move."

"No," Evans said, shaking his head. "We can't allow you to act as bait."

"I'm not asking your permission. This woman cannot be allowed to inflict any more damage, especially to people who have nothing to do with her beef against me. And I understand that for all intents and purposes I'll be on my own. As far as protection's concerned, I've broken up enough bar fights in the line of duty to know I can take care of myself. I don't have a service piece any longer, but I can use one of Duck's.

They aren't throwaways," I added quickly. "They're registered to him. And I won't use the thing unless I have to. But I've been a victim long enough. Now, if you want to waste your breath arguing with me, fine, but make it fast. I've got to get out of here."

To give them credit, they tried their best, but Nunna could have told them they were simply spinning their wheels. With three deaths on my conscience, there was nothing they could say that would change my mind.

After about a half an hour of it, they left with a promise to step up patrols starting this evening. I expressed my appreciation for whatever they could do and nudged them out of the door. With their departure, I felt more at ease than I had since the whole business had broken wide open this past Monday. Even though it had actually begun some weeks before then, tomorrow would be the beginning of the end of it.

Over breakfast, I faced an additional truth. The postponements aside, I was not happy about my wedding. As much as I loved Duck, as much as I looked forward to being his wife, I was beginning to hate more and more the three-act production my wedding had become. I'd wanted simplicity, intimacy, just family, It was still just family, but one that amounted to a cast of dozens.

The loss of that ecru suit from Bridal Bower was, on balance, as upsetting as losing our Hawaii reservations. It wasn't often that I genuinely liked the way I looked in whatever I wore, but that two-piece creation had moved to the top of the list. Therefore, having to ask my aunts to whip up something for me stuck in my craw far more than it would under ordinary circumstances. Not that I doubted their dressmaking skills; my cousin Tracy's wardrobe was equal to anything

Salina's sold. But whatever they came up with would be my second choice, not my first. And I resented that.

I showered and attacked the closet to come up with an outfit that would fool my nemesis but wouldn't make me look like a fool in my grandparents' eyes. The braids were definitely out. I flipped through Janeece's wigs and hairpieces and finally settled for a chin-length page boy with bangs. It was cute enough to make me consider letting my hair grow. That lasted perhaps thirty-seven seconds. Why bother when I could wear a wig?

It took me fifteen minutes to get the lashes on straight, but I turned thumbs down on the stuffing. I'd be wearing my Sunday go-to-meeting coat, a black cashmere that closed with a belt and was a perfect fit. It had cost too damned much for me to want to look as if I was about to burst out of it.

I was squeezing my feet into a pair of dress boots when the phone rang. I was tempted to let the caller leave a message, since I'd gotten all the bad news I cared to hear for the next year and a half, but gave in, in case it was Duck.

It wasn't. "Leigh, if I'm not in the doghouse about last night, can I ask a favor?" Tina's tone of voice could best be described as wheedling.

"Depends. What is it?" Truthfully, I was still pissed at her, but was determined to rise above it.

"I was supposed to pick up Auntie Clar from church, but I'm on my way in to work. Eva called in sick. I tried Aunt's cell phone to tell her to take a cab home, but she probably doesn't have it with her. It's not that far from you or I wouldn't ask. I don't want her standing in the cold waiting for me."

If there was a polite way to say no, I couldn't figure out how. "All right. Which church?"

She gave me directions and thanked me effusively. I sighed. Taking Clarissa home meant a detour, but it wasn't as if I was in a rush to get to Ourland, despite what I'd told Thackery and Evans.

"Leigh," Clarissa exclaimed, when I found her on the corner looking like a poor lost sheep. "I almost didn't recognize you. What are you doing here?"

"Subbing for Tina. She's having to fill in for someone at work. Get in out of the cold. How would you like to go to Ourland with me?" I asked, surprising myself.

"Oh, I'd love to." She scrambled into the car, her cheeks pink from the December chill. "Would there be time for me to see your new house? Tina told me about it. It sounds wonderful."

"Plenty of time. I'd planned to go by it anyway, to take pictures to send to my foster mom."

The ensuing discussion about digital cameras and how I came to be raised in a foster home was a pleasant distraction and made the trip seem shorter by half. I took the main route into Ourland this time, unwilling to risk damaging the undercarriage of Janeece's baby in one of the potholes that had made the back way such an enjoyable ride for Tank.

Approaching the town from this direction gave no hint that what was to come would not be your typical suburban setup, since the drive first cut through Eden's Edge. A buffer between the highway and Ourland/Umber Shores, it was barely a decade old, with sidewalks, yards all the same size to the inch, and trees resembling adolescents in that gawky stage when they're all elbows and knees. Clarissa, I could see, was not particularly impressed. Then we turned onto North Star Road.

She leaned forward, brightening. "This is more like what I expected," she said, as sidewalks disappeared. Houses sited on irregular-sized lots lost their sameness, took on personalities and character, their faces unashamed of their age. They were as neat and as well-kept as those in the buffer zone, but the swings on the decks and front porches, the occasional anchor or pair of oars leaning against a gas light in the yard, all currently wrapped in Christmas greenery, contributed a well lived-in look to this area. Since this end of town was farther from the flood zone, these homes were not elevated. The trees added the finishing touch, oaks and evergreens that had been around since the ark ran to ground on Ararat.

Without warning, this leg of North Star Road became Main Street, the commercial section, all two blocks of it. A tow truck from W. Two's service station blocked the intersection. The street itself was jammed, crowds lining the sidewalk, all practically quivering with anticipation.

"What's going on?" Clarissa asked.

"No idea." I shifted into park, got out, and approached the nearest man, a toddler straddling his shoulders.

"What's happening?" I asked, uncertain whether to be alarmed.

The man glanced down at me before pointing to the town hall, formerly a church complete with steeple. "That. Here comes my baby." His cocoa-brown face split into a grin.

The doors of the white clapboard building burst open. From inside, the sound of a band, clearly new to the exercise, began a tinny "Santa Claus Is Coming to Town," and a preschooler dressed as a majorette led them out, her little white boots practically up to her knees. She held a baton above her head, yanked it to her shoulder then up again, twirling obviously beyond her. With an ear-to-ear grin, she escorted the band down the steps, onto the sidewalk, then into the street.

The band, some of whom I recognized, my aunts among them, consisted of elves of all sizes and ages. And, man, did they stink. The crowd erupted in cheers, and I returned to a vacant car. Clarissa stood on the far side of the intersection, clapping and cheering with those around her.

I killed the engine and got out again to wait, leaning against the front of the car. The band was followed by a variety of floats from the parking lot behind the building, a couple of other bands from local schools, more elves tossing candy canes, and finally Santa, who bore a startling resemblance to W. Two and rode in a sleigh pulled by a team of ponies I suspected spent most of their time giving rides to toddlers in a petting zoo.

All smiles, Clarissa returned to the car. "That was fun! Where to now?"

Stopping by the storefront police station was out, thanks to the parade. "My grandparents, to make a formal appearance to accept the gift of the house. After that, I'll take you to see it. From there I'll need to track down my aunts. By the time they finish with me you'll be starving, so I'll have the perfect excuse to introduce you to Mary Castle and the best restaurant in town masquerading as a dump."

She greeted all that with silence, and I wondered if she was up to meeting so many people. She hadn't mentioned Claudia and neither had I, preferring to follow her lead. I wasn't even sure if she knew the results of the postmortem.

"If you'd rather not, I can probably skip stopping by my grandparents', but I really do need to see my aunts. They offered to make my wedding dress, and they'll need to take my measurements."

"Oh, it all sounds lovely." She managed a strained smile. "I'm feeling guilty because I'm enjoying this so much. Sister's lying in the morgue, all cut up, and I'm enjoying myself. Her death was so senseless, so needlessly cruel, and I'm *enjoying* myself. It doesn't seem right."

I sent up a small prayer that I could say something to help. "You spent your whole life with your sister, right? You knew her as well as you knew yourself. Do you think she wouldn't want you to revel in as much joy as you can? Wouldn't she want that for you?"

After a second, she nodded. "I always envied her that capacity. Sister got enjoyment out of every single moment, no matter what she was doing. Give her a grungy bathroom to clean and she was in sheer heaven. Give her a spoonful of vanilla pudding and you'd think she was eating a bowl of trifle. I was the serious one, attacking things as if they were obstacles to be overcome, and Sister was always chiding me about it, telling me to loosen up."

"In other words, she'd be pleased that you're having a good time today. Honor her memory by doing just that. Enjoy yourself."

Her smile was a little quivery around the edges, but it was a valiant effort. "You're right. I will. Tell me about your grandparents."

I made an embarrassingly awkward U-turn on the narrow street and tried to prepare her for the grands as I doubled back and made a detour a block over in hopes I could work my way to the other end of North Star Road far enough south to avoid the parade. It worked only because the procession appeared to have stopped for a concert and Christmas carol sing-along where Main became North Star again.

Clarissa relaxed and scrutinized the Ritch family compound with avid interest, seeming both charmed and energized. "It reminds me of Johns Island in South Carolina," she said, "minus the Spanish moss and the palmettos, of course. But the same kind of feel to it, old, well-settled."

"It has quite a history, but I'll leave it to my grandmother to spell it all out for you."

Which was exactly what happened. The candles on the tree were lit and the aroma of freshly baked cookies perfumed Ritch Manor. Both grands were home, having skipped the parade, since Granddad was still coming to grips with using a quad cane. Tall, with skin the color of cocoa and my dad's intensely dark eyes, he was a gorgeous old dude, hair graying solely at the temples despite the fact that he had to be nudging eighty.

He was, at the moment, champing at the bit to get back onto the golf course and knew that was some months away.

"I hate the damned thing," Granddad grumbled, glaring at the cane. "I keep kicking it when I'm walking, and it's a pure nuisance going up steps. I'm getting so I don't need it, but a certain someone raises hell if I don't use it."

Elizabeth ignored him, having found another avid lover of antiques in Clarissa. I settled down in a back parlor with him while my grandmother took Clarissa on a Cook's tour of the first floor.

"You've lost weight," Granddad observed, ever the M.D., retired or not. "And you look tired. You feeling okay? Want me to check you over?"

Since Granddad was an OB/GYN, I passed. No way did I wish to peer at him from between spread-eagled knees. "I'm fine, just running myself ragged. Aside from your complaints about the cane, how's your knee coming along? Are you sure you'll be able to walk me down the aisle of Arundel Woods A.M.E. on the twenty-sixth?"

"So our cousin, the reverend, got hold of you, did he?" A knowing grin lit his handsome features, and I began to suspect that Nunna and Duck's mother weren't the only co-conspirators in on the scheme to see me married in a church. "I'll be fine and raring to go," he said. "Might even manage a dance with you afterward at the reception."

I jerked upright. "What reception?"

By the time my grandmother and Clarissa joined us, I'd come to the realization that not only had I been outsmarted and outfoxed, the wedding was now completely out of my control. A part of me was touched that my new family cared enough about me to want to make it such a special event, but the major part of me was extremely annoyed and dismayed. I didn't know what to do about it.

Thoroughly distracted, I lost the thread of the conversation, belatedly picking up on the fact that the subject had become the house and Clarissa's and my itinerary for the day.

"I'm looking forward to seeing it," she was saying, "although we probably won't stay long. Leigh has to meet her aunts and get measured for her wedding dress."

My grandmother's disappointment was obvious, which I couldn't understand, given the attitude she'd exhibited about the furnishings.

"What a pity," she said. "The first floor is full of treasures you need to see at leisure. The top floor, well . . ." She wrinkled her patrician nose. "And it should be more comfortable now. I had Amalie stop by and turn the heat up a bit more." Inexplicably, her face cleared. "Leigh, dear, why don't I take Clarissa to the house? You can go on and spend as much time as you need with Frances and Bonita."

Head lowered, Granddad squinted at her over reading glasses in grave danger of dropping down onto his top lip. "Have you forgotten that you're expecting guests, Lizzie? Any time now," he said, for my benefit, "this place will be wall-to-wall elves and band members. After the parade, they come here for hot punch and cookies. Tradition, don't you know."

Elizabeth looked greatly put-upon and sighed. "He's right, heaven forbid. Every year I swear it'll be the last, and every year, I give in, bake enough cookies for an army, and pray no one breaks anything."

"Mind you," Granddad added, a twinkle in his eye, "it's not fractured arms or legs she's concerned about. I'll go with you, Clarissa. Leigh can drop us off and pick us up when she's done being fussed over by Frannie and Bonnie."

"But the steps," I said, Elizabeth's protest a beat behind mine.

"You can stay long enough to watch me, if it makes you feel better. Besides, going up is a breeze. Coming down, now, that's another matter."

Ashamed at taking advantage of his generosity, but still relieved at having a few moments to myself to deal with my growing resentment about my wedding, I agreed. "But only up to the first floor, Granddad. I'll take her up to the second when I get back. Deal?"

"Deal. Although I'll miss getting another look at that upstairs bedroom. It's a corker." He grinned at his wife. She was not amused.

I said my good-byes to her, kissed the offered cheek, and helped my grandfather down the front steps, even though he appeared to manage them with little difficulty, tongue caught between his teeth. He made appropriate admiring noises about the Cadillac and made himself comfortable in the front seat.

At the house, I followed him up the stairs to the first floor, Clarissa trailing us. He unlocked the door using a key on a ring full of them. I should have known he had one, since he had keys for half the houses in the compound, all contributed by the owners so he could check on retirees and have access to rental properties.

I left them to it and made the drive to the home of my Aunt Frances at as leisurely a pace as I could and was not particularly surprised when no one answered the door. She'd been one of the taller elves in the parade and would probably be going to my grandparents' with everyone else, including her sister, my Aunt Bonita.

Purely for form, I drove to Bonita's. No answer. I'd lucked out. I could enjoy some time alone and return later. I got back in the car and returned to Ritch Road. It occurred to me that if I parked in front of my future neighbor next door, I might be able to sneak up to the top floor and spend a few more moments in solitude. If I were quiet enough, Granddad and Clarissa would never know I was there.

Easing the Cadillac onto the edge of the adjacent lot,

with my left eye glued on the ditch between the tarmac and the grass, I parked. I'd be facing oncoming traffic, but that was a common practice here. I closed the car door quietly and hurried along the driveway on the left side of the house. I tiptoed up the stairs, hesitating at the first-floor landing, but there was no way I could be seen. The windows on this side of the great room were clerestory, tucked up under the floor of the loft.

I made it to the upper floor, relieved that the stairs didn't creak. I let myself in and just stood there. It was the first time I'd been in the space alone, and I wanted to get a sense of its ambiance, its spirit. There was a serenity about it, perhaps because of the neutral color. The walls in daylight didn't strike me as a cold white. There was a softness about them, the paintings and rugs contributing just enough vibrancy to be pleasing to the eye. I would be content here. This could indeed become my home.

I tossed my purse onto the nearest sectional and felt a twinge of annoyance from my bladder. After all, it had been a while. I dispensed with my coat and started for the bathroom. As I approached its door, I heard a series of muted thuds from directly below, even felt the vibrations in the soles of my feet. What in the world were they doing?

I saw no sense in braving the cold to go downstairs with a far more convenient means to get there at my disposal. In the utility closet I fumbled around until I located the latch and opened the door to the stairwell. Evidently we'd left the one below either open or ajar; there was a patch of gray at the bottom but it was still far too little illumination for me to see, and I had no intention of taking these steps ass over teakettle.

I was patting the wall to find the light switch when I

heard my grandfather roar, "Open this door, do you hear me?"

Ah. Granddad was stuck in the bathroom. I groped for the light switch a little more frantically and finally found it when I heard a response to my grandfather's demand.

"Just shut up, you old fool! I'm busy!"

I knew that voice, knew it well, and it damned sure wasn't Clarissa's.

21

HOW THE HELL HAD SHE GOTTEN IN? AND HOW long had she been here?

My heart hiccupped and my pulse went into overdrive. I had tasted panic on a number of occasions, but in this instance it was more than a taste, it completely consumed me. Michelle, triple murderer, nuttier than a Baby Ruth, and with, as Evans had reminded me, nothing to lose, was down there with my grandfather and Clarissa. I could take some comfort that Granddad was still alive, but what about Clarissa? Michelle had already killed her twin. If she hurt Clarissa, if she harmed one hair on my grandfather's head . . .

Between one second and the next, the panic was gone. What followed was what I can only describe as an other-body experience, an instantaneous metamorphosis into someone I didn't recognize, a cold, calculating entity who knew what she would do. Calling for help was out; the cell phone was in the car. If Clarissa and her granddad were to survive this, she would have to kill Michelle. And she just might enjoy doing it.

I blinked, startled, and felt more like myself again. But that other person was still in there, and for the moment, she was welcome. I would need her. She'd sit on my emotions, help me stay focused.

I examined my options. The only other means to get into the downstairs unit was via the front door. Unlike this floor, there was no access to the outside from the master bedroom. The matter was decided. Leaning against the washer and dryer, I pried off my dress boots, ditched the page boy wig and the lashes, paring myself down to just the essentials. As quietly as I could, I hurried back to the kitchen. I needed a weapon, and the knife rack on the wall offered a wide variety of gleaming, sharp blades. Bypassing the largest of them, the cleaver and the butcher's knife, I selected one I could hide easily in the sleeve of my sweater. I might inadvertently slit my own wrist in the process of removing the damned thing, but it was a chance I'd have to take.

Returning to the utility closet, I took a deep breath to steady myself and started down the steps, hands against the walls, as if that might reduce my weight on them. The pocket door at the bottom was indeed partly open. Amalie must have left it when she'd come to turn up the heat, because I distinctly remembered Duck closing it. Unless Michelle had found it. I had to hope that she was no more observant than I'd been when I'd seen the utility room the first time.

Praying that the hidden door would move soundlessly, I eased it open just wide enough to step through. It probably wouldn't have been heard in any event. Granddad was attacking the bathroom door again. Which made me wonder how the hell he'd gotten trapped in there in the first place. Didn't bathrooms lock from the inside?

"Goddammit!" Footsteps pounded toward me.

I froze in front of the washer and dryer. The folding door shutting the utility room off from the hall was open about halfway, the bathroom directly opposite.

If that was Michelle's destination, all she had to do was glance in my direction and she'd see me, or at least the left half of me. No fool, she'd know that there had to be a right half too. If necessary I could take her then and there, the problem with that being I had no way of knowing what kind of weapon she might have, what I'd be up against. Better to wait and find out. Of course, if she opened that bathroom door to so much as slap my grandfather, all bets were off.

Instead, she kicked it. "I'm warning you, old man! Anybody with as little time as you have left might want to make peace with his Maker. Keep that up and I'll deal with you first instead of this devious old bitch out here!" She stomped away.

I exhaled, peeked around the folding door, and saw Granddad's problem with his. A cord, probably from the blinds, was stretched tightly between the bathroom doorknob and the one on the door of the adjacent guest room, anchoring both of them closed. The temptation to slip across the hall and cut the thing was appealing, but I quashed it. While he might be trapped, for the moment he was safe, leaving just Clarissa and eventually Michelle to worry about—that is, if he kept quiet and didn't aggravate her. I had to let him know I was here.

Along with laundry-related products, the shelves above the washer and dryer held plastic baskets containing odds and ends: a sewing kit, balls of string, thumbtacks, rubber bands; one held a yo-yo, three Matchbox cars, a few marbles, tiles from a Scrabble game, and, glory be to God, a box of Crayola crayons. Most in the box had been worn to nubs but, evidently, whatever child had left them hadn't had much use for black.

I needed paper. The only things available to write on were sheets of fabric softener. I laid one on top of the dryer, hoping it wouldn't tear under the pressure of the crayon. I kept the message short and sweet, going over the letters a second time so they could be easily read:

 Granddad

  I'm here. Keep quiet!

   Leigh

I hoped getting it to him would be as simple.

Concerned now for Clarissa, I risked a peek toward the great room and saw her sitting on the chintz-covered couch, part of a conversation area clustered to the left of the window wall. Michelle had made the most of what was available. Clarissa's hands were tied with a match of the cord holding Granddad prisoner in the john. Most of the bottom half of her face was hidden under a blue print scarf used as a gag. There was no trace of fear in her body language, but even from where I stood, I could see the loathing in her eyes.

They widened when she spotted me. I pressed a finger to my lips, silly given the circumstances, but she lowered her gaze and shifted position, as if trying to get more comfortable. Her wrists were secured right over the left, right palm down, left facing up. With a move that had to hurt, she twisted her right wrist to a position perpendicular to the left, raised her thumb, and extended her forefinger. After a second, she curled the forefinger back, twice.

I gaped at her, praying I might be misinterpreting

the gesture. I pantomimed pulling a trigger and was rewarded with a nod.

Shit. Why couldn't Michelle have waited until tomorrow? I'd have been ready for her with Duck's Glock. As for the knife, I was no James Coburn with his lethal speed and aim à la *The Magnificent Seven*. By the time I got the thing out of my sleeve, I could be wearing four or five additional holes. For whatever reason, she hadn't used the gun yet, but I couldn't count on that lasting much longer. Come to think of it, what the hell was she doing?

Where is she? I mouthed to Clarissa.

She shifted position again to her left, fixing her gaze toward the side of the great room under the loft. Good enough. I stepped into the hall, slid the sheet of fabric softener under the door of the bathroom, then tapped lightly to be certain he saw it. In a second, it disappeared. I breathed a little easier.

It was time to focus on Michelle. I hadn't seen a weapon; only her left half had been visible. No surprise, she was in costume again, one I recognized, and I kicked myself for having missed yet another opportunity to confront her days earlier, considering the number of times I'd seen the outfit. Today she was the Reverend Mrs. Hansberry, lady preacher sans bucket for collecting money for presents for needy children. Frizzy black hair pulled back in a bun, frumpy black dress with white collar, old lady shoes. She was into me for a buck seventy-five. I wanted it back, every penny of it.

Envisioning the layout, I figured that if I could make it to the kitchen, I could crouch behind the sideboard that served as an island between the kitchen and dining area under the loft, at least until I could figure out how best to bring her down without sacrificing Clarissa's life and getting shot myself. The sideboard was at least six feet long, but only waist-high, if that. It was the only thing available to hide behind. Everything else was open, even the fireplace.

I gestured to Clarissa that I wanted to get to the kitchen. She seemed startled at first, then horrified, but finally gave a short bob of her head. Almost immediately she began to moan, and slumped to one side.

"Oh, no, you don't, you old bitch!" Michelle moved into view, her back to me as she yanked Clarissa upright and slapped her, hard, with an open hand. I almost lost it.

Hey, an internal voice chided me, *Clarissa's taking the heat, distracting Michelle so you can make your move. So move!*

I eased around the folding door, walked as quietly as I could, and reached the end of the wall separating the hall from the kitchen. I'd taken a couple of steps toward them when Clarissa, who'd been knocked onto her right side by the blow, saw me and shook her head. She was right. Michelle would see me coming in her peripheral vision. Even more of a hazard was the revolver nestled in her left hand, her finger inside the trigger guard. I was willing to risk her taking a shot at me if she detected my approach, but I couldn't risk startling her and causing her to shoot Clarissa by accident. Me she might miss. Not Clarissa.

I hauled ass into the kitchen, squatted behind the sideboard, relieved to see that I needn't worry about my head showing above it. Michelle had piled her coat, suitcase, hatbox, purse, three-ring binders, and makeup kit on top of it, adding to its height. Kneeling would be hell on my patella, but I'd be able to squat rather than sit or lie on the floor.

I peeked around the left end.

"I'm not falling for that dying act again," Michelle ranted, shaking Clarissa by her collar like a rag doll. "No coughing and wheezing this time. You fooled me once, had me thinking I'd killed you, and all the time you were just fine, probably laughing your head off."

Pointing the ugly revolver at Clarissa's nose, she loosened the cord around her wrists, pulled it free. "Swivel around," she ordered. "Hands behind your back. I've got to pee. Any other time, I'd take you with me." She wedged the gun under the belt of her dress. "But I've got my damned period, so I prefer privacy." She tied Clarissa's wrists together, yanking viciously on the cord before twisting her face front.

"Don't bother trying to escape while I'm gone," she said, backing away. "There's no point. With your hands like that, you won't be able to open the door, so stay put. We've got a lot of talking to do."

I heard her footsteps coming toward me rather than the steps to the loft and prepared myself for discovery. She stopped on the other side of the sideboard, however.

"Everything would be fine if I hadn't had to go to my stupid dumbfuck of a cousin practically on my hands and knees to beg her to let me hide out at her house."

She moved away. I risked a peek. She had come for her purse. Hurrying, she ran up the steps and kept talking, even after she'd reached the bathroom. "But she didn't care if I was in trouble, said it was my own fault. She turned me down."

I got to my feet, ran to Clarissa, and hauled her onto hers.

"And I knew she'd tell on me, knew it! So I had to do

what I did, especially after Bubba showed up. He never liked me. He'd have ratted on me too. So it's all your fault, not mine, yours and that cop bitch. And you're gonna tell me where she is or else, you hear me?"

Nudging her to hurry, I took Clarissa to the utility room and the stairwell, and helped her lower herself onto a step. "Stay here," I whispered, turned on the light for her, then slid the door closed. I wish I could have removed the gag and untied her hands but I had no idea how long Michelle would be in the john.

On the way back to the kitchen, I came up with a diversion I hoped might work, crossed to the front door, opened it, and left it ajar. It was a long shot, but if she went outside to look for Clarissa, I could lock her out.

"You've got to work at your craft, you know? You've got to hone it, pay your dues. And I've done that." Michelle's voice rang clearly, projected with apparent ease.

I took the time to see if there was anything else I could use as a weapon, something with more reach. Nothing heavy enough, not even a poker.

"I've played young women, old women, whores, queens. I've been in tragedies, comedies, farces, you name it. And I'm good," she said, flushing the toilet. "Damned good. Everyone says so, as if I need anybody to tell me that. I'm a star! I've always been a star!"

I heard more water and had to give her credit. At least she was washing her hands.

"I'd have made it into that repertory company if I could have gotten there on time. They'd have hired me; diversity's the big thing these days. So I *know* I could have been a principal member of the company. Juliet,

Ophelia, Lady—" The wife of the thane of Cawdor was left hanging. "Shit!"

Michelle was done, had come out, and had obviously looked over the railing of the loft.

She pounded down the steps. "Goddammit, I warned you not to move! How far do you think you'll get?"

She did exactly what I'd hoped. The front door banged open, slammed against the wall. I popped up, ready to dash the second she stepped down onto the deck. She did, darting away, and I was there in a flash, closing the door and throwing the deadbolt. Her footsteps muffled the sound.

I rushed to the bathroom door. "Granddad, can you hear me?"

"Yes, honey. Where's Clarissa? Is she all right? What the hell is going on?"

"No time to explain," I said softly, attacking the cord with the knife, listening as she stormed around to the rear, made a complete circuit of the deck, then took the stairs to the upper unit and down again, sounding as if she weighed a ton. "I'm trying to get this door open. When I do, go into the utility room and hide in the stairwell with Clarissa." I doubted Michelle would leave, not with all her belongings in here. I'd have to deal with her, but I wanted him out of the way first.

Meanwhile, I wasn't having much luck. Either the manufacturer of the blinds had used quality cord or all those nice, shiny blades were just that, nice and shiny. This one damned sure wasn't sharp. I was barely halfway through the cord.

Michelle was back at the door, and my stomach plummeted as my ears detected a sound I hadn't anticipated.

"She has a key?"

"Mine," Granddad responded. I hadn't realized I'd voiced the question.

But thank God. With all the keys he carried, she would have a hell of a lot of them to try before she found the right one. And I was getting nowhere fast with the knife. Decision time. Go or stay?

The upper half of the front door was glass covered by blinds, partially open. She, however, was engrossed with Granddad's collection of keys, eliminating those that were clearly not for doors. Using these last remaining seconds wisely was imperative. Once she got in, she would search this floor from front to back and I couldn't chance her finding the interior stairwell. She would take out her anger on Clarissa, and I couldn't ask that sweet little lady to endure any more than she already had.

Decision made, I abandoned my efforts to cut through the cord and moved quickly from the hall to the wall behind the door. I had no illusions that I'd be there for very long. I eased the knife up my sleeve again, far less concerned about slitting my wrist, now that I knew better. It probably wouldn't even break skin. Thinking fast, I unbuckled my belt, pulled it free of the loops, and draped it around my neck.

The fourth try and Michelle had caught the golden ring. She pushed the door ajar, yelling as she tried to extricate the key from the lock. "All right, where are you, goddammit?"

I yanked it open, pulling her in. "Right here, Michelle."

I looped an arm around her neck as, off balance, she hurtled into the room. Pulling her upright, I slammed her face front against the wall, my shoulder pinning her as I yanked her left arm behind her and groped for the other, the more important of the two, since the hand on the end of it held the gun.

"Drop it!" I yelled.

"Not before I *kill* you!" Grunting, she tried to hook her foot around my ankle, but couldn't gain purchase. I ignored the footwork. I had to get rid of the pistol. She held it stiff-armed, for the moment, aimed toward the floor.

"Drop it!" Gripping her wrist, I twisted the extended arm a hundred eighty degrees so that her palm faced away from her body, making sure the barrel remained pointing down. "Either you drop it or I'll wrench your arm out of its socket."

She winced with pain. "Fuck you!"

"Suit yourself." I slammed her hand against the wall, doing a number on my knuckles as well.

The pistol dropped. I kicked it aside, one eye on it as it slid across the polished wood, coming to rest against the base of the stone hearth. Relieved, I wrestled her arm up behind her back.

Now came the tricky part. Cuffing someone who would rather you didn't is usually a two-person maneuver, and trying it solo is flirting with one's mortality. Trying it solo using a belt instead of cuffs was ludicrous, but it wasn't as if I had any other choice.

"On your knees," I said. "Slowly and carefully, girl, or I'll break your arm—accidentally, of course, but it'll hurt just as much as intentionally."

"I *hate* you," she spat at me, sliding down the wall, leaving a smear of dark chocolate makeup on the white walls.

"No kidding." I moved with her, lowering myself

awkwardly. Putting my weight on the bad knee was something I usually avoided, but I gritted my teeth, settled behind her, then shifted my shoulder to bring my belt within reach of my hands.

She snapped her head back, butting me full in the face.

Stars erupted behind my eyes and my nose seemed to fill, a sensation I'd experienced on the two occasions I'd taken blows to the head. My grip on her wrists loosened, and before the fireworks subsided, she'd dropped onto her side and was scrambling to get up.

I grabbed for her hair, a stupid move, since her wig came off in my hand as she bucked, dislodging me. On all fours now, she started toward the fireplace and the gun. I grasped an ankle and tugged her back toward me. She lashed out with the free foot and clipped me on the ear. Got news for you, not only are old lady shoes ugly, they hurt.

The polished oak planking afforded her little or no resistance as she slid toward me on her face, winding up practically at my side. I hooked a leg around her and literally crawled up her backside, but she bucked me off again, and the main event began, a no-holds-barred free-for-all.

Michelle was manic, clawing, cursing, kicking, spitting, raging. It was like going up against a well-oiled octopus on PCP. She raked her nails across my cheek, went for my eyes. I drove my fist into her nose, split her lip. A new sound from outside, something completely familiar yet incongruous, penetrated my consciousness but I was too busy to identify it.

I might have kept my head if she hadn't connected with my kneecap as we tussled, the toe of her shoe slamming into it as if it had a bull's-eye painted on it. In that instant I knew she had caused serious damage. The pain was searing, intense. Everything that had gone into whipping that joint into reasonable shape, the surgery, the weeks of physical therapy, were now wasted. Not only had this woman stolen my identity, my credit rating, my wedding suit, my peace of mind, she had just stolen my future. The knee felt worse than it had when I'd injured it the first time. My days as a cop were over once and for all.

I lost it. The pain meant nothing. The cold, calculating inner being was back. I was ready to kill.

I have no idea how long the battle lasted; time had no meaning. I have no idea how we wound up on the back side of the fireplace either; we had covered a lot of territory. And I have no idea how she finally managed to get to the gun. All I know is that I was astride her, she was on her back, and suddenly the damned thing was aimed at a point between my eyes.

"Get off me, bitch. Now!"

I held her gaze, my mind clear, untainted by fear or any other emotion. "Not gonna happen."

She propped herself on her free arm. "I'm gonna kill you. I've dreamed of this for months. You ruined my big chance, the break of my life. You sided with that fat, pasty-faced bitch over me. Over me! A sister!" Her hand shook, but not enough to matter.

I grabbed her wrist, tried to shove her arm to one side or the other. Nothing doing. This girl was strong. I guess there's a lot to be said for carrying trays of food.

"Skip the race card bullshit," I said as I wrestled with her arm. "What color was that poor old woman in the trunk of my car?"

Her eyes hardened. "What difference does it make? She got out, didn't she? I could have sworn she was dead."

Her arm was trembling, weakening. "She is. That was her twin you were slapping around a few minutes ago."

She froze, and I slammed her onto her back, pinning the arm to the floor, the other one flailing.

"You killed an old lady and a sister, any way you mean it. What color was your cousin and the other man? What did you say his name was? Bubba? A sister *and* a brother. You killed them anyway."

"Yeah," she snarled, "and I'm gonna kill me one more."

She twisted onto her side, clipped me on the ear with her free hand, stunning me. Suddenly she had me in her sights again.

Time became elastic, drawn thin. She pulled the trigger. Nothing. She pulled it again. We both watched as the hammer moved back, the cylinder rotated, the hammer slammed forward. End of sequence. With no effect.

I grabbed her wrist, pried the thing from her grasp. "Forget to load it?" I panted. It was lighter than I'd expected.

I looked at it, really looked at it. And shook my head, disbelieving. "You were going to shoot me with a stage prop?"

I began to laugh, I couldn't help it. It began somewhere below my rib cage and trickled out, gaining velocity and volume until I was howling.

"Stop laughing at me!" she yelled, reaching for my throat. "You have no right to laugh at me!"

Outside, the sound I'd heard earlier registered: one

of the bands marching past, the bass drum pounding as the horns slaughtered "Deck the Halls."

It was a sign, had to be. So I did. I drew back and whacked the living hell out of her with her beloved stage prop.

It felt *good*. She was down for the count.

22

"BABE?"

I opened one eye. Then the other. I smiled at him. Closed them again. I was so sleepy. It wasn't time to get up yet, couldn't be. It was still dark. If I could snooze for just a few more minutes . . .

"Babe?"

Okay, if he was going in early, I could have breakfast with him and come back to bed after he'd left. "I'm up, I'm up. You want coffee? Bacon and eggs? What?"

"I've eaten. How do you feel?"

"Like donkey doo. Jeez, my knee's killing me. Guess it's gonna rain." I forced my eyes open, convinced them to focus by sheer force of will. It was light, in fact, glaringly bright, both indoors and out. And this was not my bed. Correction, our bed.

Confused, I tried to sit up. Wasn't gonna happen. What the hell? Then I remembered. Where was she? For that matter, where was I?

"Duck. Michelle, she's—"

"Easy, babe. She's behind bars, out of your hair once and for all. You got her."

"Granddad? Clarissa?" The fog was lifting.

"Fine, in better shape than you are by a long shot."

"Give me a minute," I said, and fixed my gaze on the

ceiling, trying to remember what had happened when. But all I had were snippets of events, pieces of a jigsaw puzzle and no idea what the big picture looked like. "I hit her—"

"More than once, from the looks of her." Smiling, he pulled a chair next to the bed and perched on its edge, folding his hands around mine.

"A band was playing. Then Granddad came roaring into the room and I got off her and stood up. Or tried to, anyway. That's all I remember clearly. How did he get out of the bathroom?"

"You had weakened the cord around the doorknob just enough. He kept yanking until it finally gave." Duck chuckled. "A bloodthirsty old dude, your grandfather. He's still fuming at missing the big fight. It must have been a championship bout. The place was a mess. So are you." He reached to smooth my cheek.

"Ow! I'd say you should have seen the other guy, except I don't remember how bad she looked."

"Worse than you," he assured me. "The broken jaw is the deciding factor."

For the first time I was fully awake. "I broke her jaw?" I thought about it. "Good. Where am I? Did she hurt me that badly? I think I remember being in an ambulance."

"Washington Hospital Center. And congratulations on your new knee."

"What?" I yanked the cover aside. No wonder the thing hurt. The top of a bandage two inches thick was all that was visible under wraps around both legs that expanded and contracted periodically to prevent blood clots. A tube snaked from under the throbbing knee and disappeared over the edge of the bed. I became aware of a slight discomfort in my back, remembered my previous experience with an epidural. I hadn't even noticed the IV in my arm.

"When did this happen? In fact, what day is it? When did you get back?"

Duck laughed, concern finally leeching from his features. "You don't remember? Your granddad said you probably wouldn't. It's Tuesday. The surgery was early this morning. I got here just before they wheeled you in. And if I'm ever hurt again, I want whatever the hell they gave you. You were one happy chick, babe, singing 'Deck the Halls' all the way. Evidently you've been caroling practically nonstop since you arrived."

I'm glad he thought it was funny. I didn't. I was missing almost a day and a half. It had to be the morphine or whatever they'd used.

A nurse who looked too young to be trusted with a thermometer came in and smiled. "Ms. Warren. You're awake. I'll go find Dr. Brady." She grinned. "I'll be sure and tell him you're not singing."

Things were beginning to make sense. Dr. Brady had pieced my knee together the first time.

"Okay, I give," I said, in surrender. I located the controls, elevated the head of the bed, and raised it. "Fill in the gaps for me before Dr. Brady gets here. After the fight is pretty hazy. How did Michelle get in in the first place?"

"Your cousin—what's her name, Amalie? She closed the door but didn't realize you have to lock it from outside with a key, like our place. Michelle had been there since she split from the Trilby. She'd been looking for you most of the day and took a chance you might have gone to Ourland again. And she'd seen you out on the deck the other night. When she found the door unlocked, she simply took advantage of it.

Your grandmother's threatening to burn the bed she slept in."

"No kidding." I couldn't imagine Elizabeth getting that steamed over anything. "They have the gun, right? One more of her dirty tricks. It fooled me, all right."

"You aren't gonna believe this, babe. She didn't know it wasn't real. And there are bullets in it, but they're fake, too. It's all in her journals, three-ring binders. She lifted the gun from a box in the manager's office of one of the theater companies she worked with. And she's used it a couple of times in hold-ups when she was low on money, a couple of liquor stores and a 7-Eleven. She's lucky she didn't get shot herself."

"Depends on your point of view," I said, wondering how much of my skin wound up under her nails. "To hell with her. How'd I wind up here? Oh, my God, Janeece's Cadillac!"

"She's got it. Tank and Tina came out, and Tank drove it back to D.C. As for you, according to Dr. Ritch, when you stood up, your leg went out from under you and you passed out from the pain. So there he is, still gimpy himself, with two unconscious females on his hands. He went outside and yelled for someone to call nine-one-one, which, I understand, put an end to the parade, then used the cord from the doorknobs to tie up Michelle. By this time, Clarissa had come out, so she was able to help keep an eye on her while your grand-dad examined you. You were bloody and bruised, but the only real problem was your knee. I'll let him describe it for you with all the technical stuff, but he could see that it was serious."

"Yeah," I muttered. The career-ending kind of serious.

"Chin up, honey," Duck said, perhaps sensing my nosedive into the toilet. "It'll be fine, in time. Anyhow, the EMTs took you to the local hospital. In the interim, Clarissa called Tank, and he called me in Seattle. I told him to ask your granddad to arrange for you to be transferred here, since I figured you'd want Doc Brady to do whatever had to be done. I took the next flight I could get, checked with Tank when I got in, and he told me you were about to go into surgery. Ten minutes later and I'd have missed you. You're gonna be fine."

Yeah, right. "And Michelle?"

"In custody of Anne Arundel county until the paperwork's done to take her back to the District. They've got her for the murders at Celebrations, found her prints on one of the wastebaskets and the heavy-duty stapler she bludgeoned her cousin with. It's all in her journals."

"Hope it's enough to hang her," I said, elevating the head of the bed even more. "Wait a minute. She killed her cousin with a stapler?"

"Heavy-duty, evidently heavy enough to do the job. She took out the other cleaner, Borden Something-or-other, with a carving knife."

"Lordy, how awful. They didn't deserve that. What's her journal say about Claudia?"

"She knew it was the day Clarissa usually came to clean and she planned to return the box and leave. After she found out last Monday that you were still living with Janeece, she hoped you wouldn't realize the box had ever been removed, and would never be able to figure out how she'd gotten your Social Security number and all the other personal information she used. Only she and Claudia arrived about the same time and got on the elevator together. Evidently Claudia went off on her as they were going up, told her she'd lied about who she was. Michelle pulled that stupid gun on her, and took her back down to the garage. All she wanted to do was stash her somewhere, keep her quiet until she could get away. She was wearing rubber gloves so she wouldn't leave any prints on the box, and there's some guesswork from this point. Evans has had to piece it together by reading between the lines. It looks like the gloves got in the way when Michelle was trying to gag Claudia with the scarf she was wearing, and she must have taken them off. There's powder from her hands all over it. With the gag in place, Claudia inhaled the particles and went into anaphylactic shock almost immediately. Michelle thought she was faking, pushed her into the trunk, and left her."

A tightness filled my chest as I imagined what Claudia must have gone through.

"In the interim," Duck said, "Clarissa leaves, figuring her sister's forgotten to come get her. Michelle's just about to make her escape in her car, and who shows up? You, Tank, and Tina."

"So she just waited, followed us around and then out to Ourland?"

"You got it, babe. Once you saw her, she hightailed it back. Then she realized she was missing one of the gloves. She had to find it, so she came back to check around the Chevy. She opened the trunk, saw that Claudia was dead and assumed she'd suffocated. She decided the best thing to do was move the car, park it in Northern Virginia somewhere, only Grandison came down to leave for work and saw her. You know the rest."

"In other words, manslaughter's probably the most she could be charged with for Claudia's death, but the stapler and the carving knife will put her under the jail for a good long time."

"Maybe, maybe not. Wait," he said, knowing full well I was about to blow. "She is mentally ill, babe, diagnosed as a schizophrenic in her teens."

"You're kidding."

"I'm afraid not. Her family—and she's lived with every relative she has—says she'd be fine for a while, then stop taking her medication. She missed her voices, the ones that told her she's a star, destined for big things. Your grandfather says that from the time the Anne Arundel boys showed up to take her away, she's been raving about how it was all a mistake, that she was a serious actress just working up a part for a play."

"Yeah, right."

"She's been going through different characters ever since. In handcuffs, and with a broken jaw, even. Dr. Ritch says she became an old crone, a Southern belle, a gospel-spouting minister, and Lady Macbeth one after the other, all in the space of five minutes, and she was astonishing. Then she went off on you, ranted about a conspiracy between you and Bev Barlowe, and the next thing she's Blanche in *Streetcar*, 'relying on the kindness of strangers.' "

"Sounds like the old multiple-personality scam to me," I protested.

"Maybe, but that's not the impression I got from talking to your grandfather. He went to the lockup to check on her. He thinks she's grounded in a different reality, fighting to survive as what her voices have told her she is, a supremely gifted actress. Survival to her means eliminating anyone in her way."

"For instance, me." Call me a poor sport, I don't

care. After what she'd put me through, I wasn't feeling generous.

"Not just you," Duck said, his voice gentle. "That business in the Silver Shaker? She was working on a character, a prostitute. The auditions were last Monday morning, and she didn't get the part, just the usual kiss-off, a 'thank you for coming.' She freaked, tried to attack the director. They should have reported it. They didn't."

"So that might have been another 'gotcha' that sent her further over the edge."

"Oh, yeah. And she takes getting into a role seriously. During that rant against you, she told your granddad it took her hours to perfect your walk."

All for nothing, I mused, since I'd never walk that way again.

"Well, it's nice to see you awake." Dr. Brady strode in, a sweet, teddy bear of a man. "But don't ever let anyone tell you that you can sing. How's the pain? Manageable?"

Duck stood, shook his hand, thanked him, then excused himself. "I'll be back," he assured me. "Got a couple of things to take care of."

With his departure, I began a slide into the doldrums again. "So what's the verdict, Doc? Will I have to use a cane from now on?"

He lowered his head, peered at me over his glasses. "I'm insulted. You doubt my work? That's a state-of-the-art knee you've got there, young lady. With physical therapy and a decent exercise program afterward, you'll walk without an aid of any sort. Not immediately, but eventually. You'll be fine, Leigh. You have my word on it."

He became a blur behind a sheen of tears. I knew

him well, knew he wouldn't bullshit me. "Honestly? I can still be a cop?"

He snorted. "You can be any damned thing you want to be. I tried to avoid total replacement before because of your age. No way around it this time, so resign yourself to going through this again in about ten years. Now let's take a look at my superior workmanship."

It's no news to anyone that they don't coddle you after surgery. I dozed most of that day but by the next day, they had removed my catheter, epidural, and the drain from above the site of the surgery and had walked me slowly but steadily to the bathroom, where getting on and off the toilet proved to be an adventure in itself.

I washed up, wondering when Duck would be back. It was late, after dark even. Janeece had called, as had Tank and Tina and my grandparents, but I was getting more and more miffed that none of them had made the effort to come see me.

I was fatigued but clean, deodorized, and lotioned when I opened the door of the bathroom, expecting to have the nurse parked outside the door accompany me and my IV tower back to bed. Waiting instead, as patiently as the day I'd met her twenty-six years before, was Nunna. I squealed and practically fell into her arms. She smelled of vanilla, Georgia Peach hair pomade, and mother love.

"Now, now, darling," she said, embracing me and the tower, "don't start blubbering. Dillon called me yesterday. I came as soon as I could. Let's get you settled. I hear you've been through quite an ordeal."

"I'm fine now. You're here and my knee will be okay and I'll still be able to protect and defend eventually and Duck and I have a new house." I grinned up at her as I wielded the walker across the room, aware that I was babbling and not caring a bit.

I maneuvered my rear onto the bed and sat, while she positioned the tower next to the headboard.

"Are you in pain, honey?" she asked, hovering. She looked wonderful, tall, regal, her snow-white hair in a spiffy new style.

"I'm fine, juiced up just enough. You cut your hair?" In all the years I'd known her, she'd always worn it in a bun or topknot.

Her smile bordered on sheepish. "I was embarrassed to go to bed in rollers. It was all right when I was sleeping alone, but now . . ."

I felt my grin widen even more. "How's Walter?"

"Doing well. He'll be along soon. Now, honey, are you sure you feel all right?"

I couldn't have felt better with a banker's check for a million or two in my hand. "I'm tired, but with you here, I'm super. I'm so glad you came."

"Thank Dillon. Otherwise I wouldn't have known anything." That was a jab, gently applied. "Do you feel strong enough to change into something else? I'll help."

"Bless you," I said. "I hate these hospital gowns but they'll have to do until Duck brings me something else." I experienced a mental hiccup, realizing that she didn't know about my new living arrangements. "Uh, Nunna, I was going to call you last night, I mean, Sunday night to tell you—"

"That you've moved in with Dillon, I know. He told me. It's not a problem, Leigh Ann. I went through the same thought process a little while back. I wouldn't allow Walter to move in with me because I was worried you wouldn't approve."

"Oh, Nunna." I reached for her and we hugged, chuckling at how silly we'd been.

"That's enough of that," she said, moving away. "Let's get you dressed." She crossed to the back side of the bed as I untied the gown.

"I'll need a nurse to disconnect the IV."

"I'm right here." A new one this time, Patricia, who had obviously been waiting just outside. She shut off the drip, disconnected the tubing. "You won't need this anymore, anyway. But don't hesitate to let us know if the pain becomes too much." She gave me a mysterious smile and left the room.

"Here, honey." Nunna dropped a lace-trimmed bra with matching panties and a half-slip onto the bed beside me. "Better hurry it up."

I fingered them. "Jeez, these are beautiful. Thanks, Nunna, but they're a little impractical at the moment, don't you think?"

"Getting married in no underwear is a trifle seedy, don't you think?"

"Huh?" I looked back over my shoulder where my foster mom was pulling my ecru peau de soie wedding suit from a shopping bag. "Nunna! Where'd you get that? Is it mine? From the Bridal Bower?"

Then it registered. I was slow, but face it, I was also doped up to a fare-thee-well.

Duck stuck his head in the door. "You aren't dressed yet? Let me tell you something, Miss Nunna, if that woman isn't decent in ten minutes, she's gonna say her 'I do' with her backside showing, because ten minutes is the longest I plan to wait."

I was next to speechless. "Duck—"

"If that's the beginning of a protest"—he cut me off, and stepped into the room—"I don't want to hear it.

We are getting hitched this night downstairs in the chapel. The people we wanted with us to begin with are all down there waiting, plus or minus a couple. We can go through it again later for everybody else if you like, but this one's for us. Now get your butt in gear or prepare to get married with it exposed to God and everybody." Turning on his heel, he left.

"I do like a man who speaks his mind," Nunna said, bemused. "And I just realized there's no way those panties will slide over all those bandages. It looks like you'll be getting married with a bare bottom after all."

So that's how I came to be Mrs. Leigh Ann Kennedy eleven days before I'd expected, in a ceremony that would always warm my heart. I was one beat-up bride, a mouse under one eye, scratches and black and blue marks here, there, and yon, but from the daffy look on Duck's face, I could tell that he thought I looked beautiful. What anyone else thought didn't matter.

In attendance, Nunna and Walter; my granddad, who pushed me in a wheelchair to the altar; and my grandmother; my brother, Jon, and his wife; Duck's mom; his sister and her husband and daughter; Eddie Grimes; Janeece; Tank and Tina; and Clarissa. Presiding, one of the hospital's chaplains, and he did a fine job, even kept it short, since I refused to take my vows sitting down, and standing for long was out of the question.

When all the important stuff had been said, rings exchanged, the papers signed and a greenback of unknown denomination slipped into the good reverend's hand, Duck helped me into the wheelchair again and knelt beside me.

"You don't mind, do you, babe?" he said in my ear. "All the way across country, I kept thinking I could have lost you. I didn't want to wait any longer. And we'll go to Hawaii as soon as you're able to travel comfortably. I know this wedding wasn't quite what we planned, but it was pretty okay, don't you think?"

"Damn near perfect," I murmured, taking the opportunity to kiss him properly. Later I would tell him that the wedding would have been absolutely perfect except for the temperature in the chapel, a little chilly for my comfort. And far too chilly if you're getting married bare-assed.

The World of Chassie West

Look for these riveting mysteries by
Chassie West
Starring African-American sleuth
Leigh Ann Warren

Killer Riches
Killing Kin
Sunrise

Killer Riches

As former D.C. cop, Leigh Ann Warren is preparing for marriage, a new career, and a new life, a low, threatening voice on the telephone sends her world spinning wildly out of control. Suddenly two innocent lives are at stake, and someone dear to her heart faces a cruel, undeserved fate.

This tragedy-in-the-making is dragging Leigh Ann back to the small African-American coastal community where the most lethal secrets of her past are hidden. And with precious time running out, she must now separate the truth from the lies about the family she never knew in order to prevent the unthinkable . . . and to live another day.

"A female Walter Mosely."
Eileen Dreyer

Killing Kin

Edgar® and Anthony Award Nominee

Out on disability leave, Washington, D.C. police-woman Leigh Ann Warren can't stay off the job and out of the game—not when her partner and former fiancé Dillon Upshur "Duck" Kennedy has vanished mysteriously, and determined and dangerous people on both sides of the law are hunting him down. The dead body she discovers in her own apartment only strengthens Leigh Ann's resolve to find Duck first.

But the trail is twisted with perilous, unexpected turns, leading her deep into the woods of western Maryland—and to the lair of a killer who'd just as soon leave behind two dead cops rather than one.

> "Chassie West creates characters so warm,
> wonderful, and delightfully quirky
> they jump right off the page."
> Janet Evanovich

Sunrise
Edgar® Award Nominee

Big-city cop Leigh Ann Warren is coming back to Sunrise, North Carolina, to escape the pressures of the job—and her guilt over nearly causing the death of her partner Duck. But things have changed here since she was a girl. Tensions over plans to develop hallowed ground for commercial purposes are tearing a once close-knit community to pieces.

Leigh Ann hoped to stay neutral, but a decades-old murder, newly unearthed, is dragging her down into a whirlpool of fear and small-town secrets. And a killer still lurking in the shadows of Sunrise is about to strike again—this time, too close to home.

> **"Chassie West has created a heroine
> human enough to appreciate a mother's hug,
> gutsy enough to solve a murder,
> and sensible enough to love Italian shoes.
> *Bravissima!*"**
> **Lisa Scottoline**

THRILLING MYSTERIES FEATURING LEIGH ANN WARREN FROM EDGAR® AND ANTHONY AWARD NOMINEE

CHASSIE WEST

SUNRISE

0-06-108110-8 • $6.99 US • $9.99 Can
Big-city cop Leigh Ann Warren is coming back home to Sunrise, North Carolina, to escape the pressures of the job. But a decades-old murder, newly unearthed, is dragging her down into a whirlpool of fear and small-town secrets.

KILLING KIN

0-06-104389-3 • $6.99 US • $9.99 Can
Out on disability leave, Washington D.C. policewoman Leigh Ann Warren can't stay off the job—not when her partner and former fiance Dillon Upshur "Duck" Kennedy has vanished mysteriously and dangerous people on both sides of the law are hunting him down.

KILLER RICHES

0-06-104391-5• $6.99 US • $9.99 Can
As former D.C. cop Leigh Ann Warren prepares for marriage and a new career, a low, threatening voice on the telephone sends her world spinning wildly out of control.